P9-DYJ-752

JOURNEY *to* RIVERBEND

DATE DUE			
OC 2 0 74			

1. Most items may be checked out for two weeks and renewed for the same period. Additional restrictions may apply to high-demand items.

2. A fine is charged for each day material is not returned according to the above rule. No material will be issued to any person incurring such a fine until it has been paid.

3. All damage to material beyond reasonable wear and all losses shall be paid for.

4. Each borrower is responsible for all items checked out on his/her library card and for all fines accruing on the same.

JOURNEY *to* RIVERBEND

a novel

HENRY McLAUGHLIN

TYNDALE HOUSE PUBLISHERS, INC.
CAROL STREAM, ILLINOIS

Visit Tyndale's exciting Web site at www.tyndale.com.

Visit Henry McLaughlin's Web site at www.henrymclaughlin.org.

TYNDALE and Tyndale's quill logo are registered trademarks of Tyndale House Publishers, Inc.

Journey to Riverbend

Designed by Stephen Vosloo

Edited by Anne Christian Buchanan

Unless otherwise indicated, all Scripture quotations are taken from the *Holy Bible*, King James Version.

The Scripture quotation in the discussion questions is taken from the *Holy Bible*, New Living Translation, copyright © 1996, 2004, 2007 by Tyndale House Foundation. Used by permission of Tyndale House Publishers, Inc., Carol Stream, Illinois 60188. All rights reserved.

Library of Congress Cataloging-in-Publication Data

McLaughlin, Henry.
   Journey to Riverbend / Henry McLaughlin.
     p. cm.
   ISBN 978-1-4143-3942-9 (pbk.)
   I. Title.
   PS3613.C5754J68 2011
   813'.6—dc22   2010040219

Printed in the United States of America

17 16 15 14 13 12 11
7   6   5   4   3   2   1

To Linda,
the love of my life, whose patience,
support, encouragement, and love
made this book possible

And to you who read this book:

May you find the shalom of our Father
in every area of your life:
Wholeness
Completeness
Nothing Missing
Nothing Broken

1

THE CROWD WAS SMALL for a hanging. Quieter than usual, as if they all knew justice would not be served today.

Michael Archer found it hard to look at the young man before him. Ben Carstairs, only twenty-two, stood like a boy grown too tall, too soon. Each strand of his sandy hair grew as if it had a mind of its own. Handcuffs encircled his fine-boned wrists in loops of heavy iron. His lips quivered. Fear raged in his brown eyes.

"You believe I didn't do it, don't you?"

Michael's throat tightened. He nodded. Many hours with the boy had convinced him of the young man's innocence.

Ben gulped air and sighed. His shoulders sagged. He lifted his cuffed hands and opened a palm. "Give this to my father when you see him. It was my ma's, and I wanted something of hers when he threw me out. Tell him I'm sorry."

It was the silver Celtic cross Ben had worn on a leather thong around his neck. Only slight traces of the delicate engravings remained. Michael rubbed the cross as he had seen Ben do hundreds of times and closed his fist over the treasured token. He slipped it into his shirt pocket, buttoned the flap, and patted the cross with his hand. "I will."

Sheriff Gideon Parsons spoke from behind Ben. "It's time, son."

Ben swallowed, then straightened. "Thank you, Michael."

Michael nodded, unable to speak.

Gideon stepped in front and slipped a black hood over Ben's head. The boy whimpered as Gideon put the noose in place and pulled it snug. He squeezed Ben's shoulder. "It'll be fast." His voice cracked.

The trapdoor sprang down. Michael couldn't look. A short, muffled sound from inside the hood ended in silence.

Michael opened his eyes. The body swayed in a gentle arc, the head at an unnatural angle.

Gideon stood on the other side of the trapdoor, his hand still on the release lever, knuckles white, eyes downcast. He shook his large head and slid his hand from the lever. Wiping his face with a red bandanna, he motioned to the undertakers, who stood like vultures beside the gallows. They moved with well-practiced efficiency to free the noose, lower the body into a plain pine casket, and load it onto the hearse.

Gideon walked over and stood next to Michael. "I feel rotten about this. It shouldn'ta happened."

"I know. Thanks for asking the judge to reconsider." Michael gazed out past the town toward the fields and the low-lying hills in the distance. Heaviness enveloped his heart like a wet blanket.

Gideon snorted. "Fat lot of good it did. The judge wanted proof, and we didn't have any."

"But you tried. Thanks for believing me."

"Well, the whole thing never added up. It was either a frame-up or bad timing on young Carstairs's part, but I couldn't prove his innocence." He shook his head. "This is one of those times I hate this job."

2

Sam Carstairs stared at the wadded lump of cloth in his hands. He slammed it on the bed in front of him, frustrated when it made no noise and just lay there, accusing him of incompetence. He cursed.

"Lupe," he bellowed over his shoulder. He smiled at the sound of his voice echoing through the house.

In seconds, he heard the patter of bare feet on the stairs. *Why can't she wear shoes like white people?*

The girl skittered into view, standing on tiptoes to prevent herself from stumbling across the threshold. "*Sí*, Señor Sam."

He enjoyed the tremble in her voice, the way her gaze darted around the room to avoid settling on him. And she was good to look at, he had to admit, with her hair so black it shimmered, her almond eyes a deep, dark brown, that nice round shape to her.

Yep, Joshua picked a pretty one, but did he have to marry her and bring her to the house? Couldn't he find an American girl? No, not Joshua Abraham Carstairs. *He makes one trip off the ranch in five years and comes back with a Mexican wife.*

Oh, well. She serves her purposes. Like now.

Sam gestured at the clothes on the bed and the open suitcase. "Finish packing for me."

Lupe stayed in the doorway and glanced over her shoulder toward the stairs. "But Josh and I were going to have breakfast."

"Never mind about that." He waggled his hand at her, calling her into the room with his fingers. "I'll have breakfast with Joshua so he won't have to eat alone." A small tinge of sarcasm colored his words. "Besides, the quicker I get packed, the quicker I'm out of here, and you two lovebirds can have the whole ranch to yourselves for three weeks."

She walked into the room with the tentativeness of a rabbit. Sam laughed. He stepped in front of her and gripped her chin. "Just be grateful that's all I want—this time."

Sam grunted as he settled himself into the chair at the end of the long table in his dining room. Going soft from too many days behind a desk and not enough on a horse.

Joshua sat in the seat to Sam's left. Next to him stood an empty chair, the plate of food in front of it growing cold.

"Morning, Dad. I was expecting Lupe."

"I know, but she offered to pack my bags for me so you and I can have breakfast together before I go."

Joshua kept his eyes on his plate.

Sam served himself from covered platters of flapjacks and bacon set on the table. He poured coffee into a mug. "Where's your brother?"

"Mark? Um . . . he didn't come home last night."

Sam's knuckles tightened on his fork and knife. He lifted one hand off the table, a backhand to Joshua's face one quick move away. He breathed deep and placed his silverware on his plate with great care, positioning it just so. He wrapped his mug in one hand and willed the other hand to stay on the table.

"Didn't I tell you to keep him here, that I needed to talk with both of you this morning?"

Joshua took a sip of coffee. He put his mug down and turned it in a slow circle, his eyes locked with Sam's. Once again Sam saw that hint of independence in his eldest son, the unspoken *I can get up and walk out of here anytime I want.* Annoyance warred with admiration as he stared back at Joshua.

"I reckon he left after we'd all gone to bed. As I recollect, all you said was for both of us to be here this morning. I'm not my brother's keeper. That's a full-time job, and I'd rather use my time for something more useful, like running this ranch."

"Don't sass me, boy. I'll run you out of here."

"Like you did Ben?"

Sam balled his fist as heat rose up his neck. He dropped

his voice to the menacing grumble he used when dealing with people who didn't move fast enough for him. "I've told you I don't ever want to hear that name. He's not my son, and he's not your brother." He waved his hand. "Now get out of my sight."

He watched Joshua grip the arms of his chair as anger and indecision warred on his son's face. He followed Joshua's gaze to the mug in front of him. *Go ahead and throw it in my face. I can still deck you with one punch.*

Joshua's jaw clenched. "I've lost my appetite anyway." He glared at Sam and stalked out of the room.

Sam barked over his shoulder, "And send Avery in here. I need him to go to town and fetch your brother."

3

Tomorrow, the long journey would end. But the hard part was still before him.

Michael Archer stood on the ridge looking down into a wide valley. In the gathering twilight, he saw a wide river flowing between broad banks. His destination, the town of Riverbend, nestled like an infant in the crook of land formed by a bend in the river. The white steeple of a church rose into the still air, a bright beacon gleaming in the setting sun.

He prayed over what lay ahead, asking for wisdom and favor in his approach to Ben Carstairs's father. He didn't expect it to be easy. Letter after letter he'd helped the young man write had never been answered. The night before the hanging, Ben had sobbed over his father's continued rejection.

Michael touched the cross Ben had given him. It hung

around his own neck now, a physical reminder of his purpose. Wearing it brought back the memories of those weeks of visiting Ben in his cell, talking with him about Jesus and heaven, listening to Ben talk about his father, Ben's claims of innocence woven throughout the conversations.

Life is strange, Michael thought. *Here I am trying to reconcile a dead son with his father when Pa and I couldn't stand each other. At least I had Ma . . . and Ellie. Ben never knew his mother, never had any love in his family.*

The rabbit in the frying pan sizzled, and he turned back to tend to his simple supper. Afterward, he read his Bible by the flickering light of the fire and sipped coffee. He closed his eyes to pray, but sleep soon enveloped him. And the nightmare returned.

Rachel Stone slipped through the small grove of trees a few yards behind the parsonage of Riverbend Church and emerged into a little meadow. It was her favorite spot for watching the sunset. She loosened her hair from its bun and shook it out so it fell to her shoulders. She leaned against a tree, her hands behind her back, the rough bark pressing into her palms, lazing in the warm, waning sunlight like a cat before a fire.

She marveled at the quiet panorama of color and light, the changes of each passing moment. *Such a simple thing. Happens every day. But each one is so different. So beautiful.*

Until six months ago, sunsets like these were something that happened outside her world. Sunset meant the time of day when more men came to survey her and the other girls like sides of beef—pick one, head upstairs. Her heart clenched at the memories.

"Thank You, Father," she whispered, "for Martha and Pastor Luke and for their courage and obedience to You. Thank You for forgiving me and rescuing me from that life." She looked at her hands. "Martha says You've blessed these hands with the ability to sew. I hope she's right. I'm scared, God. I want people to accept me. I want the past forgotten. I'm tired of the stares and whispers. Maybe my store will show them who I can be, not who I was." She closed her eyes. "Help me to trust You, God."

Tension eased as peace washed over her . . . and then, something else. Something she hadn't experienced before, something hard to understand. It wasn't heavy or oppressive. It settled on her like a warm shawl on a cold night.

"What is it, God? What's going to happen? Help me to see more clearly. Help me to understand."

4

TWO HUNDRED MILES FROM HOME. As the train rumbled through the night, Sam Carstairs enjoyed the luxury of the railroad president's private car: dark paneling, thick carpet, gold-accented lamps—all more expensive than what he had at home. Paintings of hunting scenes mixed with bold depictions of railroad engines racing along the tracks. The plush seat enveloped him with comfort. The steak dinner rivaled anything he had eaten in San Francisco.

He took one of the imported cigars offered by the ever-attentive valet, sniffed the sweet aroma, and rolled the cigar between his fingers. The outer leaf crinkled with promise. Sam drew the flame into the cigar, leaned back in the chair, and blew a smoke ring toward the ceiling. The ring floated upward before drifting apart like a cloud scattered by the breeze. He sipped a glass of the finest brandy he had ever tasted, rich and smooth as it slid down his throat.

He raised his glass to toast his reflection in the window. His trip to San Francisco had surpassed his wildest expectations. The railroads were starting to lay track again after five years of depression and had agreed to build a line to Riverbend. It would be completed in a year or so. The final deal had required more financial persuasion than he'd anticipated, but the rewards would be sweet. The town would grow, and so would his wealth and power. Track would be laid on land he owned. The station would be built on his land too, and businesses would grow around it. All those years of planning and plotting, negotiating with the railroad, buying every acre of land he could get his hands on—now it would finally pay off.

He stared past his reflection into the blackness. *Ah, Ruthie, you'd be proud of me. If only you were here to enjoy it with me.* He bowed his head and swallowed, a familiar sadness washing over him. Even after all these years, he missed his wife desperately.

The shrill whistle startled Sam back to the present as the train pulled into the station at Lassiter. His stop. He put out the cigar, took his bag from the valet, and descended the iron steps to the platform. Pools of lamplight washed the area with a soft glow that welcomed passengers and guided them through the chill night air.

Carstairs walked the short distance to the stage office and booked his passage on the next day's noon stage to Culverton, where he would catch another coach to Riverbend. He examined the hotel across the street with a critical eye. He had stayed there many times before. It paled in comparison to the one he had built in Riverbend, not anywhere near as well built or as fancy, but it would be adequate for one night.

The skinny hotel clerk greeted him with a smile and a handshake. "Good evening, Mr. Carstairs." His Adam's apple bobbed. "We're glad to have you stay with us again. Did you have a good trip to Frisco this year?"

"It was all right." Sadness enveloped Carstairs again. He was even less inclined to chitchat than usual.

The clerk handed him the key to the room he always booked, the closest thing the hotel had to a luxury suite. "Oh, by the way, I have a message for you. Someone came in this afternoon and left it with the day clerk."

Sam took the plain white envelope with his name printed in block letters and shoved it into his coat pocket. He thanked the clerk and turned away.

When he got to the room, he dropped his bag on the bed and hung his coat on a peg behind the door. He shook his head at the water-stained paneling and flaking paint. The braided rug in the middle of the floor was threadbare, the wood floors deeply scratched. *Maybe I should buy this place and show them how to run a hotel.*

Sam stood at the table in the center of the room and opened the envelope. His heart pounded as the words on the single sheet of paper seared into his eyes. He dropped the letter onto the table, sank into one of the lumpy armchairs that flanked it, and covered his face.

He looked at the paper one more time. Clammy sweat broke out on his forehead. He read the letter again, hands shaking.

> *Carstairs,*
> *Your debt is now due and it's time to pay up. You'll be contacted with arrangements for the final payment.*
> *H.*

5

MICHAEL WOKE with the sun. He stoked the embers of the fire to flame and huddled by it to drive off the early morning chill. A soft breeze brought the scent of pine, reminding him of the thick forests near the family farm in Connecticut. He shuddered and shook the memory away.

Anxious to get his mission done, he drank the last of the previous night's coffee and wolfed down a leftover biscuit, then cleaned and packed his gear on his dun-colored mare. He mounted his roan, Buddy, and rode along the top of the ridge searching for a path or trail to the valley floor.

The ridge was steep, almost a sheer drop in places. In other areas, the horses staggered on loose sand and rock that made the footing hazardous. After several miles, Michael found an old switchback trail and guided the horses to the valley floor. Spurring the animals to a brisk trot, he covered the distance to the river's edge. He pulled on the bell rope to call for the ferry nestled against the opposite bank.

A man emerged from a small cabin on the shore, waved, and pulled on the rope, bringing the boat to Michael. The ferryman was tall and broad-shouldered, with a long beard and legs like spindles. "Howdy, stranger. The fare's two bits fer you and two bits fer your horses."

Michael paid him and tied the horses to ropes along the sides of the boat.

"What brings you to these parts?" The ferryman spat a wad of chewing tobacco into the water and pulled on the rope to take the boat back across the river.

"I've come to see a man named Samuel Carstairs."

"Sam Carstairs? I know him. Whaddya want to see him fer?"

Michael glanced at the ferryman. Was he prying or just being friendly?

"I've got some information for him. Do you know him well?"

"Do I know him well? Sure do. Used t' punch cows for him up on the north range of his ranch. Worked for him after the war for nigh on ten year, tendin' his cows and horses, mendin' his fences, doin' whatever he needed doin'. He's my partner in this here business—set me up in it after my legs was stove up in a stampede three year ago. I gets to keep workin', and I splits the profit with him."

Michael let his gaze drift with the river's current, watching it ripple and catch the sun's rays. *Sure doesn't sound like the man Ben described.*

Sheriff Caleb Davis studied the desk before him, a totem of his years in Riverbend. The scratches and gouges, the dents in one corner from years of keys landing in the same spot every time they were tossed onto the desk, the coffee-ring stains, and the faint purplish smear of an old ink spill that spread like a river overflowing its banks.

The desk had seen better days. Just like him. Fatigue plagued every bone and muscle from too many years on too many horses chasing too many outlaws and breaking up too many saloon fights. Old bullet wounds and knife scars reminded him of the more serious encounters. He looked through the bars covering the dirt-streaked window and shook his head. *Sixty years on this body feels like a hundred today.*

The swish of a broom caught his attention. An old man appeared in the doorway that connected his office to the cells in the back, pushing a pile of dirt before him. Completely bald, with a grizzled beard, he was short and wiry and walked with an obvious limp, his right leg stiff. He swept his way into the office, stirring up a cloud of dust that made Caleb sneeze.

"Malachi, I know I said to sweep the place, but you don't have to raise a dust storm."

"Sorry, Sheriff." Malachi swept as hard as ever, and Caleb sneezed again. Finally he picked up his coffee cup and stomped outside.

Settling in a chair on the boardwalk, he propped his feet on an old barrel and leaned back against the wall to watch the town pass by. People opened their stores and swept the wooden boardwalks. Farmers and ranchers rattled by in wagons for their weekly visits to town, their wives next to them, their children wide-eyed at the bustling busyness, anticipating the treats waiting for them in the stores.

His internal alarm sounded like a shopkeeper's bell as a stranger rode up from the ferry landing. Early in his career, Caleb had learned to size up people, to assess quickly how much danger a stranger might pose. This man was tall— maybe six feet—and slender, with sandy-colored hair. Probably in his late twenties. His clothes and his two horses were coated in trail dust but otherwise well cared for.

Strangers weren't all that unusual for a growing town like Riverbend. Most were families hoping to start businesses, farms, or ranches, but a few were in town to take advantage of folks through gambling, stealing, or crooked business dealings. He tried to pick out the crooks right away and urge them, with the persuasion of his pistol if necessary, to move on.

This rider didn't appear to be a gambler or crook, but he sure wasn't a farmer or rancher either. *Guess I'm about to find out.*

The man turned toward him, dismounted, and tied his horses to the hitching post. He dug in his saddlebags, pulled out an envelope, and walked up the two steps to stand in front of Caleb.

"You Sheriff Caleb Davis?"

"That's me."

The stranger held out the envelope. "My name is Michael Archer. I'd like you to read this letter, and then we can talk."

Caleb raised an eyebrow. "You from out East? New York? New England?"

"Connecticut, originally. Why?"

"Way you talk. Couple of families around here come from New England. Everybody thinks they talk funny." Caleb opened the envelope, took out the single page, and glanced at the signature. "Well, this here's a surprise. I ain't seen nor heard from Gideon Parsons in years. He don't like to write much—never did—so this is something if he wrote this for you to bring to me."

Dear Caleb, the letter began.

This letter is to intradus you to a man named Michael Archer. The man that gav it to you should be almost six feet tall, kind of thin, with light brown hair and hazel eyes. I known him for several years. He works with a minister, Zechariah Taylor, that tends to the prisners in my jail and in the state prison. They both done a good job with the men and have really helped us keep things under contrl. I vouch for him as high as I can and ask you, baset on our years of riding together and trusting each other, to help him in what he's trying to do.

He's in Riverbend to see Samuel Carstairs about his son Benjamin.

Young Carstairs got in trouble here and was convicted of killing a man. We hung him April 10. Carstairs and Michael tried to reach the father but he never respnded. Michael made a promise to return his belongings and a letter Carstairs rote to his father to try to make emends.

*I'm asking you to help Michael make contact
with the father and hopefully get him to listen. His son
seemed like someone that could've been decent but made
too many mistakes. He really wanted to get back right
with his father.*

Thanks, Gideon

Caleb folded the letter and tapped it against his thigh. "Pull up a chair." He gestured to the empty chair beside him. "You want some coffee?"

"Sure."

"Malachi," Caleb yelled over his shoulder. The door to the office creaked and the sweeper stuck his head out.

"Yes, Sheriff?" he rasped.

"Bring us two cups of coffee, will ya?" Caleb handed him his empty cup.

"Yes, sir." Malachi disappeared inside.

The quizzical expression on Archer's face prompted Caleb to explain. "Malachi's one of our town drunks. Actually, he's our only habitual drunk. He's working off a sentence from the judge for public drunkenness. He cleans up my office and the jail and the town hall next door instead of paying a fine."

Malachi came out carrying two steaming mugs. He handed the mugs to Caleb and Archer and hobbled back into the office.

Archer turned to face Caleb, sipped the hot brew, and said nothing. Caleb studied him over the rim of his cup, not really sipping any coffee. The young man seemed all right. And Caleb trusted Parsons's ability to read men.

"So tell me what happened to Ben Carstairs."

Archer related a story about young Ben's trial and his hanging. Apparently he'd gotten himself saved before he died. But Caleb had been a lawman long enough to know that didn't mean the boy wasn't guilty.

"Did he really kill the horse trader?"

Archer shook his head. "I don't think so. I've worked with other men in the same situation. If they accepted Jesus, usually they'd admit what they did, to me at least. They'd say they were sorry and accept their punishment, even when it meant being hanged. Ben wasn't like that. To the end, he insisted he didn't do it. He and I talked about it a lot because I wanted to give him every chance to confess. When he didn't, I believed him. I think an innocent man was hung. But there was no evidence or time to prove someone else did it. Sheriff Parsons had his doubts about Ben's guilt too but couldn't come up with anything to postpone the hanging."

Caleb sighed. "I've known Ben since he was little. Even with all the problems with his father and the law, I don't think he'd ever kill anyone in cold blood."

"Any idea why he didn't get along with his father?" Archer asked.

"Ben's mother died giving birth to him. Sam Carstairs doted on that woman. Gave her everything she ever wanted, and she loved him just as much—always wanted to please him. Trouble was, Sam wanted a big family, and she was never a healthy woman. When she died, Sam was crushed. I don't think he ever recovered. Never accepted Ben like he did the two other boys. You ask me, he really blamed himself, but he couldn't live with that. So he blamed Ben. Threw him outta the house 'fore he was eighteen."

Archer shook his head. "Yeah, that fits with what Ben told me. How did his brothers take it?"

"Took their lead from the father—treated Ben like dirt. The oldest one, Joshua, got real quiet when his ma died. Still don't talk or smile much. Got himself a pretty Mexican wife now, which annoys Sam no end, but otherwise Josh don't have much to do with people. He runs the ranch while Sam runs the other family businesses." He gazed down the busy street. "We don't see him much in town."

"And Mark? That's the other son, right?"

Caleb snorted his disgust. "That boy was already spoilt and didn't like his mother bein' in the family way. Sam's attitude gave him reason to be as mean as he wanted to Ben. But he didn't stop there. Mark's a bully, and Sam keeps bailing him out of any trouble he gets himself into. He's just bad news—uses his name to get whatever he wants."

"You think the father will talk to me about Ben?"

"It's hard to tell. He hasn't mentioned Ben since he threw him out. It's like the boy never existed."

"Ben wanted one more chance with his father. I owe it to Ben to give it a try."

"Well," Caleb said hesitantly, "I'll do what I can to set up a meeting based on Gideon's letter. Won't happen before Thursday, though. Sam's due back then from his yearly trip to San Francisco."

"I appreciate any help you can give. Is there a good hotel

in town where I can stable my horses, take a bath, and get some decent food?"

Caleb pointed up the street. "The Riverbend is the best in town. They should take really good care of you."

Archer stood and touched the brim of his hat with a two-finger salute. "Thanks, Sheriff."

Caleb watched Archer lead his horses across the street. The man appeared lean and tough—not exactly the minister type. Still, if Michael Archer wasn't careful, Sam Carstairs would just chew him up and spit him out.

6

Sam woke early after a restless night, remembering the note he had never expected to see. It was still there on the table. He scanned it again. He knew only one "H" who might think he owed a debt.

But John Higgins was dead. Sam had paid enough to make sure of that while Higgins languished in prison on the false charge Sam arranged.

What if Higgins didn't die?

The stage to Culverton wouldn't leave Lassiter for several hours. Sam's usual routine on such mornings was to enjoy a large breakfast and spend the morning reading the papers. The hotel received newspapers from around the country—sometimes weeks old, but at least they told him news that didn't often reach Riverbend. This morning he had no appetite for food or news. His stomach churned. The thought of Higgins hung over his head like a thundercloud.

Sam pulled on his lip as he walked to the window. He peered through the dirt-streaked glass at the stage office across the street. He remembered riding the coach once on an empty stomach and knew he needed to eat something whether he felt like it or not.

As he walked by the front desk on his way to the dining room, the day clerk called out, "Did you get your message yesterday, Mr. Carstairs?"

Sam eyed the greasy-looking clerk, whose white shirt strained its buttons over an ample stomach. How could the owner let this man work up front? "Were you working when the message came in?"

All smiles and nods, eager to help. "Yes, sir. It was early yesterday afternoon."

"Who brought it in?"

"A young woman."

"Did she give her name? What did she look like? Have you seen her before?"

The clerk stepped back. He batted his eyes and held up his hands.

Sam raised an eyebrow and put an ominous edge to his voice. "Well?" He didn't have the inclination to be patient with this fool.

Sweat beaded on the clerk's forehead. He fidgeted with the bow tie that looked like a mutated butterfly under his two chins.

Sam placed both hands on the reception desk and leaned

his upper body over the counter, his face close to the clerk's. "I'm waiting."

The clerk backed up another step, pressing against the counter that held the mail slots and room keys. "Sh-she didn't give a name. I asked, but she said you would know when you read the message. Could've been in her early twenties. Didn't get a good look at her face. She wore a big bonnet, kept her head down."

Sam drummed his fingers on the counter and chewed his lower lip. The clerk kept his place against the mail slots. Sam turned abruptly and walked into the dining room, picking up several newspapers from stacks on the counter.

Breakfast tasted like sawdust in his dry mouth. He turned pages in the newspapers, not comprehending a single word. His arms and legs tingled. His mind froze, unable to focus, to think.

His gaze swept the room. No young women. But there was sure to be more than one person helping Higgins. Any of these people could be in cahoots with the man. *Somebody could be sneaking up on me now.*

He whirled around, knocking his coffee cup to the floor. The china shattered on the hardwood floor. Nobody behind him, but everyone in the room stared at him. Heat rose in his neck and cheeks. He tossed some coins on the table, picked up his hat, and walked out.

In front of the stage office, the driver and guard helped the agent load luggage and packages into the boot and onto the roof. The horses snorted and shook in their harnesses.

Two men stood on the boardwalk watching the others. *Partners with Higgins?*

One was of medium build, with a full beard and black hair that hung over his collar. He wore dungarees and a blue denim shirt with a brown leather vest. A gun in a tied-down holster hugged his left thigh. *A man not afraid of violence. Enemy or potential ally?* He dipped his chin as Sam stepped onto the boardwalk.

The other man was Sam's height but weighed about one hundred pounds less, with recently cut brown hair and a well-trimmed mustache. He wore a pearl gray pin-striped suit with a brocade vest and a gold watch chain. *Bit of a dandy. Gambler. Probably bathes in lilac water.* He gave Sam a quick glance and turned back to watching the men load the stage.

Sam consulted his pocket watch. "We gonna make it on time, Adams? Seems like a lot of gear for three passengers."

The agent stepped onto the boardwalk and shook hands with Sam. "Sorry for the delay, Mr. Carstairs. We had a lot of freight come in at the last minute." He motioned toward the other two men. "These two gentlemen will be traveling with you as far as Culverton. This is Jeremiah Turner—" he gestured toward the man in the gray suit—"and this is Philip Addison."

The three men shook hands.

Adams cleared his throat. "Mr. Carstairs, would you please join me inside. There's something I think you need to know."

Sam caught a flicker of the glare Turner directed at the

agent. Addison and Turner followed Sam and Adams into the office.

Adams leaned against his desk and looked at the three men in turn. "Mr. Carstairs, Mr. Turner is against my telling you what I am about to say. He's concerned about security. However, I know you are a loyal customer. I think it only fair for you to know there may be some danger on this trip and give you the chance to take tomorrow's stage if you want."

"What danger?"

Adams and Turner exchanged glances. Turner shrugged. "Go ahead and tell him the rest."

Adams swallowed, his face pale. "This stage is carrying a large sum of money, bonds, and other valuable documents for the banks and businesses in Culverton. There have been three robberies of similar shipments in the last two months. Two of our guards have been killed and several passengers beaten. Mr. Turner and Mr. Addison are special agents the stage line brought in. They'll be riding as passengers to provide extra security."

Sam clasped his hands together. "Let me ask you: would you have given this information to any other passengers, or have you just told me because I'm such a 'loyal customer'?"

Adams turned pale. Turner smirked in apparent amusement at Adams's discomfort.

Sam sighed. "Mr. Turner, I'm anxious to get home. I've been away long enough, so I plan to take this stage. My pistol is packed in my bags, which are already on the coach. If you can supply me with a rifle and ammunition, I'll help if trouble comes." *I feel like shooting something anyway.*

Turner nodded to Addison, who went to the gun rack behind the counter. He took down a Winchester as well as two boxes of ammunition and handed them to Sam. Sam hefted the rifle and walked over to the wall map showing the stage routes in and out of Lassiter. With the barrel of the rifle, he traced the route that ran to Culverton.

Sam tapped the map where trees were indicated. "The stage usually takes the east river road because it's several miles shorter and the road is smoother. I assume all the robberies have been on that road, probably in one of these stands of trees."

"That's right," Adams said.

"Why don't we take this west river road that runs along the ridge? It will be several hours longer and a whole lot rougher, but seeing as I'm the only paying passenger, I can sacrifice a little bit of time and comfort to get the cargo through safely. By the time the outlaws get wise to us, we should be too close to Culverton for them to try anything."

Turner called in Davey, the driver, and explained Sam's suggestion. Davey's blue eyes scrunched in his leathery face, the squint permanent from years in the sun. He crossed his muscular arms and spat. A stream of tobacco juice grazed the outside of a spittoon before dripping onto the floor. Adams frowned at him, and Davey shrugged.

"The west road's got some problems 'cause o' rock slides every once in a while. But if that happens, I reckon there's enough of us to make a way for the rig to get through. An' I think Jake and I would rather face a rock slide than deal with them outlaws again."

"Who's Jake?" Sam asked.

Davey stared at him. "Jake's the guard. Who're you?"

"All right, that's enough," Turner said. "Let's get on the road."

The five men filed out onto the boardwalk. Davey climbed up into his seat next to Jake and took the reins of the six-horse team. Once the three men were in the coach, Davey slapped the reins and gave a loud yell. The horses strained, and the stage lurched forward. By the time it reached the end of town, the team had settled into an easy trot that would eat up the miles.

Sam held the rifle in front of him, palms sweaty, hands clenched around the barrel and stock. Beads of sweat ran down his temples. Higgins or someone working for him could be anywhere. That is, if Higgins were really alive. And now there were outlaws to contend with.

Turner sat across from him. "Are you all right, Mr. Carstairs? You look a little peaked."

"Call me Sam. Just a little nervous," he lied. His heart pounded so loudly, he was surprised the other men couldn't hear it. He twisted his hands around the rifle. Above them, Davey snapped the reins to urge the team faster. Sam brought the rifle to his chest, ready to aim and fire.

7

SHAVE AND HAIRCUT DONE, Michael eased himself into the steaming hot water. He rested his head against the high end of the cast-iron tub and sighed as the aches and kinks of the trail seeped out of his muscles and joints. After three weeks of cold-water baths in creeks and rivers, the hotel's hot water, soap, and soft towel marked a pleasant return to civilization. He felt human again.

The sun shone directly overhead when Michael walked out of the hotel. He stopped and drank in its warmth, enjoying the bright sky and light breeze off the river.

He strolled down the town's wide main street, breathing in the aromas of city life—leather from the saddle maker's shop, the gunsmith's oil, the blacksmith's forge with that peculiar aroma of burning wood and heated metal. A couple of saloons that at one time would have drawn him like a cat to milk now barely drew his notice. They were part of a past he did not regret losing.

Prosperity seemed to flow from every storefront. A constant stream of wagons and riders on horseback coming down the road competed with people crossing from one side to the other. Well-dressed businessmen and townspeople mingled with simply dressed farmers. Cowboys ambled by in their rolling, bowlegged gait, spurs jangling.

Michael mused on how much he had changed—how much God had changed him. Not too many years ago, he would have been on the lookout for opportunities to steal and swindle and keep the whiskey flowing through his veins. Now he saw people instead of potential victims or threats. And all the noise and the commotion made him feel alive. Being around people was just one more reason he could never be comfortable with the isolation of a farm. *Yep, city life beats farming any day of the week.*

He smiled as he approached the church at the end of the street and the two-story house next to it. *Now that's a place I wouldn't mind coming home to.* Both buildings had fresh coats of white paint and blue trim on the windows and doors. Baskets with brightly colored flowers hung from the porch roof. A white picket fence ran from the corner of the church, in front of the house, and around to the back end.

Regret stabbed his heart at the sight of two small children playing with a puppy in the yard. *Normal kids doing normal things. Ellie should have had a puppy.* The little dog, golden with dark spots, ran after a stick thrown by the girl and returned it, engaging in a tug-of-war before releasing it so it could be thrown again. A man sat on the porch and watched. A book lay open on the table in front of him.

"Papa, look!" the girl squealed. She appeared to be about six or seven, with dark brown braids and a yellow-checked dress. *Ellie had a dress just like that.*

Her red-haired, blue-eyed brother was a few years younger. Their giggles over the puppy's antics turned to silent curiosity when they spotted Michael.

The man on the porch marked his place in the book and walked the short distance to the gate, the children right behind him. He was stocky and short, a good six inches shorter than Michael, with dark brown hair and eyes like his daughter's. Extending his hand, he said, "You must be Michael Archer. I'm Luke Matthews, pastor of the church. We've been looking forward to your arrival."

Michael stared at the man. "Excuse me. How do you know who I am?"

Luke laughed. "We received a letter from Zechariah Taylor a few days ago. He told me you were coming, and you fit the description he gave me."

Luke introduced him to the children. Abigail smiled and curtsied when introduced. Daniel stood very straight and serious. He shook hands with Michael with as much grown-up solemnity as a five-year-old could muster.

"I'm very pleased to meet you, sir. Welcome to Riverbend Church," he lisped. "Would you like to meet our new dog?"

Michael suppressed a smile. "I would like that very much."

They took a few minutes for an ear scratch. Then Luke

led the way onto the porch and opened the door into the house. "Martha," he called, "we've got company. Mr. Archer's here."

A woman emerged through a doorway at the far end of the hall. She was about five feet tall, with a compact build and bright red hair that she pushed away from her face as she came down the hall—clearly Daniel's mother. Michael basked in the warmth of her smile as she extended her hand.

"Welcome to our home, Mr. Archer. We've been expecting you." Her grasp was warm, firm, and confident.

"Thank you, ma'am. It's a pleasure to meet you."

"I was just going to call everyone in for lunch. Will you join us? It's nothing fancy, but there's plenty."

"I would appreciate that." Michael realized he hadn't eaten anything since the night before.

Luke led Michael into the dining room. The children followed and scampered to their seats around a long oval table covered with a white tablecloth. A bowl full of wildflowers sat in the middle. Places were set for five.

"Abigail, will you please get a plate and utensils for Mr. Archer?" Luke said.

Abigail hopped down from her seat and ran to a hutch along the wall, where she took down a plate and mug from the shelf and a knife, fork, and spoon from the drawer. She carefully and correctly arranged them in front of an empty chair, then glanced at her father, who beamed at her.

"Thank you, Abigail," Michael said. "You did that very well."

"You're welcome, Mr. Archer."

"Pastor Luke, you have two beautiful children." A wistful melancholy settled over him as he observed the children's happy faces. He shook it off.

Martha came in carrying a large, steaming bowl. The rich, meaty aroma reminded Michael of how hungry he was. Another woman followed Martha, carrying a tray with a basket of bread, a coffeepot, and a pitcher.

At the sight of her, Michael's hunger vanished.

She was a couple of inches over five feet, with light brown hair pulled back in a loose knot. Her eyes were dark blue, almost violet. Her nose was slim, her mouth small but rosy and plump, her chin gently rounded. A blue-checked dress revealed a trim, graceful figure.

He watched, enthralled by her movements as she and Martha served the meal. He could not take his eyes off her. He didn't know why. He didn't care why. He just wanted to stare at her for hours. Watching her was like watching the sun set behind the mountains, the colors and shadings constantly changing, drawing him further and further in. Michael forced himself to stop gawking.

When all the plates were filled and drinks poured, Luke said, "Michael, let me introduce you to Rachel Stone. Rachel, this is Michael Archer. Rachel is staying with us while she gets herself established in town. Rachel, this is the man Zechariah Taylor wrote us about."

Rachel took the seat opposite him and smiled, showing even, white teeth. She smiled with her eyes as well.

"It's very nice to meet you, sir. I know Martha and Luke have been anticipating your visit. I hope you enjoy

Riverbend." Her soft voice reminded him of honey and gentle brooks and warm breezes.

"Thank you, Miss Stone. It's a pleasure to meet you too." He stopped, not knowing what to say. He seldom had difficulty talking with pretty girls, but no girl had affected him like this Rachel Stone. He was tongue-tied, awkward, and shy. A hundred butterflies seemed to flutter in his stomach.

Luke blessed the meal. As they ate, the children chattered about the antics of their new puppy. Michael half listened, glancing at Rachel. When their eyes met, a slight smile curved the corner of her mouth. He smiled back, thankful the children's conversation provided a reason not to attempt small talk.

When the children's excitement wound down, Martha asked, "Mr. Archer, have you been able to set up a meeting with Mr. Carstairs?"

"Not yet. I found out this morning that he's out of town until Thursday."

Her fair cheeks flushed. "Well, I pray you have more success with him than we've had. Just don't tell him you're involved in any type of church work." She stabbed a piece of meat with her fork. "That man is the devil incarnate, I tell you."

Luke placed his hand on his wife's arm. "Take it easy, honey." He turned to Michael. "It's true that Mr. Carstairs has no love for God or the church. When we first got here, he told Martha she'd do more good serving drinks in a saloon than as a pastor's wife. He told me I was as useless as a one-armed house painter."

Rachel coughed. Blushing, she covered her mouth with her napkin and reached for her water glass. "I'm sorry. Carrot went down the wrong way."

Martha started to say something, glanced at Michael, closed her mouth.

What was that all about?

The grandfather clock in the living room struck the hour. Rachel stood. Michael and Luke both rose.

"If you'll excuse me," she said, "I need to leave for the restaurant. Martha, I'm sorry to leave you with the washing up. Mr. Archer—" her eyes held his—"it was a pleasure to meet you. Will I see you at the service tomorrow morning?"

"Uh . . . thank you, Miss Stone. I'll be sure to say hello in the morning." He stopped and blushed, wanting to say something profound, not able to say anything. *How could this girl leave me feeling so foolish?*

Rachel took her plate and cup into the kitchen, and a short time later he heard the front door close. The children asked to be excused, then bounded out of the room and soon could be heard playing with the puppy in the front yard. Michael and Luke gathered the dishes and cups and followed Martha into the kitchen. After everything was loaded into the sink, Martha chased them out of her domain. They retired to the front porch and made themselves comfortable as they watched the children.

"Does Mr. Carstairs know anything about why you want to meet with him?"

"I don't think so. Ben and I sent him letters, but they were never answered."

"I only knew the youngest son by reputation. He was gone by the time Martha and I moved here. But his reputation wasn't that good. We heard he was a troublemaker and hooligan."

"Yeah, he couldn't keep himself out of trouble. But just before he died, he received Jesus."

"Well, praise God for that."

"I'm trying to get a handle on the best way to deal with Sam Carstairs, but it doesn't sound like you have much of a connection with him."

"No, we don't. We went out to meet him when we first got here, even though the deacons and the previous pastor said it wasn't worth it. We wanted to introduce ourselves and invite him to our first service. He did everything but throw a punch at me or pull his gun. He practically threw us out of his house, cursing and saying preachers were the most useless people he knew. It still bothers Martha to be reminded of that meeting." He glanced back at the house and grinned. "As you no doubt noticed."

"Any idea why he's so against preachers?"

"The deacons told us it's because he blames God and Ben for his wife's death. So he has no use for God or the men and women who work for Him."

Michael sighed. "Sounds like I'm really going to have to have the Spirit's guidance and the Father's favor if I'm gonna get anywhere with him."

"Let's pray over it," Luke said. The two men bowed their heads.

As they finished their prayer, Martha came out onto the

porch and sat on the swing next to Luke. She smiled at her husband and took his hand in hers.

"You seem to have made quite an impression on Rachel," she said.

"Well, she made quite an impression on me," Michael admitted, blushing. "Have you known her long? Is she from around here?"

"We met her about six months ago," Martha answered, "and she's been living with us since then. She came to the Lord about the same time. She's a sweet, sweet person, and Luke and I and the kids all love her very much." She exchanged a glance with her husband. "She's been a blessing to us. She's learning to adjust to a town the size of Riverbend and trying to fit in."

"Where did she come from?" Michael couldn't keep the eagerness out of his voice.

"We met her in Denver." Luke brushed casually at his pants. "Since she's been here, she's gotten a job at the hotel restaurant. Next week she opens her own store. She's going to be the first professional dressmaker in town." Michael noticed the touch of pride in Luke's voice.

"Is that what she did in Denver?"

Luke and Martha looked at each other again. Martha adjusted the folds in her dress. "Yes. She made dresses for people there."

Michael waited for her to say more. Finally he stood. "Pastor, I know you probably need to prepare for the service tomorrow. Thanks for your hospitality and the delicious food." He shook hands with Martha and Luke and stepped from the porch. He said good-bye to the children and closed the gate behind him.

As he walked back to the hotel, he thought about Rachel and the conversation with Luke and Martha. *I think there's more to Rachel Stone than meets the eye.*

8

RACHEL WALKED toward the Riverbend Hotel, oblivious to the people and activities around her. She felt like a schoolgirl with her first crush. She was sure she had a silly grin on her face. What was it about Michael Archer that touched her, that made her aware of a tug on her heart?

Men never had this effect on her. Not her old customers, for sure, nor the new men she'd met at the church and the hotel restaurant. She'd put up that wall years ago when she discovered men wanted only one thing from her. They might possess her body briefly, but they would never touch her heart. The wall had kept her isolated and safe from hurt until Luke and Martha came along. Martha chipped little pieces out and ministered to the exposed parts as tenderly as she would treat a newborn child. In just a few weeks, Martha had gone from total stranger to closest friend, the sister she never had, the guide she desperately needed. She would have to talk with Martha when she got home.

A loud *tsk* caught her attention. She turned her head to see a woman take her husband's arm and half turn, half push him into the general store. Rachel wanted to laugh, though hot tears burned her eyes. She clenched her fists until the urge to punch the woman's stuck-up nose passed. She could get away with it at Red Mary's when one of the other girls acted up, but not on the streets of Riverbend.

Rachel stared at the woman's back as she passed the store's open door. *I am no threat to your marriage. How can I convince you?*

Six months she'd been here in Riverbend, and some people still treated her as though she were carrying some disease. If only that Mark Carstairs wouldn't keep spreading gossip about what she had done in Denver.

Only it wasn't gossip. It was truth.

Her stomach dropped. How would Michael Archer feel if he knew about her past? If he stayed around town very long, he was sure to find out. Why was what he felt about her past so important anyway? He was just a man, probably like all the others. He wouldn't be here long. He'd leave once he took care of business with Sam Carstairs, and she'd never see him again. The thought saddened her. Why?

"Afternoon, Miss Rachel." A man held the door open for his wife and child to precede him out of the restaurant. Rachel caught his wife's quick scowl dissolving into a plastered-on smile. The little girl stared at Rachel with wide green eyes, clutching her mother's dress. Rachel recognized them from previous visits to the restaurant. A farm family in town for Saturday. The wife always selected a table where Rachel wouldn't be their waitress.

"Good afternoon, sir, ma'am." *Keep your best city voice on, girl.* "Thank you."

The family turned to go up the boardwalk. Rachel stuck out her tongue at the woman, glanced quickly around to see if anyone had noticed, then hurried toward the back room.

"So, Fräulein, this is your last day. I hate to see you go." Mr. Gunther approached her, his hands white with flour. Though officially the restaurant manager, he was a baker at heart and produced most of the desserts they sold.

Rachel smiled as she tied an apron around her waist and reset her hair into a tighter bun. "That's kind of you to say." She bit her lower lip. "I can't tell you how grateful I am you gave me this job when I first got to town."

Mr. Gunther grinned, his gold tooth gleaming. "If Pastor Luke and Miss Martha spoke for you, then I think I could not go wrong." Rachel realized she was going to miss his German accent and the way his beefy hands danced over his pastries.

"And you stuck with me when those stories came out."

He shrugged. "We all make mistakes, and we all deserve a chance at a new start. I got mine when I came to America. You got yours when you came to Riverbend." He rubbed his hands together. "Time to get to work. Today, I make a strudel and a very nice *Apfelkuchen*, perhaps some gingerbread."

She watched him walk into the kitchen singing a German

folk song, his wooden leg thumping on the floor. He stopped at the entrance and turned back to her. He waved a finger in the air. "And remember, Frau Gunther gets the first dress from your shop."

Rachel went out to the half-empty dining room. The lunch rush was over, and most of the remaining guests were finishing their meals. Rachel cleared and reset tables, Mr. Gunther's tune rambling through her head.

In many ways, she would miss working here. At its busiest, it was the hardest work she had ever done, but also quite rewarding. The Gunthers were kind to her, and she loved being able to satisfy people and not feel degraded, abused, or fearful at the end of the day.

Come Monday, though, her life would get even better because then she would open her dress shop. Images of fabrics and patterns, needles and threads neatly arrayed filled her imagination.

A shadow of doubt intruded. *Something's not right. What am I missing?*

She shook the feeling off like a gnat, but it hovered at the edge of her mind.

9

THE STAGECOACH ROCKED and jolted over the rough road. At some bounces, the three men completely left their seats. Twice Sam bumped his head on the roof. Shouts from above told Sam that Jake was almost thrown off the stage more than once. He heard Davey urge the team to as near a normal speed as possible on the rough road.

Across from him, in the forward-facing seat, Philip Addison and Jeremiah Turner sat with grim determination, watching out their windows. Dust rising from the wheels and horses clouded Sam's vision.

Without warning, the coach slowed as the driver bellowed, "Whoa."

Before the coach came to a full stop, Turner was out the door. Sam followed him out while Addison maneuvered his frame out the other door. Turner had his pistol drawn and cocked. Sam levered a shell into the Winchester he carried.

To their right, a boulder-studded cliff rose almost a hundred feet. To their left, the road dropped off in a gradual slope to a river several hundred yards away. Rocks and boulders spilled like marbles across the slope. Trees and shrubs grew close to the river.

Sam scanned the area, squinting against the sun, finger on the trigger, alert for signs of trouble.

Turner peered up at the driver. "What's wrong, Davey?"

"Rock slide's blocked the road up ahead. We either gotta move them rocks or find a way round 'em."

"All right," Turner said. "You, Jake, and Phil scout it out. Mr. Carstairs and I will keep a watch in case it's a trap."

Addison eyed Turner up and down. "Can't get those fancy duds dirty now, can we?"

"That's right, my good man. It's all part of my disguise as the wealthy banker while you pose as the dusty cowboy."

"That's what I get for letting you flip the coin. Knowin' you, it had two heads anyway."

"The luck of the draw, my friend. The luck of the draw."

Addison chuckled and walked away. "Come on, you old ladies. Let's move us some rocks before our fancy banker here melts in the sun."

Davey and Jake climbed down from their box and, with Addison, walked to the rock slide about thirty yards in front of them. Turner climbed on top of the stage and made a deliberate complete turn. "Don't see any signs of trouble, but those rocks high up the slope would be a good place to set up an ambush."

Sam scanned the rocks, watching for the glint of the sun off a gun barrel. He cocked his head to listen for a stone being dislodged. "Seems clear."

"Yeah, it does."

Sam stood near the horses and continued to scan the cliff looming above them. Grateful to be on ground that wasn't moving and lurching, he stretched muscles cramped and tense from the ride.

Jake, Davey, and Addison walked back.

"Slide's too big to move. We gotta go round it," Davey said. "If we take it slow and easylike, we should be able to walk round on the down slope. It's not very steep, but the footing is loose."

"All right," Turner said. "We'll go around. You drive, and the rest of us will walk alongside to help keep the horses calm."

The animals didn't like the footing and the pull of the coach in the soft dirt, but the four men soothed and urged them forward. Thirty minutes later they were around the blockage. Before moving on, they drank from canteens Addison had stowed aboard to wash the taste of dust out of their mouths.

Turner gestured toward Davey with his canteen. "How much farther?"

"Well," Davey said, "if we don't have no more delays, it's about two hours till we hitch back up with the main road, and then it's another two hours to Culverton." He glanced at the sun. "It'll be after dark 'fore we get there."

Davey and Jake climbed to their posts as Turner and Addison entered the coach. Sam stood with his hand on the door, reluctant to enter the small space that rattled his bones like dice in a cup. The stage lurched as Davey snapped the reins. Sam scrambled aboard. He settled on the hard seat just as a hole in the road launched him to the ceiling.

The men maintained their lookout in silence. Conversation meant shouting over the sounds of the coach as it clattered along the road. At times the trail drifted to the right, and Sam lost sight of the river and trees. At other times, they came so close to the sloping edge that Sam feared the coach would tumble over into the water. Dust heated by the bright sun drifted in constantly through the windows, settling on their clothes and lips and in their eyes.

After a couple of hours, Davey brought the coach to a stop.

Turner jumped to the ground as the horses shook their harnesses. "What's the matter, Davey?"

The driver gestured. "Bridge is just the other side of that rise yonder. Reckon we oughta take a look-see before we go over the top?"

Turner looked up the slope. "Good idea. Phil, come with me."

Sam followed Addison out of the coach. "What do you—?"

A bullet splintered the wood next to Davey as a shot echoed. Davey and Jake jumped to the ground. Davey dived under the coach while Jake scrambled for cover in some rocks alongside the road. Turner crouched near the front wheel of the coach. Sam, rifle ready, stood at the door.

Addison edged his way toward the rear. "They're somewhere on the right—up slope. I'll see if I can get around 'em."

Another shot tore through the canvas that covered the rear of the stage, an inch from Addison's head.

Sam crawled back inside the coach and over to the door on the other side. Peering out the window, he saw sunlight glint off a rifle barrel halfway up the slope. He aimed and waited, as if he were hunting deer on his ranch.

The outlaw rose slightly to take another shot. Sam fired. The man staggered, hands covering his face. He stumbled, fell, and rolled down the slope, landing against some rocks.

Another shot, this one from the left, splintered the edge of the door, showering Sam with dust and pieces of debris.

A voice bellowed, "Throw down yer guns and put yer hands up."

Sam saw Turner jump as a shot kicked up dust near his foot. Turner moved behind the wheel, while Addison slid under the boot. Sam hunkered down, peering over the window frame. Turner fired toward the voice. His bullet pinged off a rock.

Several more shots fell around the coach. Sam saw Jake fire up the slope. A cry of pain was followed by the body of another outlaw tumbling into view. Sam sought another target but couldn't find one.

A man screamed close by. Sam turned to see Jake clutch his shoulder, blood seeping between his fingers. The guard slumped against the rocks, his rifle useless in the dirt. A shot careened off the rock near his head.

"Jake's hit. Cover me." Sam bolted from the coach. Turner

said something, but the words were lost in Sam's focus to reach the wounded man. He slung Jake over his shoulder and scurried the short distance back to the stage. He heard shots but was oblivious to where they landed.

He laid Jake on the floor of the coach, slammed the door, and dived under to join the others. His chest heaved as he sought to draw air into his burning lungs. "Been a while since I lifted anything that heavy."

Turner spoke over his shoulder. "How is he?"

Sam coughed. "Don't know. Got hit in the shoulder. Bleedin' a lot."

"It's the favor of God you didn't get hit too."

Sam shrugged. "Doubt it had anything to do with me. If God cared about anybody, He was probably watchin' out for Jake." Sam tipped his head toward the rocks. "They got us pinned down pretty good here."

Addison spat a stream of tobacco juice. "Yep. Any suggestions?"

Turner shrugged. "We could wait for them to surrender."

"They'd have to run out of bullets first."

"True. We could surrender."

Addison wiped his mouth with his sleeve. "We could. But I promised my wife I'd be home for Christmas."

"I thought that was last Christmas."

Addison arched his eyebrows. "Oh yeah. Didn't make it then, either."

They heard Jake moan through the floorboards. Turner looked up. "You know we're going to have to make a run for it."

"Yer right," Addison said. "But I'd still rather wait for them to run out of bullets and surrender." A shot clipped a piece of wood off the wheel near Addison's head. "Don't look like that's gonna happen anytime soon." He turned to the driver. "Davey, if we gave you good cover, how fast can you get back on top and get this team rolling?"

Davey paled and licked his lips. "Ten, maybe twenty seconds."

"Could you do it faster if we gave you lousy cover?"

Davey glared. "Don't fool with me, Phil. Ya know I can drive a six team better'n you, so you best keep me alive."

Turner tapped Sam on the shoulder. "First thing is to get you inside the coach. Then you can give cover on the other side. Phil will stay under here while Davey and I climb up top. When the stage starts rolling, Phil will climb inside. Everybody got it?"

Sam fumbled his bullets as they reloaded. He wiped his face with his sleeve and held tight to his rifle.

Addison nudged him. "Relax. You'll never shoot straight holding it that tight."

Sam unclasped his fingers and repositioned his hands. He forced himself to take a deep breath and relax the tension in his neck and shoulders.

Turner pointed with a jerk of his head. "I think there's three or four out there, spread out in the rocks. Probably a few more on the other side. If they see us move, they might come up out of their cover. Ready, Mr. Carstairs?"

Sam swallowed the lump in his throat. "Yep."

Turner braced himself beside the wheel. His command was sharp as a whip snap. "Go."

Sam scrambled as Turner and Addison fired from either side of the coach. A bullet tugged at the sleeve of his coat. Others splattered into the door as he opened it. Wood chips fell on his head as he dived onto the seat and closed the door behind him. He fired at the rocks without targeting his shots. The coach shook as Turner and Davey climbed up the sides. Jake, still lying on the floor, moaned.

The slap of leather and a loud "Yah!" told him Davey had the reins. The coach jolted forward. As it picked up speed, Addison climbed into the coach and lay prone on the seat across from Sam, facing the other side. "Durn fool almost ran me over. He made it in seven seconds, by the way, but don't tell him I said so."

Sam spotted a man rise up from behind some rocks and aim his rifle at the horses.

"Oh no you don't." Sam fired.

The man dropped his rifle, clutched his chest, and fell. Lucky shot. Sam levered another cartridge into the chamber as he scanned the side of the ridge.

The shooting stopped. The creaks and groans of the coach moving up the slope, the slap of the reins, and Davey's calls for more speed filled Sam's ears. No sign of any other shooters. "We made it."

Addison pointed behind them. "Don't count on it." He yelled to the top of the coach, "Jeremiah, three riders behind us."

The stage crested the slope and picked up speed as it headed for the river.

Turner yelled down, "And four in front."

Addison cursed and slapped the back wall of the coach. "Wish there was a winder here. Awright, Mr. Carstairs, you see what you can do to help Jeremiah from in here. I'll watch our back."

Sam looked out but could not find a target. The wood next to his head splintered, telling him the riders behind were gaining. From above, Turner fired. Davey's voice boomed, and the reins slapped.

He heard Addison fire several shots. Addison laughed. "How about that? One of 'em rode right into my bullet."

A horse screamed. Sam waited for the coach to lurch or tumble. Nothing happened. *Must've been one of the outlaws'.* He peered out the window. No targets. He stared at the rifle in his hands. *Useless if there's nothing to shoot at.*

Turner fired three shots in rapid succession. Addison fired again. The shooting stopped. The coach rumbled across a wooden bridge before Davey brought it to a halt.

Addison turned back from the window. A piece of wood several inches long had lanced through the skin on his forehead. Blood oozed into his eyebrows and down the side of his face.

Sam reached across the form of Jake, still passed out on the floor. "You're hurt."

Addison touched his forehead. "Ow." He probed around the long splinter. "Yep. My mother always told me guns was dangerous."

He grasped one end of the splinter and yanked. He studied the piece of wood, shrugged, and tossed it out the window. "Wouldn't even make a good toothpick."

Turner opened the door. His eyes widened when he saw Addison's face. "You all right?"

"Yep. Just a piece of wood. How'd you do?"

"Three got away. One was wounded. How about you?"

"I saw one ride away, so I musta got the other two."

Turner nodded toward Jake. "How's he doing?"

Addison turned to the wounded man. "Just fixin' to take a look. Help me get him up on the seat so's I can work on him."

It took Addison a moment to examine the guard's wounded shoulder. "It's not good," he rasped a few minutes later. "The bullet did a lot of damage to the shoulder bones. We can bandage it so he doesn't lose too much more blood, but we need to get him to a doc real quick. Ain't no way I can get the bullet out. He needs them fancy instruments."

Once Jake was settled and the horses watered, Davey started the stage at an easy canter to spare the team and give Jake as gentle a ride as possible. Addison rode shotgun. Turner and Sam rode with Jake, giving him water when he asked for it and wiping the sweat from his brow. He drifted off to a light sleep but moaned as the motion of the coach jostled his arm.

10

MEMORIES OF TENDING wounded soldiers in Mexico City almost thirty years earlier bubbled up as Sam tended to Jake. He let the man sip from a canteen and then dampened his handkerchief, folded it, and placed it on Jake's forehead.

Jeremiah Turner spoke from behind. "Thanks for your help, Mr. Carstairs. Sorry you had to go through that."

Sam looked over to see him leaning back, his head resting against the seat, jostling with the motion of the stage. "My pleasure," Sam said. "Mostly I just wanted to get through it in one piece. Didn't figure they'd let us live."

"You got family waiting for you?"

"Yeah, sort of. Ain't much. Two grown boys, although only one acts like it."

"No wife?"

The grief swooped over him like a thunderhead over the mountains, but that was nothing new. Sam sighed. "She died more'n twenty years ago, givin' birth. I still miss her. Sometimes I wonder how things would've been different if she'd lived."

"I'm sorry."

Sam shrugged and got up to sit next to Turner. He folded his arms and gazed out the window but turned at the sound of Turner's voice, soft and low with fatigue.

"It's been my experience that when someone is dealing with what you seem to be going through, it's best to seek God's help. He can bring things together and heal wounded hearts. He cares about what happens to His people in this life as well as how they'll spend eternity, in heaven or hell. He wants us all to be in heaven with Him." He leaned forward, elbows on his knees. "Do you know for sure where you'll go when you die?"

"Hell, I expect. Well deserved too." Sam shrugged. "I gave up on God a long time ago. He's the one that let my wife die and left me with one decent son, one bully, and one good-for-nothin' brat I had to throw out. The Almighty wasn't interested in me then. I doubt He's interested now."

"He never loses interest in people, Mr. Carstairs."

"Well, that ain't been my experience with Him. Besides, after the things I've called Him and the things I've done, He wouldn't want anything to do with me."

Jake moaned and stirred on the seat. Sam leaned over, checked the bandage, and lifted the canteen to the man's lips. He mopped the wounded man's brow, resoaked the handkerchief, and replaced it on his forehead. Jake muttered, "Thanks," and closed his eyes.

Sam settled into the seat next to Turner. "I wouldn't think a man in your line of work would have much use for God."

Turner leaned forward. "Couldn't do my job without God. I need His guidance and protection in everything I do."

"Well, guess that's all right for you. Like I said, I don't think He'd be much interested in me."

Turner's gaze was direct. "You'd be surprised how interested He is in you."

Sam changed the subject. "Addison is pretty good with doctoring. The bandage is good and tight and seems to have stopped the bleeding."

"You're right," Turner said. "He told me he learned it during the war when he worked in the field hospitals with the doctors. After the war, he stayed in the Army for a while and came out West for the Indian troubles. He got to practice it more then."

"You worked with him long?"

"This is only the second time. He's a good man."

Sam frowned. "Aren't you both agents with the stage line?"

"Philip is. I'm what you call a specialist. They hire me for special jobs or problems when they need extra security or an outside pair of eyes to look at something."

"You mean you're a hired gun?"

"No. I don't hire out to kill people. My job is to protect property and save lives. I work for stage lines and railroads and banks and businesses and such—help make security arrangements and plans and come up with solutions. I use a gun as a last resort. On this job, Phil and I were hoping to find who's leaking information to the outlaws about when rich shipments were going out."

"You have any luck?"

"Yes, thanks to you and your suggestion that we change the route. The outlaws knew where to meet us. And the only one who knew we were coming this way was Adams."

Sam leaned his head back against the seat. "I think we busted them up pretty good. You're pretty handy with a gun for someone who only uses it as a last resort."

"I figure if it's my last resort, I better know how to use it. With this gang, I didn't want to take any chances. The last couple of robberies, they've been getting more violent, molesting the women and killing everyone when they were done."

"Hmm, I appreciate you lettin' me know about that ahead of time." Sam crossed his arms. "So what happens next?"

"When we get to Culverton, I'll wire the headquarters of the stage line and the sheriff in Lassiter. After that, I'll get with the sheriff in Culverton and see if we can find the rest of the gang."

Sam considered that. "How can I get in touch with you if I want to hire you for some work?"

"Just wire me here." Turner took a small card out of his waistcoat pocket.

Sam studied it and tucked it away. "Actually, I could use you right now. I've received a threatenin' letter, and I think somebody might try something on my way home."

Turner angled toward Sam in the seat and fingered his dapper mustache. "Here's the situation, Mr. Carstairs. Right now I'm under contract to the stage line to stop these robberies. I have to finish this job. And thanks to your help, I believe we're very close. Adams should be arrested by tomorrow, while we try to find the remaining members of the gang. If you want, I'll come to your place as soon as I'm done here."

Sam studied his boots. "I hope it's not too late."

11

MICHAEL WATCHED from the porch of the Riverbend Hotel as the setting sun cast long shadows across the town. He remembered how he and his sister, Ellie, liked to sit in the hayloft and watch the sunset, the loft an island of peace where their father's alcoholic violence seemed far away. Tonight, that peace mingled with excitement as a brilliant palette of red and orange with yellow and purple highlights painted the sky and the underside of the clouds.

An unusual day marked by a beautiful piece of art.

He wondered if Rachel Stone was watching the same sunset, what she thought of it. *So much about her I'd like to know.*

The sun sank behind the ridge and the sky slowly darkened to deep blue near the horizon, black overhead. Glittering white stars popped out one by one.

Michael sighed and went to his room to get ready for dinner. A cool breeze through the window drove away the remaining heat of the day. He washed in the basin on his dresser, brushed his hair, straightened his string tie. *Better look my best. I might see Rachel again.*

He walked into the hotel dining room and decided the tie had been a good choice. He hadn't seen a room so elegant since he'd picked pockets at the fanciest hotel in St. Louis. Windows with heavy cream-colored curtains lined the wall overlooking the street. A set of double doors in the middle of the wall allowed patrons to enter from outside. White cloths covered the tables. Elaborately folded linen napkins marked each place setting. A candle flickered on each table, and light from the glittering chandeliers danced off the polished dark wood floor and the soft green walls. Sam Carstairs obviously spared no expense in making his property look good.

Michael spotted an empty table about halfway through the room, along the inside wall across from the door. As he sat, Rachel Stone came out of the kitchen carrying two plates of food. Their eyes met, and she almost dropped the platters. She recovered quickly, smiled at him, and proceeded to deliver the food to a nearby couple before approaching his table.

"I didn't expect to see you here," she said, a sparkle in her violet eyes. The plain white apron over her yellow dress accented her trim figure. The light from the chandeliers cast highlights in her hair.

"Funny thing happened," he said. "I got hungry, and this was the most convenient place for me. Besides, I hoped to see you again, even if you were working."

A blush crept into her cheeks. She looked away and wiped her hands on her apron. *She's nervous? About me?*

"Thank you for stopping in. Would you like to see a menu?"

"What's the best thing you have tonight?"

"The cook's been doing a good job with the steaks, and he has some baked chicken that melts in your mouth."

"I'll have the chicken."

"Coming right up."

Within a few minutes, she had brought a platter of several chicken pieces, mashed potatoes, and carrots. He nibbled at the meal and watched her wait on the other customers. Children received gentle and attentive service. Adults smiled as she chatted with them, although a few of the women seemed angry or disapproving. *Probably jealous because she's so pretty,* he thought.

Even so, she took the time to make sure everything was satisfactory. She moved with grace and ease among the tables and in and out of the kitchen. Twice during the meal she refilled his coffee and water, and each time he wanted to fall into those violet eyes. *Is this what smitten feels like?*

"How about a piece of *Apfelkuchen* to top it off?" she said on her next visit to his table. "It's apple cake—specialty of our German manager. And it's delicious."

"Ah, a temptation too hard to resist. Bring it on, please."

As he ate his dessert, the door from the boardwalk opened and three men entered, stumbling and tripping over each other. They sat in the middle row, two tables away from him. Rachel's face clouded over.

One of the newcomers banged his hand on the table. Pieces of cutlery rattled to the floor. "Let's have some service!"

He looked to be a couple of inches shorter than Michael, with a stocky build. His piercing blue eyes and straw blond hair reminded Michael faintly of Ben Carstairs. The man wore expensive tan trousers, a blue shirt, and a tan vest. Boots gleamed with a high polish. An ivory-handled pistol rested in a holster tied to his right thigh. The sneer on his face seemed habitual.

The man turned his chair so he sat sideways to the table.

Rachel approached within a few feet but not as close as she did with other customers. "What can I get you?"

"Let's start with you." The blond man reached out, grabbed her arm, and pulled her into his lap. He tilted his chair back on two legs. "You're the prettiest girl in town, you know that? I think we're meant to be together."

"Let me go." She slapped his face and struggled to get up.

He laughed and grabbed her other wrist. "Now, that ain't the way to be treatin' a payin' customer. Besides, this ain't the place for you. With your history, seems like you oughta be in business for yourself, doin' what you did when you were in Denver. And I'm lookin' to get me some free—"

"Let her go." Michael was on his feet. He took Rachel's arm and lifted her from the man's lap, sweeping out with a foot to catch the chair's rear legs. The man hit the floor with a crash.

"Ellie—I mean, Miss Rachel, get behind me." Michael braced his feet, fists ready. *Come on. Get up. Let me punch that smug look down your throat.*

The blond man went for the gun on his hip.

"Don't try it, Mark." Caleb Davis stood inside the door, his gun cocked and pointed at the man he called Mark. Everyone froze.

"We weren't doin' nothin', Sheriff. We just wanted somethin' to eat." Mark struggled to his feet. "This feller here started it."

"That dog won't hunt, Mark. I saw the whole thing through the window. You want to press charges, Miss Stone?"

"No, Sheriff Davis," Rachel said, her eyes downcast. "Thank you anyway. Just get him out of here please."

"Okay, Mark. You heard the lady. Consider yourself lucky. Now get your sorry self and your two friends outta here 'fore I run you in for disturbin' the peace."

Mark glared at Michael. "I don't like being showed up like that, friend. You had no business interferin' in what wasn't any of your business. You stay out of my way from now on." He stomped out of the restaurant.

Rachel had grasped Michael's arm. Her hands felt warm and comfortable. He took a deep breath, yet his heart still raced and his head pounded. She squeezed his arm, and calm slowly settled over him. He breathed a little easier. His fists relaxed.

"Thank you, Mr. Archer. Thank you, Sheriff." She avoided eye contact with Michael. "You came along at the right time, Sheriff. I appreciate it. Would you like some coffee and apple cake?"

"Just the coffee, miss." The sheriff sat across from Michael. "Well, you got off to a good start with the Carstairs family."

"What do you mean?" Michael found it difficult to focus. The fragile calm of Rachel's touch had evaporated. Blood still raced through his veins.

"That feller you put on the floor was Mark Carstairs, Sam's middle son."

Rachel brought fresh coffee for both of them. She touched Michael lightly on the shoulder—a butterfly landing on a leaf—and left to take care of other customers.

Davis slurped his coffee. "He'll be lookin' to pick a fight with you from now on. When he finds out you have business with his father, he'll try to mess that up too."

"Thanks for the warning. I'll keep my eyes open. Think he'll try anything tonight?"

"Hard to tell. Depends on how much drinking he does and how much he works himself up. I'll have my deputy, Pete, keep an eye on him."

"Thanks. I appreciate it."

Davis finished his coffee and stood to leave. "I'll see ya around."

"Good night, Sheriff."

Michael stared into his coffee. He held on to the fragile cup as if it were a last strand connecting him to reality. He prayed, but his prayers didn't seem to go any higher than his nose. A few minutes later, Rachel came by to clear the table.

"Miss Stone, I'm not sure Mark Carstairs is through for tonight. Would you let me walk you home just in case he tries something?"

She gave him a searching look, as if she could see what

was in his heart. Then she nodded. "I would appreciate that. I should be ready to close up and leave in about an hour."

"All right. I'll meet you in the lobby."

Michael sat on the edge of his bed, his dream still with him. He had meant to just lie down, to calm himself while he waited for Rachel to get off work. But the familiar nightmare wouldn't let go. He clenched his hands, the knuckles white, nails digging into his palms. Rapid, shallow breaths couldn't fill his lungs. He closed his eyes, and he was there again.

He saw Mark Carstairs pull Rachel onto his lap, restraining her with one arm and trying to force his other hand on her body and his mouth on hers. But it wasn't Rachel. It was Ellie—sweet, innocent Ellie. And it wasn't Mark. It was Michael's father, forcing himself on Ellie. Michael hit him, again and again, his fists like sledgehammers, going beyond stopping him this one time, wanting to stop him forever. Mark's face replaced his father's broken, bloodied face, and Michael kept hitting and hitting while yelling curses.

He took a ragged breath. Sharp pain pierced his lungs as they expanded against the tightness of his chest.

He took another breath, a little deeper. The room settled from its whirling. The lamp on the bureau burned low. His reflection in the mirror on the wall above it looked cavernous and sinister in the dim light. Shadows made his face drawn and narrow.

The hardness in his jaw and eyes frightened him. He knew the damage the man looking at him would do if Michael ever released him again. He was an ugly, brutal monster Michael had to keep buried so he wouldn't kill again.

Another breath, along with the constant prayer that haunted him. The one that both called to him and terrified him because part of him couldn't believe it. *Forgive . . . forgive . . . forgive.*

He shook his head, still willing and unwilling. Then he put a hand on his chest and touched Ben's cross under his shirt. *Remember why you're here, Michael Archer.*

12

RACHEL CLOSED THE DOOR to the now-darkened dining room and walked into the hotel lobby. Michael Archer sat by the French doors that opened onto the patio overlooking the river. Her heart constricted. Had he heard Mark's remark about Denver? Did he understand what it meant?

He seemed distracted, almost brooding. He didn't acknowledge her until she approached within a few steps. Then he jumped from his seat like a rabbit spooked from under a bush. His smile didn't spread from his mouth to his eyes. Her heart sank. *He did hear.*

"Hello, Miss Stone." He touched the brim of his hat.

"Please call me Rachel."

"Only if you call me Michael." He smiled again. This time his eyes joined in, and the tight place inside her relaxed a little.

"Is everything all right? When I walked in, you looked like you were fretting over something." She searched his face.

"Everything's fine," he said, though his expression said otherwise. "People like Mark Carstairs bother me—bullying everyone. I wish there was some way to stop it."

"The town would sure appreciate seeing that man change from his bullying ways."

Now the shadows seemed to lift from his face. He seemed as open and warm and happy to see her as when she'd first walked into the dining room. His presence gave her comfort and strength. *Hold on, girl. Don't go letting him get too close. Keep your guard up.*

They walked along the boardwalk toward the parsonage. The heat of the day lingered in the warm night air. A breeze off the river cooled her face.

"I really appreciate your coming to my rescue and now taking the time to walk me home. Mark Carstairs has been after me since I came to town."

"I couldn't stand the way he was treating you, acting like he owned you. You're too precious to be treated like that."

She felt a blush creep into her cheeks. "Thank you."

His words touched her heart. She couldn't remember anyone ever calling her precious. Yet the forcefulness in his voice surprised her. His tone carried an edge of violence, a quiet menace that reminded her of some of her old customers. *What kind of a man are you, Michael Archer? Could you possibly . . . ?*

Across the street, Mulcahey's Saloon spilled bright lights, music, laughter, and loud talk into the otherwise-quiet night.

Five men staggered through the batwing doors, smoke swirling in their wake. Mark Carstairs led them across the street. They stepped onto the boardwalk and stopped in front of Michael and Rachel.

"Well, don't you two look so sweet and innocent." He jabbed a finger at Michael. "We have unfinished business." He turned to Rachel. "Then you and I have some unfinished business too."

Michael put his hand on her arm. He spoke in a low voice, the violent undertone more pronounced. "We don't want any more trouble, Mr. Carstairs. Why don't you just let us pass, and we'll be on our way."

"No, we're going to settle this right now."

Rachel said, "Five of you against one man. That's unfair even for you."

Mark glared at her. "You keep your mouth shut. These boys are here to see that your friend don't turn yellow and try to run away." He turned back to Michael. "Now, are we gonna settle this, or are you gonna hide behind her skirts?" His finger jabbed Michael's chest with every other word.

Rachel winced as Michael's hand tightened on her arm like a band of iron.

"I don't want to fight you, sir." Michael's low-pitched voice belied the tension in his grasp.

Mark laughed. "You don't have a choice, mister. Nobody does what you did to me without some settlin'."

He swung wildly at Michael's jaw. Michael tilted his head back and the blow missed. Mark swung at Michael's stomach. Michael grabbed the fist and threw Mark's arm aside.

"I said I don't want to fight you. Just leave us alone, and you won't get hurt."

Mark's eyes narrowed. "You're the one that's gonna git hurt. Now fight like a man." He balled his fists and stepped closer.

Michael grabbed Mark's shirt with both hands and lifted. Rachel gasped at the sight of Mark raised off the boardwalk, his toes scraping the wood. Mark beat his fists on Michael's arms. Michael didn't seem to notice.

She heard the hard steel in Michael's voice, the rage under the surface, as he spoke through gritted teeth. "Why don't you people ever listen? I. Don't. Want. To. Fight. You."

He shoved Mark into the street, where the man landed on his rear with a loud thump and a swirl of dust. Rachel suppressed a giggle.

Michael's heavy breathing beside her made her turn. Fists clenched at his sides, sweat beaded on his forehead and ran down his cheek. His profile looked like a granite statue's.

He leaned forward, menace in his eyes as he glared at Mark. "Now will you leave us alone?"

Mark roared and charged.

Rachel's hands went to her chest. She heard Michael whisper one word. "Forgive." Then he swung, his arm like a whip, an uppercut that seemed to start at his knees.

His fist connected with Mark's jaw. Mark stood straight up, eyes glazed. His jaw hung slack. A tooth fell out. He started to raise his hand, but it dropped to his side. He groaned and swooned back into the street, where he lay spread-eagled in the dirt.

Michael buried his face in his hands. "I've done it again. My Father, forgive me."

Rachel placed her hand on his upper arm. Even through his clothes, she felt tension ripple in the knotted muscles. Her heart beat faster. *He protected me. I can be safe with him.* Then a familiar voice in her head whispered, *But what if he knew . . . ?*

Two of the men with Mark helped him to sit up. He tested his jaw. "You coulda broke it."

Rachel heard the childish whine and wished Michael *had* broken it.

"Yer lucky he didn't, laddie." Deputy Pete O'Brien walked up behind Mark and placed a massive hand on his shoulder. "Now, get your sorry self up and outta here. Methinks ye've made enough mischief for one night."

Mark pointed at Michael with a shaking hand. "Aren't you gonna arrest him, you dumb mick? He assaulted me."

The big deputy raised an eyebrow. "Looked like self-defense to me. Now you and these mates o' yers get off me street 'fore I throw ye all in jail."

Rachel felt Mark's eyes burning into her. "It's a fine thing when the whole sheriff's office sticks up for a stranger and a—"

"That'll be enough, me boy." The deputy cut him off just in time, then stuck out a meaty paw and introduced himself to Michael.

Rachel glanced at Michael, who blinked a few times and looked as if he had come out of a trance.

"That's quite a punch ye have there," the big man said.

"Reminded me of me da, prizefightin' in Dublin for passage over here."

Michael stared at his hands. He turned them over and clenched and unclenched them, staring as if he were seeing them for the first time. "I could have killed him." His eyes seemed to plead with her, and she couldn't fathom why.

She wanted to embrace him the way she hugged Daniel when he scraped his knee. Instead, she put her hand on his forearm. For a moment, she thought he would snatch his arm away. But he didn't. The muscles under her hand relaxed. His face eased into the smooth-skinned, on-the-edge-of-a-smile countenance that had attracted her at lunch.

"I'm sorry, Miss Rachel. I don't know what came over me."

She searched his face, trying to peer into his mind, to see what he was thinking. "It's all right. I've seen men fight before."

He shook his head. "It's just that . . . Oh, never mind." He shrugged. "It's not important. I'm just glad it's over and you didn't get hurt."

The deputy tipped his derby hat. "You folks have a quiet night. I'll be meanderin' by the saloon and keepin' me eye on young Mr. Carstairs. The lad may need help gettin' home."

Rachel linked her arm through Michael's, drawing comfort from the physical touch. What would have happened if she had walked home alone tonight? She shuddered.

"Are you chilly?"

She squeezed his arm and smiled at him. "No. Just thankful you were here tonight."

When they reached the door of the parsonage, he took her

hand. Peace and security flowed through her at the touch—along with curiosity and just a wisp of worry. She didn't know quite how to respond to him. Old habits were hard to break.

"You have a restful evening, Rachel. I'll see you at service in the morning." He lifted her hand and kissed it gently.

"You too, Michael." She stroked the place on her hand where his lips had touched. *Lord, what did that mean?*

13

SAM ROSE from his hotel bed as the first light of dawn jabbed his eyes, his mind still fuzzy with sleep.

Where am I? Then he remembered. *Culverton. The stage— almost got robbed.*

He tried to sit up. Every muscle ached from yesterday's exertion and his restless night. The attempted robbery of the stage had reminded him how easy it was to die out here.

How easy it would be for Higgins—or whoever wrote that note—to kill me.

He swung his legs over the edge of the bed and stared at the floor. *Higgins.* The whorls of wood grain drew him like a spiral downward into his past.

Hard to believe that Higgins had once been his best friend—so many years ago. Poor sons of poor farmers, they'd both come out from Kentucky looking for wealth and adventure and found the valley. They'd pooled their resources to claim the biggest piece of land they could and started a cattle herd by rounding up mavericks. John had planted corn to sell to the mountain men who came down every spring, and they'd bought more land. Life had been good except for the drastic shortage of females.

Then Sam found gold on the property. That first tiny nugget seemed so heavy in his hand. His future rested in the glittering piece of metal. No more poverty, no more struggling. Everything he could ever want in the palm of his hand.

He closed his fist over it. *Mine. All mine.*

If only John had sold out to Sam, everything would have been fine. But he wouldn't sell. Seeds of mistrust sprouted.

Then Ruth Brown came to town with her family to open a general store. *Ruth!* Even now, with fear clutching his heart, the thought of her made him smile. Delicate and beautiful, yet tough and determined, she reminded Sam of the wildflowers that graced the hillsides. The perfect wife for a man seeking to build a life from the land.

Sam fell in love with her—how could he help it? So did John. So did every man within a hundred miles. Sam managed through threats and fists to dissuade most of them— but John wouldn't back down. To make things worse, Ruth seemed to favor John.

Sam still tasted the rage and panic that surged through him at the thought of losing Ruth to John Higgins. He couldn't let that happen, could he? He had to do something.

So Sam told Ruth that John had a wife and two children back East. The lie worked. Ruth broke off the relationship without even telling John why. And John, heartbroken, sold out to Sam for less than his share was worth.

But that wasn't enough. Sam had to be sure John would pose no further threat to his plans. So he'd broken into Ruth's family's store, robbed the till, and planted the cash in John's saddlebags.

The judge had sentenced John to ten years in prison. And Sam had paid to make sure he never came home.

Had it all been worth it? All these years later, Sam still didn't know. *But Ruth—Ruth was worth it.*

She'd made him the happiest man on earth. His ranch flourished. He expanded into banking, led the development of the town.

Then she died. The light of his life went out. And only in rare moments like this did he let the truth creep close—that it was all his fault. All of it. The dark emptiness he lived with daily. The cold fear that enshrouded him now.

He shook his head violently, trying to turn the fear into something more familiar and useful. Like anger. Like a plan to stay alive.

"Seek God's help," Jeremiah Turner had told him. But Turner didn't know all that Sam had done to amass his fortune, the people he'd cheated, the crooked business deals, all he'd done to acquire more money and power.

What I did to John Higgins.

No, he'd made his choices, burned his bridges, left God behind. No chance of saving his soul—but maybe he could save his life if he acted smart. Good thing he'd run into Turner yesterday.

The sounds of horses snorting and gear jangling and men talking in the street below drifted through Sam's open window. He walked to the window, running his hand over his bald pate and massaging the back of his neck. Turner and another man stood on the sidewalk across the street. About a dozen men on horseback faced them. Another half dozen or so stood in the street.

The man next to Turner fingered the badge pinned to his vest. His deep voice rumbled. "All right, that's the deal. Those of you who are gonna ride with me and Mr. Turner, be back here in ten minutes. If we get on the road right away, we can catch these bandits while they're still lickin' their wounds. Now, move!"

Men scurried in several directions. Some of those on horseback stayed, ready to go. A few of the others spoke to the lawman, shook their heads, and ambled away. Turner crossed over to a tethered horse and started adjusting the stirrups.

What's going on? Where is Turner going? Sam scrambled to put on his pants and boots, hopping on one foot as he headed for the door. He cursed as his fingers fumbled with the buttons on his shirt, misaligning a couple of holes. He clattered down the stairs, his boots sounding like one of those Spanish flamenco dancers. He stumbled into the lobby and almost collided with Turner as the other man walked in from the street.

"You're going to ride with the sheriff?" He grabbed Turner's forearm. "I wanted you to come with me."

"Take it easy, Sam." Turner put an arm on Sam's shoulder. "I told you last night that I need to finish this. It's part of why the stage line hired me—to put an end to the holdups and killings by bringing this gang in. We hurt them pretty bad yesterday. I think we can pick up their trail real easy and bring 'em in; won't take but a couple of days. Then I'll come down to your place and help you out. I give you my word on it."

Sam shook his head as if a fly buzzed his ear. He sighed, and his shoulders drooped. "I just don't know how much time I have. These threats don't say when."

"I understand, and I'll be as fast as I can. Can I pray with you before I leave?"

Sam snorted. "Don't need no prayers. It's that gun of yours I need."

He trudged back up the stairs and unlocked the door. As he entered the room, his foot struck something and sent it skittering across the floor. Hands trembling, Sam picked up the envelope. He took out a single sheet of paper.

Soon.

H.

The note fluttered to the floor as Sam covered his face with his hands. He sank to the edge of the bed, gasping for air, heart pounding, clammy sweat breaking out on his forehead. He looked around the room, convinced someone was there, ready to attack. He calmed himself, taking big gulps of air.

After a few minutes he walked downstairs. His hands clutched the banister to support his shaky legs.

"Is everything all right, Mr. Carstairs?" the desk clerk asked. "You look like you've seen a ghost."

"Has anyone come through here in the last few minutes?"

"No, sir. It's been empty all morning except for you and that gentleman talking earlier."

Sam turned to go back to his room. *They're here and they're close by. But where are they?*

Who are they?

14

THE CHURCH SPARKLED in the bright sunlight. Rachel imagined the steeple as an arrow that would carry the praises and worship of the people through the deep blue sky to heaven. She stood at the wide double doors waiting, watching, a white lace shawl over her favorite cornflower blue dress. A few people greeted her. Most ignored her, clustering in small groups near the wagons, at the foot of the stairs, and on the porch that fronted the building, or moving past her without acknowledgment to find a pew.

Rachel sighed, wishing she had more friends but still relishing the joy of being here in God's house. Sundays in Riverbend were so far removed from the life she'd lived for so many years. She loved the way people used the Sunday service as the mark of a true day of rest. For many of the families, Sunday meant visiting with neighbors, a break from the toil of life. Many spent the whole day at the church. Picnics broke out, children played, men talked politics and the weather and crops and livestock. Women cooked over open fires and talked about children and recipes and the foibles of husbands.

And she was part of it—part of the family, even if she often felt like the immoral relative nobody knew quite what to do with. But things were definitely better now than six months ago, when she'd walked into her first service. Then Rachel had almost felt her sin radiating from her, offending these upstanding citizens. Women had glared or turned away. From the men there had been glances of curiosity, plus a few lustful leers. Martha's hand on her elbow had propelled her forward to the front pew, where she sat with the Matthews family and kept her head down, reminding herself again and again that no matter what anyone else thought, God had forgiven her.

That Sunday, Pastor Luke had preached on forgiveness and second chances. She'd resisted the urge to turn around to see the congregation's reaction. After the service, four people had come up and welcomed her to Riverbend Church—Annabelle Stewart, Vernon and Esther Phelps, and their nephew, Alexander. The ice-cold looks from others still burned in her memory.

The next Sunday, Pastor Luke preached on the woman caught in adultery. That's when the Barkstons introduced themselves.

The third Sunday, he preached on Mary Magdalene, and Isaac Walters and his wife invited her to Sunday dinner.

Since then, she'd made a few more friends, and most of the congregation had come to treat her with polite tolerance. Only a few still watched her with attitudes of disdain or worse. And in time, she knew, she'd win them over. They'd see she was a new woman.

She glanced down the street once more. Michael Archer walked toward her in a long-limbed stride. Her heart beat faster. She felt her face crease into a smile that, she suspected, made her look like a gawky schoolgirl with her first crush. She walked down the steps, holding herself back from running. *Why am I acting like this? He's just another man.*

She touched her hand where he had kissed it. *Because he might be different from the others.* She noticed his pace had quickened.

"Good morning, Michael." She extended her hand.

He took it and squeezed it firmly. "Good to see you this morning, Rachel." His voice caressed her ears like soft music drifting through a window on a warm summer night.

He released her hand, and they turned to enter the church. She enjoyed the warm pressure of his hand under her elbow as they climbed the steps. Rachel introduced him to Annabelle and the Phelpses as they made their way down the aisle to the first pew, where she took her seat with Martha and the children. Michael sat next to her.

She felt comfortable, safe, protected. Was this how it felt to have a normal relationship with a man? Would such a thing be possible for her?

Would Michael even want to know her after he found out about her past?

She wanted to reach out and take his arm, but she didn't want to seem forward. Having him beside her in church seemed perfectly natural. It was enough for now.

Sunlight streamed through clear glass windows, filling the sanctuary. Dazzling light danced off the white walls and the dark wood of the pews and pulpit. Pastor Luke took his place in the pulpit and opened his Bible. He flipped through the pages, patted his coat pockets.

Martha leaned toward Rachel and whispered, "He forgot his notes. Again."

"Martha, will you lead the people in 'Behold the Amazing Gift of Love'? I'll be right back." He dashed out the side door that connected to the parsonage.

After the song, while Luke was preaching, Rachel looked at Michael out of the corner of her eye. In profile, she saw strength in the straight nose and firm chin. She wanted to turn and look at him full on, to study and observe him, to drink in every feature. She didn't know what to do with her hands. And she certainly hoped Pastor Luke wouldn't ask her about the sermon, because she hadn't heard a word.

As they stood to leave, Michael almost bumped into a large man in the aisle. He started to apologize, but Rachel said, "Good morning, Mr. Barkston, Mrs. Barkston. Let me introduce you to Michael Archer. He's visiting us for a short while. Michael, this is Bill and Sally Barkston."

Michael shook the burly man's hand, feeling a firm grip and hard calluses on a hand that almost swallowed his own. He greeted Mrs. Barkston, a tall, slender woman, gray-haired like her husband. Crow's-feet radiated from her brown eyes. Bill Barkston stood several inches taller than Michael, larger and wider, well-muscled. Blond strands wove through his otherwise-gray hair. A widow's peak pointed like an arrow over the edge of his forehead. His pale blue eyes bored into Michael's.

"It's a pleasure to meet you, sir," Michael said. "You too, ma'am."

"Same here."

But Michael got the distinct impression that neither Barkston found any pleasure in his company.

Mrs. Barkston's voice was high and reedy. "I'm so sorry our Jeffrey couldn't be here this morning. Two of the horses are foaling, and he needed to be there for the delivery. But he expects to come to tonight's service, and he wanted me to tell you he'll see you then."

"I'll be here," she said. "I hope all goes well with the horses."

"I'm sure it will. I know he's looking forward to seeing you."

The couple walked away. Rachel took Michael's arm as they walked down the aisle. "I should apologize to you. They are really a sweet couple, but I don't think they're too happy to see you."

"Why not?"

"They're convinced Jeffrey and I should get married, the sooner the better."

"And how do you feel about that?" Did his voice reflect the jealousy and insecurity constricting his heart?

"It's something they want but Jeffrey and I don't," she said, her voice low. "We get along, but we know we're not meant to be together. Jeffrey needs a woman who likes farm life as much as he does. And I . . ." She shrugged and didn't finish the sentence.

"Do they know how you and Jeffrey feel?"

"Oh yes. Even Pastor Luke has talked to them about it, without much success. They still think they can make it happen."

When they reached the door of the church, Michael turned toward her. "Are you free this afternoon? Would you like to go for a ride in the country? I'll rent a buggy."

She hesitated, and his heart sank. Then she turned and broke into a sunny smile. "I'm free, but don't bother with the buggy. I have a horse. I can fix a picnic lunch to bring with us. I know a beautiful spot upriver."

"I'll meet you at the parsonage, then—say, in about an hour?"

"I'll be ready for you."

Sally Barkston turned from talking with Pastor Luke and walked over to Rachel and Michael. Focusing on Rachel, she said, "We'd like to invite you to join us for supper tonight at the hotel before the service. We could meet about five. Jeffrey should be here by then."

"Thank you, Mrs. Barkston. But I won't be able to make it." She stepped closer to Michael. "I already have plans for this afternoon. I do appreciate the offer."

Sally bit her lip. "All right, then, I guess we'll have to wait to see you until tonight." She shot Michael a quick, darting look and returned to her husband. They walked away, their heads in close conversation, occasionally glancing over their shoulders at Michael and Rachel.

"Well, they are persistent," Michael said.

"Yes, they are. I pray they'll be able to accept the inevitable without too much hurt or offense."

When they reached the ground, Michael tipped his hat. "I'll see you in an hour."

"I'll be ready."

15

Sam left the hotel at the sound of the stage pulling up in front of the depot across the street. The coach rocked on its springs, and the six-horse team shuffled and snorted in their harnesses. Sam studied the dusty, creaky conveyance with his businessman's eye and saw the chariot that would have him home in four more days. *You ain't pretty, and you sure ain't comfortable, but you'll get the job done.*

The driver wrapped the reins around one gloved hand and pushed his shapeless, weather-beaten hat back to show a sun-browned face and no trace of hair under the hat. He bellowed, "This is the stage for Millerville, Eagleton, March Valley, Hawkins Station, and Riverbend. We'll be leaving in fifteen minutes or whenever we're ready, whichever comes first."

Sam picked up his bags and walked to the boot of the coach. The guard helped him load and secure them. Sam jumped like a startled rabbit when he heard a voice behind him. He turned to find a young couple standing there.

"Is everything all right, sir?" the woman asked. Her green eyes stared directly into his. Her light olive skin glowed with youth and health. A brimmed bonnet covered her hair, and her neat clothes showed the wear of many cleanings. The top of her head just reached her companion's shoulder. He seemed a little older, with startling blue eyes, long black hair, and a drooping mustache.

"Didn't mean to startle you," he said.

"No harm done—just didn't hear you coming." Sam wiped the cold sweat from his face with his handkerchief and limply shook the young man's hand. "I didn't know there was going to be anyone else on the stage."

"We just purchased our tickets yesterday. We're going as far as Hawkins Station and then taking the stage east. My name's Jack Alden, and this here's my wife, Maria."

"I'm Sam Carstairs from Riverbend."

Something crossed the young woman's eyes. Sam couldn't quite catch it, but it was almost as if she knew him. *You're just getting jumpy. Seeing ghosts and shadows where there ain't any.*

Maria Alden beamed. "We're going to St. Louis for our honeymoon. We were married yesterday."

"Congratulations," Sam said without enthusiasm and turned away.

16

I FEEL LIKE A KID ON CHRISTMAS MORNING!

Dressed in blue dungarees, a light blue shirt, and his most comfortable pair of boots, Michael walked to the hotel stable. Buddy greeted him with friendly snuffles and nickers, butting his head into Michael's chest. After weeks on the trail, Michael knew Buddy's moods. This horse did not like the confines of a stall.

Michael hummed "Amazing Grace" as he groomed the horse. Buddy stamped and shook his head, eager to be out.

"Whoa. It's a good thing I'm not singing, hey, boy? With my voice, I'd spook you to the next county."

He gave another swipe with the currycomb, nervousness and excitement coursing through him at the thought of spending time alone with Rachel. His grown-up experience with women—mostly less-than-reputable types or, more recently, church ladies—had not prepared him for someone like Rachel. She was so elegant, so refined . . .

"Sure hope I don't make a fool of myself," he muttered.

Buddy whinnied and tossed his head.

A few minutes later, Buddy butted him in the chest again. Michael woke from a daydream of Rachel in his arms, her lips on his. "Sorry, pal. Didn't mean to ignore you." He gave Buddy's flanks a final stroke. The bridle came next, then the blanket and saddle.

Buddy stamped impatiently. Michael laughed and stroked the horse's nose. "All right, you're ready." He took the reins and led the way out of the barn.

Am I?

Michael was sitting with Luke on the parsonage porch when Rachel walked her sleek chestnut mare around the side of the house. Rachel wore riding boots, a dark blue denim riding skirt, and a red-and-white-checked shirt. A red bandanna fit snugly around her throat. Her long, light brown hair flowed over her shoulders, and a low-crowned tan Stetson hung down her back by its rawhide chin strap.

"Good afternoon, Michael. I hope I haven't kept you waiting." She smiled as she looped her horse's reins around the post, then stepped onto the porch.

His knees went weak as he stood to greet her. "No, ma'am—I mean, Rachel. I just got here a couple of minutes ago."

"That's good," she said. "Let me get the food from the kitchen, and then we can go."

He watched her enter the house, speechless at the subtle grace of her movement. She didn't walk. She glided.

Michael turned to find Luke grinning from ear to ear, a mischievous twinkle in his eye.

"What?" Michael felt his face flush.

"Oh, nothing," Luke smirked. "It's just the last time I knew someone to look at a woman like that was when I first met Martha. I walked around with that same silly expression on my face. Off in my own world, blind to everything else around me."

"Yeah. I guess that's it. She is one of the most beautiful women I've ever—"

The door opened, and Rachel came out with a wicker basket on her arm. "Well, I'm ready."

Luke still had that grin on his face as they secured the basket, then mounted and rode off.

They kept their mounts at a steady walk as they rode to the edge of town. Michael's tongue felt tied in knots. Rachel seemed content to ride in silence. *Say something, you fool.* "That sure is a good-looking mare. Have you had her long?"

"About three months. She was a gift from Isaac Walters."

Michael's stomach lurched. *A gift from a man? She has someone else she's interested in and who's interested in her? Of course she does! She's a beautiful woman. She's probably beating off suitors with a stick!*

A slight smile touched the corners of her mouth. "Isaac has a big ranch west of town. He's got the best horses around here. Martha and I and his wife were helping a family that got burned out. We were talking, and I mentioned how much I'd been wanting my own horse. The next day, Isaac brought Sunshine to the parsonage." She leaned forward and stroked the horse's neck. "Said his wife had been after him about it, and he didn't dare cross his wife."

"So it was really from his wife." The relief felt like a bale of hay sliding off Michael's shoulder.

Rachel laughed, and he blushed.

"Do you enjoy riding her?" Michael asked to cover his embarrassment.

"Oh, I love to." Her eyes danced. "She's so much fun, and she can go like the wind. When I'm on her, I feel free, almost like I'm flying."

"Really?" Michael teased.

"Come on. I'll show you. See if you can catch me."

Rachel urged Sunshine forward. The horse responded, sprinting into a full gallop in a few strides. Michael spurred Buddy to follow.

Rachel's hat flew off her head and hung by the cord around her neck. The wind whipped her hair. She leaned forward and settled into the rhythm of Sunshine's pace. The wicker basket bounced wildly behind her saddle.

Michael eased Buddy into a canter about twenty yards behind Rachel. She looked back and pulled on Sunshine's reins. The mare seemed to resist at first but quickly yielded to her owner's command.

"That's some horse!" Michael said as he drew up next to her. "I don't know if I could've caught you, and I thought Buddy was fast."

Rachel laughed, her cheeks flushed with excitement. "I just love riding full-out like that." She tilted her head toward the trees that surrounded the river. "Come on. The place for the picnic is just ahead."

They left the road and entered a path not much wider than a deer track that meandered through the forest. It emptied into a small clearing at the riverside. Tall, soft grass rippled in the gentle breeze. The afternoon sun dappled through the trees and glinted off the river, and cloud shadows drifted across the clearing. The lilting river music, the birds singing high up in the trees, the rustle of branches moving against each other in the breeze, the scurrying of a rabbit through the underbrush—all sound seemed softened by the peaceful aura of the clearing.

"It's beautiful," Michael whispered.

Rachel nodded, her hair glinting in the sunlight. Her hands rested gently on the pommel of her sidesaddle.

You're beautiful was what he wanted to say.

She studied him. His hazel eyes showed flecks of green and brown. His straight nose and firm mouth gave him an appearance of composure and strength. He seemed like the kind of man she could depend on. Could she let him into her heart?

Help me be wise, Lord. It was a prayer she had prayed almost continually since arriving in Riverbend, but now it seemed to have new meaning. *Help me be strong. I'm not even sure I know how to be with a good man.*

Michael hobbled the horses to one side of the clearing

and loosened the cinches on both saddles. Rachel opened the basket and spread the blue-and-white-checked cloth on the ground next to a fallen log. Then she reached in for the lunch she had packed—cold chicken, cucumbers, tomatoes, sourdough biscuits, and apples.

"I'm afraid the tomatoes are a little worse for the wear," she told him. "I must learn not to gallop with a picnic basket."

Michael smiled. "I'm not all that fond of tomatoes anyway. But that chicken looks wonderful." He lowered himself onto the log while Rachel sat on the cloth, her legs folded underneath her. He blessed the food and accepted the plate she prepared for him.

He took a bite of the chicken. "It's really good."

"Thank you."

They ate in companionable silence. Rachel enjoyed the peaceful beauty of the clearing, happy that Michael liked it. Hopefulness rose in her. This was a gentle man, not a hard-shelled bully who wanted to use her. A strong man like Pastor Luke, the strength hidden beneath a serene exterior. Was it even possible that—?

"What made you move to Riverbend?"

Her stomach dropped, and her throat tightened. She forced a breath down. *Oh, Lord, what should I tell him?* She took another deep breath, faced him, and saw concern on his face.

"I'm sorry. I didn't mean to pry," he said. "You don't have to tell me if you don't want to."

"It's all right," she said. *God, what should I do? Do I dare tell him?*

She couldn't look him in the eye. She gazed over his shoulder at Buddy and Sunshine grazing, their tails snapping to chase flies away. The right words were difficult to find. *Well, if he's going to hate me for who I was, might as well find out now.*

"About six months ago, Martha and Luke rescued me from a . . . bad place in Denver." She risked a glance at his face, saw his confusion, tried again. "I mean, a . . . house of prostitution. I was fighting with the madam and her enforcer on the street. Martha and Luke saw it and stepped in. They took me to their hotel and took care of me. They brought me here to begin a new life. And they helped me know . . . Jesus."

Tears welled in her eyes. She wiped them away with the back of her hand but didn't dare look at him. She just kept blurting the story out.

"My parents died when I was three. My aunt and uncle took me in, but when I turned thirteen, my uncle decided it was time for me to start meeting his, uh, needs. My aunt chose not to notice. Then he shared me with his friends and took money from them." She traced the pattern of the cloth with her finger, eyes downcast. "When I was seventeen, he sold me to a madam in San Francisco, who'd beat me if there were any complaints from the customers. A couple of years later, she passed me along to the madam in Denver. I was there for three years. Then I found out she was cheating all us girls by giving us less money than she promised us. So I took what I thought was mine from her safe and she caught me. That's when Martha and Luke found us, and if they hadn't come, the enforcer would've—why aren't you saying anything?"

She glanced up, steeling herself for the judgment she feared, the contempt she'd seen so many times. But he simply nodded solemnly, compassion on his face. When he spoke, his voice was gentle.

"I'm just grateful God brought Martha and Luke across your path at the right moment. And I'm grateful you came to Riverbend with them."

She felt something in her relax. "I am too," she said. "I love it here, love being saved, being forgiven. And sometimes I think I really can have a new life," she said. She tugged at blades of grass next to the blanket. "Until I get one of those looks at church or something like last night with Mark Carstairs happens to remind me that my past will always follow me."

"It may follow you, but it's not you anymore. It seems like the past will always try to come back on us and drag us down." His eyes fastened onto hers. "We can't let it."

She was curious and confused. "But you're a man of God. You don't seem like the kind of man to have a past that drags you down."

"I don't?" He chuckled and brushed a stray crumb from his pants. "Well, then, I guess it's my turn." He reached for her hand and gazed at her for a long moment before continuing. "When I received Jesus, I was sitting in a jailhouse, and I knew I was going to go right back to my old life as soon as I got out. Maybe that's why it doesn't bother me to hear you say you were a prostitute. In my old life, I was around them a lot—as a, um, customer, I mean. And I can't say I was any better than they were . . . than you were.

"Anyway," he continued, "I know what it's like to come out of a life on that side of the street. I know how turning to Jesus can change a person. I can see that in you."

Too close—don't let him draw you in. You're not ready for this. "Thank you." She slipped her hand out of his. "Go on. I want to hear the rest of your story."

His eyes took on a faraway focus. "I could already taste that first drink and was really looking forward to a fight. My life up to then had been gambling and stealing and anything else that came easy. Honest work was too hard. My pa taught me that. . . ." His voice trailed off and he sat silent. He seemed to be a million miles away.

Rachel placed her palms together almost in an attitude of prayer and held her fingers against her lips, thumbs under her chin. *Lord, what do I do? What would be wise?*

"One day, I . . . One day, we . . . One day, my pa and I had a huge fight, and I . . ." Michael looked down suddenly, eyes shut tight. He shuddered and squared his shoulders. "I started running then, never in one place too long. I'd wear out my welcome drinking and fighting and stealing. Went from saloon to saloon, town to town, staying one step ahead of the law and all those people I'd cheated. And then I got caught, and I couldn't run anymore."

A sad smile flickered on his face, then disappeared. "So there I am, sitting in jail, mad at everybody, and this preacher walks in. Kind of a heavy fellow, says his name was Zechariah Taylor. And he fixes me with these sharp, dark eyes and starts talking about Jesus. I wanted to punch him but couldn't get near him, so I cussed him and threw my slop bucket at him. Hit him pretty good, too."

His voice caught. He stopped and swallowed.

"Go on," Rachel said.

He gazed out over the river. The late afternoon sun sparkled on the water. A bird swooped at insects dancing on the surface. When he spoke again, his voice was husky, quiet, on the edge of tears.

"Zechariah kept coming back—every day for six months. He kept telling me Jesus loved me. After a while, I stopped cussing him and started arguing with him. I couldn't see how Jesus could love someone like me, someone that, uh, beat up my pa and stole from just about everybody else. Then I stopped arguing and started listening and reading the Bible he gave me."

A tear rolled down his cheek. "He led me to Jesus, prayed for me, even hugged me—can you believe that? And after that, while I finished serving my sentence, he taught me. When I got out, he and his wife took me in, and I began working with him in the county jail and state prison. That was three years ago."

"And that's how you met Ben Carstairs?"

He nodded. "More than anything, Ben wanted to patch things up with his pa. So—" he shrugged—"here I am. But I have to admit my stomach acts like a sack of rattlesnakes when I think of meeting his father. From what Ben and Pastor Luke said, Sam Carstairs sounds like one hard man to talk to."

"He's tough," Rachel said. "I went to him for a loan to

open up my dress shop. He wasn't interested at first—I think it was because I was living with Martha and Luke. He sure has no use for preachers. But Mrs. Phelps and Mrs. Walters showed him some of my work, and he showed it to some of the wealthier women in town. They told him they would buy my dresses, so he helped to set me up by becoming a partner with me. He owns 40 percent of the business, and he made it clear he expects me to make a profit from the beginning." She smiled. "He's not that unreasonable. Just don't talk about God with him. He'll drive you away with a shotgun."

Michael laughed. "Not the first time I've heard that. I've been praying about the best way to talk to him, to let him know how sorry Ben was for disappointing him."

"Well, I'll pray about that too. What will you do after you see Mr. Carstairs?"

"I don't know. Back to work with Reverend Zechariah and my regular job clerking in the general store, I guess." He turned to her. His gaze seemed to ask questions she didn't want to know the answers to. "Unless the Lord has something else for me to do."

No! Rachel suddenly fought the urge to run. *This is too close, too soon. I can't . . .*

She pushed to her feet and walked to the riverbank. Michael followed and stood beside her. Downstream, on the opposite bank, a deer approached and drank, cautious, ever alert. *That's me,* she thought. *Ever alert. Always waiting for something else bad to happen.*

The breeze had lightened. The river's surface shimmered. Even the animals and insects were quiet. Gradually her agitation settled, and she enjoyed Michael's nearness—close, but not touching. Unlike most men, he seemed to respect her. Could that be true? Or was his politeness a ploy to weaken her?

They walked along the bank. He took her hand to help her over a fallen tree. She let him keep holding it, the grip loose, as they walked. *This is all right. I can handle this.*

The tree leaves stood in sharp contrast against the bright blue sky, their different shapes and shades of green dancing in the breeze. The river water was clear as glass, individual stones easily recognizable, the water gurgling and rippling as it washed over them. The fish swam by with lazy flicks of their tails.

"Look how beautiful God makes things." Michael's voice was soft, almost hushed.

She nodded. "At times like this, I think He made it just for me."

He bent down, his lips seeking hers. She turned her head so that he brushed her cheek.

"We'd better head back," she said, "or we'll be late for the prayer service."

17

PETE O'BRIEN REMOVED his derby hat and, out of habit, slapped it against his leg to shake off the dust. His shoulders brushed against the doorframe as he glanced around the hotel dining room. No empty tables. He spotted Michael Archer sitting alone, a plate of half-finished food and a large book open on the table in front of him.

"Mind if I join ye?"

Archer looked up. He seemed flustered at the interruption. Pete realized the man had been focused on the book and oblivious to the world around him.

"Oh, Deputy. Good morning." There was a pause before Archer showed awareness that Pete had asked a question. "No, no, I don't mind. Please make yourself to home." He gestured to the seat across from him.

"Thanks." Pete plopped his hat on the table and waved to the waitress as he sat down. She came and poured coffee while Pete gave his order. He gazed at Archer, wondering where to begin, then took a sip of coffee and decided to plunge ahead.

"Well, me lad, ye've certainly made an impression on some people in a short amount of time."

"How do you mean?"

"Sheriff Caleb told me about yer wee dustup with Mark Carstairs in here on Saturday night. And I meself was there when Mark tried to start somethin' in the street with ye." Pete leaned forward. "I need to warn ye, laddie, to watch out for young Mr. Carstairs. You embarrassed him on Saturday. Twice. In here and out on the street. He's got a lot of pride, and because of his name, he can be a wee bit arrogant. Thank ye, darlin'," he said to the waitress who brought his food, then continued. "Not that he's done aught to be proud of, but that don't matter with his kind."

"Thanks for warning me." Archer poked at his food with his fork. "I'll be careful."

Pete pointed to the book still lying open between them. "Don't usually see a man reading a Bible outside of church. Seems strange."

Archer placed his hand on the book. "I read it every chance I get. Trying to understand it better, figure out how to do what it says."

Pete shrugged while he shoveled a forkful of eggs into his mouth. "Just seems like a bunch of malarkey to me. Never could understand it as a lad back in Ireland." He wiped his mouth with his napkin. "All we had was that Latin mumbo jumbo. Buncha strange-soundin' words and the priests tellin' us to obey the English, who were busy takin' everything we had. Then I came over here 'cause of the famine and ended up fightin' in the war. Both sides claiming God was on their side. Seemed to me He didn't care, just let us keep slaughterin' each other."

"I know what you mean," Archer said. "I didn't fight in the war—too young. But I remember the stories and seeing the men come home with arms and legs missing. A lot of them blamed God for it or said He didn't exist."

Pete shrugged. "Oh, I'm believin' He exists, all right. Me poor sainted mother drilled that into us every time she used the broom handle on us. God was gonna make sure we got what we deserved come Judgment Day. She was gonna miss not seeing us in heaven."

Archer chuckled. He paused while the waitress refilled their coffee cups. After she left, he pushed his plate to one side, leaned forward, and rested his arms on the table. "Before I met Jesus and made Him the Lord of my life, I was a drunk and a crook heading for worse things. I really believe it was only a matter of time before I'd kill someone, if I hadn't already, and when I did, it wouldn't mean a thing to me. Whoever I killed, I wouldn't even see him as a person, just something that was in the way of what I wanted."

Pete studied the man across from him. "You're not sure if you killed someone?"

Archer sipped his coffee. "It's a long story from a long time ago. Basically, the man was bleedin' like a stuck pig, and I was too scared to stick around and see if he was all right."

Pete forked up the last of his eggs. "Go on."

But Archer didn't really tell him what happened, just went on about a fellow named Zechariah and Jesus and such. Same malarkey Pete heard all the time from his girl Annabelle. *"Jesus loves you." Can't prove it by me.*

Pete drained his coffee cup and put it on the table, holding back the urge to slam it down. "Well, that's interestin', Reverend. I'm sure glad ye were able to find some peace o' mind." He picked up his hat as he stood. "Thanks for letting me share your table. Maybe we can talk again sometime."

Archer stood, and the two shook hands. "I look forward to it."

At the door, Pete stopped to set the derby on his head the way he liked it, using the window as a mirror. Satisfied, he looked back at Archer, who sat once again with his head bent over the Bible. *Poor lad. Someone's gonna hand yer head to ye one of these days, and I don't think Jesus will be there to help ye put it back on straight.*

18

RACHEL STRETCHED on her tiptoes to brush the tips of her fingers along the bottom edge of the sign hanging on a post outside her shop. Yellow letters on a pale blue background spelled out *Rachel's Hope*, with white flowers and greenery twirled around the edges—tangible evidence of her vision becoming a reality.

She stood in the doorway of the store and smiled. *Perfect.* The long side faced the street with white-curtained windows bracketing the door. Dressmaker's dummies displayed some of her creations. A curtain at the corner of the back wall marked the entrance to her work area. The rest of the wall held shelving with bolts of cloth behind a long counter with catalogs on it. The side walls exhibited hats and handbags as well as sewing supplies. The central space in front of the counter held small tables and chairs. A simple tea service sat next to the potbellied stove.

"Auntie Rachel." Daniel ran down the boardwalk and past her into the store. Martha followed a few steps behind, calling for him to slow down. He stopped in the middle and did a slow turn. "It's pretty."

He dashed to the counter, where a display of ribbons stood. "I like red." He grabbed the end of the ribbon and, with a sweep of his little arm, pulled several yards off the spool. The ribbon floated in gentle arcs to the floor.

"Daniel." Martha's voice was sharp, almost shrill. "No!" She yanked the ribbon from his hand and gave his rear several resounding slaps. "Bad boy."

Daniel didn't cry. Rachel covered her mouth to hide her smile at the boy's pouting lip and defiant eyes.

As Rachel finished rewinding the spool, the bell over the door jingled. In waddled Florence Meriweather, the mayor's wife. Behind her came Esther Phelps from church.

"I know you're going to like Miss Stone's work," Esther was saying as they entered.

"I don't know. How good is she?"

"Good morning, ladies." Rachel put on her best cultivated city voice. "May I help you?"

"My husband says I need a new dress for our anniversary celebration—we're making it quite the event. I want something in sky blue with lots of flowers."

Rachel directed her to a display of fabrics and stood back to let her browse. Martha turned her back to the customers and whispered in Rachel's ear, "Maybe there's a circus nearby that will sell you their big tent. Even then, you'll probably have to let the seams—"

"Shh!" Rachel peered past her friend to smile at her customer. "That's not kind."

Martha's face fell immediately. "You're right," she said. "Will I ever learn to stop saying things like that?"

"I like this one." Mrs. Meriweather held up the end of a bolt.

Rachel felt the color drain from her cheeks as she eyed the gaudy, daisy-printed fabric. *If you want to look like a balloon, that's the perfect choice. God, help me.*

"Have you seen this lovely russet wool?" Rachel directed the woman to several other options. With Esther Phelps's help, she succeeded in helping the woman pick something more suitable.

As she took Mrs. Meriweather's measurements, the woman asked, "How much experience have you had making dresses? I mean . . . in your former life, when did you get the opportunity?"

Rachel felt crimson creep up her neck. She bit back the retort that formed in her mouth.

Esther Phelps spoke. "Actually, Florence, Miss Stone made the dresses for a lot of the girls. She knows just how to make the fabric most flattering."

Mrs. Meriweather huffed. "Well, I'll give you one chance, girl, because Sam Carstairs invested money in you. He must see some potential." She shook her sausagelike finger in Rachel's face. "Just don't make me look like some cheap harlot."

"No, ma'am, I won't. I'm sure you'll be pleased."

"I'd better be." She turned and left.

Esther Phelps rolled her eyes behind her spectacles and followed the woman out of the store.

"Make her look like a cheap harlot?" Martha said. "That's a miracle I'd like to see for maybe five minutes." She placed her hand over her mouth. "There I go again. Please forgive me."

"I'm sure she didn't hear you. And I don't think Daniel was paying attention." She gestured toward where Daniel was pulling green ribbon from its roll.

An hour later, the store was empty. Rachel retreated to the back room to work on her first official Rachel's Hope dress. But the bell jingled, indicating another customer. She wiped her hands on her dress, tucked a stray strand of hair in place, and walked into the main room.

Michael Archer stood just inside the door, looking confused and uncomfortable—completely out of place. He turned his black hat around in his hands like a windmill in a strong breeze. Relief washed over his face when he saw her.

"Good morning." She smiled.

"Hope it's all right for me to stop by. I thought I'd come see what a real dressmaker's shop is like." His gaze swept the room.

She hoped he liked what he saw. *But why should that matter to me? What does a man know about a dressmaking store?*

Because this store, more than anything else, reflected who she was now. The "soiled dove," as the newspapers liked to call those in her prior life, no longer existed. She was a dressmaker, a businesswoman, and this store represented her new life.

She watched him, hands clasped at her waist, as he observed the room she had designed and outfitted.

"You seem to be all set."

"I could use some help in the back room. My worktable has a bit of a wobble, and some shelving needs to be secured."

He spread his arms and bowed at the waist. "I'm at your service, ma'am. Let me take a look and see what I can do."

She led him into her work area, tucking the curtain over a hook to keep it open.

Michael tested the table with his hand and felt the wobble. He bent down to look at the legs as he tested it again. "Looks like one leg is just a tad shorter than the others. I can make a quick shim so you can work on it today, and then tonight I can fix it more permanent."

"Thank you. That would be wonderful."

He walked to the wood box, where she had put some leftover pieces of shelving to use as kindling. He found a small piece, measured it with his eye, then placed it under the recalcitrant leg. He tested the table again, and the wobble was gone.

He was picking up the shelving unit as the bell announced someone else entering the store. "Go take care of your customer while I see if I can put this shelving up without breaking anything."

After finishing with her customer, Rachel walked into the back room, surprised to find it empty and the shelves exactly where she wanted them. She found a note weighted down by her scissors.

> *Rachel,*
>   *I didn't want to embarrass you by having you explain what a man was doing in your back room. Would you do me the honor of meeting me for lunch at the hotel? I'll be waiting in the lobby.*
> *Michael*

She looked at the clock hanging over the entrance to her back room. Two more hours until she saw Michael Archer again.

    But is that a good thing? Lord, help me be wise.

19

SAM JOLTED AWAKE when the wheel bounced over a rut. He shook his head to clear it. He hadn't meant to doze off.

What day is it? He ticked off the journey in his mind. *Tuesday. Tomorrow will be Hawkins Station, then home on Thursday.*

He looked at the young couple sitting across from him. *Sure hope I didn't snore like a bear.* He touched his chin with his hand. Dry. At least he didn't drool like a doddering old man.

Maria and Jack sat close to each other, holding hands, watching the passing scenery through the dust cloud raised by the stage. Sam studied them through half-closed eyes. They seemed innocent enough—young and in love, not really aware of the world outside the cocoon of their new marriage. But nagging doubts nibbled at the edges of his mind. *Ah, you're getting old, Sam, and those notes are driving you crazy. You're thinking everyone's out to get you.*

He realized the girl was now focused on him with more than natural curiosity, as if she wanted to see inside his head.

"I'm sorry," she said when she realized he was awake. "I didn't mean to stare. It's just that you seem so sad and lonely. Is everything all right?" Her soft voice sounded smooth and sweet, but her eyes portrayed an emotion he couldn't name— and it wasn't pleasant.

"I'm fine," he said. "It's been a long trip, and I'm feeling my age."

"Oh. I asked because you look as if you've lost someone very close to you."

Her husband spoke up in a nasal twang. "Sweetheart, don't pry." He looked at Sam. "I apologize, Mr. Carstairs. Maria has a heart as big as all outdoors and doesn't like to see people unhappy. She can pick up on it real quick just by looking at them. Then she tries to help them as best she can."

Maria glared at her husband, a split second of annoyance and irritation, so quick Sam questioned if he actually saw it. She turned to Sam. Her eyes held an intensity that belied her calm demeanor . . . and reminded him of something strangely familiar. *Have I met this girl before?*

"I do apologize, sir. My husband is right. Sometimes I let my heart lead and jump right into people's business where I don't belong."

"No offense taken, ma'am."

They lapsed into silence. The stage rocked and bounced, and when it hit a rough spot, they swayed from side to side until the coach settled down. Sam folded his arms and let his head droop as if falling asleep again, but he opened his eyes to thin slits and watched his fellow travelers. *Why does she keep looking at me like that? And why does it bother me so?*

He shifted his weight and leaned against the side of the coach, thinking of the past three weeks. The trip had been successful, beyond his wildest expectations. The railroad president had sat at his mahogany desk in his ornate office with its thick carpet and fancy drapes framing the window overlooking San Francisco Bay. He'd signed the contract with an elaborate flourish, then stood and shaken Sam's hand.

"Well, Sam, in eighteen months you'll see that big black engine steaming into Riverbend. I'm looking forward to being on the first trip."

"Yes, sir. And we'll be ready for you too. This railroad's going to make the town grow. Riverbend will be the biggest and best place to live in our part of the state."

Sam remembered his visions of money pouring in because of the railroad, but he couldn't resurrect the elation he'd felt in that moment. He couldn't summon any feeling but that familiar cold dread. John Higgins—or someone like him—was out there somewhere, lying in wait.

Isn't it enough punishment that Ruth was taken away from me?

His thoughts drifted to Ruth, so dear to him that he'd lied and cheated and even killed to get her—then she was gone too soon. And Ben, who resembled her more than either of his brothers, a burning lance to his heart. Suddenly he found himself wondering how Ben was faring. *I drove him away. And Mark's a lost cause, and who knows what Josh thinks?*

He opened his eyes to find the woman across from him still staring. Her steady gaze exposed him, slammed right through him. And in that moment he felt his carefully constructed defenses burn away. In the ashes, he realized his happiness had left when Ruth died. And nothing—not the money, not the power—could fill the void.

A tear rolled down his cheek.

He wondered what Maria Alden thought of that.

20

Tuesday evening, Rachel locked the door to her store. She rested her hand on the glass panel. A good day—with three more orders. Thank God Mr. Carstairs had advanced enough money for the Singer.

Her body ached with the satisfying fatigue of hard, clean work—her workday done instead of just beginning. She looked forward to the parsonage and Martha's cooking. Venison tonight—Isaac Walters had delivered a haunch early that morning. Her mouth tingled in anticipation of Martha's sure touch with herbs and spices.

Would Michael be there tonight? He'd spent the day with Pastor Luke, and she had to admit she'd missed seeing him today. *Remember, he's just a man.*

No, he's more than that. The debate had nagged her all day.

Two things struck her as she entered the parsonage. First, the aroma of meat cooking that triggered the rumbles of hunger. Second, the silence. Her footsteps echoed off the hardwood floor as she made her way to the kitchen. Where were the children? The house was rarely this quiet so close to the evening meal.

In the kitchen, Martha stirred a pot. She wiped her hands on her apron and turned. "I thought I heard footsteps, and I knew they were too dainty to be Luke's. The man can clomp like a horse sometimes. And smell like one too." She covered her mouth. "There I go again. I'm sorry."

Rachel reached to tie an apron around her waist. "Where is everybody?"

"Daniel's out chasing fireflies. Abigail's upstairs working on her lessons. Or more likely playing with her doll, if I know her. Luke and Michael aren't back yet."

"Michael's coming?" Rachel tried to keep her voice casual.

"That's what they told me this morning after you left. Michael said he'd be pleased to join us for supper when he and Luke returned from visiting families up the valley." She glanced out the window. "And there they are."

The sound of horses in the yard was drowned out by Daniel's yell. "Daddy's home!"

Abigail galloped down the stairs. Luke walked in, Daniel on his hip. He embraced his daughter with his free arm. "Are we late for supper?"

Martha poked at the meat, then turned with a hand on her hip. "Almost. Did you have lunch?"

"We ate at the Ramseys'. Why?"

She picked up a sack hanging from one of the chairs. "Because you forgot the lunch I packed for you and Michael."

"Oh."

"I don't care if you starve yourself, but it's not polite to force a guest to starve." She pointed at Michael, who seemed to be looking for a hole to crawl into.

"Sorry, dear."

She smiled. "You're forgiven. Again. Now get over here and give me a proper greeting."

He put the children down, took Martha in his arms, and kissed her, long and hard.

Rachel watched Michael, who was trying to look anywhere but at Luke and Martha. His eyes met hers, and his mouth twitched. She thought it was a smile that turned into a grimace at being caught in the situation. *Why does it please me that he seems embarrassed?*

After supper, Rachel and Michael sat together on the porch swing, the sounds of children being prepared for bed faint in the background. The silence between them grew until it became uncomfortable. What should she say? What did he want from her?

Well, that was easy—in a way. He was a man, after all, and she knew he was attracted to her. In her old life she would have known just how to handle that, how to manipulate him to her own advantage. But that was her old life, and Michael was different. She didn't want to manipulate him.

So what do I want?

The answer came suddenly and surprised her. *I want to be in control of my own life.* No one was going to control her ever again. But how could she tell him that?

"Sam Carstairs should be back by the end of the week," she said. Anything to break the silence.

"So Sheriff Davis told me."

Oh, what I wouldn't give to read your mind. Well, there's one thing I won't give, but beyond that . . .

She turned to face him. "Are you ready to do what you need to do?"

He shrugged. "I think so. I'll need to pray for the right words. I think I'll only have one chance to get it right."

"I think you're right."

Michael willed his fidgety hands to be still. Why so nervous? Why was it so important to impress this girl? Yes, she was beautiful, but so were many others. Why was she the first one to stir feelings and yearnings he hadn't felt in such a long time, if ever? There had been plenty of opportunities. It seemed like every family in Zechariah's church had someone to match him up with. Some were reasonably attractive.

What makes Rachel different? He thought of the picnic they'd shared on Sunday and the lunch on Monday.

"You know, you're easy to talk to."

She smiled. "I am? You haven't said more than a few words all night."

"I mean, you don't make me feel pressured to talk. You handle just sitting here real well."

"Most of what I learned to talk to men about ain't fit for polite ears." She blushed. "I mean *isn't*. I'm trying to clean up my mouth in more ways than one."

"How hard has it been? You know, giving up your past life?"

She plucked at a pleat in her dress. "Giving it up was the easy part. I would never want to go back to what I was doing. But moving past it has been hard." She ran her fingers through her hair. "The looks from people, the comments, old habits. Some of the men in the restaurant or the general store brushing up against me, trying to touch me—people like Mark Carstairs."

"Why do you stay? Why not move someplace else—where nobody knows?"

She bit her lower lip. "I've thought of it, prayed about it. Even had my bags packed a couple of times ready to jump on the next stage."

"What changed your mind?"

She stood and walked to the railing, leaned against the post at the head of the stairs, and spoke into the darkness. "Remembering I've been saved—that I'm not the same girl I was. That's real important to me. And I didn't want to let Martha and Luke down or people like the Phelpses and the Barkstons, who've been so kind."

She turned to face him, folding her arms. "And I guess a part of me was afraid that if I ran away, I'd run right back to whoring. But that's not what kept me here. Not really."

"So what was it?"

"No one knows about this—just Martha and Pastor

Luke." Her face was soft in the lantern light, her expression far away. Michael waited.

She closed her eyes. "One night I was sitting at the kitchen table, mending a dress for Abigail. I'd been here just a month. The next thing I knew, I was standing in the street in daylight, right in front of my store. Everything was exactly the way you saw it yesterday. Every bolt of cloth, every spool of thread. The tea service, the workroom. That store in that building in this town. Even the sign: *Rachel's Hope*. Then I was back in the kitchen, Abigail's dress in my hands."

She opened her eyes and looked at him, her face unreadable. "Luke says I had a vision, like in the Bible. That maybe I have a gift. But why would God give somebody like me a gift like that?"

He wanted to stand, to walk to her, to take her in his arms . . . to what? *She* was a gift, no matter what she thought, and she deserved so much better than what he had to offer—a pastor's helper, a man whose highest career ambition was clerking in a general store.

A man who couldn't seem to let go of his own past, when she had moved so gracefully beyond hers.

His heart seemed to be squeezed in a massive fist, no room to beat. How could he ever be worthy of a woman like Rachel?

And how could he convince her she was worthy of so much more?

21

Rachel tied off the thread in the lace collar she was tacking onto a dress for Esther Phelps. Her stomach rumbled, and she glanced at the clock. Almost noon. In her past life, she had never eaten this early. Of course, in her past life, she was rarely awake this early. Unless there was a big event, in which case Red Mary would expect her girls to work all night and all day. She shook her head to clear the memory, but the irritation lingered.

Food. My body wants food. Maybe I'll go back to the parsonage to see what Martha's fixing for the children. Or maybe I'll get something from the hotel and have it at the school with Annabelle.

The bell over the door jingled. *Well, hopefully this won't take long.* She walked into the store and stopped.

Michael stood holding a tray with cloth-covered dishes. A small vase in the center held two daylilies. "I thought you might like some lunch, so I asked the hotel to fix us a couple of plates." He searched the room for a place to put the tray.

"And you invited yourself to join me?" She didn't know how angry she was until she heard her own voice. Where had that come from?

He blinked and backed up a step. "I guess I did." Confusion clouded his face. "I can leave your plate and take mine back to the hotel. I, uh, didn't mean to bother you." He set down the tray on the counter and picked up one of the plates. His hand was on the doorknob, turning it.

"Wait," she said.

He stopped, hand still on the knob. She sensed that if he walked out the door, something would be lost from her life, something irretrievable. But how could she explain when she barely understood herself?

"All my life, men have told me what to do and how to do it and who to do it with. In Riverbend, I've felt like I'm free of that. I have choices. I can make decisions." She heard her voice rising, heard the hurt. And suddenly she didn't care if he heard it too. Maybe he needed to. Her temper was slipping. The closest thing to throw was the teapot.

No. I'm not going to break my own things.

She planted her hands on her hips. "When you came with food for both of us, it . . . it felt like you were telling me when to eat, what to eat, and who to eat with, and the flowers were supposed to make it all okay. Just like when my uncle expected a silver dollar to make it all okay."

His gaze went to the flowers and then back to her. "That's not—"

"I know. But that's how it felt."

"I . . . I don't know what to say."

She smiled, the irritation slipping away. "That's a good start. At least you won't be able to tell me what to do."

Michael arranged the plates on the tea table. He folded his frame into the too-small chair and blessed the food. The food was tasteless in his dry mouth. Tea passed over his tongue and down his throat without leaving any moisture.

Rachel held his attention. Her small bites of food disappearing between those lush lips. The loose strand of hair that dangled near her eyes. He longed to reach over and tuck it behind her ear, but he knew he wouldn't be content with that. His hand wanted to pull her head close to his. He wanted to kiss her forehead, her nose, her lips. He jabbed at a piece of meat.

Rachel sipped her tea. "I apologize for being rude. I do thank you for bringing lunch."

"You haven't done anything to apologize for. I wasn't thinking about how you'd see it. I just wanted to see you again."

"Are you blushing? Well, you are now." Her laugh sang to his ears. "Michael, I'm flattered you want to see me. And I enjoy being with you." She toyed with her knife. Her slender fingers on the handle fascinated him. Everything about her fascinated him.

He wanted to stop time, to prolong being in her presence,

to dream before she spoke again . . . because he dreaded what she might say next. He'd seen it coming—heard it in her hesitation.

She folded her arms on the table and leaned forward. Everything she did was beautiful.

"You don't know how beautiful you are, do you?" He blurted the words.

She straightened, and her hands fell to her lap.

He continued. "You're about to tell me you aren't ready for a man in your life, that you can't trust us, that we're only after one thing. Many men are like that. I don't think I'm one of them. Not anymore. Yes, I think you're beautiful, whatever that means. Yes, I want to be with you."

He paused, trying to control his thoughts, to figure out what to say next. But his brain was disengaged. His heart was talking.

"I want to be with you," he repeated. "I want to be in your company. I want to know you better. I want to see God as you see Him. I want to experience more of life with you. And yes, I desire you physically. But you are not, and never will be, a whore to me."

Tension tied a knot in his stomach. Had he said too much?

"I've never had a relationship with a woman like Luke has with Martha. For me, for so long, women were there to meet my needs, my desires. Until I started working with Pastor Zechariah, that is. After that . . . well, it just seemed safer to stay away from women."

He paused, took a deep breath. "Until I met you. And I

don't know what to do about it. I've never courted a woman. I doubt you even want to be courted. I don't know how you would feel about a man whose past includes using women like you've been used, and worse."

He closed his mouth. Thoughts churned; secrets nibbled at the surface, wanting to burst out. He pushed them down. She didn't need to know them.

Her voice was soft. "You're right about one thing. I'm not ready for a relationship with a man."

Her gaze met his, matching the firm edge her voice took. "All my life, men have only wanted one thing from me, and somehow they thought money was a suitable replacement for love. And I know you're different, and I like you. But I . . . I don't think I can be the girl you want me to be."

Her voice grew wistful as she looked out the window. "I dream about having a husband and children, but it feels like a fantasy. I've prayed about it too. But the hurt is still there."

She picked up the knife and tossed him a wry smile. "I will say this, though. You're one of the few men I've met where I didn't feel like I needed to keep *this* close by."

22

"WHO'S ELLIE?" Rachel said. They were walking from the store to the parsonage as dusk settled over the town. Michael had come back to walk her home and have supper with the family.

Michael's step faltered. "She's my sister. How did you hear about her?"

"Saturday night at the restaurant, you said her name when you rescued me from Mark."

He gave her a sideways smile. "I did, didn't I? I'd forgotten that."

She let him take her hand to help her step off the boardwalk to cross a side street. When they reached the other side, she hooked her arm through his. How nice to be walking together like this, like other couples. Only they weren't like other couples, and maybe she wasn't being fair.

She released his arm and asked, "Were you close?"

Silence. In profile, Michael's face seemed to take on a far-away look. His body was here, but his essence was someplace she couldn't go.

"We were close until I left home. We lost touch with each other while I was roaming around in search of my next drink or easy mark."

"And you never went back home to see her or your folks?"

Words seemed to catch in his throat. "Mom was dead, and Pa and I had that big fight when I left. I figured if I went back, I'd just be walking into a heap of trouble I didn't need."

"Sounds like you and Ben Carstairs had a lot in common."

He stopped and turned toward her, his eyes hard, his mouth grim. "Not really." He resumed walking, more rigid than before.

She had to hurry to catch up with him. "So you've never heard from Ellie?"

He sighed. "Got a letter about a year and a half ago— don't know how she tracked me down. She married a boy from the farm next door, has a couple of girls. She sounded happy. I didn't see any reason to go and bring hard times back into her life."

Rachel clasped her hands at her waist. Vague memories of her own mother and father flickered. Or were they fantasies of what she wished might have been? "It might not seem that way to her. If I knew I had a brother somewhere, I'd like to see him."

"Now who's trying to tell somebody what to do?"

Stung by his words, Rachel pressed her lips together. She hadn't been trying to tell him what to do. She'd just been trying to help.

She let the silence stand the rest of the way to the parsonage.

Michael stood alone in the room that served as Luke's office. In the kitchen, Rachel, Martha, and Abigail were preparing supper. The clatter of dishes on the table mingled with their chatter. From outside the back door came the cries of Daniel being cleaned for supper by Luke.

A family doing family things—normal, daily family things. *Ellie and her husband are probably going about the same chores.* Envy stirred. Loneliness too. *It would be nice to have a family but . . .* His work with Pastor Zechariah kept him too busy. He wasn't ready to settle down.

He heard Rachel's laughter echo down the hall. Who was he fooling?

He sighed. He was no genius with women, but he knew she was unhappy with him. And he probably deserved it too, but he still couldn't figure out what he had done.

"Go ahead. Help yourself."

It took a moment to register Luke's voice and to realize the pastor was referring to the collection of books in front of Michael.

The front of Luke's shirt was wet. He brushed at it with his hands. "Trying to get Daniel washed for supper is like wrestling a fish one-handed."

Luke sat in the chair behind the table that served as his desk and glanced at some handwritten papers. "Better remember these for Sunday." He spoke with the air of someone talking to himself. He looked at them again. "Oh, these are last Sunday's notes." He riffled through some other papers on the desk. "What happened to my notes for this Sunday? Martha will know. Or Daniel used them for his horse pictures."

He leaned back in his chair and sighed, hands laced behind his head. "Do you want to come out with me tomorrow? I'm going across the river."

"Sam Carstairs is due in tomorrow. I'd better stay in town."

"That's right. I forgot about that." Luke dropped his hands to his lap. "Are you ready for him? Do you know what you're going to say?"

Michael sat across from Luke. "I figure if I at least get him to agree to meet with me, I'll be making a good start. Once I can sit down with him, I'm thinking I'll just open my mouth and let God do the rest. I'm no silver-tongued preacher."

"Just be yourself, Michael. From what I know of Sam Carstairs, he can spot a phony before he hears a word. Keep it simple. Keep it direct. Tone down the church connection. If he hears church, he will throw you out without a second chance."

"I'm curious. It's pretty clear he doesn't like church folk, but he helped Rachel with her store. How come?"

"Two reasons." Luke frowned. "No, three." He emphasized each point with his fingers. "One, Vernon Phelps is a good friend of Sam's and on the town council, so Sam could overlook the church connection when Vernon's wife talked to him. Two, Sam had nonchurch people look at Rachel's work. They liked it." Luke grinned. "And three, she's pretty. Not that she used her looks to get the money. She wouldn't. It's just an advantage she had. Could you say no to her?"

Michael shook his head. "Can't imagine I'd ever want to."

After supper, Michael and Rachel visited on the porch. The house was unusually quiet. Rachel sat on the swing. Michael perched himself on the porch rail, leaning against the corner post, gazing at the stars. Once again, he couldn't think of a thing to say. She seemed content in the silence. At least she didn't seem upset anymore.

"Do you get the sense they're leaving us alone out here on purpose?" Rachel said after a minute.

Michael grinned. "It did cross my mind."

Rachel shook her head. "Martha seems to have a matchmaker streak in her."

"Has she tried to match you with other men before?"

"No, not me. But I've seen her do it with others. The way she was talking about you while we were fixing supper makes me think she's at it again."

Michael tried to keep the irritation out of his voice. "She hardly knows me. What could she say?"

"Mostly she talked about how you must be a good man because Zechariah Taylor likes you. She says I can't go wrong with a man Zechariah Taylor likes."

"But you told me you aren't looking for that kind of relationship."

"I'm not, but that doesn't seem to be stopping Martha."

Michael slid off the porch rail, leaned against it, and crossed his arms. "Why did you go on the picnic with me on Sunday?"

"Because I wanted to." She paused. "Partly, I wanted to thank you for what you did Saturday night. Partly, it was a test. Of me, not you. I wanted to see if I was ready to have a man in my life. Also, I was curious about you." She stroked her hand. "I've never had a man kiss my hand the way you did."

"So did I ruin it when I tried to kiss you?"

Her laugh was like the wind tinkling bells. "No. By then I knew I wasn't ready. I also didn't want you to think I might be . . . that I'm that kind of girl." She paused, the silence suddenly loud. "That I'm the kind of girl I was."

Silence again. She spoke into the darkness. "Since meeting you, I've realized something. I like you and I feel safe around you." She walked over to him. "I've also realized something else. A lot of why I feel safe around you is because you won't be here very long." She placed her hands on his still-folded arms. "But you've given me hope that maybe someday I can feel safe around a man who will be here a long time. Thank you."

She rose up on her toes and kissed his cheek.

And his heart sank.

23

A FAINT ORANGE GLOW marked where the sun had settled below the jagged horizon, the peaks reaching like misshapen fingers clawing at the sky. The stage rattled and jounced into the yard of the way station. Sam climbed down from the coach and gazed up at the never-ending sky and the myriad of stars. *One more night. Home tomorrow.*

Hawkins Station seemed like a dark hump, faint lamp-light behind coarse curtains. Beyond it and to one side, he could make out the hulking shape of the barn and the fences of the corral. Dim lanterns marked either side of the door to the way station.

He heard the young couple climb down behind him as a man and woman came out of the station.

"Welcome," the woman said. "Glad ya made it afore it got full dark. You might've missed us and driven right past."

The driver said, "Not with the smell of your stew to lead us in, Maggie."

The woman laughed, and the guard said, "Better the smell of your stew than the smell of Nate there." He pointed to the man with her. "The horses ever got wind of him, they'd run the other way."

One of the lead horses snorted and bobbed his head up and down.

"See, Nate, even Lightning agrees," the guard said.

Nate walked over to the horse and stroked its nose. "That ain't true, is it, Lightning? Ol' Nate probably smells like home to you—water an' oats an' hay."

"Enough of this jabberin'," Maggie said. "Y'all get inside and grab somethin' to eat. Nate, you help these two reprobates take care of their team proper."

The inside of the station was one big open room, with three windows on each side of the front door. To the left, two more windows flanked a bar. Shelves behind it offered a limited supply of liquid refreshment along with other supplies a traveler might need. To the right, a large fireplace separated two windows. A small fire burned in the hearth. A moth-eaten buffalo head stared mournfully from above the rough stone mantel. A series of doors lined the back wall, and several plain wooden tables with chairs dotted the wood floor in a haphazard arrangement. Lanterns hung from the ceiling, casting an uneven light through the room.

Maggie was a large, round woman whose unruly black hair was streaked with gray and white. She shook Sam's hand

and said, "It's good to see ya agin. How ya doin'? Did ya have a good trip to San Francisco and Denver?"

"You could say it was successful, Maggie, and I'm doing tolerable well."

"Couldn't prove it by me. Ya look like somethin' the cat dragged in an' then changed its mind about."

"Just tired from the traveling."

Maggie studied him, then shook her head. "I'm havin' a hard time believin' ya, ya old coot. I've known ya too long not to know when somethin's botherin' ya, but far be it from me to pry into an old friend's business. Ya just let me know if ya need anything, an' we'll take care of it for ya."

"Thanks, Maggie." He sagged into one of the chairs. "Just bring me a jug."

"You bet." She turned to the Aldens, who had seated themselves at another table. "How you two doing?"

"Just fine," the man said.

"Glad to be sitting in something that isn't bouncing," the young woman said.

Maggie laughed. "Yeah, stages can shake ya up somethin' fierce after a while. I don't think there's any getting used to it. If you're hungry, I've got some beef stew an' cornbread an' some apple cobbler. Always got a pot of beans simmerin' too if ya got a hankerin' for it. Got coffee or somethin' stronger to drink if you've a mind to. There's a washstand outside if ya want to clean up for supper, an' behind that door in the far corner is a tub an' plenty of hot water if ya want to take a bath.

"Forgettin' my manners here. My name's Maggie Johansen.

Nate's my husband. We been runnin' this station for nigh on fifteen years."

Jack Alden glanced at his companion and they introduced themselves.

Maggie studied the couple. "Newlyweds, ain't ya?"

"That's right," Jack said. To Sam, Maria looked as if she wanted Maggie to disappear.

"Knowed it right off. Can always tell." Maggie touched the side of her nose. "It's a gift. I think it's 'cause Nate still acts like a newlywed even after twenty-three years. Room number three has a double bed with a fresh straw mattress. That'll be yours for tonight."

"Thank you," Maria said. "That's very thoughtful. You know, I am feeling hungry. I think I'll wash up for supper, and afterwards I am going to use that bath you mentioned." She stood. Her husband rose a split second behind her and followed her out the front door.

"Ain't that sweet, Sam? Newlyweds," Maggie said. "You remember bein' a newlywed?"

Sam glared at her. "I do. Seems like the last good thing that ever happened to me. Get me that jug, will ya?"

Maggie put a jug of whiskey and a glass in front of him and exited through the door in the back wall nearest the bar. She returned a few minutes later carrying a tray with two plates of stew, two cups of coffee, and a platter of cornbread, just as Maria and Jack came in again. She set the food in front of them and watched as the couple began to eat.

After a couple of mouthfuls, Jack looked up and said, "This is delicious, ma'am."

Maria murmured her agreement as she continued to eat.

"Thanks. It's nice to be appreciated. You ready to eat, Sam?"

"Yeah, let me go wash up. No coffee, though. The jug is just fine."

Sam stood and walked out to wash up. He felt Maria's eyes following him.

A few minutes later, he entered with Nate, the driver, and the guard right behind him. Sam ignored the good-natured banter going on among the others. He cast a wary glance at the young couple and sat with his back to them. Maggie set some stew and cornbread in front of him. He ate without enjoyment, a mechanical action of putting food in his mouth. He kept his glass filled from the jug and grunted at the efforts Maggie and Nate made to engage him in conversation. Eventually they gave up.

His meal finished, Sam picked up his jug and glass and went outside. He walked to the corner of the building. Stars as far as he could see. The southern breeze brought warm air across his face and stirred the fringes of his hair. The aroma of wildflowers lingered in the air. A coyote howled in the distance. A horse snorted and stamped in the corral.

But the peace of the night eluded him like a butterfly that darted just out of reach. There was no comfort tonight, only oppressive heaviness. He felt like he was enshrouded in a bulky buffalo hide on a warm July evening. He didn't need it, but he couldn't shrug it off. He missed Ruth. He missed the times they would sit on the porch on nights like this or walk hand in hand through the flower garden she had planted near the house. The garden was neglected and overgrown now, another memory of her turned bitter over the years.

The door opened behind him, one of the hinges squeaking for oil. Nate Johansen passed him and made his way toward the corral. The door opened again. This time the soft swish of a skirt, light footsteps, and the wisp of flowery perfume told him Maria Alden had stepped outside. Why did she make him so uncomfortable? He moved away from the building and walked farther out. He heard her walk in the opposite direction and soon heard her speaking with Nate, but the conversation was too low for him to understand.

Sam walked across the yard of the station. He had no idea where he wanted to go. He didn't want to meander in the dark. Snorting with disgust, he went back into the station. Alden still sat at the table, a coffee cup nearby, a book open before him. The guard and driver talked quietly with Maggie at the bar.

"Maggie," Sam said, "I'm gonna turn in. Which room is mine?"

"Number four, Sam. Same as always. Have a good night's sleep. Ya look like ya could sure use it."

"Thanks. See you in the mornin'."

Sam walked into the small, neat, adobe-walled room. A narrow bed with a straw mattress stood against one wall, a table with a lantern, washbasin, and chipped pitcher against the other. A plain wooden chair stood opposite the door. Starlight through the open window provided dim illumination. He lit the lantern on the table and closed the window shutters to keep insects out of his dirt-floored chamber.

He shook off his boots, draped his jacket across the back of the chair, and stretched out on the bed. The mattress crackled and crinkled. The blanket smelled strongly of Maggie's lye soap. He wished she would let things air-dry more.

He laced his fingers behind his head and stared at the ceiling. Sleep wouldn't come. He'd known it wouldn't. His mind raced with thoughts of all that had happened the past few days, and he couldn't escape that heavy foreboding. He tried to plan his next step but couldn't. He was groping and grasping at the wind because he had no idea where his enemy was or what he would do next. He could only wait and be on guard for any sign of danger. There wasn't even any way to contact his sons for help.

Thick walls muffled sounds from the next room. Boots dropped to the floor, the mattress creaking as bodies settled into it, a man's and a woman's voices. Maria and Jack Alden were turning in. A coyote howled in the distance, and horses moved in the corral.

Sam tossed and turned for several more hours. Then physical and emotional exhaustion finally overwhelmed him and he drifted into sleep.

Cold metal pressed into his neck. Sam awoke and opened his mouth to shout, but a gloved hand clamped across it, and fingers pinched his nose. Blackness clouded the room. He couldn't distinguish shapes or patterns. He struggled, but the gun barrel pressed deeper into his neck and twisted, causing a sharp pain. A woman's voice whispered in his ear.

"Fight us and you're dead. Just be quiet and cooperate, and

you might live through this. Nod if you're going to go along with us. Otherwise, I'll have Jack here cut your throat."

The thin, sharp edge of a knife pushed against his throat. Sam nodded. The knife scraped his skin.

"All right. Not a sound," the woman whispered. "Sit up."

Sam swung his legs over the side of the bed and struggled into a sitting position. Light flared as Jack Alden struck a match and lit the lantern. The woman, Maria, pointed a pistol at his face. Jack stood next to her, his knife resting in his hand, the point aimed at Sam's throat.

Maria glanced at her husband—was he really her husband? Jack slipped the knife into its sheath and gagged Sam's mouth with a bandanna. He tied Sam's hands with a coarse rope, pulling the knots tight. Sam felt the rough fiber dig into his skin. Maria looked into Sam's eyes, the strange expression now turned to naked hatred. She swung her free hand and slapped his face.

"That's just the beginning." She swung her other hand, and the gun struck Sam in the temple, leaving a bloody gash. He collapsed onto his side, consciousness sliding away.

24

MICHAEL WALKED along the riverbank, hands clasped behind his back, a finger holding his place in the book of Psalms as the first signs of morning appeared. A cool breeze rippled the waters of the river. Soft plops marked where fish rose to the surface to snare bugs. An eagle swooped down. With a smooth, almost-effortless motion, its talons dipped into the water. The graceful predator flew away, a fish wriggling in its iron grip.

Michael felt that same grip around his heart, pressure squeezing until it seemed like it would burst. *She feels safe around me because I'm leaving. Wonder what she'd say if I told her I was staying? She deserves better than anything I can offer. But how could I possibly leave her?*

An old cottonwood with a smooth patch of grass at its

base beckoned him. He sat facing the river, his back against the tree. He read the Psalms, stopping occasionally to close his eyes and pray. A soft rustle in the nearby undergrowth distracted him. He shrugged it off as a rabbit or squirrel rummaging for food. He heard it again, closer. He turned his head and saw Rachel.

The morning light glowed around her. An orb of pale sunshine highlighted her elegant features and brightened her pale yellow dress. Released from the bonnet in her hand, her hair cascaded to her shoulders and framed her face with light brown wisps. Her eyes sparkled. Her lips moved soundlessly. She followed the path to the river.

"Good morning," he said.

She jumped. Then she smiled, a big wide smile that lit up her eyes. "Michael Archer, you seem to show up where and when I least expect you."

He stood. Waited. She made no move to come closer.

"The hotel room smelled too closed in. I thought I'd come out for some fresh air." Did he dare step closer? He wanted to. "What brings you out here?"

"I wanted to think. To pray."

"Any particular reason?" *Like me?*

"No. Just wanted a quiet spot."

"I'll leave then." He turned to go.

"No, you don't have to." She beckoned him toward the river. "Walk with me a bit."

"Still feeling safe around me, huh?"

She smiled. "Yes."

The narrow path prevented them from walking side by

side, so Rachel walked a step in front. He enjoyed her near-ness, the scent of lilacs and lavender drifting behind her.

"Would you feel safe around me if I decided to stay in Riverbend?"

She stopped, turned. "Safer than I do with Mark Carstairs. Not as safe as I feel with Pastor Luke." She paused. Her eyes drilled into him. He remembered looking through a micro-scope once at a state fair. He felt like that little drop of water under the lens.

"Are you thinking of staying?"

Michael kept his voice casual. *Pretend you're talking about the weather.* "I don't know for sure. I like the town, the loca-tion. The people." He kicked a stone in the path into the tall grass nearby. A rabbit jumped and skittered away. "I'd need to talk with Zechariah. Pray about it. I think I'd like to come back some time. See if they need a clerk in the general store. Maybe help Pastor Luke with his work."

He waited for her to say something. She stared over the river, chewing on her lower lip. Had he gone too far? She was like a rabbit, ready to skitter off. He prayed.

She turned and started back toward town. "I need to get ready to walk Abigail to school and open the store."

25

PAIN. SHARP, BLINDING, throbbing, burning. He felt like his head had been stomped repeatedly by an angry mule. He was on a horse, lying forward along its neck. He sat up and wished he hadn't. The world swam in fluid like a mucky creek. He tried to raise his hands but discovered they were tied to the saddle horn. Another rope was tied around the saddle horn and his waist. The sway of the horse intensified the pain. Bitter acid rose in his throat.

Gradually, he remembered. The stagecoach, the way station. The woman in his room. The knife and the slap, followed by the gun crashing against his head.

The sun hovered on the horizon in front of him. Ahead of him rode a man, a dark silhouette. Through Sam's pain-blurred vision, he looked like the man who had been with the woman. What was his name? And where was his wife? Sam tried to speak, but incoherent babbling came out of his mouth. Thirst burned in his mouth and throat. He tried to swallow, but a fresh wave of nausea roiled his stomach. He leaned to the side. The motion made him dizzy, and he felt himself falling. Only his hands tied to the saddle kept him from tumbling to the dry, rocky ground.

He heard a rider approach from his left rear. He turned to look. New pain streaked through his skull, down his neck, and into his spine. He gasped at the unexpected force and grabbed frantically at the saddle horn to control the vertigo.

"So you're a little more awake. That's good. We've got a long ways to go."

Through the haze, the voice sounded muffled and indistinct, like someone talking with a mouth full of cotton. It belonged to the woman. He couldn't remember her name either. Why had she attacked him with such viciousness? New pain assailed him as he probed his memory. Scattered images. Envelopes and notes. What did it all mean?

He tried to speak, but only gibberish came out.

"Hold your questions. You'll get the answers soon enough. Besides, I don't feel like listening to you. Come on. We've got to get a move on."

She took her reins and slapped Sam's horse hard across the rump. The horse broke into a rapid trot that had him swaying back and forth out of control. He grasped the saddle horn and tightened his knees against the horse's sides. Her laugh penetrated the thick gauze that encased his brain.

26

Michael walked to the stage depot, enjoying the bustle of the town around him. He liked having moments of solitude to pray, but he knew he needed people. Too much time alone reminded him of the isolation of the farm where he grew up, the loneliness. He shuddered. The violence. Being around people kept those thoughts away. He could get lost in the sights and sounds. The blacksmith's hammer provided rhythm for the music of town life, in which wagons creaked, harnesses jangled, dogs barked, horses neighed. Bits of conversation drifted by like the hum of violins he'd once heard in Cincinnati while he wove through a concert crowd picking pockets.

Several townspeople had gathered at the depot. The stationmaster, a man named Little, whom Michael had met at church, stood on the boardwalk. Sweat glistened on Little's florid features. He paced up and down, removed his visor, and ran his fingers through his sparse salt-and-pepper hair. He checked the time on his pocket watch and looked up the street. He held the watch to his ear. Then he rubbed his hand over his face and wiped it on his trousers.

Another man stood apart from the others, tall and slender with black hair and blue eyes, face and hands tanned to dark brown. He looked to be in his midthirties, dressed in clean pants, a checked shirt, and well-cared-for boots. His hat sat back on his head as he leaned against a post, arms folded, one foot braced against the post.

Little turned to him. "I'm sorry, Mr. Carstairs. I don't know what's happened. The stage has never been this late."

The tall man looked down at him. A grin creased his lips. "Calm down, Little. The stage is only about an hour late. It'll be here."

The stationmaster seemed even more flustered. "I just don't like it when I know your father's on it. It makes it seem like we don't give good service."

Carstairs placed his hand on the man's shoulder. "Take it easy. My father knows some things can't be helped. Seeing as he's on the stage, he's got a much better idea of what's causing the delay than we do." He patted the man's shoulder and his grin turned sardonic. "If there's anything that needs to be changed, he'll let you know."

Little turned to look up the street again and checked his watch once more.

Michael approached the other man. "Excuse me. Is your name Joshua Carstairs?"

The tall man studied him, his mouth a thin line, eyes shrouded, brow furrowed like he'd just seen something crawl out from under the bed. Something that wasn't supposed to be there.

"Yeah. Who wants to know?" The words were clipped, the voice hard.

"My name's Michael Archer, and I came here to meet your father. I knew your brother Benjamin." Michael extended his hand.

Carstairs gave it a brief shake. "Well, knowing Benjy's not worth much. My father might just as soon slap you as talk to you. Did Benjy send you to ask for money? 'Cause there ain't any more comin' to him."

"That's something I need to discuss with your father first."

"Well, good luck to you." He turned and walked toward the saloon next to the depot. "Little, I'm going to get a beer. Fetch me when the stage gets here."

"Yes, sir, Mr. Carstairs."

Michael sighed. *Well, that went well. It's not often I offend someone just by introducing myself.* He leaned against the post and gazed toward the saloon. *Lord, show me what to do. Give me the words.*

Late lunch settling pleasantly in his stomach, Caleb Davis sauntered out of the hotel restaurant and over to the stage depot, drawn by the crowd gathered there. Josh Carstairs sat in one of the chairs outside the depot, balancing it against the building on its back legs. Michael Archer leaned against a porch post, eyes drooping in the afternoon sun. *Yeah, a nap would feel good about now.*

Caleb's attention was drawn to Lionel Little, who fretted about like a father at the delivery of his first child. Caleb checked his pocket watch. A late stage usually caused Lionel to hop about like a three-legged rabbit.

"Afternoon, Joshua," Caleb said.

The man nodded. "Sheriff."

"Hello, Mr. Archer. Hope you're enjoying your stay in Riverbend."

"Good afternoon, Sheriff. So far it's been very enjoyable."

"I'm sure it has, even with your adventure Saturday night. With Sam Carstairs coming in today, it should get a lot more interesting."

"Yes, sir. I believe it will."

Caleb turned to the stationmaster. "Settle down, Lionel. You act like you got a scorpion in your britches."

Little checked his watch. "The stage is almost three hours late, Sheriff. I was just about to come find you and ask if you could send someone out to look for it. It might have broken down again. Hope it didn't get robbed."

Caleb rubbed his chin. "It'll take me a while to put a crew together, but we can send a few men out if it's not here in the next half hour. I'll get O'Brien started now pulling some men together."

"Thank—"

The sound of galloping horses and urgent cries reached their ears. Minutes later the stage appeared, careening down the street, horses at a full gallop. *Fool's gonna kill somebody riding into town like that.*

Caleb stepped into the street, Little beside him. The driver pulled back on the reins and pressed the brake until he lay almost flat on the roof of the stage, bringing the vehicle to a halt in front of the depot. A cloud of dust swirled behind. The lathered horses trembled on unsteady legs, tossing their heads and snorting.

Before Caleb could berate the driver for such reckless handling of the team in town, the driver blurted, "Sheriff, there's big trouble! Mr. Carstairs is missing!"

Little fainted.

27

THE CHAIR MADE A LOUD, sharp bang on the boardwalk as Joshua Carstairs rose to his feet. He strode past Michael over to where the sheriff stood. "What are you talking about?" he asked the driver.

Sheriff Davis placed a hand on Joshua's chest as if soothing a troubled horse. "Take it easy, Joshua. Give him a chance to get his breath and gather his thoughts." He shielded his eyes and looked up at the driver. "Take a deep breath and tell us what happened."

Little sat up and wiped his ashen face with a handkerchief. Michael helped him to his feet. "You okay, Mr. Little?"

The stationmaster nodded and fanned himself with his visor. Michael soaked his handkerchief in a nearby watering trough, wrung it out, and placed it on Little's neck.

"Go ahead," the sheriff prompted.

"Well," the driver began, "we stopped at Hawkins Station last night like we always do. Everything seemed fine. But when we got up this morning, Mr. Carstairs and the other two passengers was missin'. Weren't no sign of 'em. Just Mr. Carstairs's luggage."

"What about the other passengers' luggage?"

"Their bags was there, but they was empty."

"Any sign of a struggle?"

"No, sir."

"Did you or anybody else hear anything during the night?"

"No, sir."

The guard spoke up. "Nate Johansen and I thought we heard a loud thump or crash during the night. We looked around but couldn't find nothin'. We reckoned one of the horses musta kicked against a stall or somethin'."

"What are you going to do about this, Sheriff?" Joshua said, the words clipped, icy cold.

Davis rubbed his chin and the back of his neck. "We're gonna look for him and bring him back. We have to consider he might've been kidnapped, maybe the other two passengers as well. It's not like your father to ride off this close to home. I'll have O'Brien put out the call for a posse while I talk to these two—" he nodded at the driver and guard—"a little longer. I want to know more about these other passengers. Joshua, I want you to stay at the ranch and let us handle this. If it *is* a kidnapping, they may try to contact you, so you need to be there. But I can use any men you can spare."

"I'll send some hands to join you. We've got a big roundup goin' on, so there's only a few at the main ranch. I'll have the men meet you on the road to Hawkins Station."

"Any idea where Mark is?" the sheriff asked.

"Last I knew he was still passed out drunk at Becky's shack. He'll be useless until he sobers up. I'll have somebody send him to the ranch as soon as he can ride."

"Yeah, you'd better keep him with you in case whoever did this is out to get the two of you. Have a couple of men keep watch on you and Mark. Avery and Lucas would be good. They ain't never afraid of a fight, they keep their heads, and they're good with their guns."

"Good idea." Joshua climbed into the buggy he had brought to town, slapped the reins to put the horses into a trot, and rode off down the street.

Pete O'Brien approached as he left. "What's all the fuss?"

Sheriff Davis filled him in and told him to ring the church bell to let people know there was an emergency.

"Make sure the men know they may be away for several days. If he was kidnapped, whoever took him has a good head start, and we have no idea which direction they went. Make sure the men know what they're gettin' into. This might turn real nasty 'fore all's said an' done. Wives and sweethearts won't like the sound of what we're riding into."

"I don't like the sound of it meself," O'Brien said.

Michael stepped toward the two men. "I'd like to join you."

The sheriff and deputy looked at him and then each other.

"Ye've got no stake in this, lad," O'Brien said. "There's no need for ye to risk yerself for a stranger."

Michael touched his chest. "I've come this far. I owe it to Ben Carstairs to do everything I can to find his father and deliver his message."

Pete eyed him up and down. "Like the sheriff said, this could get nasty. Are ye up to it?"

"I can help with the horses and cooking and such. And I've got a spare horse we can use for hauling supplies."

"But can you shoot? Might come to that."

Michael hesitated an instant, looking at Sheriff Davis. "I can shoot if I have to."

The sheriff nodded. "Let him join, Pete. I think he's got more of a stake in this than we'll ever know."

O'Brien shrugged. "All right. Glad to have ye. Get your gear, have supplies loaded on your horse at the general store. Tell McGuffy the sheriff sent ye. Be at the sheriff's office in an hour."

Caleb motioned for the driver and guard to follow him into the saloon.

"I need to take care of the horses," the driver said. "You kin tell I pushed 'em real hard."

Caleb turned to the stationmaster. "Little, get one of your men to see to the horses. And make sure they're taken care of proper. They worked hard for a good reason."

In the saloon, Caleb ordered beers for the driver and guard and a coffee for himself. He motioned the two men to sit at a table in the center of the long room. Townspeople crowded around.

The church bell tolled in the distance. Caleb put his hat

on the table and ran his fingers through his hair. Sunlight filtered through dusty windows. The aromas of stale beer, spilled whiskey, and cigar smoke swirled about their heads like a malodorous wraith. Caleb breathed through his mouth.

"Tell me what happened," he said.

The driver drank half his beer in one gulp and wiped his mouth with the back of his hand. The guard sipped his beer. He seemed content to let the driver do the talking.

"Pauley and me"—he motioned toward the guard next to him—"got up this morning with Nate to hitch the horses while Nate's wife was a-fixin' breakfast. When we went inside to eat, weren't nobody there but Maggie. She said she called the passengers, but no one answered. Pauley and me went to get them and we found the rooms empty. All of Sam's luggage was there. The other couple's—"

"Wait a minute," Caleb said. "Tell me about this other couple."

"It was a man and a woman. She was real pretty, Mexican or half-breed. I think they was newlyweds."

"What were their names?"

The driver shrugged. "Hers was Maria, I think. I don't remember his."

"It was Jack," the guard said. "Jack Alden."

Caleb ran the names through his encyclopedic memory of outlaws. Alden didn't register. "Okay, go ahead."

"Well," the driver said, "there ain't much more. Their room was empty. Their luggage was there but it was empty too. The clothes they wore on the stage were on the bed. We looked all over the corral and barn. Pauley here rode a circle around about a mile out and couldn't find no sign of 'em."

"No tracks?"

The guard shrugged and sipped his beer. "Too many. Couldn't tell 'em apart. You know how trampled things get around a way station. Nate rode with me. Thought he saw a few that didn't look familiar, but he couldn't tell for sure."

"Anything else you can tell me about this couple?"

The driver took another mouthful of beer. He looked at the bartender, who looked at Caleb. Caleb shook his head. The driver frowned and licked his lips. "Not much. They got on with Sam at Culverton. Seemed nice enough."

"Anything go on between them and Sam? harsh words? argument?"

The driver drained his mug and studied the empty glass. "Not that I know of. I don't remember them talking to each other much at the station. Don't know what they said to each other in the stage."

The guard spoke up. "I noticed when we was eatin' supper, she looked at Sam as if she hated him. Just glared at him, real meanlike."

Caleb sipped his coffee. "Any idea why?"

"No, sir."

"Me neither," the driver said.

"What about the husband? How did he seem toward Sam?"

The driver shrugged and slid his glass from one hand to the other. "Didn't notice nothin' in particular."

"Me neither," the guard said.

"Okay. You boys go finish up your business with Mr. Little."

The guard swallowed what was left of his beer, and the two walked out of the saloon. Caleb sighed, closed his eyes, and pinched the bridge of his nose.

"What are you going to do about this, Sheriff?"

The high-pitched, whiny voice irritated like a mosquito in the night. He wanted to keep his eyes closed and wished he could close his ears too. He peered into his cup as if it would tell him the future. Then he drank the remainder of the bitter brew and focused on the man across the table. He'd rather see the bottom of a cuspidor than Mayor Malcolm Meriweather.

Caleb shook his head. Meriweather was as wide as he was tall, with chins that overflowed his collar. The mercantile business had made the man wealthy, and Sam Carstairs's considerable influence had kept him in office. Caleb knew the pompous old fool would stay in office as long as he did what Sam wanted. In Caleb's mind, the man never missed an opportunity to strut like a peacock and flaunt his position.

"Well, I plan to go to my office and see how many men answered the bell, explain what I know so far, and see who can commit several weeks to help find Sam."

"Weeks!" the mayor huffed. "Why weeks?"

Caleb felt his patience reach its limit. He restrained himself from pulling Meriweather over the table and slapping him. "Because we have no idea where they went. I think this couple may have kidnapped Sam. They may try to contact the family for money, or they may just kill him. Either way,

I've got to go after 'em, and they've got a big head start, so it may take a while."

"What about the town while you're gone? Who's going to be in charge?"

"Pete O'Brien will handle things here. Deputy Rollins will be back tomorrow to help him. I'd have a couple more deputies, but you and the town council said no. Now, if you'll excuse me, I've got a posse to organize."

He put his hat on, stood, and walked to the batwing doors. He stopped and turned back to the mayor. "We're going to need supplies: food, ammunition, packhorses. I'm going to tell McGuffy to bill it to the town. You'll find the money in the budget, won't you? This is Sam Carstairs we're searchin' for."

Caleb didn't wait for an answer.

28

SAM'S HANDS GRIPPED the saddle horn, his knuckles white. The sun glared in the cloudless expanse of sky that faded to white at the horizon. The horses had ceased their brisk pace and settled into a plodding walk. Sam swayed in the saddle, and his head jerked as if it sat on a malformed spring.

"We better rest pretty soon," Jack said to Maria. "The horses are wore out, and I don't think this old man's gonna hold out much longer if we don't get some water in him."

"Who cares about him?"

"Your father does. He's gonna want him alive so he can sign those papers."

She sighed. "You're right. Let's head for those trees to our left. There should be water there."

Jack spurred his gelding into a trot, pulling on the lead

rope attached to Sam's horse. After a short distance, the horses once again slowed to a walk, too fatigued to maintain a faster pace.

"Let the horse set the pace," Maria said. "He'll pick it up when he smells the water."

Within a few hundred yards, Jack's horse sniffed and raised his head, nostrils flaring. He walked faster but wouldn't break into a full trot. The other horses followed his lead.

Trees lined both sides of a narrow brook. The sluggish water ran over rocks, and tree branches littered its bed.

Sam watched Jack help Maria dismount. For a moment they froze, Jack's hands on her slim waist, her hands on his shoulders, their eyes locked. Maria slid from her saddle and leaned into Jack, their bodies in full contact as he lowered her to the ground. Sam remembered Ruth and their rides around the ranch. They would find a secluded spot, and Ruth would dismount and slide into his arms just as Maria had slid into Jack's. They would spend several hours lying together.

Maria walked over to Sam, untied the rope around his wrists, and pushed him off the saddle. He landed with a loud thump on the soft ground. More pain. He stifled a moan.

Jack loosened the girths and led the horses to the water, where they drank with loud slurps. He filled the canteens upstream. Maria lay on her stomach on the bank of the brook and drank.

Sam croaked through parched lips, "I need . . . to drink."

Maria sat up and sniffed. "So help yourself. Nobody's stopping you."

Sam rolled onto his stomach, but after several attempts

to rise up on his elbows and push with his feet, he collapsed and coughed on a mouthful of dirt.

"You don't have to be so mean to him." Jack walked over to Sam and helped him drink from a canteen.

Maria stood and wiped the dust from her man's shirt and trousers. Her shiny ebony hair cascaded to her shoulders, framing her face with its waves. Her green eyes flashed as she glared at Sam.

"You don't know what my father suffered because of this man. He broke Papa's spirit and sent him to prison for a crime he didn't commit just so he could get him out of the way for that woman they both wanted to marry."

Sam stirred and tried to shout for help but only managed a hoarse grunt.

"Aaahh." Maria waved her hand in his direction. "He's useless. Not even worth pitying. I'll be glad to get rid of him when Papa's done with him."

She went over to the horses and removed some biscuits, cold bacon, and dried fruit from the saddlebags. She gave some to Jack.

"What about the old man?"

"You feed him. I don't even want to go near him. He makes me sick."

Jack helped Sam into a sitting position against a fallen tree and placed some of the food at his feet. Sam shoveled the food into his mouth. His stomach gnawed. His head throbbed, pounding like a hammer beating hot metal into his brain. He retched, and everything he'd eaten came back up. He turned his head just in time to avoid getting it on his clothes.

"Useless. Just like I told you. I'm going to go clean up. There's a nice, deep spot upstream."

She walked about fifty feet and stood at the edge of the stream. When he saw her remove her clothes, he looked at Jack, who seemed to think it a normal, everyday occurrence for his wife to strip naked before strangers.

Sam managed to lift the canteen to his lips. The water soothed his parched mouth and relieved the burning irritation in his throat.

"Has she no shame?" He couldn't raise his voice above a hoarse whisper.

Jack shrugged. "It's her way of saying she don't care about you. You don't even exist to her."

Sam averted his eyes when she climbed out of the water. Jack stood between the two of them while she dressed. When she finished, Jack tended to the horses, tightened the girths, and topped off the canteens. When all was ready, Jack helped Sam onto his horse while Maria stood gazing off in the distance.

"Where are we going?" Sam asked.

"You'll find out when we get there," Maria snapped.

29

THE AFTERNOON SUN beat down, but a soft breeze drifted through the town, just enough to ruffle hair and cool the skin. As he walked back to his office, Caleb already missed the caressing evening breezes and fishing for his supper. The crowd cleared a path so he could walk up the steps to the boardwalk that fronted his office.

Pete O'Brien waited for him. "Ye got here fast, Sheriff. I ain't said anything to 'em yet. People are still gatherin'."

Caleb glanced at his chair, wondering how long it would be until he could once again sit and watch the town go by. He turned to face the group of about thirty men and women gathered before him. More people joined them. A multitude of conversations jabbered.

Caleb took off his hat, scratched his head, and ran his

fingers through his hair. Pete stood next to him, thumbs hooked in his belt. Caleb expected Pete was surveying the crowd, deciding whom he would select for the posse if it were his responsibility.

Caleb held up his hands. When the crowd quieted, he spoke, slowing his cadence and raising his voice so all could hear. "Something has happened to Mr. Sam Carstairs. He was on the stage, and according to the driver, he was missin' when they woke up at Hawkins Station this morning. I don't think he would take off of his own free will this close to home, so I gotta suspect foul play. Now, we all know what Mr. Carstairs means to this town, and I'm sure all of y'all want to help. I'm planning on riding up to Hawkins Station and start looking for him. It may well be dangerous. I'll need about ten to twelve men to ride with me. I don't know how long this is going to take, but I figure a couple of weeks or more. I'd expect those of you that can't ride with us to help out those who can by taking care of their families and their chores and suchlike."

The crowd murmured its agreement. One of the women spoke up. "You can count on that, Sheriff. You know we take care of our own. People in town will adopt the families of the men who go so they won't have to fret none while they're gone."

Charlie Atkins, the carpenter, added, "We'll take care of 'em, Sheriff. Sam's important to this town. You do everything you can to find him and bring him back."

Intense conversations bubbled up to Caleb as husbands and wives discussed the situation. He waited, knowing from experience the wives needed to agree for their husbands to join the posse. Otherwise, the men would be distracted by what they'd left behind. Wives would worry anyway, but a heated parting would put a burden on the posse that he didn't need. A few worried men would put the whole group at risk.

Two men rode up to the back of the crowd. Bill Barkston straddled a horse that seemed too small for him. To Caleb's eye, every horse seemed small under Bill. Next to Bill rode Vernon Phelps, a rail-thin man that Caleb knew to be stronger, pound for pound, than any other rancher in the area. He sat his rangy buckskin mare with the ease and grace of a man who spent more time in a saddle than on the ground.

Bill spat a stream of tobacco juice. "Howdy, Caleb. Havin' a party?" He crossed his hands on his saddle horn.

Caleb told him what he knew. Bill looked at Vernon, who kept his eyes on Caleb. A quiet man, he seemed to ponder each word before he spoke. His soft voice carried over the heads of the people. "We can't have that. Count me in. My nephew, Alexander, will join us."

"You sure the missus is gonna be okay with that?" Caleb said. "She's raised that boy since he was a pup."

Vernon nodded. "I know. But she knows he's ready to step out as a man. She'll fuss, but she'll let him come."

Caleb eyed the two men. Vernon was the first friend he'd made when he came to Riverbend. Over the years, the man had volunteered for every posse and proved himself capable of leading men in tough situations. The only man he trusted more than Vernon was Pete O'Brien.

Like Vernon and himself, Bill Barkston was a war veteran. Unlike the two of them, Bill was an experienced officer and a Yankee. He'd ended the war as a colonel under Sherman.

A Yankee, but a good man. Barkston's large ranch north of town rivaled the Carstairs place as an example of efficiency, organization, and profitability. Another leader with wise counsel in any situation would be welcome on the posse. Caleb grinned at Bill. His greatest strength was that he was the best trail cook in town.

Then Caleb remembered that Jeffrey Barkston had broken his leg on Tuesday. "Bill, is the ranch gonna be all right if you leave it right now?"

Bill resettled himself on his horse. "Jeffrey can run it from the front porch just fine."

Caleb addressed the crowd again. "Any more volunteers?"

About half the men in the crowd raised their hands. Caleb pointed at several of them, calling their names as he made his selections. "You men be back here in half an hour with your horses and weapons. The town will supply food and ammunition."

He pointed at five other men. "I'm deputizing you men to help O'Brien and Rollins keep things under control here. O'Brien will give you your assignments after we leave."

He pointed to one of the men in the crowd. "George, run up to the Ace of Clubs and tell Malachi I need him. Tell him to bring Old Thomas too."

Caleb turned to Pete as George took off down the street. "Who would you have picked?"

Pete scratched his chin. "Well, sir, I think the only mistake ye made was leaving me off the list." His eyes crinkled as a grin spread across his face. "I think ye picked the best. Why're ye askin' me?"

"Just makin' sure you're learnin'. This job will be yours someday. Maybe sooner than we think."

As the crowd dispersed, Michael led Buddy and his now-loaded packhorse to the sheriff's office and tied them to the hitching post.

He stepped onto the boardwalk. "Mr. McGuffy was very generous, Sheriff. He wrote everything down and said he'd send the bill to the mayor's office. He also said he'd load up more packhorses if you needed them."

The sheriff turned to his deputy. "Pete, will you take care of that? Get three or four good horses from Johnson at the livery and have him saddle Caesar for me."

"Sure thing." Pete broke into a trot as he headed for the stables, passing two characters who approached from the direction of the bar. Michael recognized Malachi, the old man who had been cleaning the sheriff's office on Saturday. Beside him walked a short, powerfully built man of indeterminate age.

Michael studied the stranger. He could be fifty. He could be eighty. His iron-gray hair was tied in a braid that reached his waist, secured with a leather thong. A wide band of red cloth encircled his head just above his eyes, which gleamed black in a round brown face with distinctive cheekbones. Wrinkles etched his cheeks like deep gullies. He wore dungarees, a loose-fitting buckskin shirt, moccasins, and leggings that ran halfway up his calves.

"You wanted to see us, Sheriff?" Malachi said as the two men stepped onto the boardwalk. "I ain't even had time to get drunk yet."

"I ain't arrestin' you, Malachi. I need you and Old Thomas. You two are the best trackers I know, and we've got to find somebody who's got a big head start."

"Who we hafta find? Somebody rob the bank?"

"No. Mr. Carstairs has gone missing up at Hawkins Station. I'm askin' you to be in the posse."

Malachi exchanged glances with Old Thomas, who nodded once. "All right, we're in. I'll go get our horses."

Old Thomas sat in Sheriff Davis's chair as Malachi turned to leave. He hadn't gone but a few steps when the sheriff called after him.

"Malachi, this is going to be a dry trip—just coffee and water. There's no need for you to bring your own personal supply."

Malachi looked past the sheriff to Old Thomas, who turned his palms upward and shrugged. "Have it yer own way," Malachi said, "but a drop or two has always been good for my eyesight and Old Thomas's hearin'."

"Yeah," the sheriff answered, "you see three of everything going in five directions, and Old Thomas hears his ancestors tell him to kill us white devils in our sleep. Just get going."

"That only happened once," Old Thomas said as Malachi left. His voice was deep and resonant. He gestured in Michael's direction. "Who is this?"

The sheriff introduced Michael to Old Thomas. They shook hands, and the old man peered into Michael's face for a long moment. Then he turned away and spoke to the sheriff. "This is a good man, Sheriff Caleb. The Great Spirit of your people favors him. You can trust him."

Embarrassment crept up Michael's neck. The sheriff studied Michael. "You ain't gonna get a much better compliment than that. Old Thomas reads people as good as he reads signs."

Michael swallowed. "Sheriff, do I have a few minutes to say good-bye to someone?"

"Yeah, but don't take too long. I wanna get on the road as soon as everyone's here. We need to make Hawkins Station before dark."

Rachel pulled another bolt of fabric from its slot on the wall and held it out for her customer to feel.

"Ooh, this is nice and soft, just right for my new Sunday dress. Cut me enough for the dress and a bonnet."

"Yes, ma'am." Rachel rested the cloth on the counter and measured out the desired amount. Two other women sat at the little table, half-empty teacups before them. The conversation was more about Mr. Carstairs than dresses.

The bell on the door jangled and all conversation stopped as Michael walked in. He was dressed for the trail: dungarees, plain blue shirt, and riding boots. His mouth and chin looked determined, his eyes calm. An aura of resolute strength emanated from him.

"Rach—" His voice cracked. He removed his hat and took a step forward. "Rachel, you heard about Mr. Carstairs?"

"Yes," she said. "I did."

"I feel like I'm supposed to go with the posse to look for him."

Her voice was a soft whisper. "As soon as I heard about it, I knew you were going to go." *And I don't want you to.*

The idea dropped into her mind without warning, leaving her openmouthed with surprise. If it had been Luke or Mr. Phelps or Mr. Barkston, she could understand. But this man had been a stranger five days ago, and she had already decided he was not for her. Why did she even care if he joined the posse?

But she did care. She cared deeply, and denying it did no good at all. Without realizing it, she had dropped her guard and let him into her heart—closer, she now realized, than any other man, even Pastor Luke. And she couldn't bear the thought of his riding on a dangerous mission. She was afraid for him and, she discovered in this moment, afraid he wouldn't come back.

Confusion reigned. Part of her wanted to open her arms to him. The other part said, *Don't let him any closer. He'll only break your heart.*

But maybe it was too late.

Rachel walked over to him, holding one hand in the other with a knuckle-squeezing grip to keep from reaching to touch his arm, his hand, his face. She glanced over her shoulder. The customers were watching, some with sympathy, some to see just how brazen she might get with a man in front of them. *You'll get no satisfaction today.*

"Please excuse me for a moment, ladies. I'll be right back." She motioned for Michael to follow her out to the boardwalk.

She knew the ladies could see them, but at least they wouldn't be able to hear the conversation.

She kept her hands together. "Michael, I . . ."

She stopped, her tongue stuck. She stared at a place on his sleeve, unable to look him in the eye. She swallowed. "I . . . I . . . want you to be careful. And come back . . . so we can get to know each other better." She bit her lower lip. Weak as it was, it was the strongest commitment she'd ever made to a man.

Now she met his eyes and put her hand on his arm. "Travel safe. And . . ."

She couldn't finish. She didn't know what to say. She just gazed at him as he covered her hand gently with his.

"Wait for me," he said.

She watched him walk away. *Lord, what have I done?*

30

MICHAEL JOINED a small group of men gathered outside the sheriff's office. While they talked, Malachi rode up on a gray mare, leading a small paint. Old Thomas rose with a youthful grace from his chair and, grabbing the saddle horn, swung up onto the paint's back without using the stirrup.

Pete O'Brien walked up the street leading four well-laden packhorses and a magnificent palomino. The horse tossed his head and skittered in little side steps as if insulted to be walking with mere packhorses. Pete handed the reins to Sheriff Davis, who stroked the animal's neck. The palomino butted his head into the man's chest. The sheriff produced a sugar cube from his pocket and let the horse take it from his hand.

One by one, the rest of the posse arrived, many with

families to see them off. Michael and Sheriff Davis swung into their saddles. A couple of the riders took charge of the packhorses. The send-off from the townspeople was somber, with hugs and tears exchanged before the men mounted.

The sheriff turned to Pete. "You know what to do. Keep your eye on Joshua and Mark Carstairs if you can. Somebody may be contacting them, and I don't want them going off half-cocked on a rescue mission. Let Pastor Luke help with any negotiations."

"Sure thing, Sheriff. You keep your eyes open too. Don't need to have you riding into any traps."

Sheriff Davis led the posse out of town at an easy trot. When they passed Rachel's store, Michael saw her standing in the doorway. Her face seemed clouded with worry. He waved and smiled. She returned the gestures, but her smile looked weak and tentative. He couldn't suppress a glow of satisfaction at seeing her. He didn't want her unhappy, but it was gratifying to know she cared.

The posse rode north, the river on their right placid except for small riffles where rocks protruded above its surface. Open land stretched toward the ridges that surrounded the valley, lines of trees marking where small creeks wound their way to the river. The sun was warm, the sky a deep, clear blue. Small, high clouds cast galloping shadows when they crossed in front of the sun. *This is a good place to call home.*

A piece of the ridge pointed like a disjointed finger from the main ridge and extended almost to the river. Where they met, the river took a sharp bend to the northeast. The road made a tight curve around the outcrop, forcing the riders to slow their pace almost to a walk. After they rounded it, the land opened up again, stretching far to the west.

"That's the beginning of the Carstairs place," Vernon Phelps said, catching up to Michael. "It runs right along the river for about ten miles and then all the way back to the ridge."

"Mighty big place."

Phelps nodded, his lanky body swaying easily in the saddle. Sandy brown hair framed his weathered, squarish face and blue eyes. A bushy mustache hid his upper lip until he smiled.

Sheriff Davis signaled for a halt as five men rode toward them, Joshua Carstairs in the lead. The men slowed and walked their mounts toward the posse. The sheriff rested his hands on the saddle horn. "Hello, Josh. What're you up to?"

"Me and my men are gonna ride with you to find my father. I can't stand sittin' at the ranch like an old lady. It don't feel right." Joshua's voice was level and firm, his eyes fixed on the sheriff as if challenging him.

Davis scratched his jaw. "We talked about this in town. I ain't sure that's a good idea, Josh. You'll be puttin' yourself in danger, and who'll be here if kidnappers try to contact you?"

"Mark can handle it."

The sheriff raised an eyebrow and pushed his hat back on his head. "That ain't your head talkin'. Mark can't even handle himself. When's the last time he was sober for more'n three days straight? That boy's been looking for trouble ever since he could crawl. If your father really has been kidnapped and they contacted the ranch, Mark'd only make things worse. Josh, I'll take as many of your men as you can spare, but I really think you need to stay."

Joshua dismounted and walked toward the river. The sheriff did the same. Michael and the others watched the two men talk out of earshot. Davis put his hand on Joshua's shoulder. Joshua stood with his arms folded. After several minutes, the two men shook hands and walked back to the riders.

Joshua pointed at three of the men who had come with him. "Shorty, Frank, and Martin, join the posse. Do whatever Sheriff Davis tells you and bring my father back alive."

He turned to the fourth man, who sported a thick beard and looked to be somewhere in his midthirties, an inch or two over six feet tall, with the lean, muscular build of a longtime cowboy.

"Avery, your job is to be Mark's shadow. He doesn't go to the privy without you being with him."

Avery spat a stream of tobacco juice onto the ground. "I'll give it my best shot, boss. But keepin' track of that boy is like trying to lasso a tornado."

Joshua turned to Sheriff Davis. "I'm gonna set up in my father's office in town, and Lupe and I'll stay at the hotel till this is over. I'll let Pete know where I'm gonna be and if I hear anything." The two men shook hands, and the sheriff waved the posse forward, setting a fast pace.

31

SAM'S HEAD THROBBED, an incessant pounding that beat in his temples like an Indian drum. An unexpected jolt in the horse's step sent a sharp bolt of agony from his brain down his spine. Blinding light flashed. Nausea churned his stomach. A moan escaped his lips despite his efforts to bite it back.

"Weak old man." The woman's scorn tainted each word. With a slap of her reins on his horse's hindquarters, she sent the animal into a brief, agonizing trot. Sam gripped the saddle horn like a rope that kept him from falling off a cliff.

Late in the afternoon, they stopped at a narrow creek. A grove of trees provided some shade from the relentless sun. Jack helped Sam down, set him against a tree, and handed him a canteen. Sam swallowed the lukewarm liquid in large gulps while Maria and Jack unsaddled the horses and let them drink their fill. Jack gave them some oats and let them graze in the grass along the bank. *They sure don't seem to be in much of a hurry to get wherever it is we're going. Wonder why.*

"Where are we heading?" Sam asked again after he found his voice.

Maria shushed Jack before he could answer. She stood over Sam and stared down at him. If he had met her under different circumstances, he would have thought her quite beautiful with her long black hair, emerald eyes, and slender yet well-rounded body. But hate hardened her features and marred her beauty.

She took the canteen from him and secured the stopper with a firm push. She dangled it from her hand by the strap. Then she swung the canteen with a swift, quick movement of her arm. It hit him on the side of the head where the gun had struck him. Pain shot through his eyes.

He slumped over, waiting for unconsciousness to come, but it didn't. He lay in the dirt, vision unfocused, the smell of damp earth filling his nostrils. A spider skittered across his nose.

She dropped the canteen and walked to the fire. Jack shook his head.

"What's eatin' you?" Her voice was harsh and brittle like out-of-tune brass.

Jack added more wood to the fire. "I don't know how I'm going to stop you from killing him before we get back to your father."

"Don't worry about that. I'm not gonna kill him. I just want him to feel some of the pain he's caused Papa."

She sat next to Jack and watched him fry bacon in a pan. A small pot at the edge of the fire boiled, and the aroma of coffee wafted.

She stretched her arms overhead and arched her back. She rubbed the base of her spine and bent to one side, then the other, stretching her torso. Her lithe movements mesmerized Sam.

She smiled and leaned forward to give Jack a kiss. "Later, you can give me one of your wonderful back rubs. I'm going to need it after all these hours riding."

He took her in his arms and kissed her long and hard. They fell to the ground together and kissed some more until the lid on the coffeepot rattled.

Jack prepared two plates of bacon, biscuits, and dried fruit. He pointed with his chin toward Sam. "I'm going to fix him a plate of something to eat."

Maria shrugged and flicked her hair over her shoulder. "Go ahead. I'm going to sit by the water. I'd rather watch a pig at a trough than see him eat."

Jack helped Sam to a sitting position and placed a plate in his lap and a cup of coffee on the ground next to him.

As Sam ate, he watched Maria as she sat on the creek bank, chin resting on her drawn-up knees, hands holding her ankles. She placed her hat on the bank next to her. Thick hair flowed over her shoulders and down her back, hiding her face from view. She looked fragile, more like a little girl than a violent, hate-obsessed woman.

Jack walked over and sat next to her. She snuggled into the arm he put around her shoulders and rested against him.

The warm air and his full stomach lulled Sam into a doze. Something touched his foot, and he started. His head jerked up and banged into the tree behind him, the bark rough against his bald scalp.

Jack stood over him. "Get up, old man. Time to get back on the trail."

"Where are we going?" Sam leveraged himself on Jack's outstretched arm until he stood. His knees buckled, and he leaned against the younger man for support.

"You'll see soon enough. Until then, do like Maria says. Be quiet and enjoy the ride."

I slept sounder than I thought. He saw the horses saddled, the fire scattered and mixed with the surrounding earth. Maria sat on her horse and watched Jack help Sam mount his. After Jack secured Sam's hands to the saddle horn, Maria leaned over and gave the knot a hard tug. The rope dug into Sam's wrists.

They rode in the creek, Maria in the lead, the splash of the horses' hooves the only sound. The sun on his right cheek told Sam they were headed south. He did not recognize this country. From the creek to the mountains on the horizon, the land was barren—no trees, no familiar rock formations, no abandoned buildings. Home seemed so far away, he might as well have been in China.

They followed the creek bed for several miles. When the stream made a turn to the east, they left the water and continued southwest. Maria sought out hard-packed places and stony areas, and she never seemed to ride in a straight line.

They meandered for hours. Sam's skull pounded as if

a blacksmith were using it for an anvil. His wrists burned. Blood stained the ropes.

The sun sank below the horizon, and still they rode. Sleep scratched at Sam's eyes. They rode single file, Maria in front of him and Jack behind. An occasional snort from the horses and the jangle of bits and bridles broke the silence.

The stars gave enough light for Sam to make out the shapes of rocks and boulders. The horses' hooves told him they were once again on stony ground. Maria stopped without warning. And Sam almost rode into her. She scanned the area, nodded, and settled back into her saddle.

Soon they entered another creek, and Maria led them down it for several miles. The current of this stream flowed swifter than the previous one, and the bottom was rockier. Sam's horse stumbled twice but righted itself. Pain lanced from his head to his knees as he struggled to stay in the saddle. Splashing water from behind told him Jack's horse had the same difficulty. That fact gave him small comfort.

A grove of trees curved around a small pool that had formed where the creek had eaten into the bank. Maria led the way onto dry ground. She barked at Jack, "Leave him on the horse until we get a fire started. Just tie the horse to a tree so he won't be tempted to get away."

While Jack started the fire, Maria prepared the coffeepot. She wedged a small pot of beans into the fire and set some biscuits baking in another pan. Jack helped Sam down and settled him near the fire.

The three of them ate in silence.

Later that night, Sam struggled to get comfortable on

the hard ground. He couldn't remember the last time he had roughed it like this. It felt like all the stones and half the sticks for miles around were gathered under his blanket. He dozed until the hoot of an owl woke him. As he drifted off again, the sound of rustling clothes disturbed him. He opened his eyes to see Maria lift Jack's blanket and settle down on top of him, murmuring quietly to him, a soft tenderness in her voice.

Sam squeezed his eyes shut and turned his back to the fire, but their sounds penetrated his ears. *So this strange woman is capable of loving someone.*

As he drifted back to sleep, memories of Ruth flashed, her own voice husky in his embrace.

32

THE STARS GLIMMERED like diamonds scattered on velvet in the pale light of the half-moon. Michael pulled back on Buddy's reins as Sheriff Davis slowed the group to a walk and called out. "Hello, the station."

The door to the main building of Hawkins Station opened. Lantern light washed the ground in a small semi-circle. "Who's there?" an older man's gravelly voice called from the shadow behind the lantern.

"Hello, Nate. It's Caleb Davis from Riverbend. I've got a posse with me. We've come lookin' for Sam Carstairs."

The men formed a line with the sheriff in the middle. Nate lifted the lantern high and walked toward them. "Been expectin' y'all. C'mon inside and get somethin' to eat. Maggie's got a pot of stew on. Don't expect you'll be able to start yer search till mornin'. I'll get my Mexican boys to help me with your horses. You men go in and rest."

Old Thomas spoke up. "If I could borrow a lantern, I would like to take a look around tonight. It will help me focus in the morning."

Nate squinted at him. "Speaks right good for an Indian," he said to the sheriff.

"Yep, government educated him at some fancy school back East, so he's a lot smarter than most of us too. Sure would appreciate you sharing your lantern."

"Sure thing, Sheriff. Anything for you. 'Specially if it'll help get Mr. Sam back."

Old Thomas dismounted. As he took the lantern from Nate, he muttered some words in a language Michael didn't recognize.

"What'd he say?" Nate asked.

The sheriff shrugged. "Ain't got any idea. Don't speak Creek."

"He said he sure appreciated all your help, sir," Malachi said, dismounting to join Old Thomas.

Michael caught the smirk on the sheriff's face as he turned to the others. "The rest of you men dismount and leave your horses with Nate here. Get some food and rest. Tomorrow the work really starts."

Michael lagged at the rear of the group, not sure where he fit in. The sheriff treated him with respect. Vernon Phelps was friendly, Bill Barkston barely civil. He sensed the others were withholding judgment until they saw how he handled himself.

Vernon Phelps stopped at the door. "You coming in to get something to eat?"

Whiffs of the stew floated out the door. Venison and vegetables. Michael's stomach rumbled, but he said, "I think I'll stay out here for a few minutes. Enjoy the night air."

Barkston shrugged. "Suit yourself." Vernon and Barkston walked inside.

The door closed, leaving Michael in near darkness. The road they'd come in on shone as a pale strip lighting the way back to Rachel and safety. *Was I right to come?*

Malachi and Old Thomas moved into view, breaking Michael from his reverie. The Indian held the lantern at arm's length in front of him, and he and Malachi bent over and examined the ground. *What can they see in this light?*

About a hundred yards from the station, they turned to the right. Every once in a while, one or the other of them would bend to inspect something on the ground. Sometimes they would look at each other and shake their heads or shrug and continue walking. After making a complete circle around the station, they went out another hundred yards and completed another circle.

The station door creaked. Nate came out and stood next to Michael. "Food's hot, and there's plenty of it. You should go get you some." Nate poked a toothpick into his mouth and sucked his teeth.

"Thank you. I will in a few minutes. Want to let my legs stretch after being in the saddle." Michael kept his voice flat. He couldn't think of how to discourage the old man from talking.

Nate squinted one eye. "You a stranger here? I don't recall seeing you around."

"Got into town Saturday."

Nate spat tobacco juice. "Five days ago? What made you hook up with this bunch?" He jerked his thumb over his shoulder.

Michael hesitated. The need for caution spiked in his mind. The old man was probably just trying to be friendly, but there was no sense in everyone knowing Ben's business. "Seemed like my civic duty."

Caleb Davis came out and leaned against a post that supported the roof overhang. Nate spat on the ground. "Stranger here sure don't talk much."

The sheriff shrugged as he rolled a cigarette. "I expect when he's got somethin' to say, he'll let you know."

Nate made a guttural noise of complaint and went back inside. The sheriff struck a match and cupped the flame in his hands to the end of his cigarette. "Don't pay Nate no mind." The cigarette bobbed in his mouth, and he squinted one eye against the smoke. "He's just a harmless old gossip."

The two stood in companionable silence while Davis smoked. Then the sheriff stood away from the post. "Looks like our wanderin' minstrels are comin' home."

Old Thomas and Malachi walked back toward the station buildings, their heads close together, Malachi's hands and arms gesturing. Sheriff Davis flicked the remains of his cigarette into the night. "Didya find anything?"

Malachi spat and wiped his mouth with his sleeve. "Nary

a clue, Sheriff. Some critter tracks and a stray hoofprint or two. Don't amount to nothin'."

"I think we will find that they rode the coach road for a good ways before branching off from it," Old Thomas added. "That will make it more difficult for us to pick up their trail."

Davis nodded. "I expect so. 'Course, we got no way of knowin' if they went south toward Riverbend or north or took the road goin' east or west."

"I think they went south." Michael inclined his head in the direction they'd ridden from.

The sheriff arched an eyebrow. "What makes you say that?"

"Something I feel in my spirit. I've been praying and asking the Lord for some guidance about which way we should go. I get a strong stirring that they headed toward Riverbend."

The sheriff looked at Old Thomas and Malachi. Malachi shrugged and spat again. Old Thomas eyed his friend with disgust. "I do not know what is worse: when you drink or when you chew tobacco. I am grateful you do not do both at the same time." He turned back to Davis. "Sheriff, we are going to have to pick a direction because they did not leave us anything to start with here. South is as good a direction as any."

The sheriff nodded. "Makes sense in a way. If they're gonna make demands, it'd be best to do it closer to Sam's home. We'll start at sunup and spread out on both sides of the road, try to find where they may have turned off. I'll go in and tell the others."

Old Thomas and Malachi followed him inside.

Michael lingered, gazing up at the star-filled sky. Thoughts of Rachel flooded into his mind. The sparkle in her eyes, her smile that dipped to one side, the warmth and softness of her hand in his. The sweet memory of her last, tender words to him.

He missed her. He'd known her only a few days, yet he longed to be with her. Loneliness pierced him; his heart ached as if someone squeezed it in a fist. He'd last felt this alone the first few nights after he'd run away from home, knowing he would never see Ma or Ellie again.

What would the next days bring? If Sam Carstairs had really been kidnapped, there could be violence ahead.

Images sped through his mind, uncontrollable. His father bleeding, his overalls dark with blood. His fists striking other men, the satisfaction of it, the pain he'd caused bending them to his will.

For three years that monster had been caged. It almost escaped Saturday night. Could he control it now?

He looked down at his hands.

He prayed.

33

MICHAEL'S EYES POPPED OPEN. Where was he? What were those noises?

He sniffed the air. Coffee. Bacon. Biscuits. Hunger rolled in his stomach. His heart slowed as the familiar aromas cleared the fog of sleep from his head.

Hawkins Station. Posse. Sam Carstairs. Rachel.

Soft gray light poked at the shutters on the window. Metal plates clattered in the main dining room. Voices murmured. He picked up his Bible and walked outside. In the east, the sun peered over the rim of the earth, turning the undersides of the few clouds delicate shades of pink and red.

Nate came out, yawning and scratching his stomach. The two men acknowledged each other; then Nate moved off toward the stable and corral. "Pedro, Enrique," he called, "get your sorry selves up. There's work to be done."

Two men walked out of the stable, each leading two

horses. The pair exchanged smiles and shook their heads. One of them spoke in a broken singsong accent. "*Sí*, Señor Nate. We started as soon as we knew you were awake. We wouldn't leave it all for you."

They led the horses over to the corral and tied them to the rails, then went back into the barn and reappeared a short time later with four more horses. Buddy snorted and nickered when he saw Michael.

"Breakfast is ready." Sheriff Davis emerged from the station door. "Better get some before Malachi gets to it. When that man's sober, he can put more food away than anyone I've ever seen."

Michael turned to follow him back into the building. The sound of approaching hoofbeats stopped them. A single rider, shrouded in the dusky gloom, appeared down the road from the east. Next to Michael, Davis exhaled. He adjusted the holster strapped to his waist and rested his hand on the pistol grip. Nate walked over and stood on the other side of the sheriff, squinting up the road.

"Hello, the station," the stranger called.

"'Lo, yerself," Nate answered.

The rider stopped about a hundred feet from the station and dismounted. Holding his hands out from his sides, he drew near. Michael studied the man—lean build, neat mustache, pistol and holster tied down above the knee. Capable and confident? Yes. Dangerous? Not to them. Michael relaxed. Not a threat, but a possible ally.

"Is this Hawkins Station?" The man's voice was friendly, and he smiled.

"Yep," Nate replied.

"Name's Jeremiah Turner. The agent in Culverton said I might be able to get a meal here on my way to Riverbend."

Michael waited for the sheriff to relax, but he didn't. Gideon Parsons always struck the same attitude with strangers. Calm on the outside. Tension coiled inside like a rattler ready to strike.

"Ya sure can," Nate said to the stranger. "Have to charge you two bits, though, seein' as you ain't on a stage."

"That's fine."

"Well, come on in, then." Nate opened the door.

Turner wrapped his reins around the hitching post and walked past Nate. Michael and the sheriff followed.

Lanterns hanging from the ceiling cast a dim light throughout the room. The men of the posse sat spread among the tables, cups in front of them. Some were silent, while others held murmured conversation. Michael saw Vernon, Barkston, and Vernon's nephew, Alexander, huddled together around an open Bible. Frank, Martin, and Shorty from the Carstairs ranch stood at the bar, heads bent, studying a pistol that lay in pieces before them. Old Thomas and Malachi sat at the back of the room like two statues carved from different shades of wood. Harold Miller, Mitch Jones, and Dave Roberts, the other townsmen on the posse, sat at a table near the door talking quietly. Michael studied the group and wondered why Sheriff Davis had selected these men. What did he see in them that made them valuable on a posse?

A woman's voice bellowed from the kitchen. "Nate, git

those shutters open and let some daylight in here. Then come help me serve this breakfast."

"Be right there, Maggie."

Nate opened the shutters, allowing the strengthening sunlight to pour in. He disappeared into the kitchen and returned carrying a stack of plates, which he placed at the end of the bar.

Jeremiah Turner walked to the coffeepot standing on the bar. He nodded to the cowboys, picked up a worn and chipped cup, and poured from the pot. He blew across the top of the steaming liquid, then took a tentative sip.

The sheriff walked over and stood at the bar facing him. The stranger pointed at the pot and gestured in Davis's direction. The sheriff held a cup while Turner poured. He poured a cup for Michael as well.

Turner motioned toward the badge on Davis's shirt. "You the sheriff in Riverbend?"

"That's right. Caleb Davis is the name."

"Pleasure to meet you." Turner extended his hand. The sheriff looked at it for a second before grasping it in a brief handshake. "You've got a reputation for being fair," Turner continued, "and for being dogged determined to get your man, no matter what."

The sheriff shrugged. "I've heard of you too. You've got a reputation for being a hired gun. What's your business in Riverbend?"

Turner sighed, put his cup down, and rested his hands on the warped planking of the bar. He spoke in measured, well-educated tones. "Not exactly accurate, Sheriff. I *am* for hire, and I use my gun when I have to, but I don't sell myself as a gunslinger. That's the farthest thing from my mind. I help people and businesses with security problems, and I always make sure I work on the right side of the law."

"Be that as it may, you didn't answer my question."

Turner put his hand to his chest. "My apologies. I'm on my way to meet Sam Carstairs. I met him on the stage between Lassiter and Culverton. He asked for my help with some trouble he was in. I had to stay in Culverton to finish some business, and I told him I'd get to Riverbend as soon as I could."

The sheriff's eyes narrowed. "You're a little late, my friend. Mr. Carstairs went missing from this station between Wednesday night and sunrise yesterday. I'm working under the assumption he was kidnapped by a couple of other passengers. I've brought a posse here to start looking for him."

Turner stared at him. "Then we must pray in the name of Jesus that we find him soon before something happens to him."

Michael choked on his coffee. He coughed to clear the liquid from his throat. *Did this man just pray? A Christian gunslinger?*

Sheriff Davis raised his head. "Did he say what the trouble was?"

"Nothing specific. Just talked about threats and wanted my help in dealing with them. If I had known the danger was this immediate, I would have stayed with him."

The sheriff nodded. "You had no way of knowing."

"Come an' get it." Nate's wife, Maggie, emerged from the

kitchen carrying several platters of food. She placed them on the bar near the stack of plates.

Malachi led the attack on the food like a well-coordinated cavalry charge. Michael selected some flapjacks and bacon and remained near Sheriff Davis at the bar. He noted the sheriff's tension—spasms along the jaw muscle and twitching in the mustache as the sheriff chewed on the longer hairs.

Davis motioned Maggie to come near him. "Did Sam give any indication he was in trouble?"

Maggie folded her arms across her chest. "Like I told ya last night, Sheriff, he didn't say nothin'. A little quieter than usual. Kept pretty much to himself. Drank a little more than I've seen him in the past. Acted like he had something on his mind. But he didn't say what it was."

"What about the other passengers?"

Maggie wiped the bar with a stained towel. "They seemed like a nice young couple. Said they was newlyweds. She was real pretty—long dark hair and beautiful green eyes. Her husband was kinda quiet."

"Did they talk with Sam?"

Maggie frowned. "Not that I recall. Like I said, Sam wanted to be alone."

"Notice anything unusual about them?"

Maggie rubbed her chin. She arched an eyebrow and waggled a finger toward the sheriff and Michael. "Ya know, there was somethin' in the way the girl looked at Sam. Like she knew him and didn't like him."

Davis drummed his fingers on the bar. "Did you and Nate hear anything yesterday morning?"

"Not a sound, Sheriff. We was shocked to get up and find all the passengers gone."

"How about your Mexican boys?"

"They weren't here. They'd gone to visit their families and didn't come back until about noontime yesterday."

The sheriff turned to the room. "All right, men, eat up." He grabbed a plate of food, topped off his coffee, and went to sit with Vernon and Barkston. Michael refilled his plate, drinking in the aroma of the bacon, and joined them. Turner stood facing the room, his elbows on the bar. The three cowboys from the Carstairs ranch had put the pistol back together and were piling second helpings on their plates. Forks scraped metal plates as the men gulped down the breakfast.

Barkston wiped his mouth with the back of his hand. "That new man gonna ride with us?"

The sheriff looked over his shoulder. "'Spect so. I've heard he's real good with his gun. Don't know how he'll be at takin' orders. I've heard he's a bit of a loner, likes to be in charge."

Barkston snorted. "We'll keep an eye on him. He won't cause you no trouble."

Vernon glanced around the room. "I think you picked a good crew, Caleb."

The sheriff swallowed a mouthful of eggs. "I picked the best I could, men I could rely on." He eyed Michael. "I hope."

Michael assured him, "I won't let you down, Sheriff."

Davis sniffed. "I'm countin' on it, and so are these men."

Michael clasped his hands under the table. What would he do if he had to fight? Would he run? Could he release that ugly brute inside? Could he control it once it was out? *Father, be with me. Show me what to do.*

The sheriff rapped the side of his cup with a fork, and the room fell silent. He stood. "Let's get on the road. We're gonna head south and try to pick up Sam's trail. Malachi and Old Thomas will take the lead, and the rest of us will spread out on either side of the road behind them, searching for tracks.

"We don't know what we're riding into. Sam could be out there, out of his head, wandering around. I don't think that's likely. Or he could have been kidnapped. That's my thinkin' because the other two passengers are gone too. If it's a kidnappin', we don't know how many there are, what they want, or where they're goin'. And we don't know how long it's gonna take to find them."

He paused and surveyed the group. "I'm expectin' this to be a long, hard ride. And I 'spect there'll be shooting before we're done. So if any of you want to leave, now's the time. Nobody'll hold it against you."

There was a silence. Then Vernon drained his coffee and slammed the cup back on the table. "Caleb, we appreciate the offer, but we're sticking with you no matter what. I don't like the idea of anyone coming in and thinking they can take one of our people and get away with it."

"Okay. Mount up."

Michael watched Jeremiah Turner approach the sheriff. "Thanks for letting me ride along, Sheriff."

Davis cocked his head to one side and placed his hands on his hips. "Well, I still ain't all that sure about it." He jabbed a finger at Turner's chest. "You do what you're told, when you're told. I see any sign of you going lone wolf on me, and I'll shoot off your kneecap and tie you to your horse till we're done. Are we clear?

"Yes, sir."

34

Sam woke at the sound of Jack rekindling the fire. The gray light of dawn suffused the clearing, muting the colors, reminding him of a photograph. He watched Jack through narrowed eyes, a small victory in hiding his wakefulness. Jack set the coffeepot to boil and stirred up a batch of biscuits, glancing in Sam's direction a couple of times. Maria still slept, her face beautiful and peaceful.

The trouble with feigning sleep was having to be awake. Stones dug into Sam's hip. Twigs pinched his side. Sam struggled into a sitting position. Pins and needles coursed through his bound feet. His wrists chafed from the coarse rope. He scratched the bristle of his unshaved chin, longing to soak in a hot bath with Lupe tending to him.

Maria sat up and stretched. She shook her head and ran

her fingers through her hair. She smiled at Jack, then turned to look at Sam. Coldness filled her eyes like a veil blocking out everything bright and good. She stood, gathered some clothes, and walked to the water. Soon Sam heard her splashing and washing herself.

Sam yearned to have his hands untied, to shave, to wash off the sweat and grime. He knew it would be fruitless to ask. When he had sought relief the day before, they'd ignored him. He still felt the welts on his face where Maria slapped him with her reins after he asked to have the rope around his wrists loosened.

Despondency overpowered him. Lost, alone, at the mercy of this quiet man and this hateful, violent woman, hopelessness enveloped him, stifling any expectation of rescue.

By now, the town must know something had happened, but they would have no idea where he went. He himself had no idea where he was. Their meandering path had left him confused and disoriented. The constant pain in his head, his back, his legs made it impossible to concentrate.

I'm my only hope for rescue. No one else will ever be able to find me. Fight back! He inhaled and held the breath before releasing it. The hint of a resolve formed. They would not break him. He'd show his strength by not asking for anything, by not sinking to the level of a groveling peon, begging for scraps.

Whatever they wanted, he would not give it to them.

Combing her still-wet hair, Maria came back from the river in a mannish outfit of faded and patched dungarees, a tan cotton shirt, and boots. She took a plate of beans and bacon from Jack, picked up a biscuit and a cup of coffee, and sat on her blanket, eating in silence. Jack brought Sam a plate of food and put a cup of coffee near his feet. The pain, the stiffness of his muscles, and his bindings made eating without spilling an arduous task.

Jack picked up his gear and headed to the water. He returned in a few minutes clean-shaven and in clean clothes. He prepared a plate of food for himself while Maria saddled the horses.

"Let's go." Maria walked the horses to where they sat. Jack took Sam's half-filled plate and his untouched coffee and went to the river to wash them, along with the rest of the cooking gear. Jack came back, stowed the gear, and helped Sam onto his horse.

As Maria rode past him to take the lead, he leaned over and spat on her boot.

The back of her hand cracked into his cheek. "Pig," she hissed.

He tasted blood. She spurred her horse and trotted away.

Whatever they want, don't give it to them.

Sam smiled.

35

THE SHIMMERING SUN balanced on the edge of the horizon. Caleb scanned the group gathered around him. Good men. Men he could trust.

His days as an Army sergeant flashed before him. Once again, men under his command might die. He shivered at the thought of telling their wives and girlfriends he'd led them to their deaths. He shuttered his mind at the vision of children left fatherless. He shifted in his saddle trying to think of something to say.

Jeremiah Turner cleared his throat. "Sheriff, before we head out, can we have a word of prayer?"

Can't hurt. Doubt it'll help. Caleb nodded.

"Heavenly Father—" Turner lifted his face to the sky— "we come before You today in the name of Jesus. Lord, we ask for guidance and protection as we start this effort to rescue Your child, Sam."

Caleb bit back the urge to snicker. *I can see Sam spittin'* *and snortin' at that one.*

"We need Your help to be successful. Let Your Holy Spirit guide and direct us. We ask You to send angels forth to clear the way for us and command the angels to surround Sam and protect him from harm. We pray this in Jesus' name, and we believe we receive. Amen."

A chorus of agreement rumbled through the group.

Caleb straightened in his saddle. "All right, men, here's the plan. First, we find their trail. Second, we find them. We're pretty sure their intentions ain't good, so be alert and watch out for each other. Malachi, Old Thomas, let's get going."

The two old men started out, one on each side of the road. Caleb rode between them in the road. The rest of the posse followed in a loose group, a few yards behind.

Tension stretched tight as they rode, the silence oppressive. Even talkers like Malachi and Shorty were silent. Caleb watched Malachi and Old Thomas ride with deliberate slowness, scanning the ground.

"Ya know, if they went this way and stayed on the road, we shoulda come across 'em last night," Malachi said.

Old Thomas nodded. "That is what makes me think they left the road at some point."

"Well, if they went thisaway, you'll find 'em."

"Thank you for your vote of confidence."

Malachi sighed. "'Course, my eyesight'd be a whole lot better if that puritan of a sheriff'd let me have a wee nip to stimulate my senses."

Caleb chuckled. "I heard that, old man. Just keep your eyes open."

"Old? I ain't much older than you."

"That may be true, but I ain't pickled myself for thirty years. And besides, I'm better-lookin'."

Old Thomas's eyes never left the ground. "He is correct about that, old friend."

Malachi spat. "Ah, what do you know, you heathen Indian?"

They rode for another couple of hours. Caleb sensed the posse's restlessness over the creeping pace. But he trusted his trackers, and their work took precedence over anyone else's comfort.

Old Thomas raised his hand to signal a halt. He and Malachi rode several yards to the west and then made a slow circle to the road. They went back to the starting point and did the same on the east side.

"What'd you find?" Caleb asked when they returned.

Old Thomas looked at Malachi, who shrugged. "I ain't telling him."

"I ain't got time for games," Caleb said, annoyed. "Tell me what?"

Old Thomas pointed to the side of the road. "They turned off here." He paused, his face troubled. "And rode off in three directions."

Caleb cursed.

He waved for the posse to join them. "Go ahead, tell them."

"Gentlemen," Old Thomas said, "we have found their tracks."

Murmurs of gratitude. Vernon exclaimed, "Hallelujah."

The Indian continued, "We do not know which ones were made by Sam."

Caleb put up his hand to still the grumbling. "Hear him out."

Old Thomas pointed to the western side of the road. "There are three sets of tracks. Each goes in a different direction. Each set has three horses, and each set seems to carry the same amount of weight."

Caleb saw his own frustration and anger mirrored on the men's faces. He drank from his canteen to calm his emotions. He needed to show control to his men. He could see only one thing to do.

"All right. These people are smart. They planned this well. Two of these sets are decoys, but we don't know which. So we're gonna have to split up into three groups and follow each trail."

He surveyed the group. How to assign them? Who would work well together? Archer and Turner remained unknowns, potential jokers in the deck.

"Vernon, you're the next best tracker here. You take Alexander, Shorty, and Dave and follow the trail to the east. Bill, you take Malachi, Martin, Harold, and Mitch and follow the trail that leads west. Michael, you and Mr. Turner and Frank will ride with me and Old Thomas. We'll take the one heading southwest. If you find anything, stay put and send a rider back to find us. Don't risk firing a shot."

The riders gathered in their designated groups and started on their assigned trails. Caleb's group set off at a brisk pace.

After a few miles, however, Old Thomas slowed as the terrain became rockier. The tracks lead to a creek, then failed to come out on the other side. Old Thomas shrugged and spread his arms, palms up.

Caleb sighed. "I don't like it, but we need to split up again. Michael and Frank, you ride upstream. The rest of us will go downstream. If you find the trail, one of you come back and get us. The other one stay where you found the tracks. Don't do anything until we're all together."

What would I do if I were a kidnapper? "Y'all be careful. Keep one eye open for a trap."

Michael glanced at the cottonwoods and brush as Sheriff Davis had instructed. He leaned forward and stroked Buddy's neck. "Let me know if you hear anything." His eyes roamed the ground before him, searching. *Lord, guide me. Reveal hidden things to me.*

No birds sang. No breeze disturbed the branches or rippled the water. Sweat ran into his eyes and he wiped them with his sleeve. After a couple of hours, his throat felt like sandpaper. "Need a break."

Frank straightened his hat. "Me too."

They stopped to refill their canteens and let their horses drink.

"You're new around here, ain't ya?" Frank said. "What brings ya out here anyway? Why'd you join up with this here posse?"

Michael studied the man. A few inches shorter than Michael's six feet, slender and wiry, early twenties, shaggy blond hair, sun-darkened skin. *A cowboy. And enjoys it. How much money did I cheat your kind out of over the years?* Frank's friendly, open face offered friendship and encouraged trust.

"I have some business with Mr. Carstairs. When he turned up missing, I felt like I should be part of helping find him. Didn't I see you in church on Sunday morning?"

"Yep, that was me. I go every chance I get. Ma raised us to always make time for church. I don't always understand all of it but I know it makes her happy. Besides, did you see that redhead sittin' with me?"

"I think so."

"Well, she's Harold Miller's daughter, Mary, and I'm sweet on her. I think she's sweet on me too, but the only way she'll see me is if I go to church with her every Sunday. I have to admit, it keeps me out of the saloons on Saturday night."

Michael chuckled. The light in Frank's eyes when he talked about the pretty redhead showed how smitten he was. *I bet I have the same look when I talk about Rachel.*

Frank took another swallow of water and wiped his mouth with the back of his hand. "I hope we find Mr. Carstairs quick. I don't have a good feelin' about the way this is goin'."

"Me neither. We have to trust the Lord to guide us. Have you worked for Mr. Carstairs long?"

"I've been at the ranch about five years. Don't see much of Mr. Carstairs, though. He stays in the house or in town. Mr. Joshua runs the ranch. He's a good boss but don't talk much."

Michael started to ask another question when the sound of hoofbeats interrupted him. Frank whipped his pistol out of the holster, hammer cocked. Michael reached for the rifle in his saddle scabbard. He grabbed the stock, praying he wouldn't have to use it.

Jeremiah Turner rode into view. He threw his hands up when he saw Frank's gun.

Frank relaxed and holstered his pistol. Michael let the rifle slide back into its sheath.

"We found the trail a few miles down the creek."

Caleb watched the receding figure of Old Thomas as the Indian walked away, his head bent toward the ground. He admired the man's skill and patience. Old Thomas never lost focus. He was more determined than a bloodhound and not as smelly or noisy when he found his prey. Malachi was almost as skilled, when he was sober. This search would be impossible without them.

Caleb heard the other three gallop up. He turned as they reined to a halt. "It's the same three horses."

They walked their horses as Old Thomas followed the trail on foot. He stopped when the trail faded on hard ground. He walked in a slow circle until he found a mark on the edge of a stone that showed the way.

"How does he do that?" Michael asked in wonder. "I don't see anything."

Caleb grinned and pushed his hat back with a forefinger. "Me neither. Him and Malachi scouted for the Army for years. They know every which way there is to see signs and figure out where to go. Old Thomas told me once that learning to track and how to hide his own tracks was part of his initiation into manhood."

The day drew on, the sun warm. They chewed beef jerky and sipped from their canteens. Around midafternoon, Caleb swiped a bandanna across his brow, then settled his hat back on his head. "We're not gonna take any breaks. As long as there's daylight, we'll keep goin'."

Their shadows lengthened as the sun continued its slow plunge toward the mountains. Caleb saw the fatigue and tension in the men's faces. He smiled as Michael and Frank drifted off at times and startled themselves awake. Jeremiah Turner rode next to him, back straight, eyes narrowed against the sun, following Old Thomas's every movement. The man hadn't spoken since they found the trail. Caleb still didn't know if he trusted Turner. He certainly wasn't fooled by that praying business.

The ground softened, and Old Thomas mounted his paint. They picked up the pace to an easy trot. Caleb's spirits lifted. Moving somewhere at last.

They rounded a rock outcrop, and Caleb cursed again.

Vernon Phelps and his group stood waiting for them on the stage road to Riverbend.

Anger and frustration rose like a sudden thunderstorm on a summer evening. A full day on the road, and they were no closer to finding Sam Carstairs than when they started. Caleb wanted to lash out at someone or something, to drive his fist into some no-good crook's face. He settled for slapping his hat against his thigh. The sound startled Caesar and caused him to rear. Caleb almost tumbled off.

Vernon pushed his hat back. "Can you believe it?"

"Kinda hard not to when it's staring me right in the face."

"They sure are slick."

Caleb wrestled between giving vent to his frustration and setting an example for the posse. Physical and mental exhaustion drained him. He repressed the desire to quit.

Caleb straightened his shoulders and pulled himself erect. His vow rang in his mind: *Never stop bringing lawbreakers to justice, no matter what the cost.* "Any sign of Bill and his men?"

Vernon shook his head. "Maybe they've had more success."

Caleb looked at the darkening sky. "Vernon, you and Old Thomas use what daylight we've got left and ride down the road a ways, see if you can find any sign of the trail. The rest of us will set up camp and keep a lookout for Bill's group."

36

DUSK WRAPPED its light gray cloak around the town as Rachel closed and locked her store. She rested her fingers on the doorframe and bowed her head. *Thank You, Father, for blessing my business. I hope it brings You glory and honor.*

She walked to the post office to see if a letter Luke was expecting had arrived. As she walked, several townspeople greeted her with nods. Others ignored her, and still others stared and frowned. She squeezed her fingers while doing her best to keep a smile on her face. Would it always be like this? How long would people hold her past against her?

The letter hadn't arrived yet. As she left, Mayor Meriweather entered. He held the door for her.

"Thank you, Mr. Mayor."

He touched the brim of his hat. "You're welcome, Miss Stone."

She moved to step past him. He moved also as if to give her more room. Then he stumbled toward her, hands reaching out. She turned slightly so that he grabbed her arm. She knew that look in his eye.

He released his grip, one hand moving toward her chest. She took it in her hands as if shaking hands with him.

She smiled. "Watch your step, Mayor. Some of these floorboards can trip you up." Then she leaned forward, lowering her voice to a whisper, watching the pain register in his eyes as she squeezed his bread-dough hand. "I'm making dresses for your wife. I can make her look like a laughingstock while convincing her she looks like Queen Victoria."

She straightened and spoke in her normal volume. "Please thank your wife for ordering two more dresses. I'm sure she'll be pleased with them. And I hope you like them too."

She smiled as she left him standing there. But the surge of victory quickly drained away. *It will never stop. I'll be fighting this battle the rest of my life.*

Was it worth it? Would it be easier to give up and go back into the business? It seemed like it sometimes. She cursed. Out loud. *God, why is this so hard?*

Before she reached the church, she turned down a path that led to the river, the same path that had brought her to Michael yesterday morning. *Was it only yesterday?* She sat by the cottonwood where he had been, wrapped her arms around her knees, and lowered her head. She wanted to pray. She cried instead.

After several minutes, she lifted her head to look at the patches of sky beyond the leaves. White clouds hung motionless. She prayed a halting, stammering prayer asking for release and strength to go on.

She waited. Michael's face came into view, his hazel eyes warm, his smile gentle. No leering. No demand for what she no longer sold. A face she could trust. *Really? I can trust him?* She remembered his boldness in trying to kiss her on the mouth. Then she remembered his acceptance of her refusal.

He seemed willing to accept what she could offer. Which wasn't much. She was willing, even eager, to see him again. But she couldn't make any promises—not yet. Not when the thought of a man touching her sexually sent contradictory waves of revulsion and confusing desire through her. She shivered. The only honest prayer she could manage was *Help me.*

Several minutes later she walked into the parsonage kitchen. Martha was preparing supper, checking the chicken roasting in the oven, the bread baking. A pie sat cooling on the windowsill. Rachel washed her hands, picked up a knife, and began peeling potatoes.

"Easy there," Martha said. "They don't need to be bite-size, and I don't want you cutting your fingers off. What's got you so riled?"

"Men." Rachel sliced more skin off the potato.

"Did Mark Carstairs try something?"

"Haven't seen Mark since Saturday night. It was the mayor this time."

Martha made a face. "That's disgusting to even think about. Did you leave him in one piece?"

"He'll have a reminder every time he shakes hands the next couple of days."

They worked in silence for a while. The sounds of Luke playing with the children drifted from the front room. Martha began humming a little tune as she washed the bowl where she'd mixed the bread. Rachel looked around the peaceful room and felt a wave of envy wash over her. *Why did God bless you with a good man while I have to deal with people like my uncle and Mark and so many others who only want one thing?*

She bit back the tears of self-pity. There was a reason. Maybe she'd understand it someday.

37

MICHAEL AND JEREMIAH TURNER gathered firewood from a small copse of trees that bordered a narrow, muddy creek a few yards off the road.

"I don't think I've ever heard of a Christian gunslinger before."

Anger flashed in Turner's hazel eyes. Then he sighed, a long, deep exhalation that seemed to come from his toes. "I don't think I'm ever going to get rid of that reputation."

"What do you mean?"

Michael felt weighed and measured in the other man's steady gaze. Turner shrugged. "I see my gun as the last tool in my bag, my last resort. So I've learned to use it that way, to be better with my revolver or rifle or shotgun or whatever than the other man, because at that point my life depends on it."

Michael nodded. Made sense. A farmer wouldn't last long

if he didn't know how to use a plow. "What led you into this kind of work?"

Turner examined a piece of wood as if it held the answer. "The war more than anything else. I was in Missouri, assigned to stop Quantrill's Raiders. Always felt like we were behind enemy lines. Never saw such cruelty. Drove some men to disbelief, but somehow it drew me closer to God. And I think that led me to what I'm doing now, defending people and their property." He added the piece of wood to the pile in the crook of his arm and picked up another.

"Seems like a tough job."

Turner stacked another piece on his armload of wood. "Yep. Especially when the law sometimes thinks I'm as much an outlaw as the men I'm fighting against."

The two men walked back to where the others had set up camp. As they drew near the picket line of horses, Turner spoke. "So what's your connection to Mr. Carstairs?"

"I have some things to deliver to him, along with a message."

"Bad news?"

"His youngest son was hung. They were estranged. I'm bringing his son's belongings back to him with some letters the boy wrote looking to be reconciled."

Michael gave him the rest of the details about his relationship with Ben and their efforts to contact his father before the execution.

Turner shook his head. "Seems like a mighty long trip to take, especially when it could end with the door being slammed in your face."

"I know. But I'm hoping God's going to make a way for me to speak to Mr. Carstairs's heart."

They stacked the wood near the spot Shorty had cleared for the fire. Turner continued. "Carstairs is carrying a heavy load. I could see it, but he didn't want my prayers. Said God didn't want anything to do with him and he didn't want anything to do with God. He just wanted me to take care of the threat to his safety." He straightened and turned to Michael. "It's something to pray about."

"I've been doing that every day, Mr. Turner."

"Guess we need to start praying together. And by the way, you can call me Jeremiah. The way I look at it, a man that prays with me can call me by my Christian name."

They walked over to where Shorty was coaxing the fire to start. Sheriff Davis set a coffeepot at its edge and surveyed the group. "Anyone here know how to cook?" Jeremiah shrugged, and Dave Roberts raised his hand. "Dave, you're elected. Shorty, Michael, see what McGuffy packed in there for food."

Michael and Shorty rummaged through the packages. Michael found a small ham, and Shorty held up cans of beans and a sack of flour. "You know how to make biscuits?"

Michael shook his head. "Not that this group will eat. My horse won't even eat 'em."

Shorty patted the bag. "Sure wish Bill Barkston was here. The man knows how to cook on the trail."

They carried the supplies to the fire. Dave Roberts took the flour and soon had biscuits baking. Shorty started the beans heating and rigged a spit for the ham.

The sheriff approached Michael and Jeremiah, who stood

a little apart from the group. "Is the water in that creek any good?"

Jeremiah shook his head. "Not right here, Sheriff. Too low and muddy. Looks like it's getting ready to dry up. There may be better water farther upstream."

"All right. We'll check it out in the—"

A voice boomed from the darkness on the north side. "Hello, the camp!"

The sheriff gripped his pistol, but he didn't draw. Jeremiah slipped the leather thong off the hammer of his Colt and adjusted the pistol in the holster. Michael's fingers tingled, and he took a side step toward Buddy and his rifle resting in its scabbard.

"Who's there?" the sheriff called.

"It's Bill Barkston from Riverbend. That you, Caleb?"

"Come on in, Bill. Was wonderin' what happened to y'all."

The group of five riders stopped a short distance from the camp and dismounted. Fatigue and frustration showed in their faces and the stoop of their shoulders. They unsaddled their horses, and Alexander Phelps led the mounts to the picket line that had been set up between two of the trees.

"I'm tellin' you," Barkston said in a rumbling voice that seemed to start at his toes and then work its way up the considerable distance to his mouth. "That was the most miserable ride I've been on in a long time. I bet we ain't more than five miles from the stage station, but I know we rode at least thirty miles, none of it in a straight line. If it weren't for ol' Malachi here, we'd still be moseying around out there looking for tracks."

"How'd ya find us?" Frank asked.

"Wasn't looking for ya. The trail led us back to the stage road. We were gonna head back to the station when Harold here spotted the fire. I figured no kidnappers are gonna light a fire out in the open this near the road, so I decided to check it out."

Sheriff Davis had started to speak when Vernon and Old Thomas rode in.

Vernon eyed Barkston as he and the Indian dismounted and handed their reins to Alexander. "This isn't good if your trail brought you back here. I was hoping one of us was on the right track."

Barkston shrugged. "Stinks having to start all over again."

"Find anything, Vernon?" the sheriff asked.

"Nah. Couldn't find a sign of them 'fore it got too dark. Have to try again tomorrow and see what we can find."

"They keep doing this," Dave Roberts said, "we don't have a prayer of finding 'em before Christmas. And that's if we're even on the right track. We don't know that these trails have anything to do with Mr. Carstairs."

"Right now they're all we've got to work with," the sheriff said.

Vernon crouched by the fire next to the sheriff. "There's always hope."

"What're you gettin' at?" the sheriff asked.

Vernon turned toward Michael and Jeremiah. Michael's shoulders tensed as everyone in the group stared at him. "Mr. Archer, I understand you're a religious man and that you've worked as a minister some. Would you pray over us for the Lord's guidance and a quick resolution to this problem?"

Michael scanned the group. Some of the men wore hopeful looks, a few seemed hostile, others curious. *Soften their hearts, Lord. Prepare them to receive or at least not reject.* He stepped to the edge of the fire, the waves of heat warming his face. Sheriff Davis scrutinized him and then stared into the fire. Jeremiah Turner came and stood on one side of him. Vernon Phelps stood on the other. Michael looked up into the dark night and extended his arms, palms open.

"Father—" he kept his voice soft, in awe of his God and the responsibility resting on him at this moment—"we worship and thank You for Your goodness and mercy and love. We come into Your throne room with boldness in the name of Jesus as Your Word says we can." He raised his voice as the power of prayer rose in him. "Your Word tells us to believe we have what we pray for and we will have it. Father, we pray for Your wisdom and direction as we seek Sam Carstairs and those who may have kidnapped him. We pray for Your divine guidance to protect us and show us the right trail. We thank You, Lord, that as we journey tomorrow, You will guide us every step of the way. We thank You that You hear our prayers and that You do answer them. We believe we receive what we pray for, and we give You the praise and the glory and the honor for it. In Jesus' name. Amen."

The chorus of *amens* ranged from muttered and mumbled responses to clear, affirmative statements of agreement.

"Well, that was to the point," Sheriff Davis said. "Tomorrow we'll see if it does any good."

38

Sheriff Davis rattled a spoon inside a cooking pot as the first blush of sunrise lightened the sky. The men stirred at the racket. Shorty threw a boot in the sheriff's general direction, while mumbles and groans rose from several of the others. Michael, already awake, prayed as he watched the horizon brighten. He envisioned Rachel rising with the dawn and preparing for her day. Would he be a part of her life one day? Could he give her what she needed and wanted? give up his own needs? Could he be worthy of her?

He stowed his gear. The aroma of coffee brewing made him hurry to cinch Buddy's saddle and return to the fire, ready to eat.

"Let's eat quick, gentlemen. I don't want to waste any daylight." The sheriff kicked the feet of Mitch Jones. "Come on, you old barkeep. Most folks consider this the beginning of the day."

Jones muttered something unintelligible and rolled over, pulling his blanket up over his shoulders. The sheriff pulled the blanket off and tossed it several feet away. "What'd you say about my mother?"

Davis's lighthearted tone brought a chuckle from Mitch. Michael admired the way the sheriff treated the men with an easy camaraderie. The mantle of leadership rested easily on his rounded shoulders. He held their trust and respect with a light hand.

Jones sat up and rubbed sleep from his eyes. He sighed, shook his head, and shrugged. "If God wanted me up at the crack of dawn, He shoulda made it later in the day."

Before the sun rose fully over the horizon, they were mounted and on their way, fanning out as before on either side of the road behind Malachi and Old Thomas.

At midmorning, they reached the intersection of the stage road and a well-traveled side road. Their hearts sank at the myriad of tracks in the churned-up dirt.

Malachi's shoulders slumped. "This is gonna be impossible."

Old Thomas looked up, his face expressionless. He shrugged.

"Nothing is impossible with God."

Everyone turned as Michael spoke, the words out of his mouth before he realized it. Some of the men glared at him, unbelief on their faces. Others looked at him as if he had two heads. From experience with Zechariah, he recognized these as the ones who put God in that place they visited once a week and didn't expect Him to show up anywhere else. Jeremiah Turner and Alexander Phelps gave him encouraging nods. Bill Barkston raised one eyebrow and nodded. Vernon Phelps murmured, "Amen."

Everyone seemed to be waiting on Sheriff Davis. *What is this man's relationship with You, Father?*

The sheriff turned with an expression Michael could not decipher. Michael waited, hands resting on his saddle horn, hoping to convey confidence and hide the anxiety churning in his stomach.

A few seconds ticked by in agonizing slowness. Then the sheriff removed his foot from the stirrup and hooked his leg over the saddle horn. "What's on your mind?"

"Well, sir, the Bible teaches us that we can do all things through Christ and that Jesus will supply all our needs. The key thing is to not give up hope, but to believe. This crossroad isn't some test from God. It's a tool of the devil to discourage us, divide us, and lead us astray. As believers, we have authority over the devil and his weapons. We can turn this setback to our good if we wait on the Lord to show us the way."

Mitch Jones spat tobacco juice onto the road. "And just how long is this waitin' gonna take? Every minute we sit here, Sam gets further away."

Michael turned to the man. "If you're prepared to wait forever, it won't take very long."

Silence. Some of the men squirmed in their saddles. Leather creaked as horses shifted their weight. The sheriff grinned and swept his arm in a gesture that invited him to go ahead.

Michael cleared his throat and turned to Old Thomas. "Sir, why don't you take another look at the tracks and see if there isn't something familiar."

The Indian nodded slowly. Head bent, he began walking in a slow circle around the intersection. He squatted a couple of times, his hand hovering over some of the prints. He got on his hands and knees, his face only a couple of inches from the ground, one hand extended over the road, palm down, making small circular motions. He cocked his head to study a print from a different angle.

Then he sat up, resting on his haunches. "I would not have believed it if I had not seen it with my own eyes. One of the horses we trailed yesterday had a nick in one of his shoes—the right rear, if I am not mistaken. That same print is here. Now that I found this one, I can see the others. They head east."

Caleb looked at Old Thomas and then at Michael. He shook his head. "Let's head out, same as yesterday. Slow and easy. We don't want to lose the trail." He nodded at Old Thomas. "Lead on, old friend."

Old Thomas and Malachi rode ahead. The posse followed about a hundred yards behind. A half mile down the road, the scouts stopped.

"What now?" Caleb said when the posse drew near, his voice edged in irritation.

Old Thomas pointed to the side of the road. "They have split up again."

Caleb cursed. "Guess we'll have to split up again too."

39

SAM'S EYES ITCHED and burned from lack of sleep. The sun peeking over the horizon and warm air brushing across his cheek brought no relief or comfort.

The blacksmith in his head continued to bang away. Pain coursed through his body, his mouth dry, his stomach always threatening to heave. His clothes reeked of fear-driven sweat. The beard on his face chafed, and no amount of scratching provided any relief.

The thought of another full day on this ungainly horse over rough terrain filled him with dread. A vision of a long, hot bath and a close shave tantalized him.

Jack broke the vision like a child smashing a piñata. "Time to move on, old man." Once again, he secured Sam's hands to the saddle horn with a length of rope snugged around his wrists. Fresh pain pierced skin still raw from the day before and the day before that. Blood seeped into the stains on the rope.

"Where are we going?" Sam asked for the hundredth time, not really expecting an answer. His chafed lips and dry throat made his voice hoarse. He couldn't put any volume into the question. But asking it had become a little act of defiance.

Maria slapped him, a hard blow that snapped his head. "Shut up. You'll find out when we get there."

He tasted blood. "If I live long enough."

She grabbed his jaw, her leather-clad hand like a vise, her fingers digging into his cheeks. "Oh, you'll live, all right. Jack and I will see to that. I don't want you to miss any of the treats my papa has for you. He's had a long time to think about it."

She glared at him, her hate and disgust so tangible he wanted to pull back. He couldn't. She'd break his jaw if he tried to move. She squeezed tighter and spat in his face. He blinked the sputum out of his eye but was powerless to wipe it from his cheek. Nausea roiled again as some of the spit trickled into his mouth.

"Let's go." She turned and spurred her horse into a trot. Jack slapped the rump of Sam's horse and fell in behind.

Another meandering day. For a time they rode north, although Maria took numerous detours over hard ground and along creeks wherever she found them. They made elongated loops. Sam's only point of reference was the mountains to the west.

At midday, they met six other riders. No meal break. They sat in their saddles and gnawed on jerky. Maria spoke to the others in a Mexican-Indian dialect he couldn't understand, then dismissed them. They broke into two groups of three riders each. Sam's heart sank as he realized their plan—leave three trails to confuse and delay anyone who might be following. He admired their planning but realized with overwhelming dread that he might never be found.

He slumped in the saddle, body sagging and wanting to fall forward onto the horse's neck. He watched Maria riding in front of him, her back straight, one hand holding the reins while the other rested on her thigh, her body in rhythm with the animal beneath her. *Come on, you old coot. You're as good a rider as she is. Are you gonna let her show you up like this?*

Pride swelled, and he forced himself to sit straighter, head high, eyes straight ahead. After a short distance in this position, his stomach heaved, and he leaned over and left his lunch on the side of the trail. She looked back at him and shook her head.

His head swam in a befuddled haze. Nausea churned and acid burned the back of his throat. Cold, clammy sweat broke out on his forehead. He cursed to himself. Fear and loneliness gripped him; helplessness hovered around him like a swarm of gnats.

So is this how it ends? All that work to build his fortune wasted because he wouldn't live to enjoy it. Ironic that John Higgins would be the one to do it. What did John want? How much?

Whatever it was, he wasn't going to get it. John wasn't all that innocent when they started. He would've done the same to Sam, but Sam was simply better at it. Smarter. Quicker.

With John out of the way, Sam had thrived. He'd been able to make sure whatever deal he made brought him more money or land or power. And people liked him for it. He convinced them he was doing it for their benefit. Nobody saw the real Sam inside. He even hid it from Ruth and his sons.

That whole part of his life was gone now. Ruth dead. Joshua had as little contact with him as possible. He loved the ranch but seemed to enjoy it best when Sam was gone, and though he followed Sam's orders well enough, he kept his own counsel. Mark had the ability to be another Sam but wasted it. He had no discipline, and Sam only saw him when he was in trouble or wanted money.

Who knew where Ben was? Sam didn't want to know. Ben had always been a knife in his heart anyway—ever since that night he'd killed Ruth.

Ruthie . . .

Sam's heart raced as he relived the fear and panic of that night.

The screams of pain had pierced the wooden door to their bedroom and plunged like a dagger deep into his heart. He'd wanted to be at her side, but the midwife kept shooing him out. So he'd paced the hallway, stopping each time he came to the door, willing as hard as he could for her pain to ease.

His sons hovered in the doorway to their room, their eyes wide with fear. Little Joshua's voice quavered on the edge of tears. "Is Momma gonna be all right?"

"I don't know," Sam snapped. "Look, you boys don't have to hear this. It could go on for a while. Go downstairs and tell Magdalena I said for you to have some pie and milk."

The two boys hurried down the stairs. Sam resumed his pacing. Another scream, followed by a long, drawn-out moan.

The midwife yanked the door open. Sweat glistened on her face and plastered her hair to her head. "Send someone for the doctor. I'm gonna need his help."

"It'll be at least two hours before he can get here, and that's if he's in his office."

"I know that, you fool. That's why you better send someone now." She slammed the door in his face.

He stood there dumbfounded.

The door opened again. "Move!" She gave him a shove.

He ran down the stairs and almost tore the front door out of its jamb. Several of the cowhands had gathered on the porch, waiting for news. Sam pointed at his foreman.

"Take my horse and ride into town. Bring the doc back here as fast as you can. Hog-tie him over the saddle if you have to, but git him back here."

"Yes, sir, Mr. Carstairs." The foreman ran for the barn.

Sam bolted upstairs again. As he reached the bedroom door, he heard his horse gallop away. Sam walked into the room. The midwife turned to chase him out.

"I want to see my—" He stopped at the foot of the bed. Ruth lay limp as a rag doll, her face white, her beautiful pale hair like strings of matted weeds strung out on the pillow in a bizarre halo. Her blue eyes were bloodshot and swollen from tears. Her nightgown was soaked with sweat and pulled above her waist. Blood pooled on the sheet beneath her.

His voice trembled, barely above a whisper. "What's going on?"

"She's having a real hard time. The baby is all twisted inside her, and I can't get it to straighten out. She's just not strong enough to keep having babies."

Sam glared at the woman. "It's a little late for that now, isn't it?"

She looked at him, not flinching, someone he could never intimidate. "It well may be. Now that you're in here, give me a hand. There's a bowl of water and a cloth on the bureau. Keep wiping her forehead with the damp cloth. It might ease her some."

Sam had never felt as helpless as he did over the next few hours. Ruth's cries and moans grew weaker. The midwife worked to get the baby turned in the right direction.

Footsteps clattered up the stairs and down the hall. Then the short, pudgy doctor burst into the room. He examined Ruth and consulted with the midwife, then turned. "Sam, you need to leave us. I have to cut into Ruth to get the baby out. Have your cook boil plenty of water and get some clean towels ready."

Sam didn't argue. In a few minutes, he was back pacing the hallway.

God, please help her. Please . . .

Soon he heard the weak cry of a baby.

The midwife opened the door, the tiny infant cradled in one arm. "It's a boy."

Sam barely glanced at the child. The sight of Ruth on the bed commanded his attention. Her face was paper white. Her long lashes rested on hollow cheeks. The doctor shook his head. Sam sat on the edge of the bed and took Ruth's hand. It felt like a feather, the blue veins in stark contrast to the ivory skin.

"Ruth, honey? It's me, Sam." His voice cracked as he fought down the sobs that collected in his throat. "It's a boy. We'll call him Benjamin like you wanted, after your grandpa."

Ruth's eyes fluttered. She looked at him. He stroked her cheek. The corners of her mouth twitched.

He squeezed her hand. "Stay with me, Ruthie. Help me raise him."

Her breathing was shallow, and her lips moved. He leaned closer to hear her whisper, "Sorry, Sam . . . sorry I wasn't stronger." Then she was gone.

And nothing had been the same since then.

Trust God, people kept telling him after that. But Ruth's death had destroyed what little faith he had. How could anyone let someone as gentle and beautiful as her die and expect Sam to believe in Him or want to have anything to do with Him?

Sam's heart had hardened as he watched the dirt shoveled onto her coffin. And no matter how hard he'd fought to build a life after that, the best part of him still lay in that grave with her.

He knew she wouldn't be proud of all the things he'd done—to Higgins and to others. He hadn't done it to please her, but to please himself. *I'll make it up to you, Ruthie, somehow. If I survive this. I'll put things right with all of 'em. Maybe I can even find Benjy, make things right with him too.*

Somewhere in Missouri. That's what he remembered from the envelopes he had tossed in the fire, unopened. *Maybe that Jeremiah Turner can find him.*

They rode on in silence, Maria's back ramrod straight, at one with her animal, Jack loose-jointed but obviously not a skilled rider, Sam hanging on to his saddle horn in pain-riddled fear.

They made camp that night in a group of boulders. Jack ranged far and wide to gather enough scrub wood to make a small fire. Sam could only choke down a little of the beans and hard cornbread they gave him. He just kept his head down, trying not to vomit. When they stretched out to sleep, Sam found the ground hard and unyielding.

He lay on his back, his head resting on his saddle, and gazed at the stars that sparkled far above him. He felt a huge weight on his chest. His mind reeled out of control.

I should've died with my Ruthie.

40

MICHAEL CINCHED HIS SADDLE and reached over to scratch behind Buddy's ears. The horse turned his head and nuzzled Michael's hand.

"Sorry, boy. No treats this morning. I'll see if I can find something along the trail." The horse shook his head, rattling the metal on his bridle.

Frank slid the bit into his horse's mouth. "What day do you think it is?"

Michael paused, his mind blank. He didn't know. The days blended together. He couldn't remember how long they had been searching. "I dunno. I can't tell them apart anymore."

"Me neither." Frank mounted and walked his horse to join Sheriff Davis and Jeremiah Turner. Michael saw Old Thomas out ahead, studying the ground.

Frank pulled up next to them. "Any idea what day it is, Sheriff?"

The sheriff shrugged. "Nope."

Jeremiah Turner took a small book from the inside pocket of his vest. He flipped a few pages. "It is Monday, May 27."

Frank gave a low whistle. "Almost three weeks we've been out here."

The sheriff turned to him. "You can go back anytime."

Frank shook his head and held up a hand. "Ain't that, Sheriff. We need to find Sam. I was just curious is all." He stood in his stirrups and looked around. "'Sides, I don't think I could find my way back even if I wanted to."

They rode off, Old Thomas in the lead. Michael reflected on the routine of the days: up at the crack of dawn, follow a trail that meandered all over the place but generally moved westward, stay in the saddle until it was too dark to see. Eat a cold supper. Sleep. Start all over again the next day.

The divided posse still followed three trails. Michael couldn't remember how long it had been since they had seen either of the other groups.

Day after day, tension battled fatigue. The men drowsed in the saddle, snapping awake when they almost tumbled off their horses, looking around to see if anyone noticed. The novelty and humor of that wore off after a few days of the relentless ride. The weather was clear, warm in the morning and hot in the afternoon, the heat adding to their sluggishness. The few meandering streams were almost dried up.

On this day, Michael rode with Old Thomas. Sheriff Davis wanted one man riding with the tracker as a lookout.

The sheriff, Jeremiah, and Frank remained about thirty yards back. They would not come closer unless beckoned by Old Thomas.

The sun's rays reflected off the almost-white stones and light-colored sand. Michael's eyes burned from squinting. Even with his hat brim lowered over his face, the light dazzled.

For the last hour, they had moved with deliberate caution over hard, rocky ground. Old Thomas spent much of the time off his horse, searching the ground for the slightest indication of the kidnappers. Now he squatted on his haunches, staring at a small indentation in the rock. He turned his head and scanned the landscape, then stood slowly, as if in pain. A loud pop sounded from one of his knees as he straightened. He rubbed the small of his back with both hands, lifted his canteen for a long drink, and splashed some water in his face.

"The spirits are not being kind to me today, young one." He replaced his canteen and rested his head on his arms on his saddle. Then he straightened, the lines in his face like canyons gouged by a glacier now long gone. Fatigue showed in his eyes and in the droop of his shoulders.

Peering into the distance, he said, "Those we are following have strong spirits. Dark and evil spirits are hiding them from my eyes."

Michael took off his hat, wiped his face with his sleeve, and replaced his hat. It was a breezeless day, and the silence was eerie. He watched an eagle drift on the air currents, wings spread, gliding. Old Thomas followed his gaze.

"Yes," the Indian said. "It would be wonderful to see from

where he is, to see the whole world laid out before us, to see those we seek plainly and without being seen by them."

Michael studied the aged man, a man whose quiet strength he had come to respect. He admired the man's strong spiritual presence, the belief in an almighty creator that was not too far from his own beliefs, except the Indian had not yet met Jesus as a personal Savior.

"Watching that eagle reminds me of something from the Word of God," Michael said. "'They that wait upon the Lord shall renew their strength; they shall mount up with wings as eagles; they shall run, and not be weary; and they shall walk, and not faint.'"

Old Thomas nodded gravely. "Unfortunately, time to wait is something we probably do not have—not if we are going to safely rescue Mr. Carstairs."

Buddy shifted his weight unexpectedly, jostling Michael so that he grabbed the saddle horn. "It means more than just time. To me, it means being sensitive to Him, to hearing Him. It means blocking out distraction and focusing on what He has to say. There are times that can happen very quickly."

"You draw a lot of strength from your God and from His writings. I can see this God of yours has changed you from a bad man to a good one. You are strong, Michael Archer. And you will grow stronger as you keep on the path your God has set before you. Stay true to your God and pray He helps us find these people who have taken Mr. Carstairs."

"It's been my constant prayer."

Old Thomas mounted his horse and, with a heavy sigh,

settled into his saddle. He gathered the reins and set his paint to a slow walk. He pointed to a large rock that rose out of the ground like a huge mushroom cap about one hundred yards to the north.

"I want to see if we can climb that and get closer to the view of the eagle." He said it with a wry chuckle in his voice. He examined the ground while they approached the boulder. The stone rose perhaps fifty feet at the most and was about two hundred feet long, rounded at both ends. A web of cracks and fissures worn by rain and wind covered the side.

Old Thomas perused the face of the rock for several minutes, scanning the patterns of the cracks, searching for a path to the top. Speaking softly to himself in Creek, he reached into his saddlebags and took out a pair of moccasins. He shucked his boots with a soft thud onto the ground, slipped the moccasins onto his feet, and securely wrapped the leather thongs around his legs. When he was done, he swung his leg over the saddle and slid gently to the ground.

Approaching the rock face, he spoke to Michael. "Bring the looking glass, young one. I think your eyes will be better at distance than mine."

Michael pulled the spyglass from his bag and dismounted, then followed Old Thomas over to the huge rock. The Indian tested a couple of cracks with his hands and toes, then started to climb, his fingers and feet finding openings just large enough to get a grip.

"Come, my young friend. Follow me."

Michael began following the same route and soon learned why the Indian had changed his footwear. His boots had difficulty getting purchase in the cracks. Several times he slipped and hung on by his fingertips until he regained balance and control. After fifteen minutes of climbing, he reached the top, sweating profusely, fingers raw and knees bruised.

Old Thomas lay flat on the rock, facing west, and motioned for Michael to do the same. He raised himself up on his elbows and used his hands to shade his eyes. Before them the land stretched toward the mountains, the shades of gray and tan and brown around them turning green in the far distance near the mountain streams. Behind them, to the east, the land looked deceptively flat as it merged into the great plains. To the south lay the way to Riverbend and the valley that nurtured and protected and gave prosperity to the community. But all Michael could see where they lay was emptiness—no sign of human or animal life anywhere.

He handed the spyglass to Old Thomas. The old man slowly scanned the area in an arc from north to west to south, stopping occasionally if something caught his interest. He repeated the process from south to north and then focused the glass on an area toward the southwest. He handed the instrument to Michael, pointing to that area.

"Tell me what you see in that direction."

Michael held the piece to his eye and adjusted the focus. He pointed the spyglass in the direction Thomas had indicated and did a slow scan to either side of it. He paused to wipe away some sweat and lifted the glass again, praying silently for guidance and clear vision. He concentrated on a line of trees several miles distant. There was something there, dots drifting in the sky.

He rubbed his eyes again and peered one more time. He lowered the glass and handed it to Old Thomas. "There's something over there."

"Buzzards." The Indian continued to scan further to the left. He glanced at the sun and then back to where the buzzards circled lazily.

"Come. We must go back to Sheriff Davis."

They made their way to the side of the rock, staying low and close to the surface. Old Thomas easily maneuvered down the side. Michael once again lost his footing and fell the last five feet, landing with a decided thump on his rear.

"Are you hurt?"

"Just my pride." He stood, slapped the dust off his pants, and mounted Buddy.

Old Thomas waved his hat to signal the others. Michael settled in his saddle as the others approached.

"What have you got?" Excitement and anxiety tinged the sheriff's voice.

Old Thomas's voice was level and calm as he pointed past the rock. "We saw buzzards circling about five or six miles away."

He squatted and drew a crude map in the dirt with his finger. "We cannot ride straight there. It is all open ground, and if there are people there, we will be seen. There is an arroyo a short distance from us that we can follow. It will take us to a creek, and we can ride through the water and trees without being seen."

Frank held up his hand. "Wait a minute, Sheriff. Won't that take us off the trail? How do we know they even went that way?"

The Indian's voice was calm. "This ground is very hard. The trail, if there is one, is slow and difficult to follow. The creek is the first good water we've seen in several days. They will want water as much as we do. They either went straight ahead or followed the path I suggest. Either way, that's where we will find the trail."

Frank shook his head. "I dunno. Seems we're puttin' a lot of faith in one old Injun."

The sheriff's voice was sharp, like a whip snapping. "Let it go, Frank." He paused. "Anything else?"

The cowboy shook his head.

The sheriff nodded, combing his thinning hair with his fingers. He resettled his hat with the brim lowered over his eyes, then climbed back on his horse. "All right, let's ride. Lead on, friend Thomas."

41

THE ARROYO WAS NARROW, with steep sides of soft sand. The group slid as much as they rode to the bottom. The sand was churned with so many tracks, Michael couldn't distinguish one from another. Sheriff Davis and Old Thomas studied the ground.

Old Thomas stood from a squat. "Several riders have come through here recently."

"I can see that." The sheriff rubbed the back of his neck. "Y'know, part of me just wants to ride right in there. This bein' slow and cautious is wearin' on all of us." He turned to Michael. "If that God of yours is still up there, you'd better pray He gives me patience."

Michael said nothing. This was not the time to give Sheriff Davis a lesson on the existence of God.

The sheriff turned back to Old Thomas. "Do you recognize any of them?"

Old Thomas didn't speak. He walked slowly along the bottom edge of the slope, careful not to disturb any of the tracks. "They are right on top of each other, so it is hard to tell. All are heading for the creek, though. None are heading toward us. I believe I see at least one of the horses we have been following. Others look familiar, but I am not sure."

"All right. Let's keep goin'."

They headed off in single file with Old Thomas in the lead and the sheriff right behind. Michael rode next, with Frank behind him. Michael heard Jeremiah, at the rear of the line, slide his rifle from its scabbard. Michael glanced over his shoulder and saw the weapon resting across the saddle. Jeremiah scanned the top of the arroyo.

They rode in silence, the soft sand muffling the horses' hoofbeats. The only sounds were the creaking of saddles, the jingle of bits, and an occasional snort when one of the horses blew air through its nostrils.

Tension was a knot between Michael's shoulders. No amount of twisting or stretching could relax it. He watched the top of the arroyo. *What a perfect place for an ambush.*

No breeze disturbed the air or cooled their skin. The washed-out blue band of sky above the arroyo was cloudless. The riders pulled their hats low, squinting against the glare. The air smelled burnt and dry.

Sweat ran through Michael's hair, down his face and neck. It found its way under his shirt to trickle down his back. His bath at the hotel seemed a lifetime ago. He smiled at the thought of the steaming water, the lilac aroma of the soap, and the softness of the towels. He knew he stank, and only the thought that everyone else smelled the same kept him from being embarrassed. He was grateful Rachel couldn't see or smell him now.

He thought of her, the brightness of her smile, her shining hair, the gentle touch of her slender fingers, the honesty of her eyes. She was so beautiful, so brave. If only—

A buzzing sound broke through his reverie. The sheriff's horse reared, sending her rider tumbling to the ground, and Buddy jumped at the commotion. Michael heard Jeremiah cock his rifle. Sheriff Davis put one hand out to stop him and his other hand to his mouth to silence them. The buzzing sound continued.

A few feet up the slope, a rattlesnake raised its head, tail rattling, eyes focused on the sheriff.

No one moved. The snake's tongue darted in and out, and the rattle increased its vibrations. The snake pulled itself into a tighter coil, its eyes still riveted on Sheriff Davis. Michael prayed silently, *Father, protect him.*

The sun glinted off a darting sliver of metal that flew from Old Thomas's hand. The blade penetrated the skin below the snake's broad head. The reptile writhed and thrashed, driving the blade even deeper. After a few moments, the snake lay still, its head almost severed.

The silence was the most deafening Michael had ever heard.

The sheriff seemed to shrink as he relaxed. He wiped his

mouth with his hand. "Thank you, old friend. You saved my life."

Old Thomas bowed his head. "You are most welcome, my friend. Obviously your time here is not over. The spirits guided my hand because the sun clouded my vision. I threw at the sound."

Behind him, Michael heard Jeremiah. "We know what Spirit it was."

The sheriff's eyes flashed as he cast a quick glare in Jeremiah's direction.

Old Thomas dismounted. He retrieved his knife, cleaned it in the sand, and slipped it into the sheath in his boot. Then he reached down and held up the snake's drooping body. "Perhaps we should save it for our meal tonight. It tastes just like chicken."

Michael's stomach lurched.

Frank said, "I wouldn't eat that thing if you pickled it in whiskey for a year."

The sheriff took up the reins of his horse. "That might be the only whiskey Malachi wouldn't drink. Let's ride."

They rode in silence. After a time, the meandering arroyo emptied into a lovely little creek bottom. After watering the horses and filling canteens, the posse followed the creek upstream, winding through the cottonwoods and live oak that hugged its bank. Through occasional breaks in the trees, they could see the circling carrion birds.

They kept the horses at a steady walk at the edge of the stream to minimize noise. A slight breeze cooled the back of Michael's neck.

The sheriff whispered, "Breeze feels good, but it'll carry our scent forward. We smell so bad it'll let 'em know we're comin' half an hour 'fore we get there."

They came to a bend, and Old Thomas motioned for them to halt. He slid to the ground, walked a short distance, and disappeared around the bend. The men waited in silence. Michael could see the tension in their faces and posture. *Oh, Lord, let this end soon.*

Time dragged. Restlessness churned in Michael. He could find no channel to release it.

The sound of someone running through water came from up ahead. The sheriff drew his pistol. Jeremiah cocked his rifle. Michael pulled his own rifle from its scabbard and levered a round into the chamber. *Lord, don't let me have to shoot anyone.*

Old Thomas trotted round the bend. He mounted his horse and looked at the sheriff, grief etched in the lines of his face.

"Come. It is very bad."

42

RACHEL LEANED FORWARD in her saddle and stroked Sunshine's neck. The coat was warm and soft from the constant brushing Rachel and the children gave the animal. Firm muscles rippled at Rachel's touch, telling her they were ready to go. Rachel gazed at the open range that stretched from behind the parsonage to distant foothills shimmering in the sun. Wide-open. No hindrances.

She tapped Sunshine's side with her heel. "Yah," she called.

The mare sprang forward and within a few strides was at a full gallop. Rachel pulled her hair ribbon and shook her head, letting her hair catch the wind.

Learning to ride was her only pleasant memory of life on her uncle's farm. Galloping through the pastures and into the forests had offered a brief respite from the torment. Back then she'd ridden astride and bareback, often barefoot, her feet and legs feeling every pounding step. It had taken a while to get used to the sidesaddle.

She leaned forward now and urged Sunshine to more speed. The horse responded with a burst that made Rachel laugh until the wind took her breath away. It was the closest thing to actually flying that she knew.

For years she had dreamed of flying away from the pain and abuse and degradation of her life. Meeting Martha and Luke and coming to know Jesus had opened the door of that cage. But now, too often her flight was clumsy, the learning painfully slow.

The Bible told her to forgive her enemies. She could not forgive her uncle.

The looks and words of people in Riverbend hurt. She wanted to lash out.

A good man had found his way to her, knocking on the door of her heart. Part of her wanted to let him in. The fear kept her backing away.

She was a long way from being free to fly.

But out here, for now, riding Sunshine gave her just a taste of the delicious freedom she longed for. She hadn't been able to find mention in the Bible, but surely there were horses in heaven.

After several miles, she eased Sunshine into a trot and then a walk to cool down. Her eyes swept the landscape. Open and free space. No barriers to lock her in. Behind her, the parsonage snuggled unseen beyond the undulations of the prairie. The steeple, like a slender needle, stabbed into the late-afternoon sky. How fitting a symbol to guide her home.

She released the reins and let Sunshine meander to a nearby stream. Rachel inhaled the fragrance of wildflowers while the horse drank and grazed. Like a sponge, Rachel's senses absorbed the aromas of the earth, the bright colors of the grass and flowers and sky, the friendly sounds of her horse munching grass. She hugged each sensation in her mind and heart, savoring as if she might never taste such beauty again. *If only life with people could be like this.*

The lengthening shadows brought Rachel out of her muse. With a heavy sigh, she tugged on the reins and turned Sunshine away from the water.

"Come on, girl. Time to head home. We'll come back again soon." She guided the animal into a loping gait, heading toward—

Pray.

The word shouted like a thunderclap in her mind as the parsonage came into sight.

Pray.

There it was again.

Urgency clouded her mind as the thought repeated itself.

We need to pray. There's danger. Where? Who?

An image of Michael filled her mind. Behind him, Vernon Phelps and his nephew, Alexander, wavered as if caught in heat waves rising from the ground.

Pray.

Get to the others and pray.

Dear God, let them be all right. Let Michael be all right.

She kicked Sunshine into a gallop.

43

THEY SAW THE BUZZARDS FIRST—big, ungainly birds on the ground at the edge of a clearing bordering the creek. They were pecking and tearing at something in the clearing. Something dead.

Michael followed Old Thomas and Sheriff Davis as they galloped into the midst of the birds. The buzzards scattered only to land a short distance away. They crept closer, seeking the opportunity to resume their feast.

The horses stamped and snorted at the smell of blood and death. Michael pulled deep breaths through his mouth as he fought to keep his stomach under control. The riders dismounted, and Jeremiah tethered the horses near the creek. The animals calmed down and began to drink. The men tied bandannas over their mouths and noses to ward off the stench as they walked toward the four bodies in the clearing.

Michael recognized Vernon Phelps and those in his group. The four men lay in grotesque positions, hands tied behind their backs, throats cut. Dried blood blackened the earth. The buzzards had committed further mutilations. The remains of a cook fire formed a neat circle in the middle of the clearing. Old Thomas walked over and felt the ashes. "Two days old at least."

Sheriff Davis gestured toward the trees. "I think at least two of the groups we're chasin' joined up for this little party. Three people couldn't have caught Vernon like this."

Frank's face had turned ashen behind his dark blue bandanna. His shallow breathing came in gasps. He bolted into the trees. After a few moments he returned and took a long pull from his canteen before pouring water on his bandanna and washing his face. He replaced the bandanna around his mouth and nose. "Sorry. Thought I'd seen just about everything, but this is too much." He looked at the bodies again and turned to the sheriff. "What do we do with them? We can't leave 'em like this for the buzzards and varmints."

The sheriff pushed his hat back on his head. "We'll have to bury them here the best we can. After this is over, we'll try to get 'em to bring back to Riverbend." He turned to Old Thomas. "See if you can find the trail they took out of here while the rest of us tend to these men."

The old man rode off to make another of his circular searches for signs and tracks.

Three hours later, the four remaining men stood over

four humps of dirt and stones. Michael hoped the graves were deep enough to keep coyotes and other scavengers away. They'd carved the names into tree branches to mark them for a return trip.

The sheriff stood with his hands jammed in his back pockets. He kicked at the dirt. "Michael, I think you're the closest we have to a preacher here. Would you mind saying a few words?"

They removed their hats. The breeze didn't disturb a strand of Michael's sweat-matted hair. He cleared his throat, feeling all eyes upon him. His mind went blank. *What do you pray at a time like this?*

He quoted the Twenty-third Psalm. Then he prayed. "Heavenly Father, we believe these four men are now in a far better place with You. We grieve for the ones they left behind. Comfort them, Lord. And, Lord, help us find those who did this and bring them to justice. Amen."

There was a silence. Then the sheriff began to speak, his voice choked with grief and anger. "Vernon Phelps was a good man, a good friend. Always willin' to help others. When my wife died, Vernon and his family made sure I had meals and somebody to talk to. He'd sit with me for hours. Sometimes neither of us would say anything, but he was a comfort to me just being there. Other times, he'd just let me talk and talk, lettin' the hurt and pain come out, lettin' me cry like a baby."

He paused and swallowed. He wiped his eyes with his knuckles. "Young Alexander was growin' up the same way. Vernon and Esther took a boy that lost just about everything and could've headed down the same dead-end road his daddy took. But they turned him around, taught him to be a man. Gave him a future. Vernon was training him up to be a first-class rancher. But now they're gone. The town'll have a smaller heart now."

Silence again. Frank coughed, turning his hat round and round in his hands, his eyes focused on his boots. "I don't think anyone ever knew Shorty's last name. He was just Shorty to everybody. Kinda quiet but could outwork any three men. Didn't never get drunk or rowdy like the other hands. He'd have maybe one beer on payday. He told me once he was savin' his money to buy some land up in Wyoming and start a ranch. Plannin' on getting married, though he didn't have a girl yet. Shorty worked hard and stood by his friends. He was never afraid to stick up for a buddy if trouble came. At his size, he took some lickin's but he gave as good as he got." Frank sniffed. "We're gonna miss him out at the ranch."

"Dave worked hard at the hotel," the sheriff said. "Did whatever Mr. Carstairs asked him. Took good care of the guests. Kinda kept to himself. Doted somethin' fierce on his wife, Sarah. Buying her little gifts. Bringing her flowers. She's expectin' their first. He was real excited about that. Now that kid's gonna have to grow up without a father."

The men stood there a long minute, hats in their hands, pondering the graves. Then Frank set his hat on his head, pulled the brim down low, hefted his gun belt at his waist. He walked over to his horse and mounted, gathering the reins in his fist.

"Where you goin'?" the sheriff called after him.

"We gotta git the guys who did this. I'm not gonna sit here while they git away."

"Calm down. I want to get 'em just as much as you do, maybe even more." Sheriff Davis looked at the four graves and then at the sky. "But it's gettin' too late in the day, Thomas ain't back with their trail, and I don't want us riding hog wild into another ambush."

Frank glared at the sheriff, twisting the reins tighter. Michael sensed the turmoil in the man, the drive for revenge battling to outweigh common sense. Finally Frank's shoulders dropped, and his hands relaxed. "I guess you're right, Sheriff. I don't like it, but we'll do it your way."

Frank dismounted and stomped into the trees. Michael took the reins and tethered the horse with the others.

Jeremiah built a fire and put a pot of coffee on to boil. He soon had some biscuits baking while he heated the beans and fried up some bacon.

Michael still stood by the graves. He gazed across the creek but saw nothing. Sweat and filth seemed to ooze from every pore on his body. He looked at his hands, at the dirt in every crease, the grimed nails. He shuddered, then headed toward the creek.

He found a secluded spot upstream. The water, cold from the mountain snows, stung, and he thought twice about going in, but the need to get clean won out. He'd do the best he could without soap. He stripped off his clothes and washed them, but the shirt shredded under the scrubbing. One clean shirt left in his saddlebags would have to see him through. He hung his pants and underwear on tree branches to dry.

Back in the water, he scoured his skin with his fingers. Weeks of sweat and dirt washed out of his hair and off his body, but the despair of man's inhumanity and the stench of death still clung to his soul. No amount of scrubbing could lessen it. *Father, I need You,* he prayed. *Help me to know Your peace.*

Dusk whispered in the softer light and cooler air as he returned to camp. The sun sat on the tips of the mountain peaks, about to be impaled on the jutting formations. Crimson, orange, and yellow reflected off the few clouds. Night birds and insects began their soft songs.

Frank tended the fire while Jeremiah Turner stirred the beans and tested the biscuits. Michael found a place next to him, while Frank and the sheriff squatted on the other side of the fire.

"We're gonna have to put that fire out soon," the sheriff said. "I don't want to give any sign we're here. Also, we'll post a guard in case the kidnappers double back. They must be figurin' there's more of us after them. Frank, you and Mr. Turner here take the first watch. Michael and I will take the second. We'll let Old Thomas sleep whenever he gets back. We'll do four-hour shifts starting right after we eat."

Frank served the bacon and biscuits while each man poured himself a cup of coffee. Michael added water to his. They waited in respectful silence while Jeremiah spoke a blessing over the food. They ate without a word.

44

RACHEL SKIDDED Sunshine to a halt and ran into the kitchen. Martha sat at the table shelling peas. Their friend Annabelle Stewart sat across from her with Daniel in her lap, watching him draw on a paper. The domestic peace of the scene flashed across Rachel's vision before the urgency in her spirit shattered it like fine crystal falling on flagstone.

Annabelle looked up. "Rachel, there you—what's wrong?"

Rachel gulped. The words came out in a rush. "We need to pray." She took a deep breath. *Calm down.* "Something's happening or going to happen. I don't know what. All I know is, we need to pray. It came to me while I was riding back."

Martha put down the pod in her hand and stood, wiping her hands on her apron. "Daniel, go get your father. Now."

Daniel broke from his wide-eyed stare, jumped to the floor, and ran into the hallway. "Paaaaa," echoed behind him.

The next minute, Luke hurried into the room, followed by Pete O'Brien. Daniel and Abigail slipped through the doorway and pressed against the wall, their eyes round as full moons.

"What's goin' on?" The sound of Pete's brogue shocked Rachel. His unexpected presence drove the words from her mind. Fleetingly, Rachel remembered Martha had invited him and Annabelle for supper.

Annabelle put her hand on Pete's arm. "Rachel says we need to pray."

"Oh." Any other time, the befuddled expression on Pete's face would have made Rachel smile, if not laugh out loud. Now, the sense of urgency pushed amusement aside.

She looked at Luke, pleading for guidance. His dark brown eyes held hers. His gentle tone soothed her. "What did the Lord tell you?"

Rachel clamped down the shiver that wanted to course through her body. She clasped her arms at the elbows. "All I heard clearly was 'Pray.' Then I had this sense that someone is in danger. I saw Michael and Vernon and Alexander, and I knew I needed to get back here so we could all pray."

"Why don't you get us started then and we'll join in as the Lord leads us." Luke reached for Martha's hand.

Rachel folded her hands together at her waist, fingers interlocked, head down. Her hair fell around her face. She ignored the strands brushing her eyes and touching the sides of her mouth. "Father, we come before You in Jesus' name. I'm not sure what to pray for, so I lift up the situation You placed in my heart. Someone is in danger."

She paused. People flashed through her mind in a confusing swirl, too fast to tell one from the other.

She swayed. A large, strong hand grasped her elbow. She opened her eyes as Pete guided her to a seat at the table. Tears flowed. She received Annabelle's embrace like a blanket and snuggled into the warmth.

Martha came to stand behind them and placed her hands on Rachel's head. Her voice croaked through sobs. "Lord, we lift up Rachel. Comfort her. Strengthen her."

Rachel sensed that Luke had come to stand beside his wife, but his voice sounded far away. "Let's all sit down. Daniel, please go get my Bible."

Rachel straightened up as the others took their places. Annabelle on her left held her hand while Martha on her right stroked her back. Luke sat on the other side of Martha, leaning forward, holding Martha's other hand, his lips curved in the gentle smile that always gave her peace and comfort. Pete sat across from Annabelle, his hands clasped on the table. He looked at them as if he wasn't quite sure what to do with them. Abigail seemed tiny next to him.

The patter of bare feet on hardwood announced Daniel's return. He handed the Bible to Luke and climbed into his father's lap.

Rachel and the others waited. Her back and shoulders relaxed, the tension seeping away. But concern still troubled her spirit. She wanted answers. Who was in danger? Was it Michael? How could she warn him? She rubbed her forehead. *Lord, help me.*

Luke turned the pages of his Bible, the sound like poplar

leaves rustling in a breeze. He cleared his throat. "When Rachel prayed, I also felt in my heart that someone is in danger. I don't know who. So we need to keep praying, first for Mr. Carstairs and the posse, and then see where the Lord leads us." He leaned around Daniel to read. "These words from Philippians 4 came to me. 'My God shall supply all your need according to his riches in glory by Christ Jesus.' And, 'I can do all things through Christ which strengtheneth me.' Let's pray."

Luke led them in prayer, naming Sam Carstairs and each member of the posse. Rachel felt the heaviness lift from her spirit as she joined in. She didn't have the peace she sought, but the oppression dissipated like smoke tugged apart by the wind.

Luke's prayer faded into the background as Michael's image filled her mind. *What, Lord?* What was that feeling in her heart? She had never felt it before, at least not for a man. It was more than just caring, almost a yearning. She wanted him to come back. To come back to her. And after that? She still didn't know.

She squeezed her fingers, crushing the knuckles together. The pain didn't distract this time.

Just let him be safe, she prayed. *Bring him back to—*

A gasp from Martha made her eyes fly open.

Luke stopped praying. "What is it?"

Martha turned to her husband, her eyes wide. "I think someone at this table is in danger too."

45

A REDDISH GLOW MARKED where the sun settled behind the mountains. Stars appeared, little pinpoints of cold light. Jeremiah extinguished the fire with the dregs of the coffee.

The grisly scene of the afternoon flooded Michael's mind. In the jails, he'd seen a great deal of cruelty among the inmates and between the guards and inmates. Fights and beatings were commonplace in the confined and degrading surroundings. But nothing he'd ever witnessed could explain what they'd found today. It seemed like something only Satan could do.

He prayed from Isaiah, thanking God for His promise that no weapon formed against them would prosper. He also prayed the Ninety-first Psalm, seeking comfort in the promise of protection. But his mind kept returning to Vernon's bloated face, to young Alexander dead before he had a chance to live.

Michael lay on his back and stared into the sky. There had been a time when death held no significance for him. Death simply marked the final phase, the end of a meaningless existence. He'd mourned no one. He'd encased his heart in a cold, hard chamber of granite that let no one close. And he had wanted it that way. People were things to be used to get what he wanted, tossed aside when they no longer served his purpose.

Then he met Zechariah, who introduced him to Jesus, and everything changed. Suddenly death was the enemy. And he mourned. First for his mother and then for others. He repented of the pain and hurt and death he had caused. He believed God forgave him.

Yet every time the image of his mother or Ellie flashed across his mind, the guilt of not having done more weighed. When he thought of his father lying on those steps, the guilt crushed his chest. The voice scratched in his brain like loose boards creaking in the winter wind: *How could you take up a weapon against the man who brought you into the world? How could you leave your own father to die?*

He closed his eyes. Sleep eventually came, and with it came the nightmarish memory. The one he kept trying to put behind him.

The one he couldn't seem to forget.

He'd been fourteen at the time, tall and slim, with skinny wrists and too-big hands poking out from too-small shirts. Walking home from fishing, he'd heard the screams. His sister's screams, coming from the barn, shrill with pain and terror.

He burst through the door and struggled to make sense of what he saw. Two bodies, writhing on the floor. Their father on top of Ellie, pinning her while he grappled at her clothes. Her tangled hair spread out wildly on the boards.

Fury filled him, almost without warning. A guttural roar erupted from his throat as he rushed forward, bowled into the older man, knocked him to the side. He pulled his sister to her feet. She was sixteen, and the dullness in her dark eyes told him she had already experienced far too many of their father's drunken, lustful rages.

"Run, Ellie. Take the horse and go to the Brownings'."

"But he—"

"Run!"

His father, a small, wiry man with thinning hair and a scraggly beard, staggered to his feet, the stench of mingled alcohol and sweat overwhelming. He reached for the ax propped in the corner.

"I've had it with yer interferin', boy. I'm gonna take care of ya like I shoulda years ago. I shoulda drowned ya when you was born. I knew just lookin', you was gonna be trouble."

He swung the ax. Michael ducked away from the wild blow and saw the pitchfork. He picked it up. "I'm tired of you hurting us, old man, tired of you beating up on Ma and messing with Ellie. It ain't right, and it's gotta stop."

"You ain't man enough to stop me." His father lunged at him, ax held high.

"Somebody's got to."

The pitchfork plunged deep into his father's thigh. The tines hit bone. Blood spurted from the wound. His father screamed and clutched his leg.

Michael dropped the pitchfork and ran to the house, tears flowing, sobs catching in his throat. "Ma!"

His mother lay on the kitchen floor unconscious, blood oozing from her nose and mouth. He knelt beside her and touched her face. Her eyelids fluttered and she looked at him. Then her breathing stopped. He heard his father yelling. Through the open door, Michael saw him hobbling toward the house using the pitchfork as a crutch, carrying the shotgun he kept in the barn. Wet blood stained his pants almost black while curses poured from his mouth. Michael scurried to his room, grabbed a handful of clothes, and bolted out the back door as he heard his father stumble up the steps to the front porch.

Silence.

Michael crept around the side of the house and peeked around the corner. His father lay on his back on the steps, the pitchfork on the ground, the shotgun in his hand.

Michael didn't go any closer. He took off through the fields.

He had never looked back.

Michael lay awake in the darkness that enveloped the campsite, waiting for his heart to slow down as the reality of where he was registered. He wasn't on that farm anymore. He wasn't that boy. Or was he?

The distant stars cast a dim light in the expanse above

him. Sounds seemed magnified. Buddy snorted. Another horse stamped his foot. Sheriff Davis snored on the other side of the cold fire ring. Michael turned his head at the sound of footsteps to see Frank walking near the creek. Jeremiah was on watch too, probably somewhere in the trees. A smattering of insects chorused near the water. An owl hooted. The forlorn call of a coyote echoed in the distance. He closed his eyes again, but sleep hung back in the shadows at the edge of his mind.

A branch snapped. Sheriff Davis sat up, his pistol cocked.

Jeremiah whispered from the edge of the trees. "Good evening, Thomas. I'm glad you could join us."

The Indian spoke in a hoarse whisper. "Hello, Mr. Turner. You are very good, or I am getting older than I thought. I did not see you. Frank, on the other hand, makes himself too easy a target."

The sheriff released the hammer on his pistol and holstered the weapon. "Do you have news for us?"

"Yes, but I am not sure how good it is."

Michael took the Indian's horse and tethered the paint near the stream with the others. He returned to the fire ring. Frank and Jeremiah stood near enough to hear Old Thomas's report but kept their focus outward, continuing to watch. Sheriff Davis and Old Thomas sat facing each other across the cold fire. They looked so solemn, Michael expected one of them to produce a peace pipe to seal a treaty.

The sheriff spoke first, his questions abrupt. Old Thomas didn't seem to mind, his stoic peacefulness draped over him like a shawl.

"What did you find?"

Old Thomas munched on a biscuit and sipped cold cof-fee. "They rode down the stream for several miles before they left it, heading south."

"How many riders?"

Old Thomas chewed, swallowed, sipped. "There are nine. It looks like the three groups met here."

The sheriff stared off into the darkness. "And murdered Vernon and the others. The snakes."

The insects seemed to grow louder in the silence that fol-lowed. The sheriff straightened his legs. "Any sign of Barkston and his men?"

"No."

"Let's hope they're still behind us. How far ahead are the kidnappers?"

Old Thomas shrugged. He spoke around a mouthful of biscuit. "Maybe two days. No more than three. But they are moving fast."

Michael sat in silent awe of these two men. Tired, yet comfortable in each other's company. Older, almost past their prime, some might say. Yet they had pushed themselves for three weeks on a grueling, frustrating, and seemingly end-less search. He prayed for them to receive the strength and endurance to continue.

"Any sign some of them might have doubled back on us?"

Old Thomas shook his head. "I saw no sign. I think they want to get to wherever they are going soon."

"All right." Caleb looked at the other men. "I don't think

they'll be comin' back. Let's all get some sleep. We have some hard ridin' to do tomorrow."

Michael woke once more. Wind-tattered clouds scudded overhead. He held his breath. What had disturbed him? He listened and heard a slight scraping near the fire ring. He turned his head to see Sheriff Davis sitting cross-legged and poking at the cold remnants of the fire with a stick. He watched for several minutes as the older man absentmindedly moved the stick. His hat shadowed his face in the dim light. Michael sensed a deep melancholy in the set of his shoulders and the angle of his head.

Michael rose and sat across from him. "I don't mean to intrude, but you seem to be carrying a heavy burden."

The sheriff stopped his poking and looked at the tip of the stick as if it held the secrets of the universe on its ash-covered point. "This ride's been tough. Wanderin' around like this has me angry enough to bite the head off a rattler. And then findin' Vernon cut up like he was and left to rot—hangin's too good for these people. I'd like to slow roast them on a spit."

He laid the stick outside the rocks of the fire ring with a tenderness that made it seem like a fragile reed. "Vernon Phelps was a good friend, probably the best I had in Riverbend. I'm gonna miss him somethin' fierce. He was always there for me. It felt like everyone else ran off after my wife died. Even God, when the sickness took her."

Sheriff Davis picked up the stick and wagged it in Michael's direction. Michael wanted to shrink back at the bitterness he saw in the thin line of the sheriff's mouth. "Y'know what always bothers me about you preacher types? You're always spoutin' that God's a good God. Well, if He's such a good God, why did He make her get sick and suffer so much? I was helpless. She was in a lot of pain, and I couldn't do nothin' to help her. Doctors couldn't do nothin' for her neither. And then God left me all alone to deal with her dyin'. Haven't had much use for the Almighty since then, though Vernon was always tryin' to talk to me about Him."

Michael prayed, *Lord, give me the words and the wisdom.* "Sheriff, I can't tell you why your wife died. I believe that God does not put sickness and disease on people. Satan does. He does it not only to hurt people, but also to make the ones who love them and have to watch them suffer turn against God. But God doesn't leave us to deal with our suffering alone. God hurts when we hurt, and He does show up to help us. He just doesn't always do it in the way we expect. A lotta times, He uses other folks to minister to us. I think that's what Vernon was to you—someone God used to help you deal with your wife's dying, to be a friend and comfort and support to you. I only knew Vernon from being on this ride, but he struck me as a man who loved God and who would be a great friend to anyone."

The sheriff sighed. "Yeah, he was. So you think God uses people like that?"

Michael reached for the kindling pile and arranged some of it in the fire ring. "God wants His people to show His love to each other by doing things like Vernon did for you. It's His way of saying He loves you and cares for you. I know He's used people like Zechariah Taylor to show me how much He loves me. It's the only way He could've reached me, to be honest—I was so far gone. And then He used me to reach Ben Carstairs, and I believe He's using me to somehow reach Sam Carstairs. He wants everybody to be right with Him and be saved by the blood of Jesus and live well on this earth, then spend eternity with Him."

The sheriff rubbed his chin, staring into the small flames of the fire Michael had started while they talked.

Michael wiped his hands together to rub off the debris from the wood. "Was your wife a Christian?"

"Oh yeah. That woman did her best to get me to church. She was there every time the doors opened. I told her I'd seen too much evil in the world to believe church would do anybody any good. But I went with her every once in a while to keep her happy."

"Well, she's with God in heaven now, in a much better place."

"Anyplace'd be better than this earth."

Michael took a deep breath. "You know, Sheriff, God wants you to be with Him and your wife and Vernon in eternity. He wants you to know He loves you while you're on earth and that you have a place with Him in eternity."

The sheriff cocked his head to one side, a flicker of interest in his tired face. "You really believe there's a life after this one?"

"I do. And I believe your wife did too and so did Vernon."

The sheriff crossed his arms. "Can you prove it?"

Michael shrugged. "Well, the Bible tells me there is. Jesus promises we can be with Him in eternity if we believe and confess Him as Lord. Another thing that convinced me there has to be more after we die is that if this is all there is, it's pretty worthless."

"You got a point there."

Michael took a deep breath. "Would you like to be in a place to be with your wife in eternity with Jesus?"

The sheriff didn't answer right away. He poked his stick back in the fire. "Yeah," he finally said, "I guess I'd like that. But I gotta warn you, I've got a bunch of sins under my belt, and I'm not sure I'm sorry about all of 'em."

Michael laughed. "I'm right there with you, Sheriff. If the only people that got saved were people without sins, none of us would make it. That's the whole point. You come to the Father with your sins, and He takes care of 'em."

"So how does it work?"

"With a simple prayer."

"That's all?"

"That's where you start. I can lead you in it, if you'd like."

The sheriff sat and considered some more, then nodded.

"All right," Michael said. "Repeat this after me."

At the end, Davis looked into Michael's eyes. "Young man, I'm much obliged."

46

Sam woke screaming. The gag in his mouth smothered the sound to a hard, smoldering lump in his throat. A clammy sweat permeated his clothes, saturated his hair, and covered his face as the nightmare of the posse's brutal murders scalded his mind.

He struggled to a seated position. The fire burned low in the early morning light. His eyes stung and burned from sweat and drifting smoke. Maria sat by the fire, staring at him. As he looked at her, the scene he'd witnessed replayed itself once more in a vivid recollection of blood and cries for mercy. He squeezed his eyes shut but could not stop the images.

Jack and Maria had kept him in that clearing for a day. He was unable to fathom why they'd stopped moving. He'd gotten his answer when six more riders joined them.

The riders had dark skin and spoke to Maria in a mixture of English, Spanish, and some kind of Indian language he didn't recognize. One of the groups reported that a posse was close behind them. A ray of hope burst in Sam's heart like the sun breaking through thunderclouds. Then Maria laid her trap.

She gagged Sam and tied his hands behind his back and left him with Jack and one other rider at the fire. She and the other riders hid in the trees.

Sam watched in helpless agony as Vernon Phelps rode into the campsite, gun drawn, on the alert. Vernon had his nephew with him, plus Shorty from the ranch and Dave Roberts from the hotel. Sam tried desperately to warn his would-be rescuers, to no avail. Jack and the other man stood and raised their hands in mock surrender, and Sam saw the posse relax. Sam gestured with his head toward the trees, but Vernon and the others didn't grasp the warning.

At Maria's signal, the other riders stepped from behind the trees and dashed in from across the creek, surrounding them.

"Drop your guns," she called out. "If you don't, that sack of pig guts Carstairs will get it first."

The weapons fell to the ground.

"All right. Dismount."

After the men were on the ground, Maria walked into the circle, her pistol steady in her hand. She motioned for her men to collect the weapons and take the horses. Then she leveled her pistol at Vernon and ordered the posse to kneel. "How many of you are there?"

"Just us," Vernon answered.

Maria's hand lashed out like a rattlesnake's strike. Her pistol caught Vernon on the side of his head and toppled him over. Blood gushed from a cut that ran from his nose to his ear.

"Get up and don't lie."

Vernon straightened himself up and stared at her.

Looking at Vernon, she placed the barrel of her pistol on the forehead of his nephew, Alexander, and cocked the gun. "How many?"

Sam heard the tremble in Vernon's voice. "There's ten more in two groups following different trails."

"How close are they?"

"Don't know."

She moved her gun slightly and fired it, nicking the bottom of Alexander's right ear. She centered the pistol on his forehead once more.

"How close?"

Vernon straightened his shoulders. "I told you I don't know. We haven't seen any of them in weeks. But if we found you, it won't be long before they do too. You might as well surrender now."

She stared into his face and caressed the trigger. Abruptly, she lifted the gun and released the hammer. Putting it back in her holster, she turned to the men behind her.

"Tie them up. Hands and feet. Leave them kneeling."

She walked back to the fire and poured a cup of coffee. She swallowed some and poured the rest on the ground.

Jack took the cup from her. "What are you going to do with them?"

Maria rubbed her jaw, frowned. "We can't take them with us. They'll just slow us down and cause trouble every chance they get."

She walked back to the four men and stood with her hands

on her hips. Then, without warning, she stepped behind Shorty. She pulled a long knife from her boot, pulled Shorty's head back, and slit his throat in one smooth motion.

Jack took a step toward her, hands outstretched.

"We're going to do this my way," she said as she stepped behind Dave Roberts and cut his throat.

Sam turned his head. He heard Alexander's whimper turn into a gurgle, overridden by Vernon's cry of "No!"

"Make him watch."

One of the men turned Sam's head so he could see where she stood behind Vernon. Vernon's eyes were wide, locked on Sam's. His lips moved in what Sam thought to be silent prayer. Maria grabbed him under his chin and tipped his head back. Sam watched in horror as she murdered a fourth time. Vernon's blood joined that of the others pooling on the packed earth. She wiped her knife clean on Vernon's pant leg before returning the blade to her boot.

The color had drained from Jack's face. "Couldn't you have just left them here? gagged 'em and hidden 'em in the trees?"

"No witnesses." She mounted her horse and waited, drumming her fingers on her thigh, while Jack helped Sam onto his horse. Then she gave her horse a hard kick and galloped ahead. Sam fell in line behind Jack. The others arrayed themselves after them. No one spoke for a long time.

Helplessness, despair, and shame engulfed Sam as he relived those moments, remembered the faces of the men who had died. Joshua always said Shorty would make a good foreman one day. Dave Roberts worked in the hotel like it was his own. Alexander Phelps was young, so young, all his life still ahead of him. And Vernon—the closest thing he had to a best friend. A wise man whose counsel Sam didn't always take. A man who almost made Sam believe God might have a sliver of goodness in Him.

Sam had caused those deaths. His greed and deceitfulness had brought all this on him and now on his family and townspeople. He couldn't stop those deaths and was incapable of avenging them.

Loneliness and fear overwhelmed him.

Maria kicked one of the sleeping men in the ribs and knocked his sombrero off his face. The man reached for the pistol on the blanket next to him, but his anger morphed into fear when he saw Maria standing over him. She prodded him with her boot. "Fix breakfast. We have a long way to go today."

"*Sí*, señora." He scurried to the fire to rekindle it.

Maria woke the other men in the same gruff manner. She ordered two men to ride back down their trail to see if anyone followed. Then she walked to the fire, shaking her head. She checked the coffeepot and nibbled on a leftover biscuit, dipping it into the spattering bacon grease.

Jack walked over and squatted next to her, sliding an arm around her shoulder. She nestled against him.

"I'll be so glad when this is over," he said.

She straightened, her back stiff. "He's got to pay for what he did to Papa."

He stroked her hair. "I know he does."

She nodded and leaned once again on Jack's shoulder.

Jack took the cup of coffee offered by the cook and sipped it, looking over the rim at Sam, an unreadable expression on his face.

Maria stood, brushing her hands on her jeans. "I'm going to go wash." As she walked toward the stream, two of the men turned their heads and watched her go.

"You two!" Jack snapped. Their heads spun around. "Finish eating and then take some grub out to Felipe and Pedro and help them watch our rear."

When they had left, Jack removed Sam's gag and placed a metal plate of food at his feet. Sam tucked in, too hungry to let his misery interfere with his appetite. He noted with grim amusement that he was getting adept at eating with his hands tied.

The men began to break camp. The cook doused the fire and scattered the ashes, took Sam's plate before he was half-way through, and put Sam's gag back in place. Tears stung Sam's eyes as the cook caught a few strands of hair in the knot and pulled the cloth tight.

Sam's heart sank as he watched Jack secure Maria's saddle on Vernon's horse, a tall black mare with a magnificent head and mane. She had claimed it for herself. Sam knew the horse—gentle yet fast, with a heart that would never quit. A fresh wave of grief shot through him at the thought of that she-devil riding the beautiful friend of a good man.

Jack tied Sam to his saddle once more. Sam remembered the salve Lupe made from plants in her garden. He wished he had some now for his chafed wrists and other body parts. His thighs and rear felt rubbed raw, as if someone had used coarse sandpaper on them. His legs felt like lead-filled sacks, unable to give him any support. There was no comfortable position for his back. Pain ranged from a constant dull, throbbing ache to a shooting lance of agony straight up his spine to his head. He concentrated hard on not throwing up in his gag.

They headed south and southwest, deeper into the foothills. The land was barren away from the creek. Sage and prickly pear sprouted hopefully from the sandy earth. Rocks of all shapes and sizes surrounded them. The air had the acrid smell of dust burned by the sun.

Maria led the way with Jack and Sam right behind her. The sound of clopping hooves was all that broke the stillness. They rode all day, keeping a steady canter that covered miles without tiring the horses. There was no more meandering about, no leaving a long and useless trail. *We must be close to their hideout, or else Maria thinks the rest of the posse is close behind.*

They ate their midday meal in the saddle—leftover breakfast with a swig of warm water from their canteens. Maria sat next to Sam while he ate, her gun pointing at his stomach, a silent warning not to call for help.

47

RACHEL STOOD in the Riverbend Cemetery, flanked by her friends Martha and Annabelle. The noon sun beamed on the small crowd gathered around the three graves of the town's Civil War veterans. Two Union and one Confederate, buried side by side.

Martha whispered in her ear. "I hope Luke keeps this short. It's hot out here. At least he remembered his notes."

Rachel suppressed a smile and reached down to squeeze Daniel's shoulders as he shifted from foot to foot in front of her, trying his best not to chase the butterfly that danced nearby. Abigail held a small bouquet of wildflowers. The rest of the schoolchildren were arrayed in an undulating semi-circle around them—boys on the left, girls on the right.

Luke's prayer and sermon were both short and poignant

as he began the ceremony. Mayor Meriweather followed with a speech, his eyes roaming the gathering. When he found Rachel, she smiled. He stammered over his last few words.

Abigail laid her flowers at the base of the weathered board marking one of the graves. Isaac Walters played a wavering rendition of taps on a dented bugle.

A time for the healing of old wounds. Was healing working in her?

Annabelle took her arm as they walked up Main Street. "Pete almost proposed to me last night."

"How do you know?"

Annabelle leaned close, excitement on her face, a flush behind her freckles. "When he walked me to my house after dinner, he was real quiet and fidgety like he gets when he's got something on his mind. Then, at the front door, he took my hand, real formal-like. And he said, 'Annabelle, there's something I want to ask you.' And then a gun went off somewhere and he left."

Rachel laughed with her friend. "He's a deputy. He must answer the call of duty."

"Don't remind me. Anyway, he didn't have to be so relieved about it."

"He'll ask. Don't worry."

"I know." She squeezed Rachel's arm. "Someday someone will be proposing to you."

"I doubt it."

Annabelle stopped and faced her. "Rachel Stone, you can have any man you want. You know that."

"I know they think they can have me, but not for a wife."

"What about Michael Archer?"

Rachel opened her mouth, then closed it. She sighed. "He's nice, but we barely know each other, and he won't be staying long. Besides, I need to keep my mind on my work, build the business. I'm probably better off without a man."

Annabelle rolled her eyes. "Are you trying to convince me or yourself?"

48

MICHAEL WOKE before the others. Clouds had moved in during the night, delaying the dawn. He slipped away from the camp and walked to the stream. Sitting on the bank, he prayed, his voice a soft murmur. He lifted his face to the sky, eyes closed, his Bible against his chest. "Lord, help me be Your instrument today to minister to these men." Peace washed over him like a soft, warm light, driving back the darkness that skulked at the edges of his spirit.

The rest of the camp stirred as the overcast sky took on the rosy color of sunrise. Michael rekindled the fire while Jeremiah put coffee on to boil and prepared breakfast. Frank and Sheriff Davis—Caleb—saddled the horses. Michael joined them and secured the dwindling packs of supplies to one of the animals. Caleb patted the supplies and looked toward the nearby foothills. "Maybe we'll find some deer to help stretch these out a little more."

Frank turned from cinching his saddle. "I wouldn't mind doin' a little huntin'."

Caleb shook his head. "Nah, we best stick together. 'Sides, Thomas'll have to get it with his bow. Can't risk a shot lettin' the kidnappers know where we are."

Michael studied Caleb as the posse gathered around the fire. It had been four days since the two men had prayed together, and the man looked unchanged on the outside. Lines and creases made his face seem long and somber. His heavy-lidded gray eyes reflected the burdens and grief he carried. Michael wished he could open Caleb's head like a jar and pour in all that God had for him, but Caleb would have to learn it as Michael was learning it, one lesson at a time. Rebuilding the foundation of his life brick by brick, making corrections along the way.

"Some eggs and steak and flapjacks would sure taste good about now," Frank said as he spooned beans over his biscuit and bacon. "Wash it down with some good chuck wagon coffee."

"Just close your eyes and imagine," Caleb said. He turned to Michael. "Would you say a blessin' for us?"

Frank halted the spoon an inch from his lips. He canted one bushy eyebrow. "Sheriff, I ain't never heard you ask for blessin' before." He looked at Jeremiah. "If I'd cooked this delicious meal, I'd be insulted."

Caleb shook his head. "I . . . um . . . just feel like we oughta let the good Lord know we thank Him for all He's given us. Go ahead, son."

Michael bowed his head. "Lord, we thank You for this day and for food to nourish our bodies. Thank You for guiding and leading us and sending Your angels to minister to and protect us. We ask You to be with us today. Help us find Mr. Carstairs and bring him home safely. In Jesus' name. Amen."

When he finished, Frank shoveled a spoonful of beans into his mouth. "Caleb, what happened to—?"

Caleb shot him a look from under lowered eyebrows. Frank shrugged. "Oh, well. 'Tain't none of my business anyways."

Caleb met Michael's eyes and smiled.

Old Thomas stood in one fluid motion, his knees cracking just a little. "Caleb, old friend, I do believe you have had a transformation. This is a good thing. May your God bring you comfort and peace and wisdom."

Caleb nodded, and Frank opened his mouth, then closed it and shrugged again. He poured a cup of coffee and spoke to Caleb. "Are we going to push on or wait for Barkston to join us?"

Caleb swallowed his last bite of biscuit. He brushed crumbs off his hands. "Good biscuit, Jeremiah. 'Course, I remember my wife addin' honey to the dough. Made 'em extra sweet." Scratching his chin through his beard, he glanced skyward through half-closed eyes.

"I think we push on," he said, answering Frank's question. "There's no telling where Bill and his men are. With Malachi tracking, he'll get here eventually. The trail from here is pretty hard to miss, so he should be able to catch up to us. If the trail peters out or splits, we can leave him some sign." He pushed to his feet and gave another upward glance. "Hope it don't rain, though."

The group rode out with Old Thomas and Jeremiah in the lead. Caleb, Michael, and Frank followed about a hundred yards behind. They maintained an easy trot for several miles, altering their straight course only to follow the contours of the land as they entered the foothills.

After several hours, they stopped at a small brook to water the horses.

"They sure are makin' this easy," Frank said. "Why do you suppose that is? Think they're leadin' us into a trap?"

Caleb remounted and looked across the brook to where the tracks continued. "Could be. Could be too they're getting close to wherever they're headed and want to get there quick."

Jeremiah said, "They might have panicked after murdering Vernon and the others, or they might think Vernon was the only one following them and now they're safe."

"Could be any of those things," Caleb said. "This outfit is tough to read. We best figure they may be laying an ambush somewhere up ahead and keep our eyes open."

As they rode off again, Frank lagged a little ways behind. Caleb paced his horse to keep in step with Michael. "Thanks for, you know . . . the other night."

"You're welcome."

Caleb tugged his hat lower over his eyes. "I can see now what my wife would talk about—the peace, that feeling like a heavy load's been lifted. It feels strange after all these years, especially since she died. It's like the bitterness just kept building. But that's gone now. It feels good to be able to talk about her without wantin' to bawl my eyes out."

Michael nodded. "I know what you mean. It's a good thing to lay your burdens down."

They rode on until dusk, enjoying the respite the cloud cover provided from the relentless sun. Old Thomas and Jeremiah finally stopped at the top of a small rise that dipped between two taller foothills.

"What do you see?" Caleb asked as the others joined them.

Old Thomas squinted at the sky and then down the other side of the rise. "It is getting dark. These clouds will hide the moon, so the trail will be hard to follow. If they are planning an ambush, the next few miles would be the place to do it. There are plenty of places for them to hide, and we will be moving very slowly."

"I reckon you're right, old friend. Let's ride on a little ways to find a place to camp. It'll have to be a cold camp, and we'll mount a guard again."

At the bottom of the small slope, the trail turned around the hill to their right. A small spring gurgled from the rocks, forming a shallow pool that fed a small green meadow. The men dismounted and tended to the horses, their movements hushed and tense. Michael brushed Buddy and checked his hooves for stones or damage. The others did the same. The packhorse rolled on his back, happy to be released from his burden.

Michael took the first watch with Frank. He held his rifle

across his chest, a round in the firing chamber, his finger on the trigger guard, praying he'd have no need for it. The clouds blotted the stars and dimmed his vision. Every sound seemed magnified and a potential danger. Time crawled. But nothing happened.

After a quick, cold breakfast, they were on their way again.

49

EVEN IF I COULD ESCAPE, I'd never find my way out of here.

Sam looked around, unable to place any landmark. He knew they were somewhere in the mountains, but he'd never been here before. Was anyone still trying to find him? He alternated between hope of rescue and fear that what had happened to Vernon could happen to the others. He didn't want them on his conscience too.

Late in the afternoon a week after the ambush, they scrambled up a steep incline, loose dirt and stones hindering their progress. Jack pulled Sam's horse behind him. After struggling for several minutes, they reached the summit and halted next to Maria. They rode single file on the narrow crest of the ridge for several miles, Sam between Maria and Jack. Yesterday's overcast had evaporated, and the sun now beat down on them relentlessly.

Finally Maria led them off the crest down a gentle slope. The slope leveled off into a trail that took them to another ridge overlooking a lush, verdant meadow. Three streams crossed it, joining into one to flow out of the area to their left. Deer fed at one of the streams, a doe and two fawns, the buck standing watchful guard some distance away. He eyed the riders warily, ready to signal his family at the first sign of danger. Across the stream at the far edge of the meadow, a group of wild goats grazed. It was one of the most beautiful spots Sam had ever seen.

A weathered cabin with a sagging roof stood at the junction of the three streams, looking like it had been abandoned years ago. The whole structure leaned to one side. One good gust of wind might topple it into the stream. Behind it stood a roughly built corral. Two horses nibbled at the grass. A third stood erect, head up, as if it had spotted the intruders on the ridgeline.

Maria motioned for two of the men to remain on guard. She led the rest of the group farther down the ridge to where a path had been worn in the hillside.

There was no sign of human life, but dread rose up in Sam anyway. This, clearly, was their final destination.

Sam rode across the meadow between Maria and Jack, his stomach churning as he eyed the cabin. What waited for him there? He felt dread and also, strangely, a kind of relief. *This is it. It will all be over soon. But how?*

Two men stepped out of the cabin, rifles braced on their hips, fingers on the triggers. Maria, Jack, and Sam stopped a few feet from the building. One of the men on the ground turned and spoke into the cabin. Out of the corner of his eye, Sam saw Maria fidget with the reins of her horse as if trying to keep her hands busy. She bit her lower lip. Jack sat up straighter, expectant.

After a few moments, Sam heard shuffling from inside the cabin. A black oblong pierced the gray walls of the cabin as the door opened wider, squealing on broken hinges.

A figure moved forward into the light, emerging in stages. First a foot, shod in a boot scuffed and scratched from long wear. A left hand grasped a cane in a white-knuckled grip. The cane wobbled as the figure took another step. A tan corduroy shirt over a gaunt frame topped faded dungarees.

In two more steps, the figure emerged from the shadow. An old man stepped into the sunlight—tall and thin with the wasted appearance that came from illness, not choice. His face was creased and weathered, eyes muddy brown and glazed. Sparse gray hair struggled for a foothold on a smooth skull. A ragged salt-and-pepper mustache occupied the upper lip.

"It's good to have you back, Daughter." His husky voice sounded damaged and never healed.

So this is John Higgins. They were the same age, but Higgins looked to be in his eighties, not his early sixties. The man clung to the cane, his breathing labored. Sam expected to see him fall over dead any minute.

Maria's voice cracked as she held back a sob. "It's good to be back, Papa."

Sam couldn't help staring at her. He'd never dreamed such tenderness could come from someone so evil. And he'd certainly never felt such devotion from his own children. Why was that?

Higgins turned to face him. "You remember me, Sam?"

Maria yanked the gag from Sam's mouth. Sam tried to get his jaw to work. "Answer the man!"

Sam tried to speak. His tongue felt like an old woolen sock stuck in his bone-dry mouth.

Higgins laughed, a short, dry chuckle like autumn leaves crinkling underfoot. He took the rifle from one of his men by the door and cocked the hammer. He held the weapon at his waist, pointed at Sam. "Yeah, I expect you do. But I'm not the fine figure of a man I was the last time you saw me. Prison'll do that to a man. People is mighty mean in prison. Even meaner when someone outside is paying them to do their best to make sure someone doesn't get out alive. They tried, Sam, but they couldn't finish the job. I'm sure they told you they killed me, but they lied just to get your money. They stopped trying after I killed one of them with my bare hands."

He stared into Sam's eyes. "Yep, prison can sure change a man." He gestured with the rifle. "Sure am tempted to use this on you right now and get it over with, but we got some business to discuss."

He coughed and spat a reddish brown stream onto the ground.

Maria gasped and jumped from her horse. "Papa!" She put her arms around the old man. "Get a chair."

One of the men brought out a straight-backed chair from the cabin. She settled her father in the chair and glared at

Sam. Contempt and loathing filled her eyes and distorted her face. "You're the reason he's like this. Your lies and scheming put him in prison and almost killed him. And you're going to pay for it."

Her words stung. Could he be responsible for the man John Higgins was now? Yes, he'd connived to get him out of the way, but that was over thirty years ago. Had he damaged the man this much? Had he damaged others?

But what he'd done benefited others, he argued silently, not just himself. The town benefited. Ruth and the children benefited.

Not all the children.

The thought came out of nowhere, almost as if someone else had spoken it. And suddenly he was thinking back to the last time he saw Benjamin. Ben lying under a tree at the edge of the ranch, unconscious, nose bloodied, eye swollen shut. Sam had pinned a note and money to his shirt and left him. He hadn't seen him since, had done his best not to think of him. Even when the letters started coming months ago, he'd burned them.

Who had his treatment of Ben benefited besides himself and his need for a scapegoat?

He hung his head, unaccustomed to this kind of thinking. Was it too late to make amends?

Looking at John Higgins, he was pretty sure it was too late for much of anything.

50

RACHEL PUT AN *X* through the square for Monday on the calendar that hung on the wall over her worktable. She stared at the square for Tuesday, the fourth of June. Her neat handwriting told her Mrs. Phelps was due in for a fitting today.

The rows of *X*s marched across May and into June like a split-rail fence. Almost a month ago the posse had left, Michael with them. All this time and not a word. She hugged herself as goose bumps pimpled her arms. She bit her lower lip. *Lord, where is Your peace?*

Rachel walked around her store. Her mind didn't register what her eyes took in. Without conscious thought, she opened curtains to let in pale sunlight. She arranged bolts of cloth to display their patterns and colors. Her fingers smoothed the fabric but didn't linger as they often did to enjoy the softness of the cotton and the silkiness of the satin. She straightened a display of lace that didn't need it.

Her mind dwelled on Michael, not on her store.

"Father, You know my heart. You know how worried I am, how I need Your peace and strength. Can You guard me? I don't want to be hurt again." She stood still, a bolt of cloth forgotten in her hands. "Please protect Michael. Don't let any harm come to him. Be with Sam Carstairs and the posse and bring them home safe." She paused, just breathing, waiting to know what to pray next. "And when they're home, help me to know what to do about Michael. Because I think I may love him, and I just don't know if I can handle that."

Finally, with that, she felt a little sense of release. Of benediction. "Thank You, Father."

She went into the back room and resumed her work on Mrs. Phelps's dress. Soon, the rhythm of the work soothed and absorbed her. She heard muffled voices in the alley but paid no attention until the back door crashed open.

Mark Carstairs stood in the doorway with two other men behind him.

Rachel froze. She opened her mouth to scream but the sound stuck in her throat. Mark sauntered into the small room, his fingers hooked in his belt. Rachel sensed the arrogance in him, fueled by the whiskey she could smell. She could smell the lust on him as well.

"Well, ain't you a pretty sight." He swaggered up to her. "Sittin' here pretendin' you're just like regular folk. But we know what you were, and I don't think you left it far behind you. I've watched how you walk and bat your eyes at that preacher man you're tryin' to impress."

Before she could speak, he grabbed her wrists and forced his mouth on hers. He pushed her down onto the table.

"Me and the boys figure it's time you got back into the business you're really good at."

He released her wrists and began to tear at her dress. Buttons popped and flew in the air. She raised her hands, her fingers seeking his face and eyes. He tilted his head back. She screamed. He clamped his hand over her mouth and continued to rip at her clothing with the other hand. She brought her legs up to fight him off, but he pulled her to the edge of the table, lifted her dress, and spread her legs. She thrashed against him even as he pressed down on her.

"Lie still, whore." He tore at her undergarments.

Her hands flailed around the table seeking something, anything, to use as a weapon. Fear and rage warred within her. She would not give in to him. No one would take her body again.

He was strong. Too strong. She kicked at him but hit only air. She tried to bite his hand, but he kept her mouth shut.

"You're a feisty one; I'll give you that. You boys better come hold her down before she hurts herself."

Her hand closed on something smooth and metallic. Her scissors. She stabbed at him before the others could get to her, driving the point into his upper arm. He took his hand off her mouth and pulled back his fist, the punch aimed at her face.

She screamed. "God, help me."

She swung the scissors again and plunged them into his chest.

Everything stopped. Rachel brought her hands to her mouth, transfixed, as Mark stood straight, staring at the scissors in his chest. Blood seeped onto his shirt. He looked at her, bewilderment and confusion on his face. He turned white, a dreadful shade of death, and his lips moved. He raised his arm as if to point at her, but it flopped back to his side. His eyes rolled back in his head, and he swayed and fell. His head made a hollow thump when it hit the floor.

Rachel sat up and pulled the remains of her dress about her. The other two men stood dumbfounded, immobilized. All three stared down at Mark, unconscious on the floor.

Pete O'Brien entered through the back door, his gun drawn. Mrs. Phelps stood behind him in the alley. Pete fell to one knee and examined Mark. Then he stood and holstered his gun. "Are ye all right, lass?"

Rachel stared at him, his words incomprehensible. "You're not Michael."

"No, lass, I'm not." He glanced over his shoulder.

Mrs. Phelps entered the room, stepping over Mark as if he were a dozing snake. She slipped her arm around Rachel's shoulders and drew the young woman to her. Rachel welcomed the embrace but couldn't take her eyes off Mark. The blood on his shirt kept spreading. He didn't move.

Her hand went to her mouth again. *Is he breathing?*

She heard Pete speak to the other men. He sounded as if he had a wad of cotton over his mouth. "You two, pick 'im up and take 'im over to Doc Palmer's. Maybe he can patch 'im up. I'll be right there. Both of ye wait there for me."

He turned back to the two women. "By the saints above, Mrs. Phelps, 'tis a good thing you came along when ye did and ran to fetch me. We're lucky we got here in time so it didn't go much further."

Rachel watched the two men lift Mark and carry him out the door. The scissors protruded from his chest, a grim reminder of what she had done.

"Is he dead? Did I kill him?"

51

Sam sputtered and spat as cold water splashed in his face. He shook his head to clear his eyes. Shards of pain sliced through his brain, and shivers rippled through his body in the cool evening air. He moaned.

A fist slammed into his stomach. The hard blow sank deep into his soft flesh. Acid rose in his throat and the coppery taste of blood filled his mouth.

"You're disgusting." He heard the contempt in Maria's voice. He tried to look at her but saw only a blur. Paper rustled. "Are you ready to sign this?"

He forced himself to focus. It was the same paper Higgins had showed him the day they arrived at the cabin—and every day afterward. Precise feminine handwriting instructing Joshua and the bank to prepare the enormous sum of ten thousand dollars in gold to purchase Sam's release, plus a space for Sam's signature. He'd wondered where they got the money figure. Sam wasn't even sure how much he was worth. Didn't matter anyway.

"No." His throat burned. The word croaked out.

She grabbed his hair and lifted his head so he faced her again. More pain. He cried out. Her hand slapped his cheek, and his head snapped back. Pain shot from his skull to the base of his spine.

She brought her face an inch from his. "You will sign it."

He just shook his head.

She released his hair, kicked the inside of his knee, and walked away. Sam sagged against his bonds, wondering how long this could go on.

The first two days, they had tied him to a chair and presented him with the paper to sign. His refusal brought slaps, fists, and a belt used as a whip. The third day, they'd stripped him to the waist and laid him on a bed of stones in front of the cabin, his arms and legs stretched and tied to stakes with leather straps. The leather had been wet when they first tied him. It shrank as it dried and brought new and searing pain to his wrists and ankles. He felt his arms and legs being pulled from his body with excruciating slowness.

Yesterday, they had tied him between two of the posts supporting the porch roof of the cabin. They stretched his arms and tied them just above the height of his head. His shoulders screamed, and pins and needles coursed through his arms like insects in a high-speed race.

Several times a day, he toyed with the possibility of simply signing the paper and getting it all over with. Maybe he did owe John Higgins something. Maybe he didn't want to fight anymore. After all, Ruth was gone. Ben was gone. Mark was more or less a lost cause. And Joshua—if Joshua ever found out about Lupe, Sam didn't know what he'd do.

So why am I holding on? He didn't even know anymore. Plain old cussedness, probably. He just couldn't let them win. Not now.

Sam dozed, his chin on his chest. Several loud clangs startled him. A woman stood a few feet away, rattling a metal spoon around the inside of a triangle. She wore a dirty, faded dress with one sleeve torn away and the other half-ripped from the shoulder, the skirt torn, the front ripped from her neck to the top of her breasts. Snarled blonde hair, stringy with oily dirt, framed her expressionless face. Pale eyes peered out dull and lifeless from blackened sockets, and bruises mottled her mouth and cheeks. Once a day she brought him a meal of cold rice and beans and a cup of water.

He'd tried to speak to her a few times, but she never answered. Though not bound, she was as much a prisoner as Sam, a slave used by the men to cook, wash their clothes, and provide whatever other services they required.

She turned to go back in the cabin. Their eyes met.

"Run," Sam croaked. "Go for help."

She stared at him. *Does she even understand English?* He jerked his head to indicate the entrance to the valley, the only means of escape he saw. She looked down the valley, then around the camp, eyes twitching, then back to him. She shook her head, the slightest movement, before disappearing back into the house.

Sam studied the camp. Anything to take his mind off the pain. Maybe he might even find a way to escape. With the blonde woman's refusal, escape seemed even more impossible, but he had to do something.

Over the several days at the cabin, he had counted at least fifteen men working for John and Maria. All were as lean as the cowhands who worked his ranch. He knew the type—used to long hours and hard work, tempered by physical labor and danger, ready for a fight, ruthless. Maria had chosen her gang well.

Jack, John, and Maria slept in the cabin. The rest camped out in the triangle formed where the creeks came together. He'd have to be as quiet as a field mouse to slip past them. One always guarded the cabin, and Maria kept two or three on guard at the entrance to the valley.

There had to be another entrance. Maybe over the ridges that formed the side walls of the valley. Riders patrolled them and, he assumed, the wooded area behind the cabin. Not an airtight prison, but he would need a great deal of luck to get out.

He tugged at the bonds that held him to the posts. The leather chewed into his wrists and pain shot the length of his arms. Forget luck. He'd need some sort of miracle just to get out of his bonds.

Mealtime brought most of the gang together. Sam heard murmurs of conversation broken by occasional laughter. Other than a furtive glance from time to time, they ignored him. Sam found it ironic that some of this group who obviously planned to kill him would stop and pray over their food and cross themselves.

As he looked at them gathered for the meal, he realized he hadn't seen Jack since the day after they arrived. He remembered Jack had ridden off with another man but had yet to return.

The blonde woman brought a plate with beans and rice to him. Some of the rice seemed to be moving. She lifted a spoonful toward his mouth.

"Wait."

The blonde froze at the sound of Maria's voice.

Maria stood in front of Sam. She held up the paper. "Will you sign?"

He shook his head.

Maria took the food from the blonde woman and flung it to the ground. "No food or water until you sign."

52

Pete O'Brien hesitated, his hand on the doorknob. No matter how many times he came to this small brick-fronted building on a side street near the hotel, he had to brace himself for what lay on the other side of the door. The smell of ether and the sight of instruments and bandages brought it all back—the clamor and confusion of the field hospitals, the stench of rotting flesh, the screams of wounded and dying men.

He shook off the memories and walked in. The waiting room stood empty, its straight-backed chairs lining the walls like mourners at a funeral. Curtainless windows overlooked the street. The whole room felt stark, as if designed to keep patients uncomfortable while they waited.

Pete made his way to the examining room down the hall. Mark Carstairs lay on the long, narrow, padded table, moaning like a newborn calf caught in a thicket. He tossed his head from side to side. Blood seeped from the wound on his bare chest, his shirt spread open like a bizarre butterfly. Doc Palmer's rotund body hovered over him. The physician guided a needle and thread through Mark's skin to bind the wound. The ash on the cigar clamped in Doc's mouth dangled over the wound like an apple about to fall from the tree.

Pete looked away from the sight. His eyes rested on Doc's bookcase, jammed with texts and journals without any sense of order that Pete could detect. He wondered how the doctor ever found anything in here. A sea of papers flooded Doc's rolltop desk, leaving only an island of bare wood in the center for Doc to write on.

The area with the counter and glass-fronted cabinets along the wall opposite the door contradicted the disorder in the rest of the room. It was clean, almost pristine. Instruments gleamed. Bottles and vials behind the glass stood in rows like soldiers in formation, their labels squared to face front.

One of the men who had brought in Mark now slumped in Doc's office chair, a sheen of sweat on his blood-drained face. He looked as if he might slide onto the floor at any moment. The other man leaned the upper half of his body out the window.

Pete kept his eyes averted. "How is he, Doc?"

The doctor continued to stitch. "Oh, he'll live, but it was close—very close. A quarter inch or so to the left, and she would have got his heart. Might have punctured his lung too. Definitely cracked a couple of ribs. Must be one strong girl."

"That she is, I wager, havin' to fight off these hooligans." Pete pointed to the other men. "What happened to these two?"

Doc focused on his patient but gestured with his head. The ash fell from the cigar and landed in Mark's navel. "Apparently these two brave cowboys and intimidators of women can't stand the sight of blood. One fainted, and I told the other one to stick his head out the window because I didn't want him puking all over my floor."

"Well, I best get these two lads over to the jail, and then I'll come back and talk to ye about Carstairs."

"Take your time. He ain't going anywhere soon." Doc did not look up from his patient as he worked the needle and thread. He ignored the gray cylinder of spent tobacco that lay a few inches away.

Pete took a pitcher of water from the counter and poured it on the face of the man in the chair. He jumped and sputtered, brushing the water from his face with both hands.

"Whatcha do that for? You tryin' to drown a man?" He looked at Doc and Mark, and for a moment, Pete thought he would faint again.

"McCreedy," Pete said to the other man, "get yer head in from that window. Think what yer poor sainted mother would do if she saw the shenanigans ye was gettin' up to. She'd be spinning in her grave, an' the priests and sisters'd be wearing out their rosary beads prayin' for yer soul. Now, help your pal Owens over to the jail. Yer both under arrest."

"What for?" Owens protested. "We didn't do nothin'."

"Ye were about to. Now git."

McCreedy came over, his head turned so he wouldn't have to look at Mark. He helped Owens stand and draped the man's arm around his neck.

Owens pushed him away. "I can do it myself. I don't need no help from a dumb mick that can't keep his lunch down." He staggered to the door that led to the kitchen. Pete took him by the shoulders and pointed him toward the other door.

Minutes later, Pete locked the cell door. Owens sat on the bottom bunk, his head down almost to his knees, his face pale and drawn.

McCreedy grabbed the bars and glared at Pete. "You can't lock us up. We didn't do nothin'. It was all Mark. He just wanted to have some fun with that gal."

"He weren't planning no fun, and ye know it. Ye were gonna help 'im do it and probably have some yerselves. I'm ashamed we're of the same race. No wonder the English think we're baboons. Now sit yerself down and be quiet. I'll be back directly."

McCreedy mumbled something as Pete closed the door that separated the cells from the main office. He tossed the keys in the bottom drawer of Caleb's scarred desk and had to jiggle the old, warped wood several times before it would slide back in. *Man's worked for this town as long as Caleb has, and they won't give him a decent desk.*

On his way back to Doc Palmer's, Pete stopped at Charlie Atkins's carpentry shop across from the hotel. The smell of fresh-cut wood and paints evoked the memory of his grandfather's workshop in Dublin, where the old man labored with fastidious precision to make fancy furniture for the English lords. The wood curls scattered on Charlie's floor reminded Pete of the blonde curls of his baby sister, who'd died during the famine. He shook away the melancholy memory.

"What can I do for you, Deputy?" Charlie appeared from behind a set of plain sawdust-coated curtains that divided his workshop. The carpenter ran a hand over his bald head, then stroked his luxurious, curving mustache.

"There was some trouble over at Miss Rachel's dress shop. I need you to put a new knob and lock on her back door. Bill it to Mark Carstairs."

Charlie didn't blink. "Still up to his old tricks, huh. Did he hurt Miss Rachel?"

"Don't know. Mrs. Phelps is taking her back to the parsonage."

Pete turned to go but stopped with his hand on the doorknob. He took a five-dollar piece out of his vest pocket and tossed it to the carpenter. "I want ye to build a new desk for Caleb and bill the town for what that doesn't cover."

Charlie flipped the coin. "He'll have it in a week."

"Thanks, Charlie."

As he walked to the hotel, Pete smiled and imagined the look on the mayor's face when he got the bill for the desk. He went into the dining room and arranged for supper for the prisoners. Then he walked back to Doc's house to check on Mark Carstairs.

He was surprised to find the door to the examining room open. Doc always kept it closed when he had a patient. He drew his pistol and peered in. Doc sprawled on the floor, an ugly gash on the back of his head. Blood matted his gray hair and dripped onto the floor. Mark Carstairs was gone. *That fool. Now he's just gone and made it worse on himself.*

Pete holstered his gun and grabbed a cloth from the

counter. He bent down to the doctor and dabbed at the wound. Doc groaned, and his eyelids fluttered. He reached out his hands, and Pete helped him sit up. Doc looked at the cloth and probed his scalp with his fingers.

"Doesn't seem too bad." His voice was weak and soft. "Sure does feel like a pack of mules had a hoedown in my head, though."

"What happened, Doc? I didn't think Mark was in any shape to do something like this."

Doc shook his head. "He didn't. Two men came in and told Mark to come with them. I tried to tell them he was in no condition to be moved. I guess one of them didn't care for my medical opinion and whacked me with his gun."

"Do ye know who they were?"

Doc shook his head, then winced. "They had bandannas over their faces. I didn't even see which way they went."

"I've got to go look for 'em. Will ye be all right?"

"I'll live. Just give me that bowl of water off the counter so I can start cleaning myself up." He put his hand on Pete's arm. "Deputy, he's in bad shape. He shouldn't be out riding for at least a week. Find him soon or he might not make it."

The door to Doc's kitchen stood open. Pete drew his gun and peered over the threshold. Empty. The back door stood open. He crossed over to it and scanned up and down the alley that ran behind Doc's house. At the foot of the porch steps, he saw where horses had been tethered. Drops of blood dotted the porch and steps.

Pete sighed and kicked at the dirt. He dreaded having to break the news to Joshua.

53

DIFFERENT TERRAIN. More hills as they neared the mountains. Like blind men, the posse probed the unfamiliar surroundings. They no longer had the far vision of the plains where a figure on the horizon was visible miles away. Here, hills confined and constrained. Trees and boulders provided too many hiding places. Heads turned constantly, and eyes strained to catch the smallest sign of warning.

Lord, protect us, Michael prayed. *Open our eyes to see danger.*

As always, Old Thomas led the way, his gaze fixed on the ground. Michael and the other men formed a ragged line across the trail behind him. Caleb and Jeremiah rode the outside flanks with Michael and Frank between.

Michael scanned ahead and above them. He wondered if the others were as frightened as he was. Did they feel the tension as much as he did?

Jeremiah Turner showed no outward signs. His rifle lay across his saddle, his hand resting on it, his body moving in unison with his mount's gait. Caleb rode ramrod straight, his brow furrowed in concentration, his right hand on his pistol handle. Frank's head swung back and forth like the pendulum on a clock, eyes focused upward.

The smell of leather and sweat mingled with the faint scent of pine as they moved into one of the small evergreen groves that dotted the hillsides. Old Thomas stopped in the shade and drank from his canteen.

He turned as the others joined him. "Let us . . ." His eyes narrowed suddenly, and he nudged his horse back out on the trail. He stood in his stirrups and peered through the trees, his hand shading his brow. He pointed back the way they had come. "Riders."

Michael saw nothing. But he knew the Indian wouldn't imagine such a thing, so he squinted and peered again, cupping his hands to shade the sun.

There. Several miles back, a smudge of light brown touched a sky bleached almost white where it met the horizon. His stomach lurched, and his mouth went dry. His right leg tingled at the feel of the rifle in the scabbard, reminding him a tool of death lay within his reach.

Jeremiah lifted his rifle so that it pointed skyward, the butt on his thigh, his finger on the trigger. Frank slid his pistol from the holster and cocked the hammer.

Caleb held up his hand. "Y'all take it easy, men. Let's see what we're dealin' with." He took out the spyglass and watched for several seconds. He closed it with a snap and returned it to its case in his saddlebag. "It's Barkston. We'll wait here for him. Frank, ride out and tell him to come in slow. We don't want that dust drawin' any extra attention."

Michael leaned over in the saddle before his light-headedness caused him to tumble. After a couple of deep breaths, he dismounted and joined Old Thomas and Caleb to watch the riders approach. He noticed that Jeremiah scrutinized the trail ahead, rifle ready across his chest.

Hope surged in Michael's heart as the riders drew closer. "It looks like they're all right."

"Yep," the sheriff said. "I count five riders, and they all seem to be sittin' straight. Now we can go on together and not worry about runnin' into each other when the shootin' starts."

Michael felt the blood drain from his face. "I pray it doesn't come to that."

Caleb placed his hand on Michael's shoulder and squeezed. "After what they did to Vernon and the others, I don't think they'll come peaceful-like. Are you up for a fight, Reverend?"

Michael swallowed his irritation at the name the men had taken to calling him. He hesitated. *God help me.* "I said I wouldn't let you down."

Caleb patted him on the shoulder. "Good. I'm goin' to need you." He paused. "Ever kill anyone?"

The memory of his father coming at him flashed through his mind. "I don't think so." He clenched his fists and hurried to add, "I've been in a few fights, but no one ever died from them that I know of."

Caleb looked at him, eyes narrowed, lines deep around his mouth. "Someday, you're gonna have to tell me what all happened to you."

Michael nodded. "Someday."

He resumed watching the riders, sensing that Caleb still studied him out of the corner of his eye.

Barkston and his group approached at a slow walk—the riders covered in dust, the horses rimmed with dried sweat on their flanks and haunches. Michael wondered what they all must look like after several weeks of riding with few opportunities to wash clothes and bathe. Barkston's large shoulders drooped. All the men looked pinched and shriveled with fatigue.

Caleb and Barkston exchanged the brief greetings of men who had ridden together for years.

"Glad you caught up to us," Caleb said.

Barkston straightened his shoulders and touched the brim of his hat with his finger. "Yeah. It took us a while." His voice boomed like a bass drum even in a normal tone. "Those riders we were following led us on a pretty wild trip. If it wasn't for Malachi here, I know we woulda lost them a long time ago."

"Same here," Caleb said. "Old Thomas kept us on the trail when there wasn't a trail to see."

Barkston scanned the men and jerked his thumb over his shoulder. "From the signs back at that creek a ways, it looks like Vernon got to them first."

Caleb leaned over and spat on the ground, his grief simmering in every movement. He cleared his throat and spat again. "Yep. The kidnappers must've laid an ambush, caught 'em, and murdered 'em in cold blood. Slit their throats, all four of 'em."

Harold Miller and Martin stirred in their saddles. "Let's get after 'em," Martin said, revenge in his voice.

"Hang on there, son." Caleb held up his hand. "We'll catch 'em, but we'll do it careful. I don't want to lose any more men. There's at least eight of 'em, and we know they're killers, and they still have Sam. We're goin' to go slow because I don't want to ride into an ambush like Vernon did."

He turned his attention to the others. "Malachi, go up with Old Thomas and help him track. Mr. Turner, Michael, Martin—you ride lookout for 'em. Keep your eyes open for trouble. The rest of you take a rest here. We'll catch up with the trackers in a little bit."

54

RACHEL SAT next to Martha at the kitchen table, her hands twisted in a handkerchief in her lap. She stared into her untouched cup of tea. A shawl draped over her shoulders provided a modicum of modesty over her torn dress and undergarments. Esther Phelps sat across from them, her glasses smudged, her large, work-worn hands resting on an open Bible. From the living room, the grandfather clock sounded the quarter hour.

Rachel stiffened at Martha's attempt to embrace her. She turned her head away.

Several minutes passed. Rachel wanted to be alone, but she dared not face the emptiness of her room. The memory of Mark's attack stabbed at her. Other scenes flashed through her mind—men wanting to be as rough, playing out some fantasy. Red Mary standing in the background, laughing, encouraging the men, her enforcer Scar joining in.

Esther cleared her throat. "It says here in the Psalms, 'Because thou hast made the Lord, which is my refuge, even the most High, thy habitation; there shall no evil befall thee, neither shall any plague come nigh thy dwelling. For he shall give his angels charge over thee, to keep thee in all thy ways—'"

Rachel's head snapped up. "Really?" She spoke through clenched teeth, the sarcasm oozing like black tar. "I can't see that Mark Carstairs encountered any angels on the way to my shop. And I'd say that evil came pretty close today." A single tear leaked from her eye.

She turned to Martha. "Maybe Mark's right. Maybe whoring is all I'm good for and this little . . . *experiment* of yours is a failure." Bitterness and sarcasm made *experiment* sound like a curse.

Rachel rose from the table and rushed out the back door. Martha called her name, but she ignored it. She hesitated in the middle of the yard. Where to run to? She shucked off the shawl, hugged herself, headed for the barn.

Sunshine poked her head over the railing of her stall and whinnied. Rachel opened the gate and wrapped her arms around the mare's neck, burying her face in the horse's mane. Her body shook as sobs poured from her. Sunshine nickered gently and nuzzled her back.

A few minutes later, someone touched her shoulder. She turned and threw her arms around Martha, sinking into the warm tenderness of her embrace.

55

THE DOOR TO THE SHERIFF'S OFFICE slammed into the wall, the noise like a rifle shot. Pete O'Brien jumped. His pen scratched across the report in front of him, leaving an inky trail through half the words. His hand grabbed his pistol from its holster on the desk as Joshua Carstairs stomped into the room. Spurs jangled to the beat of his boots on the wooden floor. Pete laid the pistol down.

Joshua loomed over the desk. "What's this about my brother disappearing? I thought you had him under arrest. Can't you keep your eye on one good-for-nothin' lousy excuse for a cowboy?"

Pete sighed, wishing he could trip a lever and just drop right through the floor, chair and all. It would be nice to have a leprechaun's tunnel underneath. He hoped he projected an image of calm and control, although he knew he possessed neither.

He nodded toward a straight-backed chair opposite the desk. "Sit ye down, Joshua. I was just about to ride out there, soon as Rollins gets here to relieve me."

Joshua tossed his hat on the desk as he sat down. He ran his hands through his thick black hair, his blue eyes boring into Pete. "Avery came in a while ago and told me Mark had given him the slip out at the ranch. Left him feeling like a fool. He figured the boy was headin' for town to have some of what Mark calls fun. So he gets here and finds out Mark tried somethin' with that dressmaker gal and ended up at Doc's office . . . and then disappeared from there. What happened?"

Pete clasped his hands together on the desk, inspired by the image of Caleb, who always seemed to maintain control no matter what the situation. *Does Caleb's stomach do flip-flops like this?* "Mark and a couple of his pals had in mind to, um, assault Miss Stone in the back of her shop."

"Dang fool."

"Are you referrin' to Mark or Miss Stone?"

Joshua's head snapped back. He leaned forward in the chair, his hands on the edge of the desk. "Why, Mark, of course. Why'd you ask somethin' like that?"

Pete kept his voice calm and his hands clasped. *Stay in control.* "Just makin' sure that Mark's attitude toward women isn't a family trait, as we say."

Joshua touched the ring on his left hand. "It ain't anymore. Not with me anyway." He folded his arms across his chest and crossed an ankle over a knee. "Now tell me about Mark."

"Miss Stone stabbed 'im with a pair of scissors. I showed up right after it happened. I had his buddies bring him to

312

Doc's. Then I put the buddies in here. When I went back to check on Mark, he was gone." Pete took a deep breath. "Two men pistol-whipped Doc and took Mark out the back way. They were long gone by the time I got there."

"So what're you gonna do about it?"

Pete wished once more for that magic lever. He turned back to Joshua. "It galls me to say this, but I don't think there's much I can do right now. I can't go after 'em because that'd leave the town too short of lawmen. Most of the best men are already out on the posse, searchin' for yer pa, and I got no idea which way they went. I doubt even Malachi or Old Thomas could find the trail. Besides, I think this might be connected to your father's kidnapping."

Joshua stared at him. Pete returned his gaze, grateful the other man couldn't see his knees shaking under the desk. Pete did not want to fight him.

Joshua seemed to struggle inside. His jaw muscles twitched. He looked right at Pete, but the deputy sensed that Joshua's mind saw other things. Finally the man gave a quick, sharp move of his head, then sighed and relaxed in the chair.

He's made a decision.

Joshua sat back and picked up his hat. He gazed at his silver ring as he spun the hat in his hand. "I expect you're right, but I hate to admit it. I've got no use for the boy myself, but I'd hate to have to face Pa if anything happened to him. Did he hurt Miss Stone?"

"Roughed her up a bit—she's gonna have some bruises and scratches. She stabbed him before he got much further. But there's no tellin' what he did to her mind. She was pretty upset. I had Mrs. Phelps take her back to the parsonage. I'm goin' up there in a wee bit to see how she's doing and let her know Mark's been taken."

Joshua scratched his chin. "I'll send Lupe over too. Miss Stone's been makin' a dress for her, so they've gotten friendly. Besides, Lupe don't have much use for Mark either."

He walked to the door, then turned back to Pete. "Who were the other two with Mark?"

"Owens from the livery stable and Dan McCreedy."

Joshua's mouth gaped. "McCreedy? McCreedy from my place?"

"The very same. A disgrace to his race, he is."

"Where is he?"

Pete jerked his thumb in the direction of the cells. Joshua opened the door that led to the cells. "McCreedy?"

A voice answered in the distance. "That you, boss? You come to get me out?"

Joshua looked at Pete and shook his head. "Not too bright, is he? And I hired him." He turned back toward the cells. "McCreedy, you're fired. I don't want you back on the ranch again. I'll send your gear into town tomorrow."

Joshua settled his hat on his head and walked out. "Good night, Deputy. I'll be at the hotel with Lupe if you need me."

"Good night, Joshua."

As Pete closed the door to the cell area, he overheard McCreedy speak to Owens. "I'm gonna kill Mark Carstairs for gettin' me into this."

Pete shook his head as he walked back to the desk. "Nope, not too bright."

56

PETE STARED into the sputtering lamp. He adjusted the wick without thinking about it, his mind elsewhere. *What a mess. Way to go, ye dumb mick. Way to let yer boss down. Can't even keep one cowboy under control.*

Someone knocked on the door. One of the waiters from the hotel came in carrying a tray with two covered plates. "Supper for your prisoners, Deputy."

Pete picked up his pistol from the desk and led the waiter to the cell area. "You two back against the wall," he barked.

The two complied. When the waiter left, Pete stayed in the room.

"I don't like somebody watchin' me eat," McCreedy said.

"I'd rather watch pigs at the trough than you two, but somebody's got to count the utensils. So just hurry up and eat."

The men ate in silence. McCreedy cast sullen glares at

Pete. *Go ahead and try something, ye big ox. I feel like hittin' someone, so just give me a reason.* As if he read the deputy's mind, McCreedy turned his head and focused on his food. When they were finished, Pete once again made them stand against the back wall while he removed the plates and made sure all the knives and forks were present.

"How long you gonna keep us locked up?" Owens's nasally whine reminded Pete of English lords complaining about their fox hunts.

"Ain't decided yet. 'Twas a pretty serious crime ye lads were involved in. I might just have to keep ye here till the judge comes in a couple or three weeks."

Owens grabbed the cell bars. "A couple of weeks? I'll lose my job. We was just havin' a little fun, gettin' a free sample afore she started sellin' agin."

Pete advanced to the cell door in one stride, the tray balanced in one hand, his pistol in the other, cocked and pointed at Owens's stomach. "She wasn't selling nothin' 'cept dresses. I hear you talk about Miss Stone like that again, and it may be the last thing ye say for a long time."

Owens backed up several steps. Pete thought the man might faint again. "Just shut up, and ye might get out of here sooner than later."

The tray of plates rattled as he carried it into the outer office and placed it on the desk. He reached for the coffeepot on the potbellied stove. The pot clattered against the side of his mug, and coffee spilled on his hand. He gripped the mug with white knuckles. One more word, and he would have shot that man.

The door opened. Annabelle walked in. "Oh, good, I was hoping . . . Pete, what's the matter? What happened? Are you sick?" She put down the cloth-wrapped package she carried and placed the palm of her hand on his forehead. "No fever." She stroked his hair and caressed his neck. She lifted his chin to see his face. "What is it, Pete?"

"I'm just sick of the kinds of people I have to deal with sometimes." He motioned toward the cells.

Annabelle rested her hands on his shoulders, her round face full of concern. "I don't know what to say. I wish I had some words to encourage you. But there are bad people in the world. I just want you to know that I appreciate you being willing to protect us from them."

Pete looked up at her, shocked. "You are? I thought ye didn't like the idea of me being a lawman."

She bit her lower lip. "I'd rather you weren't, but I know it's what you want, and it's what God wants you to be."

God again. Will she ever let it go? He decided to change the subject. "Did ye hear what happened to yer friend Rachel today?"

Annabelle sat down in the chair across from Pete. "I've just come from there. Rachel's still upset. She was even talking earlier about going back to her old profession. Now she won't talk—just kind of sits there, staring off into space—but at least she'll let us pray for her. Martha and Mrs. Phelps are still with her. Lupe Carstairs came in just as I was leaving." She lifted the cloth from the package. "Martha sent you some supper."

The sight of the plate of steak and potatoes and a thick

slice of apple pie set his stomach rumbling. "Praise be. That Miss Martha sure takes good care of people." He started to cut the steak. "Can ye sit with me a bit?"

"I'm going back to the church. Pastor Luke called a prayer meeting." She kissed the top of his head. Her soft brown eyes seemed to search his soul. She took his face in her hands and kissed him. Her lips lingered.

"I love you, Peter O'Brien." She left, her skirt swishing through the door like a summer breeze through the pines. He looked at the piece of steak impaled on his fork, hesitant to spoil the taste of her lips.

57

An HOUR LATER, Pete paced the floor. The half-finished meal sat on the desk, congealed into an unappealing lump. His mind raced in turmoil at the cruelty men could inflict on each other. What had Rachel ever done to warrant the treatment Mark Carstairs gave her? Pete knew others in town talked of her past, but they wouldn't do what Mark did. And why the kidnappings? Why beat on Doc? None of this made any sense.

He thought of Annabelle and her church and the peace she always seemed to have. *How does she do that? And why didn't that peace protect Rachel? If God was as good as Annabelle says He is, why did all these bad things happen?*

But Annabelle had something to say about that. What was it? *"There is evil in the world because of man's sin and free will, but God, if you turn to Him, can turn all things to good."*

Pete couldn't quarrel with what Annabelle said about sin and evil. And he knew man sure couldn't keep evil away by himself. There was too much of it, and too many men and women willing to cooperate with it.

But what about the "turning all things to good" part? Could that be true?

The morning they shared breakfast, Michael Archer had talked like he had a personal acquaintance with God. He'd talked of God's love and said He wanted to be close to His people. Was that possible? The image didn't agree with what Pete remembered about God from his childhood.

Was that what Martha and Luke Matthews had that helped them keep going when they first got here and Sam Carstairs opposed them? They didn't moan and complain. Luke just kept visiting the farms and ranches, talking with the people, helping out where he could. Now over half the town attended his church. And now they were gathering people at the church every night to pray for Sam and the posse. Pete had to admit that things seemed calmer since the Matthews family came.

The office grew too small and confined for the energy that churned inside him. He picked up his hat, threw the cell keys in the drawer, and walked out into the night. Whatever he passed on the streets registered only in the periphery of his mind. His inner dialogue continued. Frustration grew as the questions and debate failed to produce answers.

He found himself at the end of the boardwalk. He turned around. He didn't remember passing any of the buildings or people. Ahead, the church glowed with a soft luminescence in the pale starlight. A golden glow lit the windows and spilled out the open doorway onto the top step. Other than for funerals, he had never entered the building. He mounted the steps, his tread light. *Why am I doing this? There are no answers for me here.* Something pulled at him, drawing him.

People gathered in the pews at the front. They knelt, some with heads bowed and hands clasped. Others lifted their faces to the ceiling. Pete spotted Annabelle's pink bonnet to the right, bent low over the pew in front of her.

Luke Matthews knelt on the floor in front, his back to the people. Most everyone prayed on their own, some loud, some with barely a whisper. The voices rose in a babble he couldn't understand. *Is this what it sounds like to God? No wonder things are a mess down here.*

He wanted to run, but his feet wouldn't move. He sat in the last pew and watched, trying to understand. After several minutes, the praying tapered off and silence crept over the room. No one moved until Luke stood and turned. "Thank you all for coming and for your faithfulness and dedication. We believe as the Bible tells us that our fervent prayers will avail much. We are in agreement for the quick and safe return of the posse and Mr. Carstairs and Mark. And we are in agreement for the healing of Rachel Stone and Mark Carstairs. We'll meet again tomorrow at the same time. God bless you all."

The people stood and filed out, some engaged in soft, murmured conversations. Some lingered to share a few words with Luke. Several smiled and greeted Pete as they passed. He looked for Annabelle, but she had slipped out the side door without even seeing him.

Luke followed the others down the aisle. "Good evening, Deputy. I'm glad you could join us." He extended his hand.

Pete shook hands with the pastor, feeling like he was violating some sacred commandment. You never touched a priest, not even to shake hands, unless he was a relation. "Evening, Fa—I mean, Reverend. Hope I didn't disturb yer meeting."

Luke smiled. "You didn't. What brought you in here tonight?"

Pete scratched the back of his head. "Don't know. I've had a lot on my mind today, and this place seemed so peaceful in the starlight. I thought I might be able to clear my head."

"Were you?"

"Huh?"

"Able to clear your head?"

Pete's fingers danced on the brim of the hat he held in front of him. "Not really, if ye don't mind my sayin' so. Comin' here just seemed to add more questions."

Luke gestured to the pew. "I have some time if you want to talk. I'd take you over to the parsonage, but Martha and Annabelle and Lupe Carstairs are tending to Rachel there."

Pete looked over his shoulder at the open doors as he settled into the pew. They beckoned with the call of his world. He could still escape. He put his hat on to signal he didn't plan on staying. "I need to get back on patrol."

Luke sat in the pew in front of him and turned so he could face Pete. "I understand. Stay as long as you can. We can always make some time to get together later." The man's voice was warm with the compassion and gentleness and strength Annabelle had told him about.

Pete sat on the edge of the seat as part of his mind told him to walk out. His eyes darted around the sanctuary while he wondered where to begin or what to say. He felt like a schoolboy asked to recite his lesson. Finally he decided to go for safe ground. "How's Miss Rachel?"

A frown passed across Luke's brow. "Physically, she's in pain from scratches and bruises. She'll recover from those in a few days." He rubbed his chin. "It's hard to say how she's doing emotionally and spiritually. I'd say she's very fragile right now. The ladies are praying for her and doing whatever else they can to help her. We're believing she'll be fine, but it may take some time."

Pete licked his lips, which felt dry as sand. "Does she know Mark Carstairs has been kidnapped?"

Luke nodded. "She blames herself for that too. We're trying to help her see that Mark put himself in danger by the choices he made."

"Do you think she'll be all right with that?"

Luke rubbed his jaw. "With prayer and patience, I think she will be. She's under a spiritual attack right now. We're standing with her, helping her to be strong."

Pete felt a frown crease his face. "What do you mean, 'spiritual attack'?"

Luke studied his hands. After a moment, he sighed. "I mean Satan is attacking her at the foundation of her faith. He's trying to get her to believe that she's no good, that she only got what she deserved, and she might as well go back to her old way of living because she'll never be able to escape it."

Frustration crept over Pete's mind. "But how do ye fight an attack like that? How do ye fight the devil?"

"Prayer and the blood and the name of Jesus. Jesus will never let you go once you accept Him as your Savior. No matter what you do, He's always ready to forgive you and bring you back into His fold."

"Simple as that, eh?" Pete couldn't keep the skepticism out of his voice. "Just pray to Jesus, and everything'll be all right?"

Luke leaned forward. "It will if the person believes. Deputy, it all comes down to believing that Jesus died for our sins and that through His death we are forgiven and cleansed and can walk in eternal life with Him. We can't do anything by ourselves to earn salvation. All we can do is accept Him as our Lord and Savior."

"Beggin' yer pardon, but I just can't see that it makes all that much difference. I still see people who are Christians do bad things or get attacked for no reason. Like the little Simmons boy who died of the fever last week and Miss Rachel today and all my folks back in Ireland dyin' of famine. An' the war—that was really bad, and Christian men on each side, fightin' each other. That don't make no sense to me."

Luke didn't say anything. And suddenly Pete couldn't stop talking.

"Sometimes when my Annabelle talks about Jesus, He seems too good to be true, especially with all the evil I see even in this little town. Ye can't imagine what goes on in the saloons and back rooms around here. And then I see some of the same men goin' to church on Sunday morning, acting like they're clean as just-washed laundry, when the night before they was drinkin' and cussin' and whorin' like there was no tomorrow.

"I guess it's hard for me to see God being Someone who really cares for us. I think He just set it all in motion and then sits back to see what happens. I remember the priests back in Ireland telling us to be careful because ye never know what God's gonna do. He's just looking for any opportunity to punish you for every little sin."

Pete stopped, breathless after the rush of words. Anger churned, but he pushed it down. The pastor believed and preached all those lies just like the priests did. No sense in taking it out on him.

"Let me ask you this." Luke ran his hand along the back of the pew. "Why do you care about people?"

Pete scratched his head, bewildered. He felt like he had back when the nuns tried to teach him Latin. "What do you mean?"

Luke smiled. "Well, I know you care for Annabelle in a special way. I can see it when you're with her and in how you talk about her. I can hear in your voice that you care about Rachel. You care about the people in this town—otherwise, why would you risk your life to protect them? You even care about Mark Carstairs, and you feel bad he was kidnapped. That goes beyond just feeling guilty because it happened on your watch. At some level, you care about him and you want him returned safe. So why do you think that is?"

Pete exhaled and adjusted his hat, pulling the brim lower on his forehead. "I don't know how to answer that. I think people have a right to live free and safe. I'm thinkin' some of us have to step up to be the protectors and the keepers of the law."

"So you want to help make things right for people?"

"Aye, I guess that's one way to put it."

"God's the same way. He cares for people, and He wants them to be free to care for Him. He wants their love to be genuine. He doesn't want to force them to love Him. Because He gave us freedom, we can make choices that go against what is best for us. God wants to protect us and make things right, but He can only do that to the extent that we let Him."

"So why didn't He protect Miss Rachel? Why didn't He protect the doc?"

Luke smiled. "He did protect Rachel today. He gave her the strength to fight off Mark, and He arranged for you to arrive at the right time to take control before it got worse. I don't know about Doc Palmer, although I know he's doing all right, and it could've been worse. But the point is, for God to make things right, He needs that opening from us to work in us. When we give it to Him, He can do marvelous things even when we're going through our worst nightmares. The nightmares, the attacks will happen, but He will see us through them if we trust and rely on Him."

Pete flicked a minute piece of dirt off the edge of his boot. He didn't want to reveal more of himself to Luke. "Annabelle talks about God turning things for good. It seems to me that He puts bad stuff on us so He can fix it and come up smelling like a rose."

"I know it can seem that way sometimes, but I promise, God has a good and perfect plan for our lives. And if we turn to God and trust in Him, He will see us through those—"

Before he could finish his sentence, a gunshot echoed in the distance.

"I better go see what that's all about. Thanks for your time, Fa—I mean, Reverend."

Pete heard the words "Come by anytime" as he darted out the door and ran up Main Street.

58

THE NEXT TWO DAYS passed with agonizing slowness for the posse. They moved through terrain marked by gullies and hills, following a trail that twisted and turned through the foothills. Constant vigilance frayed nerves and heightened reactions. More than once, a pistol was drawn and cocked, then lowered as a rabbit emerged from the undergrowth along the trail.

The air cooled and the pine scent grew stronger as they climbed higher. They rode in near silence, communicating with hand gestures and whispers. When they stopped for the evening, they ate cold suppers and settled into restless sleep, taking turns on guard duty. The slightest noise woke them. Michael felt the bone-aching, heavy-headed exhaustion brought on by weeks of interrupted sleep on uncomfortable ground.

On the third morning, Michael heard heavy footsteps
behind him as he saddled Buddy. He looked over his shoulder to see Bill Barkston approaching, his saddle on one shoulder. They worked in silence, focused on the task at hand.

When he finished, Barkston turned to Michael. "Caleb
told me how he accepted Jesus with you. I can't tell you
how much that means to me. Caleb's a good friend. Me and
Vernon have been after him for years, but I guess he needed
a stranger to get to him."

Michael smiled. "I think I just followed up on the seed
you and Mr. Phelps planted. I wouldn't have been able to
reach him if you hadn't gone first."

Barkston rubbed the back of his neck. "Maybe so. Well, I
just wanted to say thanks." Barkston extended his hand and
they shook. Then, instead of moving away, Barkston stood
looking at him. Michael felt as though the man were assess-
ing him for an important position on the ranch.

Finally Barkston spoke. "I owe you an apology for the way
my wife and I treated you at church that Sunday you came
to town." He held up his hand to stop Michael from talking.
"My Sally's had her heart set on getting Jeffrey married, and
when Rachel came to town and grew to be such a good person
under Pastor Luke and Martha, Sally did everything she could
to get them together. Then you showed up, and Rachel only
had eyes for you, and . . . Anyway, like I said, I'm sorry."

Michael grinned. "Apology accepted. But I don't think I'm
the one for Rachel, much as I want to be. She's made it pretty
clear that she doesn't want to be with anyone right now."

Barkston wheeled his horse around so he could mount.

He grinned as he swung into the saddle. "Don't give up too easy, son. She could change her mind."

Two days later, the posse climbed a gentle slope, the kidnappers' trail still clear. Michael rode with Caleb a few yards behind Old Thomas and Malachi. A storm had threatened earlier, but now the sun beamed from a cloudless sky. A gentle breeze dried the sweat on their brows.

On the far side of the slope, they entered a narrow gully that forced them to ride single file. Small shrubs dotted the sides. Pine trees ranked along the tops like soldiers on a march. Each sound seemed amplified by the close confines.

Michael saw Caleb sit straighter and slide his pistol in and out of his holster. Old Thomas and Malachi seemed to pay more attention to the terrain around them than the tracks in front of them. Behind him, Michael heard shifting that told him the others were more alert. He kept looking right and left, ears and eyes straining for signs of ambush.

He heard and saw nothing. The gully was still. *No one—*

Old Thomas suddenly spread his arms as if nailed to an invisible cross. The sound of a shot echoed through the hills. He tumbled backward, a slow-motion somersault that ended with him flat on his back, arms still spread, a dark stain on his chest.

Malachi jumped from his horse and stumbled toward his friend, while the others dismounted and scrambled for cover. Another shot kicked up dust next to Malachi. Then a third shot entered his shoulder just as he reached Thomas, knocking him forward. Michael ran and slid one arm around

Malachi's chest. A bullet shrieked past his ear and ricocheted off the rocks as he dragged the older man out of the line of fire.

"Gotta help Thomas," Malachi moaned. He clenched his shoulder, his face twisted in pain as blood seeped down his shirtfront.

"You wait here. I'll get him." Michael ran back to the Indian. Old Thomas's eyes stared at nothing.

More shots came, and the posse returned fire. Michael dragged Old Thomas to where Jeremiah tended Malachi. The old man wept. Caleb glanced over from his place a few yards forward. Michael shook his head.

Caleb bowed his head for a moment, then moved back to where Bill Barkston, Frank, and Martin had taken cover. "Bill, you three backtrack a ways and see if you can find a way to come up behind 'em. I think they're to the right of us, but I can't be sure."

Bill listened as a few more shots hit dust. "I think they're on both sides, hoping to catch us in cross fire, but I don't think there's more than two or three of them."

Caleb cocked his head toward the gunfire. "You're right. My ears are gettin' fooled by the echoes. But there's probably reinforcements on the way now that the shootin's started."

Bill spat on the ground. The dark brown tobacco juice took on a coat of sandy dust. "I expect you're right, so we best try to get control of this while we can." He motioned to Frank and Martin. "Come on, boys. Let's see if we can take some authority here."

The three men started off, hugging the gully wall. Frank

and Martin followed the husky, gray-haired rancher in single file, rifles at the ready. In other circumstances they would have looked like a father and his two sons on a hunting trip. Now they were the hunted. Michael watched and prayed as they disappeared around a bend.

The gunfire stopped. The silence dragged on for several minutes, tension hanging in the still air like a sopping wet blanket. A trickle of sweat slid down Michael's spine.

A voice with a heavy Spanish accent broke the silence. "You might as well give up, señors. We have you trapped, and we can just wait you out. You'll either starve or walk into our guns. If you surrender, you might live."

"Highly unlikely," Caleb muttered.

Three shots rang out so close together, they sounded almost like one. Silence echoed as loud as the shots.

Barkston's voice boomed out. "Come on up, Caleb. But you'd better hurry."

Caleb and the others scrambled around a slight turn in the trail. Two bodies lay in the dirt. Brown-skinned young men, Indian or Mexican. One had a large hole in the center of his forehead. The other had two holes in his chest. Their eyes stared unseeing into the clear blue sky.

"Mitch and Harold," Caleb barked, "you go gather the horses. And be careful."

The two men ran back down the trail where the horses had scattered when the ambush began.

Barkston pointed forward. "Our shots must have alerted others up ahead. There's a dust trail rising, and it's moving our way fast."

"Everyone take cover."

The men scrambled behind rocks and shrubs that dotted the sides and top of the gully. Michael lifted Malachi under his good arm. The old man leaned on Michael, tears streaking down his wrinkled cheeks. His gaze lingered on Old Thomas's body.

"We can't just leave him here. I need to stay with him."

"I know." Michael grunted as he shifted Malachi's weight. "We won't leave him. But I need to get you to cover right now and patch you up. We'll come back and get Thomas as soon as we take care of this business."

Harold and Mitch came back with the horses. Caleb motioned for them to get to high ground. The men tugged and pushed and pulled the animals up the soft slopes of the gully. Michael followed, swatting the rumps of the slower mounts, Malachi's arm around his neck, Michael's other arm around his waist. They tied the horses to some pine trees that had established a toehold in the rocky, sandy soil.

Michael laid Malachi under a pine and went to get a couple of blankets from the packhorses. One blanket he folded into a pillow. The other he spread over Malachi's torso. The old man's teeth chattered, and he shivered despite the blankets and warm air.

Michael ripped open Malachi's shirt and rolled him on his side to examine the wound. The bullet had gone right through but had left a gaping hole in the front of Malachi's shoulder. Blood ran down his chest and shoulder blade.

Michael ran to the packhorses and rummaged in the packs until he found some cloth to use as bandages. He found a half-full bottle of whiskey wrapped in the cloths. He grinned, shook his head, and darted back to Malachi with the cloth, the whiskey, and a canteen of water.

Malachi's eyes lit up at the sight of the liquor. "Boy, I was wonderin' where that got to. I can sure use some of it."

"I'm going to give you some." Michael opened the bottle and poured some of the contents over the entrance and exit wounds.

Malachi grunted behind gritted teeth. "That's not where I meant."

"I know, but it's where you needed it." Michael wrapped the cloth around the shoulder and under the arm of the wounded man. He pulled it tight and tied it off.

Malachi moaned again. "I need a drink."

Michael held the canteen to his lips. Malachi sputtered as the liquid entered his mouth. "Not that, you fool!"

"This is all you get for now. I need you sober if you're going to recover."

"Dang preachers. Never know when to let a fellow have the medicine he needs." But he drank from the canteen like a calf hungry for its mother.

When he finished, Michael capped the canteen. He placed his hands on the wounded shoulder and prayed for a quick healing. "Now you just lie here and rest as best you can. I'll be back to take a look at you in a little bit."

59

RACHEL STOOD in the entrance to her workroom. She clutched the dividing curtain, her knuckles white, and suppressed a shudder.

Four days since the attack, yet Mark's image dominated the room, an almost-physical presence that cast a gray fog and distorted all the shapes. Again, she felt his hands on her, grasping, tearing. His beard scratching her face as he forced his mouth on hers. His fingers probing and pinching. His hand over her mouth, the smell of sweat and whiskey assailing her nostrils.

She gasped, a cry like a weak kitten, and pulled the curtain closed with a fierce snap of her wrist. She wished the fabric were a door she could slam and lock to banish the nightmare forever.

She hugged herself and bit her lower lip. She stroked a bolt of satin cloth on the counter, then jerked her hand away. The luxurious material reminded her of the dresses Red Mary had made her wear, especially the white gown the mine owners requested on the nights they passed her around like a tray of pastries. And Mark had planned to do the same.

Darkness gripped her soul, holding her tight. She could barely see.

She felt Lupe's arm around her shoulders. Annabelle's arm encircled her waist. She wanted to shake them off, but the need for comfort won out.

She sighed. "Three times I've been back here, and I still can't go in that room. Maybe I should just give up."

"No, Rachel," Annabelle urged. "You can't give up. You have to keep trying."

Lupe tightened her grip. The musical lilt of her accent couldn't hide the sadness Rachel heard in her halting words. "I know . . . I know how difficult it is to face things like this."

Rachel glared at her, resisting the urge to slap her. *How could you know how what I went through feels like—you with your privileged life and rich husband?*

Lupe must have known what she was thinking. She took her hand away and bent her head. After a few moments, she raised her head and looked out the window. She spoke into the distance, her voice flat. "I know what it's like to have a man force you to do things when your husband is out on the ranch somewhere, to grab you and . . . touch you and . . ." Her voice trailed off as if she had no more strength to speak.

Rachel grabbed her arm. "Mark did that to you?"

Lupe shook her head.

"Then who? I can't imagine . . ." The truth dawned. "Mr. Carstairs?"

Lupe nodded and squeezed her eyes shut. Then the tears began. Annabelle helped her to a chair near the stove. Rachel sat next to her and held her hand while Annabelle gave her a handkerchief.

"Please, you must not tell. My husband . . ."

Rachel stroked Lupe's hand, her own face still streaked with tears. And somewhere inside, she felt a door open in the blackness. A tiny glimmer of light shone into the despair of Rachel's soul.

"So I'm not as alone as I thought."

Lupe gave a half smile and nodded. Annabelle pulled up a chair and took Lupe's other hand. "But why do you stay? Why do you . . . let him?"

Lupe shrugged. Her accent thickened. "Because I love my husband and I don't want to lose him. Señor Sam, he threaten me. He say he tell Josh I seduce him and have me thrown off the ranch." She took a deep breath and exhaled. "And I don't want to make trouble between my Josh and Señor Sam. If I tell, maybe Josh hurt Señor Sam or maybe Señor Sam throw Josh out like he throw out Ben."

Confusion raced through Rachel's mind. Her emotional pain still seared, but something was different. The hard shell that encircled her spirit like a block of ice had cracked—a tiny fissure, to be sure, but still an opening. Warmth and compassion stirred. For the first time since the attack, she looked outside herself and her pain. Before her sat a woman who was trapped, who could not fight back.

But I'm not.

The thought came quietly, but the power of it made her

take a step back. She was not trapped by her past. People might try to lock her into that life, but she did not have to go there. She would not go there. What people thought or said or did to her didn't matter.

Unlike Lupe, she could fight back. She looked at the curtain to her workroom. Mark's attack flashed through her mind. *I did fight back.*

God had given her the strength. He had even placed a weapon near her. Afterward, He'd sent people to help her, people who had been there for her since her arrival in Riverbend. Those people still wanted to help her.

And God did too. God still cared for her and loved her. He kept standing there, arms open wide, ready to embrace her when she finally found the courage to run to Him.

Rachel took a deep, ragged breath. *I'm sorry, Father. And thank You. And help me . . . please. Help us both.*

Rachel saw Annabelle's lips move in quiet prayer. Rachel took another breath, then turned to gaze into Lupe's tearful black eyes. "You are not alone anymore either. We are here for you. And when Sam Carstairs comes home, we will deal with his sorry carcass so that he'll never bother you again. Right, Annabelle?"

Annabelle looked shocked, but she swallowed and nodded. Then she reached out and gathered Lupe into her arms, while Lupe just shook her head doubtfully.

Rachel stood. She brushed the skirt of her dress smooth, gulped another big breath, then walked toward the curtain that hid her workroom.

60

Michael slid his rifle from its scabbard and trotted along the top of the gully to where Caleb and Jeremiah hid behind a rock. Across the gully, he could see Barkston, Mitch, and Harold. Frank and Martin were a little ahead of them, Martin up in the branches of a tree.

"They're coming," Martin called. "Looks like about ten or eleven of 'em. Ridin' hard."

"Let 'em get close so we can do maximum damage the first time," Caleb said.

Michael grasped his rifle. The weapon felt slippery in his clammy hands. *Oh, Lord, don't let me have to shoot anyone. I couldn't take another person's blood on my hands, no matter what he's done.*

He thought of Rachel. *Could she love a killer? What will she say when I tell her about my father?*

Horses galloped up the trail. *What a beautiful blue sky. Lord, this is too beautiful a day for anyone else to die. Angels, protect us.*

The riders slowed as they approached the site of the failed ambush. Michael heard them but couldn't see anything because of the bend in the trail.

Across the gully, Martin whistled. Michael turned with Caleb and the others. Martin raised his hand, five fingers splayed. He raised it again the same way, then held up one more finger. Eleven riders and eight in the posse—nine counting Malachi.

Michael swallowed the lump in his throat. The rifle felt like a blacksmith's hammer, heavy and unwieldy. Jeremiah peered over a small rock, his rifle cocked and ready. Caleb wiped his face with his hand and spat in the dirt. He cocked the hammer on his rifle and bent behind a shrub. Across the way, the others prepared their weapons. The riders drew near, their horses' hooves clomping in the stones and sand.

Silence. Everything stopped. The breeze faded. Birdsong ceased midnote. Sweat ran down Michael's neck and forehead and into his eyes. He shook his head and blinked to clear the stinging moisture that blurred his vision. He looked at Martin, who motioned with a sweep of his arm that the riders had left the trail and split into two groups, one on either side.

Then Martin's eyes went wide like a child seeing its first rattler. He pointed past Michael and yelled, "Caleb."

Caleb swiveled his head toward Martin, but Michael looked in the direction Martin had pointed and spotted the head and shoulders of a man wearing a black sombrero, his rifle aimed at the sheriff. Michael fired. The bullet pinged into a tree several feet to the man's left. The man flinched. At the same instant, Jeremiah rolled onto his back, pointed his rifle, and fired.

The man fell back. The sombrero flew from his head. Stones scattered as he slid. Heavy, oppressive silence followed the concussions of the gunshots.

Barkston sighted his rifle on a spot in front of Caleb. The shot echoed like a bass drum in a circus parade. As the echo faded, a body tumbled to the floor of the gully.

A shot kicked up dirt inches from Michael's face. He rolled away, blinking to clear the painful particles. Martin fired from his perch, and another body tumbled into the gully, rolling into the body of the first man. The two lay there, a bizarre dance frozen in death.

The sound of retreating hoofbeats broke the eerie silence. Martin strained from his perch. He looked at Caleb and held up four fingers and pointed ahead of him, then four more fingers and made a walking motion with his fingers.

"Four rode away. There's still four out there waitin' for us to follow," Caleb croaked. He reached for his canteen. Michael's throat tightened. He wondered if he'd ever draw a full breath again.

He heard a soft moan and turned to see Malachi reach for the trunk of the pine sapling as he tried to stand. Michael sprinted over to him and guided him back into a sitting position.

The old man tried to push him away. "I gotta help . . .

gotta do my part. They killed Old Thomas. Best friend I ever had." The old man's eyes pleaded with Michael.

"You're too weak—you'll only get in the way right now. You need to stay here and rest."

"Then give me a gun, a rifle, anything I can use to defend myself and watch your back."

Michael gave him a pistol and gun belt from the supply pack. "Here. These should hold you."

"You betcha." Malachi's eyes brightened. "Hey, hows 'bout giving me that medicinal bottle you found. It sure would ease my pain and help my eyesight so's I can shoot straighter."

Michael shook his head. "Just focus on not shooting yourself or any of us." He headed back to his position near Caleb.

Caleb called in a loud whisper, "Martin, can you still see the ones that rode away?"

Martin looked and nodded.

"Keep watchin'. Let me know if they turn to get behind us."

Martin nodded again.

Barkston looked at Caleb. His eyes smoldered. "Not a good spot."

"Nope."

Barkston scanned the area. "Any ideas?"

Caleb shrugged. "I'm open to suggestion."

"I can't think of anything either."

Michael prayed, his voice a low murmur. Jeremiah removed his hat, wiped his forehead with his arm, and prayed too.

Caleb looked at the two of them. "How's Malachi?"

"He'll make it," Michael said. "He's asking for the whiskey bottle."

"Whiskey bottle? Where'd that come from?"

Michael shrugged. "Don't know, but it was in the supplies we had with us."

Caleb laughed. "Serves him right, the old coot. Smuggled it in but then couldn't get at it."

Michael gestured in Malachi's direction. "He asked for a weapon. I gave him a pistol. He told me the whiskey would improve his marksmanship."

Caleb snorted. "Sober, that man couldn't hit the side of a barn if he was standing inside it."

He looked up the trail, staring hard as if that alone would make it possible to see through the rocks and trees. But evidently no revelation came. He sighed and cursed, then looked at Michael. "Sorry. Guess I ain't s'posed to use them words anymore."

Michael smiled. "Old habits die hard." He paused. An idea percolated in his brain, loose threads he reached to grasp. "Sheriff, if those other riders turn to come up behind us, won't that take them away from us for a little while?"

"Go on, Reverend."

"If they turn, I think it would give us an opportunity to ride out and take care of the ones that are waiting for us."

Caleb looked across the gully at Barkston. "You hear that, Bill?"

"Yep. It'd be a real small chance. We'd be riding through single file, and they could pick us off one at a time like they did Old Thomas."

Michael said, "Not if a couple of our better shots stayed on the high ground. You could spot the shooters by the smoke."

Caleb rubbed his beard. "Bill, I want you and Martin to stay on the high ground. Scoot on ahead as far as you can without gettin' spotted. When y'all are in place, the rest of us'll ride as fast as we can down the gully."

"How about Mr. Turner staying there on your side? I'd feel more comfortable knowing I had some cover over there."

Caleb looked at Jeremiah, who nodded. Caleb turned back to the others. "What are they doing, Martin?"

"Still riding straight away."

"Keep your eyes on 'em."

Michael's stomach knotted and churned. He took a deep breath and held it for several seconds before exhaling to relieve some of the tension.

Jeremiah scrabbled sideways to crouch next to him. "You all right?"

Michael met the other man's eyes. "No, I'm scared. I don't want to have to shoot anyone, but I don't want to get shot either."

"You think God would bring you all this way just to have you get killed?"

Michael shook his head as if trying to chase a bee away. "No. But I might do something to mess it up."

Jeremiah smiled. "I know what you mean, but you've got to remember God has a plan for you and the devil wants to stop it. Stay focused on what you know you're supposed to do—tell Carstairs about his son. Trust in the Holy Spirit and let His peace lead you into what you need to do."

Michael managed a smile too. "Thanks." *All right, Lord, that's what I'm asking. Show me what I need to do. And—*

Martin whistled, and all eyes turned in his direction. He made a sweeping motion with his right arm. "They turned off the trail to your side. I've lost sight of 'em, but it looks like they might be doublin' back."

"All right, then," Caleb called. "Let's go."

Martin, Barkston, and Jeremiah moved along the tops of the banks of the gully. The others headed to the horses. Michael checked the bandage on Malachi's wound and helped him onto his horse. "It looks like the bleeding's stopped for now, but we'll need to keep an eye on it. Any rough riding may open it up again."

"You better ride last with him," Caleb said.

"I understand."

Caleb put his hand on Michael's shoulder. "You're a good man, Reverend. I'm glad you came on this ride with us, and I sure don't want nothin' bad happenin' to you. I'd hate to have to break that kind of news to Luke and Martha Matthews and Miss Rachel. Besides, Gideon Parsons would have my hide if I didn't send you back to him in one piece. You take care of Malachi and the packhorses and ride as fast as you can."

Michael placed Malachi on the horse behind him, then tied the lead rope for the packhorses around the tracker's saddle horn. Malachi sat with his shoulders slumped, his head down.

"You all right, Malachi?"

He turned to Michael, tears brimming. "It don't seem right to leave Thomas here out in the open."

Michael looked over to the trees where Malachi had rested. Old Thomas's body lay wrapped in a blanket. He studied the packhorses. "Sheriff, give me a minute."

He dismounted without waiting for an answer and shifted the load from one horse to the other. He climbed the gully wall, picked up Old Thomas, and lugged him back down, draping him over the empty packhorse and securing him with leather thongs. He remounted and gathered Buddy's reins.

"I thank ya." Malachi's voice was soft and shaky.

"You're welcome." Buddy shifted beneath him. Michael knew he didn't like Malachi's horse so close or the packhorses at his heels, and the smell of blood made him jittery. Michael leaned forward and patted him on the neck, sending a burst of dust into the air. "Boy, do you need a bath."

The horse snorted and bobbed his head up and down. "Easy, boy," Michael soothed. "Just give me all you've got for the next little while and then I'll take good care of you when we get back to town."

Buddy snorted again. The horse seemed to quiver with excitement and anticipation.

Caleb took the lead. He motioned forward. "Let's ride!"

61

THE AIR FELT HEAVY and moist. Rain threatened but never fell. Its moisture hung in the air, a haze that distorted the sun. Sam's eyes burned and itched, and his parched throat begged for water. His body sagged in pain and fatigue, torturing his muscles and bones—a slow process of tearing his arms from his shoulders.

He added more bricks of anger to his wall of stubbornness. He would never sign those papers. He wouldn't give Maria or her father any satisfaction.

There were only a few men in camp now. Jack had not yet returned from his mystery mission. Others had ridden off to the east that morning in response to news that riders were approaching. Rescuers? Had someone found him? Old Thomas or Malachi must have led them. No one else could have followed that corkscrew of a trail. *Those two will never have to buy whiskey again.*

The blonde woman approached him stealthily and brought a tin cup to his lips. Her vacant stare showed her shuttered soul, her mind closed to any hope of normal human contact. But she was bringing him water in defiance of Maria. That had to mean something.

"Help me," he whispered, trying to get through to her. She just shook her head while she let him drink some more. Some of the water ran down his chin and dripped on his chest.

Maria approached and pushed the woman aside. She sprawled to the ground. The tin cup bounced away, its contents spilled in the dirt.

"Go take care of my father."

The woman scurried into the cabin without looking back. Maria turned to Sam. "Are you ready to sign those papers?"

Sam glared at her, hatred and disgust welling up inside him. He spat at her.

She backhanded him in the mouth. Blood spurted from a cut on his lip. Then she grabbed his hair and lifted his head. Pulling a knife from her belt, she pressed the blade against his throat.

"Daughter, stop." The voice was sharp and clear, carrying more force than Sam thought John Higgins could muster.

Maria hesitated, then pulled the knife away. "Papa, he deserves what's coming to him."

"He doesn't deserve that."

He hobbled the few steps from the door, his cane wobbling

even when he set it in the dirt and leaned on it. Sam expected him to fall over with each step.

John stood in front of Maria, looking up into her face from his shrunken posture. "I'm ashamed of what I've turned you into, girl. When did you become so cruel?"

Maria pointed at Sam. "When you told me all the things he did to you. He cheated you, robbed you, had you sent to prison, did everything he could to ruin you and kill you."

"But I lived. And if those things hadn't happened to me, I might not have met your mother, and you might not be here."

Her mouth hung open, and she sputtered something Sam didn't understand. John didn't seem to understand it either. He patted his daughter's arm. "Let me talk to him one more time."

Maria threw her arms in the air and walked off. "It's not going to do any good," she said over her shoulder. "He's as stubborn as you are."

Sam waited as John slowly turned to face him. Higgins's eyes were sunken into dark folds of his skin. One side of his face seemed to sag.

"Well, Sam, what's it gonna be? Sign over what you owe me, and I'll let you go."

Sam stared at John. "If you had come to me, maybe we could've talked and reached an agreement." The words rasped in Sam's throat. It hurt to speak more than a few words. *Are they true?* Sam didn't even know. He doubted it.

John motioned for the blonde woman to give Sam more water. Sam drank it gratefully, gulping its coolness, swallowing it slowly.

"You can't let me go," he told Higgins. "I watched your daughter murder four men—did you know that? If I live, I'm gonna make sure she hangs."

John seemed to contemplate Sam's words.

Maria walked up to stand beside her father. "Well?"

"You're right, Daughter. He is stubborn. But maybe we can persuade him another way. Jack, bring him out here."

Sam heard a scuffing sound accompanied by the moans and mutters of someone in pain. Jack walked into view and stood next to Maria. Behind him walked two men supporting a third man. Sam wanted to scream but could only moan and gasp when he saw his son.

Mark was pale, his lips colorless, a bloodstained bandage around his chest. Sam's heart turned to a lump of lead in his throat, its beating a painful pounding. Mark's head hung down. He appeared to be unconscious.

"What did you do to him?" Sam croaked.

"Nothing," Jack said. "We just brought him here. Rode day and night. I want to get this done and over with as quickly as possible before the rest of the posse finds us. We did have to take him from the doc's office. Apparently some female he was interested in didn't share his enthusiasm and stabbed him. He didn't take to the ride too well, and he might've popped some stitches."

Maria's laugh held a bitter edge. "Like father, like son. Well, Mr. Carstairs, are you ready to reconsider your position?"

"I want to talk with my son."

Maria looked at her father. John said, "Give them some time. I need to rest."

The blonde woman came over and helped him back to the cabin.

Maria shrugged. "It's not going to change anything, but I'll give you a little time with him." She nodded at Jack and the other man, who let Mark slip from their grasp until he knelt on the ground. When they released him, he fell on his side. Maria used the toe of her boot to turn him on his back and motioned for one of the men to bring her a bucket of water. She poured the water in Mark's face. He stirred as if he were fighting through bales of cotton to wakefulness.

"Ow." He cursed. "That hurts." He reached for the bandage on his chest, gasping for air. Then he slowly became aware of his surroundings.

"Where am I? Who are you people? Pa, what've they done to you? What's going on?" His voice was weak, his eyes confused. Sam thought he looked feverish.

"Shut up," Maria said. "Your father and I are discussing a business deal, and you're here to help us cinch it."

"I . . . I don't understand."

"You don't need to. Just be quiet and lie there." Maria turned her attention to Sam. "Well, do we have a deal?"

"Don't hurt him." Sam hated the plea for mercy he heard in his voice.

"That's entirely up to you. We'll let you two visit for a while, and then we'll talk some more. Mark, tell your father he'd be doing the right thing by signing. It might just keep both of you alive."

Mark tried to roll on his side again, then groaned and clutched his chest. "Who is . . . she? What does she want?"

Sam shook his head at the sight of his injured son. "What happened to you?"

Mark worked himself up to his elbow. "I was havin' some fun with that whore you gave money to, and she stabbed me."

"Rachel Stone? Rachel's no whore. Not anymore. What's the matter with you, boy?"

Anger flared in Mark's eyes. "I'm not a boy. Stop callin' me one. And you know she worked at Red Mary's. She may not be whorin' now, but she should be."

Sam shook his head. "You're still a fool."

Mark coughed and spat blood-tinged mucus into the dirt. "Hurts to breathe." He coughed again. "Who are these people? Whadda they want with you?"

Sam struggled for the air to speak. "An old business partner. Thinks I cheated him. Wants me to sign over half of everything I own to him."

Mark's voice trembled. "Half? What about me?" He paused. "And Josh?"

Sam squeezed his eyes shut to block out the image of his son. *It's true. What did that old preacher say years ago? Oh yeah. You reap what you sow.*

Mark coughed and spat again. He rubbed the bandage, and blood smeared his fingers. He wiped his hand on his pants. "So did you?" He looked into Sam's eyes with a yearning Sam couldn't understand.

"Did I what?"

"Did you cheat him?"

Sam lifted his head and winced as fresh pain shot down

his spine. He nodded. "It was the only way I could get your mother."

Mark barely managed an insolent smile. "Was it worth it?"

Sam glared at his son. "Sometimes, when I look at you, I wonder."

Sam sighed. He looked at each hand bound to a post, his wrists raw and bleeding. The pain throughout his body surged to an intensity that made him feel alive for the first time in days. He gazed out over the small valley, and for the first time, he couldn't quite remember her face. "I thought so at the time. Now, I'm not so sure."

After several minutes, Mark coughed again. "So are you gonna sign what they want?"

Sam shook his head.

"But, Pa, they're gonna kill us if you don't."

"Son, they're gonna kill us if I do."

62

AT FULL GALLOP, Michael felt like they rode through snow up to the horses' bellies. He and Malachi were last in the line of riders, the packhorses running close after him on their lead ropes. Michael leaned low on Buddy's neck, every rapid breath a silent prayer.

He saw Mitch's horse go down in a slow, graceful dance, Mitch's arms windmilling in a vain attempt to keep his balance. Martin slid down the gully and ran to Mitch. The cords on the cowboy's neck stood in stark relief, his mouth open in a silent scream as he tried to pull the other man from under the horse.

Another shot. Blood erupted from Mitch's neck, a slow-moving fountain, each drop visible in the air as it splattered Mitch and Martin. The next shot hit the horse.

Michael felt removed from the scene, watching from an eagle's nest as the posse ran the gauntlet of the confined gully. Movement on the gully wall caught Michael's attention. Jeremiah stood and fired three shots in rapid succession from his Winchester. A yelp of pain came from behind a small boulder, and a rifle tumbled down the slope. But another shooter fired at Jeremiah, who dived behind a shrub that clung for dear life in the thin soil on the side of the gully.

Barkston's position did not give him a clear shot.

Martin rolled away from Mitch and took cover behind the dying horse's hindquarters. He pulled Mitch's rifle from its saddle scabbard and dashed to the other side of the gully. When he reached the other side, he turned, brought the rifle to his shoulder, and fired toward the gun smoke. Jeremiah rose to one knee and fired in the same instant. The shooter dropped his rifle, clutched his chest, and fell to the gully floor in a flurry of stones and dirt.

Michael slowed enough for Martin to climb up behind him. Buddy took a couple of strides to adjust to the increased weight and then resumed his pace, hindered by the slower packhorses and Malachi's mount, who seemed as old as its rider. He guided Buddy around Mitch's downed horse, praying none of them would stumble and wishing there was time to put it out of its misery.

More shooting. A body tumbled down the wall on their left. Michael leaned forward, Martin pressing against him. Not as many shots now. A small column of dust sprouted in front of him as a bullet smacked the dirt.

"I see him." Jeremiah's voice echoed as a shot sounded.

Another cry of pain came from Michael's left. *Too much death, Lord.*

About fifty yards farther on, the gully widened as it reached the entrance to a clearing. Caleb called a halt and waited for the others to join them. Barkston walked up, brushing dust off his jeans and shirt with his hat.

"Where's Turner?"

"He went back to get Mitch."

A shot rang out behind them. All reached for their weapons, searching around them.

"That was a pistol shot, not a rifle," Martin said. "I think Turner finished off Mitch's horse."

A few minutes later, Jeremiah walked into view, the butt of his rifle braced against his left hip, Mitch's body over his right shoulder. Michael helped him wrap the body in a blanket and secure it to the packhorse that carried Old Thomas. They paused a moment, hands on the shrouded body, heads bent.

Caleb walked up to Malachi, who still sat on his horse, hunched over. "Malachi? Can you keep going?"

The old man looked at the sheriff, his face pale and pinched with pain, his mouth a thin line, his lips colorless. He spoke in a voice more frog's croak than anything else. "Yes, sir. But a nip of the medicinal whiskey would sure make me stronger."

Caleb shook his head. "Well, I guess one nip wouldn't hurt."

He nodded at Michael, who held the bottle so that the old man took only a little.

"You sure got a small definition of *nip*, boy."

63

MICHAEL STOOD with Caleb as the sheriff spoke with Jeremiah and Barkston. "Any sign of those other riders?"

Barkston looked back down the trail. "Didn't see or hear any. They should be comin' up behind us anytime."

"Martin," Caleb said, "climb one of those trees up on top there and see if you can see anything."

Michael handed Martin the spyglass. "You might need this."

Martin hefted the cylinder and slid it into his pants waist. "Thanks."

The cowboy reminded Michael of a squirrel as he mounted a tall pine and glided from branch to branch. At times he seemed to disappear. He stopped about thirty feet in the air, wrapped one arm around the trunk, and peered down the trail through the spyglass. Michael's stomach lurched as he watched the tree sway in the breeze, Martin a large lump on its trunk. To be up that high and moving did not appeal to Michael. He prayed for clear and quick vision for the cowboy.

After several minutes, Martin clambered down, snapping off weaker branches in his hurried descent. He slid down the embankment and scurried to Caleb, his shirt and pants streaked with pine sap and dirt.

He took a deep breath. "They're 'bout a quarter mile back. Ridin' kind of slow, watchful-like."

"They don't know where we are," Barkston said.

Caleb spat in the dirt. "Well, soon as they find their companions lyin' in the dirt, they'll know somethin' ain't right, and we ain't got the time to hide 'em. How many more riders are there?"

"Four comin' up behind us," Martin said. "I'm pretty sure we got all the ones that was waitin'."

Caleb rubbed his chin. He studied the terrain. "Well, there's seven of us able-bodied. I think we might be able to do a little divide and conquer if we make a stand here."

Michael realized the clearing was really a widening of the gully. The sides tapered to ground level over a space of about thirty yards. Pines and scrub plants marked the edges.

Michael saw Caleb's eyes narrow. The sheriff pointed. "Michael, take Malachi and the horses into those trees." He pointed to a group of pines farther along the trail. "Go in maybe twenty or thirty yards. Make Malachi as comfortable as you can and secure the horses. Then come back up to the edge of the trees and find some cover."

"Yes, sir." Michael waited while Caleb gave instructions to the rest of the men.

"Bill, you and Mr. Turner climb up to the high point on the gully wall. Martin, climb back up that tree. Frank, you go on the same side as Michael 'bout halfway between him and where the gully widens. Harold, you and I will do the same on this other side."

The men checked and reloaded their weapons as they went to their assigned positions. Michael wondered at their calm determination. Except for Caleb and Jeremiah, they were ranchers, cowboys, townsmen, ordinary peaceful people. They didn't even seem to like Sam Carstairs much. And yet they were ready to face death to save him. Why?

He knew, for him, it was his promise to Ben—keeping his word after so many years of lying and cheating.

But why did the others do it? After so many weeks on the trail, he had a glimmer. For the cowboys, it seemed to be part of their code of loyalty. "It's what we do," Frank had told him as they rode alone one day. "Mr. Joshua is our boss, the best boss most of us have ever had. This is his father. No matter what the old man is like, we do it for Mr. Joshua."

For the others, it was to protect one of their own. Sam Carstairs may not have been universally loved, but he was still part of the community and he was in trouble. They were willing to do what they could to help him.

Michael thought of Vernon and Alexander, Dave and Shorty, Mitch and Old Thomas. *They're even willing to give their lives. Lord, help me draw strength from You and from their example.*

Michael spurred Buddy and led his caravan to the spot Caleb had indicated. He guided Malachi to the largest tree and settled him against the base. The tracker was pale and feverish. Michael placed a bedroll behind the old man's head and gave him some water. He put the canteen on the ground next to him and laid a pistol in his lap.

"You're going to have to be on your own for a little bit, Malachi. I'll be back to get you as soon as I can."

The old man lifted his hand, let it drop into his lap, and closed his eyes.

Michael checked his rifle as he returned to the edge of the trail. He found a place behind a tree that gave him a good view up the gully. Short, tight breaths made him light-headed. He forced himself to take a deep breath to ease the constriction in his chest. Small relief. *Don't faint. Stay calm.*

He could see Harold across from him and Barkston on the higher embankment on the same side. He knew Jeremiah and Martin were farther ahead on the same side as him. Frank stretched out behind a rotted tree trunk about twenty yards in front of him.

Caleb walked over to him. "Martin says they're still comin' in slow and easy, real cautiouslike. I'd like to try to take as many of them alive as we can so we can find out where they're keepin' Sam."

"Yes, sir."

Caleb trotted across the clearing to take up his position. Michael waited, his mouth dry, his palms sweaty. He wiped a hand on his pants, then looked down and flexed it. He remembered the hand under Rachel's elbow as they walked up the church steps. He remembered Rachel holding it as he helped her step over a log and across the street. He remembered it bringing Rachel's hand to his lips.

More than anything else, he wanted to see her again and earn her trust. His heart was hers if she wanted it. *Lord, I'm going to have to leave that in Your hands. Please be with me now. Show me what to do next.*

Michael heard the creak of leather and the soft shuffle of horses. He tightened his grip on his rifle. He was surprised to find his breath held steady.

"Stop right there," Caleb commanded in a loud voice. "Drop your weapons."

The riders looked around in confusion. One raised his rifle and fired in Caleb's direction. Splinters flew from the tree next to the sheriff's head.

Barkston fired, and the rider fell in the dirt.

Other riders shot into the trees, not aiming, as they milled in a circle, confused, their horses terrified.

One more fell as the posse returned fire. The others made to ride away.

More shots. As they neared Michael, he raised his rifle, hesitated, then aimed again. *Sorry, fella.* He fired.

Blood burst from the horse's chest and the animal stumbled. The rider flew over the horse's head. All the other noise of the gunfight faded. Michael was transfixed on the rider, on his wide eyes, on his open mouth as he flailed his arms. His sombrero flew off. The man landed on his back with a loud *whuff* as the air was pushed from his lungs by the force of his landing. He shook his head and reached for the pistol on his hip when he saw Michael.

Michael pointed his rifle at the man's chest. "Please, don't."

The man stretched his hands over his head.

Caleb's hand slid the pistol from the kidnapper's holster. He squeezed Michael's shoulder. Michael forced himself to focus on the sheriff's words. "It's all right. We can take it from here."

The fight was over. It had lasted less than two minutes, Michael guessed, though it had seemed like an hour. The silence felt different now, not oppressive. Gun smoke drifted in the air. Somewhere behind him a cardinal sang.

Michael pulled his sweat-drenched shirt away from his chest. He looked at the man lying at his feet. *Thank God he's alive.*

Gradually, he became aware of the scene around him, the bodies sprawled in grotesque positions. Jeremiah bent over one of the riders, who moaned and clutched his side. Martin and Frank gathered horses. Barkston and Harold moved among the other riders.

Caleb pushed his hat back on his head. "So much for taking them alive and quiet. Sure wish we'd caught that one that got away."

"Sorry, Sheriff," Barkston said.

"It's all right, Bill. We did the best we could. Maybe we can get some information from the one Jeremiah's tendin' to—" he jerked his thumb at the man at Michael's feet— "and this one the Reverend brought down."

Jeremiah spoke over his shoulder. "This one might make it, but it's gonna be close."

"Do what you can to keep him alive."

Barkston and Michael lifted the other rider to his feet. Caleb stared at the man for several seconds, while the man's expression turned from apprehension to sullen defiance.

Caleb spoke, his voice quiet and slow. "I want to know where the rest of your gang is. Where are you holding Sam Carstairs?"

The man responded in a stream of Spanish. Michael recognized several curses and references to body parts. Caleb's fist lashed out. The man fell to the ground, blood flowing from his nose. Martin and Frank stood the prisoner back up.

Caleb again asked the man about Sam's location. The dark man shrugged his shoulders. Caleb spoke again, this time in Spanish. The prisoner continued his silence.

Frank drew his pistol, cocked it, and placed the barrel against the man's knee. "Tell us what we want to know, or you'll lose the kneecap. And that will only be the beginning."

The man flinched and looked at Caleb. The sheriff translated, then shrugged.

"Frank, you really shouldn't threaten the poor man," Barkston said.

Frank looked at the man and pushed the barrel against his leg. Sweat formed on the prisoner's face. Fear danced in his eyes.

"I ain't threatenin' him," Frank said. "I'm—what's the word?—oh yeah, I'm *negotiatin'* with him. Helpin' him to see the value in tellin' us what we want to know."

Caleb folded his arms and leaned toward the prisoner. "He will do it, and I'm far enough out of my jurisdiction that I can't stop him."

The prisoner spoke a rapid stream of words, fear etched on his face.

Caleb extended his arm. "All right, Frank. You can ease up. He's willing to talk now."

Caleb and the man spoke in Spanish for several minutes. Caleb gave him a stick and pointed to the ground. The man sketched in the dirt, and the posse gathered in a rough circle around the crude map the outlaw drew.

Caleb took the stick and gestured at the map. "Accordin' to our prisoner here, they're holdin' Sam in an old cabin in a small valley about two miles away. This trail leads right to it. He says there's 'bout ten to twelve men left there now besides the leaders and a servant woman. That rider who got away will let 'em know we're comin', but he won't have any idea how many we are. That should help us some."

Jeremiah gestured toward the prisoner. "Can he tell us anything about how the valley is laid out? Where's the cabin, any creeks, any trees?"

Caleb repeated the question and gave the stick back to the man. The man drew as he spoke. Caleb asked him a few questions about different areas of the sketch. "Here's what we're facing. This trail enters the valley from the east end and follows this creek. About two-thirds of the way up the valley, it joins up with two other creeks to form a bigger one. The cabin sits where this Y is formed. The land is open in front of the cabin. Trees pretty much cover the land behind and around it. On the north side, the ground slopes up and is covered with trees. The south side is pretty level, from what he says."

"It'd be good if we can get some of us into the trees on the north side and sneak down to the cabin. It'd give us good cover for a surprise," Jeremiah said.

"With that rider gettin' away, we're not gonna have much chance for surprise. They'll be waitin' for us. But maybe it'll work. We'll scout out the place better when we get there." Caleb sighted the sun. "Maybe we can get this finished before the day is done."

"What about Sam?" Barkston asked.

Caleb questioned the prisoner again. "He says they're keepin' him at the cabin, tied between some posts that support the porch roof. The leader is an old man named Higgins—seems he's an old enemy of Sam's. Anybody remember him?"

They looked from one to another. "Doesn't ring a bell," Barkston said.

"Not with me either," Caleb said. "Anyway, he has a daughter that really runs the show, givin' orders, makin' decisions. Our prisoner here says she's real mean and cruel to everybody 'cept her father and her husband. Nobody dares cross her."

"She must be the one that kidnapped him at Hawkins Station," Jeremiah said. "If we capture her, everyone else may just give up."

"We'll see," Caleb said. "Let's ride."

64

"RIDER COMIN' IN."

Sam stirred at the guard's voice. The faint sound of hoof-beats grew louder. Through the narrow slits of his swollen eyes, he saw Maria step out of the cabin, tucking her shirt into her pants.

She spoke to someone behind her in the cabin. "What I wouldn't give to wear a dress again. How do you men stand these things?" She ran her fingers through her disheveled hair and tossed her head.

Jack fastened the last button on his shirt as he came to stand beside her. "I hate getting interrupted when we're just getting started."

She jabbed an elbow into his ribs. "Quiet."

Mark lay staked out on the ground, arms and legs stretched

to their limit, held with strips of leather to wooden pegs. Blood soaked the torn and dirty bandage around his chest. More blood oozed out of stripes on his chest and stomach from Maria's whip and from her technique of dragging her spurs across him.

The men gathered at the cabin as the rider yanked hard on the reins and skidded his sweat-lathered mount to a stop just before Mark, scattering dust and debris into the open wounds. Mark twisted and moaned in renewed pain.

The rider leapt to the ground. The horse shuddered, its sides heaving as it tried to breathe. One of the men stepped forward, took its reins, and stroked its nose.

Maria approached the rider. "What is it, Felipe?"

"Many men coming, señora. They ambushed us." His lungs strained to take in enough air to speak.

"Are you the only one still alive?"

Felipe drank from a dipper of water one of the men handed him. He was breathing as hard as the horse and looked about to pass out. "I think so. They shot us up pretty bad. It was like they knew right where we were and what we had planned."

Maria put her hands on her hips and leaned close, her face inches from Felipe's. "How many are there?"

Felipe spread his arms weakly. "Many."

"Did you count them?"

"No, señora. They were hiding and it happened *muy rápido*. I ride as fast as I could to warn you."

Maria chewed on her lower lip and looked up the valley. "How close are they behind you?"

Felipe shrugged. "Not far, I think."

Maria turned to Jack. "See anything?"

He shaded his eyes with his hands. "Nope."

Sam squinted in the same direction. Everything was a blur. But there were men out there, coming this way. They must be coming to help, to rescue them. He looked at his son stretched out before him, skin white as new milk. Would they get here in time? Would Mark live? Would Sam live to correct the things he had done?

Was that even possible?

"We've got some time, then." Maria turned a slow circle. "We can make some preparations." She turned to the cabin, where the blonde woman stood in the doorway. "Get Felipe something to eat."

John Higgins emerged from the cabin and worked his slow way over to Maria.

"We've got some trouble coming, Papa."

The old man nodded.

"We'll have to get ready to fight them off. I think the best place for you would be in the cabin."

Jack jerked his thumb at the ramshackle building. "That isn't going to be much cover. Those walls won't stop a rifle bullet."

Maria eyed the weathered boards. "You're right. But we can make them thicker."

She turned to two of the men gathered around her and pointed at Mark. "Tie him between the other posts, just like the old man. I don't think they'll try anything that might harm these two fine upstanding citizens."

Maria turned to Sam. "If you had signed when you first

got here, you'd be home by now. Now your stubbornness will get you and your son killed. But if you sign now, we'll just leave the two of you here and ride away."

"No, you won't." Sam's tongue was thick with thirst as he forced the words through battered and blistered lips. "You never intended to let us live."

Maria walked over, leaned close, and leered at him. "You're right, old man; I didn't want to let you live. But Father was willing to let you go after you signed and we had gotten what was ours. We were going to head for our home in Mexico and let you go on the Rio Grande. And I would have obeyed him because he's my father and I love him and he's a much better man than you'll ever be."

She drew back her hand, and Sam winced. But the blow never came. She spun around and walked off.

For the next hour, Sam watched Maria and Jack make preparations. Their ten remaining men gathered in front of the cabin. Maria assigned three to the creek, where they took up positions behind logs piled in a low wall, and sent a man up each of the ridges that bordered the valley. Then she and Jack took the remaining men behind the cabin and returned without them. John Higgins emerged from the cabin as if he'd been watching for their return.

"Are you ready, Father?" Maria said. "This is going to be rough. There's still time for you to get away. Jack and I and the men will hold them off."

Higgins coughed. "I know, Daughter. But I started this, and I'll finish it. I want you and Jack to leave. Ride out the west end of the valley. Get away. Go home and raise a family."

"I won't leave you. I'll finish this with you." The tender emotion in her voice surprised Sam, as did the sight of her blinking back tears.

Higgins took her hand in his.

"I love you, Papa."

"I love you too, Maria."

65

RACHEL DISPLAYED a bolt of cloth for Lupe Carstairs, a soft green cotton. "I think this is a good shade for you. It brings out the honey color in your skin."

Lupe fingered the material. She cocked her head to one side. "I am not sure. Can you make, perhaps, green down here—" she gestured—"and white up here?"

"A white bodice? Of course—that would be beautiful on you. Let me show you some options."

As she reached for another bolt of cloth, the bell over the door rang. Joshua Carstairs closed the door behind him. He took off his hat and gave a slight bow of his head toward Rachel. "Afternoon, Miss Stone."

"Mr. Carstairs." This was the first time she had seen Joshua Carstairs since Mark's attack, and it was the closest she had ever been to him. The hard planes of his face softened when Lupe skipped over to him, wrapped her arms around his neck, and kissed his cheek.

"*Mi marido,*" she said, taking his hand, "come see what Rachel is showing me."

He walked to the counter, his gaze not leaving Rachel's.

"Miss Stone, I apologize for what my brother did to you." He stopped as if unsure what to say next. "There's no excuse. I shoulda been keepin' a better eye on him."

"There's no need to apologize. It wasn't your fault."

"Well, I knew he had designs on you. I just never expected him to go that far."

"Mr. Carstairs, you've got enough on your mind without fretting over me." She took a deep breath. "I'll be all right." She looked at Lupe. *And I will stay all right with friends like Martha and Annabelle and now Lupe. And God.*

He turned to Lupe. "I've got a meeting at the bank, and then Avery's comin' in to talk about how the ranch is doing. I'll probably be tied up until supper." He sighed. "I'll be glad when this whole business is over and we can get back to normal. I ain't got the head for this business stuff."

Rachel noticed the tightness in his jaw. "What a burden you must be carrying."

He looked at her, shrugged. "Kind of goes with the territory in this family. I'm just glad I got my girl here."

He kissed Lupe and left.

Lupe's shoulders sagged as her husband walked out. She turned to Rachel. "You are right. He carries too much, and he worries about his *padre.*"

"Have you told him what Sam did to you?"

Lupe lowered her eyes and shook her head. "It would not help anything now. I will wait until Señor Sam comes back." She looked up. "You will help me, *sí*?"

"*Sí*. Yes. I will help you, and so will Annabelle and Martha."

"You are very kind." Lupe brushed her hands over the green fabric Rachel had been showing her. "And you are better now?" she asked a little shyly. "Not so . . . afraid?"

Rachel smiled a little sadly. "I'm better. Still afraid sometimes, still sad, but I'm not going to run away. I'm not going to let Mark or anyone else keep me from what God wants for me."

Lupe tilted her head, a quizzical look on her pretty face. "And you know this? You know what God wants?"

"I know He wants me to be free." Rachel reached over to take her new friend's hand, daring to whisper what the Lord had been teaching her as she studied and prayed the last few nights.

"And I know He wants me to love."

66

IT'S BEAUTIFUL. The vibrant colors dazzled Michael's eyes. The verdant valley floor, the dark green pines, the lighter green poplars contrasted with the grays and browns of the surrounding mountains and the white-capped higher peaks. Cool, crisp air brought the clean aroma of evergreens.

He focused on the cabin, a small dot between two strings of water, and fresh dread rose in his throat. The trail of violence and blood they had been following ended there in that small gray smudge.

Caleb stood beside him and trained the spyglass on the scene. He slammed the cylinder shut and rammed it into the carrying case.

"Bad news. Looks like they kidnapped Mark Carstairs too. He and Sam are tied between posts on either side of the cabin door."

"Are they still alive?" Harold said.

"Well, they're still standing. But they look pretty beat up."

"Mark?" Michael heard the surprise in Frank's voice. "Avery was supposed t' keep an eye on 'im."

Martin kicked a loose stone. "Probably gave Avery the slip first chance he had and headed for town."

Caleb sipped from his canteen and spat in the dirt. "And got himself into a heap of trouble, the fool. The boy never would learn."

"What do their defenses look like, Sheriff?" Jeremiah said.

"Can't tell how many they have. Our prisoner thinks there's around ten men besides the woman, her husband, her father, and a servant woman left in the camp. I can see three, maybe four along the creek bank. Hard to tell how many are in and around the cabin or in the trees. We can't attack 'em head-on. That'll just put Sam and Mark in a cross fire. I'd like to see if there's some way we can get in behind 'em."

Caleb pointed to the north. "Mr. Turner, I want you and Martin to scout up the north side of the valley and see if there's a way to get into those trees without being seen. Bill, you and Frank do the same on the south side."

A small copse of trees near the trail provided shade and gave Michael and Caleb a secluded place to watch the valley unseen. Michael squatted next to Malachi. "How you doing?"

Malachi gave him a weak smile. "Doin' okay for an old man with no whiskey. What's all the commotion? Where'd everybody go?"

Michael poured some water on a cloth and mopped the old man's brow. "We've found the kidnappers' hideout. The others went to scout out the best way to come at them."

Michael removed the bandage and examined the wound. He washed it with some whiskey.

"Hey, don't go wastin' that stuff." Malachi reached for the bottle with his good arm.

Michael held the bottle away and placed his hand on Malachi's chest. "Believe me, old man, this whiskey's doing a lot more good where I put it than where you would put it."

"Try telling my mouth that." He drifted off again.

Caleb walked over. "How's he doin'?" He held his voice to a low whisper.

Michael stood and looked down at the dozing man. "All right, I think. The wound looks clean, but he's still running a fever."

Malachi's eyes fluttered open. "A little whiskey would sure help, Sheriff."

Caleb gave him a slight kick in the foot. "We need it to keep your wound clean. You just keep drinking water, old-timer. You'll get some whiskey soon as we get back to Riverbend."

"Waste of good whiskey, if you ask me."

Quietness settled over the area. No one spoke. Malachi slept. Harold stretched out under a tree and covered his face with his hat. The horses dozed in the warm, still air. The stomp of a hoof and the swish of a tail to ward off flies were the only sounds.

Michael watched Caleb as the sheriff paced. The man

checked his watch and glanced at the sky. He looked north and south as if wishing the scouts would reappear. The lines on his face seemed etched with a chisel.

Time crept. The sun moved across the sky, but it seemed that time stood still where they were.

Buddy snorted and raised his head. Michael reached for his rifle. In an instant, Harold had jumped into a crouch, his pistol cocked. Caleb grabbed his pistol but didn't draw it.

Jeremiah and Martin walked into view, and relief swept over Michael like a cool breeze.

Caleb stood with his legs apart, hands on his hips. "What'd you find?"

Jeremiah jerked his thumb over his shoulder. "It doesn't look like there's a way in on the north side. About halfway to the cabin, there's a deep crevasse. It's too wide to jump and too steep to climb down. The sides are all loose rock, and they'd hear us coming."

Martin nodded. "He's right. We could ride north a ways and find a trail in the back way, but it might take us all night or longer to get back here."

Caleb shook his head. "They know we're close. They ain't gonna wait around for us to find some other way in." He chewed the edge of his mustache, looking straight ahead as if hoping an answer to his dilemma would appear before him. "I've had it with these people. Tryin' to catch 'em has been like trying to catch air in your hand. Maybe Bill and Frank will have better luck."

Michael watched an eagle soar and drift on high currents of air, graceful and slow. He remembered his conversation with Old Thomas on the rock and envied the view the bird had of their situation. He glanced at the Indian's body wrapped in blankets, and his heart grew heavy thinking of a friend gone too soon. He whispered a prayer of protection as they waited for Bill and Frank to return.

Caleb paced. Jeremiah sat next to Malachi and offered him the canteen. The old man groused about the lack of whiskey like one of those birds with an irritating squawk that you didn't really notice until it penetrated your consciousness. Then you wanted to shoot it.

The tension between Michael's shoulders returned, tightening like the mainspring of a watch wound to its breaking point. It moved into his neck. He stretched and twisted his upper torso without relief.

Caleb drank from a canteen and spat on the ground. He rammed the cork back into the neck with a hard slap. The sun moved a little farther across the sky. The waiting wore on everyone except Malachi, who had drifted off into a restless sleep after Jeremiah and Michael prayed for him.

Michael stood with Caleb looking into the valley. *Such a peaceful place. Lord, show us the way in.*

A call of "Hello, the camp" interrupted his thoughts. Bill and Frank walked into view. The others gathered around them.

Bill grinned. "We can get close to the cabin by goin' along the south wall of the valley. The goin' will be slow, but there's good cover. We can get around behind the cabin if we go on the other side of the south wall, where they can't see us."

"How long will it take to get into position?" Caleb said.

"'Bout an hour, maybe an hour and a half. We'll have to go slow so we don't raise any dust or start rocks moving."

"Do they have any men on the south wall?"

Bill shook his head. "Didn't see any. They seem to be concentrated along the creeks and around the cabin, but they're watchin' everything."

"All right then," Caleb said. "Let's move."

They gathered their rifles and extra ammunition. Caleb made sure Malachi was awake and had his pistol and rifle. He gripped the old man's shoulder. "Be back as soon as we can."

"Just get them killers, Sheriff."

67

They walked in single file, Bill in the lead. Michael gripped his rifle with sweaty palms and concentrated on walking across the slope. The sensation of one leg always being longer than the other made him uncomfortable, but shrubs and trees provided something to grab hold of when he sensed he lost his balance.

Caleb and Bill held whispered conversations as Bill gestured to indicate what lay ahead.

After about half an hour, Bill angled up the slope to where some boulders stood like stoic sentries. He cautioned the men to keep low as they crossed over to the back side of the valley wall. When all had skirted the outcropping, they resumed their journey.

Michael admired Bill's leadership. He proceeded with

caution. He checked that all the men were in place behind him. He tempered Frank's urge for speed by pointing out the kidnappers might have placed guards along the valley wall since the two of them passed earlier.

The stillness of the air magnified the slightest sounds. Michael realized that he had not heard a bird call or the rustle of smaller animals since they began. He squinted in the sun, the tension in his neck and shoulders a sharp ache, the muscles tight as a fully drawn bowstring. Dull pain crept from his eyes to his forehead. He tried to relax, but adrenaline kept him alert. Jeremiah gave his shoulder a squeeze. He acknowledged the gesture with a quick smile, then returned to following Caleb's back. The sheriff's loose-jointed gait handled the difficult terrain with ease.

Barkston put up a hand. Everyone froze. The rifle slipped in Michael's hands. He wiped the barrel and trigger area with his bandanna, then used the cloth to dry his hands. Barkston smiled at him and gestured to one of the men behind Michael. Martin slipped past him to squat near Barkston as the rancher whispered in his ear, pointing farther up the valley. The cowboy nodded and moved off.

Time hung in the air like heat on a windless day. Michael waited, holding himself as still as possible, resisting the urge to stretch his cramped legs. Never had the urge to cough and clear his throat seemed so strong.

After what seemed like an hour, Martin reappeared, grinning, carrying another rifle. A gun belt and holster hung over his shoulder.

"All right then. Let's go." At Caleb's signal, they moved

forward again. Ten minutes later, they passed a man lying on the ground, unconscious, gagged with a bandanna, hands tied behind him with his belt, feet tied with a *bandolera* emptied of its shells. A crushed sombrero lay near the man's head.

Caleb turned to Martin. "Good work."

Martin shrugged. "He was sleepin' when I found him."

Half an hour later, Barkston and Caleb scurried up the valley wall to check their position. After several minutes, they slid back down to the others.

"We're near the cabin." Caleb gazed at each of them. "Michael and Jeremiah, I want you to go straight up to the top right here. You'll have a good view of the creek and the men behind it. The cabin will be to your left about twenty-five yards back from the creek. Your job will be to take out those men at the creek. Bill, Martin, and Frank will go on a little further up and then get down into the trees behind the cabin. Harold and I will keep on until we're right across from the cabin. Give us a little time to get in position. Then, Bill, you fire the first shot to get their attention."

He held up one finger toward Barkston. "Don't actually shoot anyone—not at first. I want to see if they'll surrender. If they don't, you'll create a distraction behind the cabin and draw their people away so me and Harold can go down and get Mark and Sam. If you have to shoot, be very careful. We don't want to hit either of them. Keep in mind that the walls on that cabin are probably paper thin and a stray bullet will go straight through, so if you have to shoot, make sure you hit a person. I'd like to take these animals alive, but rescuing Sam and Mark is more important.

"Any questions?"

Nobody spoke.

"All right. Let's get into position."

68

MICHAEL GRIPPED HIS RIFLE and peered into the flat valley below him. The grass between the creek and cabin was a beaten-down, greenish brown muck. The creek water ran deep and clear. The cabin with its weather-bleached walls stood to his left. A thin wisp of smoke rose from a rusted chimney that poked through the sagging roof. On the porch, between the posts, two figures slumped. *Sam and Mark Carstairs.* Michael's heart climbed to his throat as he continued to scan the valley.

Three men lay behind some logs along the creek bank, rifles focused on the eastern approach to the valley. Michael saw no one else. Up the ridge from his position, Caleb and Harold moved down the side, careful not to disturb rocks or snap twigs. They sheltered behind some thick shrubs about halfway down the slope. Bill Barkston and his group had already disappeared into the trees behind the cabin.

Jeremiah tapped Michael's shoulder and pointed to a small group of young pine trees about two-thirds of the way to the bottom. "Let's head for that spot," he whispered, his voice loud in the still air. "It will give us good cover."

Jeremiah moved out, planting his foot before placing his weight on it, watching for any object that might be disturbed by their movement and raise an alarm. Michael followed, putting his feet in the same places, watching the cabin and the men at the creek.

The door to the cabin opened when they were halfway to their goal. Michael and Jeremiah froze behind a small shrub. Michael watched a dark-haired woman come out, a rifle braced against her hip, a holster and pistol strapped to her waist. She surveyed the valley floor and the ridges. Then she walked over to the three men behind the logs and spoke to them.

On her way back to the cabin, the woman stopped in front of Sam. She spoke to him and he shook his head. She spat in his face and hit him in the stomach with the butt of her rifle. Michael winced at the sight.

She went over to Mark and raised his head with the barrel of her rifle under his chin. She said something to Sam and then punched Mark in the chest, directly on the bloodstained bandage he wore. Michael heard his cry of pain. The woman removed the rifle from under his chin, and his head dropped. His body sagged even further.

The woman swept her glance around the area once more. It

seemed to Michael that her eyes rested momentarily on the area where Caleb and Harold waited. She took a step, stopped, shook her head, and walked behind the cabin. After several minutes she reappeared from the other side and went back inside.

Michael took a deep breath, his first normal one since the woman appeared. He and Jeremiah started to move again. Michael wanted to run to the trees, but he forced himself to follow Jeremiah's example of slow and determined steps.

The cabin door opened again. They froze. Exposed. Nowhere to hide.

A blonde woman came out, carrying a metal pot and some plates. She crossed over to the men at the creek and served them from the pot. Michael's own stomach growled at the sight. He'd had nothing since the previous evening but jerky and water.

As the woman filled their plates, one of the men fondled her, laughing. The woman didn't even protest, just stood with head down and shoulders slumped. Anger surged through Michael at the way they treated her. Then Rachel's face filled his mind. For the first time he realized what her previous life must have been like. *Lord, I thank You for delivering Rachel from that degradation and for bringing Martha and Luke into her life to teach and protect her.*

The blonde woman finished her duties and returned to the cabin. No one else came out.

Michael and Jeremiah waited, shifting shadows marking the passage of the warm afternoon sun across the valley. Michael relaxed his grip on his rifle to relieve the cramps in his hands. He tried to stay as motionless as Jeremiah, who lay prone next to him, watching the men at the creek. A disciplined calmness seemed to permeate the man.

A shot echoed from behind the cabin. The men at the creek turned in confusion, seeking the source. The dark-haired woman appeared, rifle at the ready. She advanced to the corner of the cabin and cautiously peered around it.

Caleb called from his hiding place. "Hello, the cabin. You are surrounded. Throw down your weapons and come out with your hands up."

Fury snarled the woman's face. She fired in the direction of Caleb's voice, her shot wild and flying over his head. She fired again, joined by the three men from the creek.

Jeremiah fired, and one of the men dropped his rifle, grasped his chest, and tumbled into the creek, bobbing away on the slow current.

Michael sighted his rifle and fired as well, hitting another man in the shoulder.

The third man realized where the shots were coming from and shifted his aim. Jeremiah and Michael both fired, one bullet hitting the man in the forehead, sending him backward. *Lord, I pray that wasn't my bullet.*

The second man had a pistol in his good hand and began firing. Jeremiah fired again. The man grasped his throat, blood gushing between his fingers as he collapsed.

The smell of gunpowder filled the air, and gun smoke formed clouds that hung like fog. More shots came from behind the cabin, and the woman on the porch kept firing at Caleb and Harold. Michael realized that Caleb and Harold could not fire back because of her proximity to Mark and Sam.

Jeremiah nudged Michael. "Let's see if we can get behind her."

He moved from the covering trees. Michael followed. They descended the slope in a controlled rush. As they reached the floor, the woman turned and fired. Michael dived to the ground and rolled toward the creek.

Jeremiah crouched over, unable to fire because of the captives. The woman took a position behind Sam Carstairs and fired again.

The cabin door opened. A youngish man with a drooping mustache came out of the cabin, took a position behind Mark Carstairs, and joined in the shooting.

Michael heard a grunt and looked over to see Jeremiah. Blood flowed from his shoulder. Michael scrambled to him. Jeremiah grimaced with pain, his hand clasped to his shoulder, blood seeping between his fingers.

Michael moved him into a slight depression formed by the land's slope to the creek. Bullets spit up dirt around them. Some splatted into the creek. Michael looked up to see Bill, Martin, and Frank come trotting around the cabin. A shot from a window sent them scrambling for cover. They joined Caleb and Harold.

"That's it," Caleb called out a few minutes later. "We've taken out all your men behind the cabin. You've got nobody left in front either. Time to give it up."

The woman took a knife from her belt and held it against Sam's throat. "*You* give it up, or I'll cut him and gut him like a pig."

Jeremiah spoke. It sounded like a shout in Michael's

ear. "You're going to have to shoot her, Michael. Nobody else has a shot, and she'll kill Sam before anyone can get closer."

Michael looked at the other man. "You're crazy. I'm not that good a shot. I might kill Sam. There's got to be another way." His mind reeled. *I can't kill again. I can't.*

"Listen to me."

Michael focused on Jeremiah's hazel eyes. There was a fire in them that bored its way into Michael's conscience.

"I don't have time for a lecture. You have to do it to save lives. Remember, she's probably the one who killed Vernon and the others, and she will kill Sam rather than give up. She's keeping her head over his shoulder, so that's your only target. Now, pray, breathe, and shoot."

Michael raised his rifle and aimed at the small oval peering over Sam's shoulder. *Lord, forgive me.* He squeezed the trigger.

The bullet entered her right eye and exploded out the back of her skull. The knife slipped from her grasp and clattered to the ground.

Michael turned and vomited. He threw his rifle into the creek. He knelt in that small depression, hands at his sides, and wept. Dim awareness of what happened next crept through his tear-fogged eyes.

The man behind Mark cried out and ran to kneel beside the fallen woman on the porch. He touched her face, seemingly oblivious to the gunmen surrounding him. Seconds later, the cabin door flew open, and an old man appeared in the doorway.

"Maria!" A long wail escaped his lips, grief and pain

echoing in the hushed air. He seemed to stagger forward, then stiffly regained his feet. Maria's knife glinted in his hand.

He took a step toward Sam. "You took Ruth, and now you've taken my girl." He swung the knife toward Sam's stomach.

Caleb fired, hitting the man in the side and spinning him around. He fell, but the knife still found its mark.

Harold levered a round into the chamber of his rifle. "You . . . on the porch. Throw that gun away and stand up. Do it slow."

A pistol skittered into the dirt in front of the cabin. The man turned to face them, hands rising like flags to shoulder level. Even at a distance, Michael saw the tears on his cheeks. *Oh, Lord, he loved her.*

He started to stand, thinking it was all over, but a shot rang out, and a bullet skipped off a rock a few feet from Caleb.

"Up on that slope," Martin yelled, pointing to the ridge wall opposite the one they had followed into the valley. He raised his rifle and fired.

The man scampered over the top of the slope and disappeared.

"I missed?" Martin stared at his rifle as if he had just seen the sun rise in the west.

Frank started toward the slope.

"Let him go, Frank," Caleb said. "We've got plenty to do here as it is."

Rachel handed Lupe a cup of tea and poured one for herself. "I think one more fitting should do it."

"I hope Josh likes it. I think green is his favorite color."

The door to the store opened with a loud swoosh, the bell clanging. Annabelle rushed in and threw her arms around Rachel, then reached to embrace Lupe. Excitement reddened her freckled face. Pete O'Brien walked in behind her.

"He didn't!" Rachel said, looking from one to the other.

Annabelle's head bobbed up and down.

"When?"

Annabelle took a deep breath. "Last night. We had dinner at the hotel, and he walked me home. Knelt down on one knee, said he loved me, and asked me to marry him."

Rachel looked at Pete. "Well, it took you long enough."

"I know." The big man was actually blushing. "I was afraid she'd turn me down. Then I got more afraid someone would snatch her up from under me nose."

Rachel laughed. "Like she would fall for anyone else."

"I am very happy for you both," Lupe said. "May you have many years together and many beautiful *niños*. When—"

Rachel gasped. Her teacup clattered to the floor.

Lupe jumped. "What's wrong, Rachel?"

Rachel put her hand to her chest to calm her pounding heart.

"I don't know. Something's happened. Michael's face flashed through my mind. Let's pray." She joined hands with Lupe and Annabelle, then realized Pete had joined the circle as well. She only wondered about that for an instant. Her mind was focused on praying protection for Michael and the posse.

After several minutes, the urgency passed. She dropped her friends' hands and smiled an apology.

"I hate when I get those flashes, those images. I wish God would be more specific."

69

MICHAEL STOOD numb as they laid Sam Carstairs on the ground, a blanket for a pillow. The old man was alive, but just barely, and bleeding heavily from a wound in his abdomen.

Jeremiah winced in pain as Harold tied off the bandage he'd wrapped around the man's shoulder and upper arm. Jeremiah pointed his other hand toward Sam. "Come on, Michael. This is what you came here for."

Michael shuffled to where Caleb and Bill knelt next to Sam. Bill applied pressure to the knife wound, desperate to stop the bleeding, while Caleb washed Sam's other wounds with cool water from the creek.

Caleb squatted near Sam's head. "Who were these people?"

"Man I wronged many years ago," Sam croaked, "and his crazy daughter." He coughed, and blood trickled from his mouth. "How's . . . Mark?"

Mark Carstairs moaned from where he lay a few feet away. Frank and Martin held cloths against the wound in his chest.

"He's hurt bad, Sam," Caleb said. "I don't know if he's gonna make it."

"What about John?" Sam asked.

"Who?"

"The old man in the cabin."

Caleb looked at the frail body lying a few feet away. "He's dead, Sam. I had to shoot him."

"It's my fault, Caleb. All of it. I've done so many bad things, hurt so many people." He took in a breath. It seemed to rattle in his throat. "Ruth. Ben. John. That girl. An' now I'm dyin' and I can never . . ." A spasm of coughing racked his body, and more blood ran out the side of his mouth. Tears slipped from his sunken eyes and ran down his temples to settle in his ears.

"Don't talk," Caleb said. "As soon as you're able, we'll take you back to town and get Doc to fix you up. Right, Bill?"

Barkston looked at Caleb and shook his head. Caleb turned to Michael and mouthed, "Not much time."

Something grabbed and shook Michael's shoulder. His vision focused on Bill Barkston in front of him. "Are you with us, boy? The man you rode a thousand miles to see is right in front of you, but he ain't gonna be here much longer. Do what you came to do. Do it for Ben, like you promised."

Michael glanced at the cabin. The dark-haired woman still sat against the wall, legs splayed, head erect, the vacant eye staring at him, accusing.

"Now," Barkston urged.

Michael shook the fog of guilt from his mind. *Lord, help me.*

He moved forward and knelt next to Sam's head. "Mr. Carstairs, you don't know me, but I knew your son Ben, and he wanted me to talk to you."

Sam opened his mouth to speak, but Michael placed his hand on the man's shoulder.

"Don't try to talk. It will take too much out of you. Ben wanted you to know he loved you very much and he was sorry for all the pain and disappointment he caused you."

"Dead?" Sam murmured.

"Yes, he is. I'm sorry."

"How?"

Michael sighed. He looked into Sam's eyes and saw the man's pain and remorse. "He was hung for a crime he didn't commit, but we couldn't prove it."

Sam turned his head away. "My fault. All my fault."

Michael reached into his shirt and lifted the Celtic cross from around his neck. "He wanted you to have this back. He took it because he wanted something of his mother's."

Sam looked at the cross. He whimpered. "Ruthie . . . so sorry."

Michael placed the cross in Sam's palm and wrapped his fingers around it. Sam's hand dropped to the ground. He stared upward into the darkening sky.

Michael stared at the man who lay before him, the man he had traveled so many miles and days and weeks to find, the man whose journey might end this day. His own father's face flashed before him, there and gone in an instant. Michael swallowed and closed his eyes, pushing back the tears. "I'm sorry, Pa."

"Caleb." Sam's voice was barely a whisper. Caleb leaned forward. "Tell Josh there's a journal in my desk. It's the record of every business deal I've done these last thirty years. Tell him to make amends with everybody. And—" his voice was barely a whisper—"tell Lupe . . . sorry . . ."

Sam rested a long minute, his breaths ragged and shallow. Then he looked directly at Michael and rasped, "You . . ."

Michael knelt and leaned over, his ear close to Sam's mouth as Sam whispered. Michael's heart sank as he heard the words. *Lord, this is too much.* His head hung heavy on his aching shoulders as he got to his feet.

Sam drew another ragged breath. His eyelids fluttered. Then he gasped and was still.

Caleb reached down and gently closed the old man's eyes.

They stood looking down at Sam's damaged, lifeless body. The silent grief hung heavy around them.

Mark Carstairs moaned. Frank and Martin knelt next to him.

"I don't think he's going to make it," Martin said. "He's beat up pretty bad."

Caleb bit his lip and blinked back tears. His voice cracked. "Do what you can for him. We'll wait a couple of days to see if he improves enough to travel. Then we're going to head back. We've all been out of Riverbend long enough."

Michael sat at the edge of the creek, staring at the water's slow ripple as it joined the other streams before flowing out of the valley. Behind him, Mark lay near his blanket-shrouded father, moaning, mumbling weak calls for his mother. Martin, Frank, and Harold had been sent to fetch Malachi, the horses, and their prisoners. The man who called himself Jack Alden had been tied to one of the posts on the porch, and the pitiful blonde servant woman had been coaxed out of the cabin and now sat silently near him. Behind them, the dead woman had been laid out on the porch, awaiting burial.

Michael sighed. It was over. The posse's mission was complete, and he had fulfilled his promise to Ben. But—he glanced back at the porch—he had done it again.

He held up his hands. Hands that wanted to hold Rachel, touch her cheek, tuck her hair behind her ear, grasp her hand. Hands that had killed again.

And he felt . . . nothing. Hollow.

Footsteps came from behind. Jeremiah Turner lowered himself to the grass next to Michael with a grunt and a groan. "How are you doing?"

Michael didn't answer, didn't turn to face the man.

"That's what I thought," Jeremiah said. "Killing someone is the worst thing in the world, especially the first time."

"I killed my father."

"Oh." Jeremiah's voice was small. Michael heard the shock and disbelief in it. He told Jeremiah the story.

"So you've been carrying this load of guilt around since then?"

Michael nodded.

"Let me guess. You feel like you've got an evil monster inside you that you have to control so it doesn't kill again."

Michael faced Jeremiah. "That's right. How did you know?"

"Because I had him too. Joined the Army early in '65, when I was seventeen. First man I killed was with my bayonet. He was an officer. He came charging over the wall, screaming, shooting his pistol until it was empty. He saw me and swung his sword. I reacted. Didn't even think about it—just ran my bayonet into him. I still see his face in my dreams."

"How'd you get rid of the monster? I've prayed and prayed, and it . . ." He put his head in his hands. "It just doesn't work."

Jeremiah grimaced and touched his bandaged shoulder. A small red splotch showed on the cloth. He turned his gaze to the valley. "I think maybe you're praying for the wrong thing."

Michael stared at him. "What are you talking about?"

Jeremiah's face had an intensity that mesmerized Michael. "There is evil in the world. And it doesn't go away because we wish it would or even because we pray about it. Jesus died and He defeated the devil—He won the war—but there's still skirmishes out there. The evil keeps trying to hang on. And we need to fight it. It's our responsibility."

He carefully shifted his position, awkward without the use of one arm. "Let me ask you a question. Why did you kill your father?"

Michael hesitated. "Because he was hurting my sister. He would've . . . would've . . ." He couldn't go on, just hung his head.

"So it wasn't just for the thrill of hurting him, of seeing another person die at your hands, to exercise your power of life or death over him?"

Michael shook his head.

"No, you did it to protect your sister. If you could have stopped it without killing him, you would have."

Michael nodded.

"From what you told me, if you hadn't stopped him then, he would have done it again the first chance he had. Killing him was the only way you had at that moment to permanently protect your sister."

"I guess so."

Jeremiah pointed toward the cabin. "Did you shoot that woman for the pleasure of seeing someone die? I saw you. I think you would have shot yourself rather than her if it would have saved Mr. Carstairs."

"I would have."

"You shot her because it was the only way you had to save Sam."

"I guess you're right."

Jeremiah leaned closer, his eyes locked on Michael's. "So don't look at that thing inside you as a monster. Look at it as a tool God gave you to defend and protect people. Control it like you would a hammer. Pray for wisdom, for God's hand on you as you use it. And if it really does get out of hand—and it might sometimes—pray for forgiveness. The Lord will forgive you—He promised in His book. But then you have to accept that He forgives you, not keep dwelling on it."

Michael thought of the confrontation with Mark Carstairs his first night in Riverbend. Even then the monster had come out to protect Rachel. Hitting Mark was the only way he could do it. He nodded slowly as his thoughts turned to Rachel. How long would it be before he could see her face?

I asked her to wait for me. Will she do it?

Jeremiah interrupted his thought. "One more thing."

"What's that?"

"Like I said, I watched you shoot that woman. Next time, keep your eyes open. For my sake." Jeremiah clapped him on his shoulder with his free hand. He carefully got to his feet and turned to go, then stopped. "By the way, what did Sam Carstairs say to you at the end there?"

Michael sighed. "He asked me to clear Ben's name."

70

JUNE 15, 1878

RACHEL PLUCKED a piece of lint from Annabelle's skirt. "I wish I'd had the time to make a whole new dress for you."

Annabelle turned to the mirror in the bedroom of her small house tucked behind the school and examined the navy blue frock she wore. "This one is fine—my favorite Sunday dress. And the new trim you added is wonderful." She looked up and grinned. "I figured once Pete proposed, I didn't want to give him any extra time to change his mind."

Rachel brushed the hem, arranged the skirt into neat folds, and stood back, her critical eye seeking any flaw. "He won't change his mind. You look beautiful."

Annabelle blushed. "Thank you. But are you all right? I know you're worried about the posse . . . and Michael."

Rachel sighed. "We're all worried. They've been gone over a month."

"Yes, but you've been so concerned for Michael. Especially since last week."

"All I know is I'm supposed to pray. And I'm praying."

Annabelle reached for her hand. "You looked so sad just now."

Rachel shrugged. "Maybe I'm a little envious. You're getting married. You're going to settle down with a good man and raise a family. People in town like you, respect you. That's the kind of life I want, a life where my past isn't constantly thrown in my face, where I can be like everybody else." She stopped herself as she heard the anger edging her voice. She took a calming breath, then released it slowly. "I'm tired of being alone."

"Oh, Rachel." Annabelle pulled her friend into a tight embrace. "Sweet one, you are not alone, and you know it. You have me . . . and Pete . . . and Martha and Luke and the children . . ."

"You know what I mean," Rachel murmured against Annabelle's crisp blue bodice.

"Yes, I know." Annabelle released her and held her at arm's length. "And I know you just have to keep on trusting God. He will *bring* you the right man, just like He brought me Pete." She chuckled. "Of course, it did take me a while to convince Pete of that."

Rachel couldn't help smiling. "That was just a matter of time. And I have to admit God's done all right by me so far. He got me out of Denver, and He brought me you and Martha and Luke, my shop, the church. He's done so much, and it must seem like I'm never satisfied—I just keep on asking Him for things. I must sound like a spoiled brat sometimes."

"You are not spoiled," Annabelle insisted. "And there's nothing wrong with asking. God *wants* you to ask, doesn't He?"

Rachel brushed at the skirt again. "It's just that . . . I don't even know if Michael is coming back. Or if he will stay in town. Or if he will want me." She sighed. "What if I just don't know how to be with a good man like him?"

Annabelle placed a gentle hand on her cheek. "Rachel, you'll know. The Lord will guide you."

"But it's not just that. I'm also . . . well, a little scared about what being with someone means. What if he wants to change me—not back into what I was, but something different from who I am now—from the life I'm making here with the shop." She felt tears welling and reached up to wipe them before they fell. "Oh, dear, I know this is silly, and I shouldn't be crying on such a happy day."

"Nonsense," Annabelle said in her practical schoolteacher's voice. "Everyone cries at weddings. Now, we should be going. It's almost time."

She reached for her bonnet and settled it over her brown curls. Then she turned to Rachel. "I'm no preacher, but doesn't it say somewhere in the Bible that the Lord will give us the desires of our heart? Don't you believe that?"

Rachel settled into the pew between Martha and Daniel, who snuggled against her. She put her arm around his shoulder, pulling him close, and kissed the top of his head. *Will I ever have a child of my own?*

Martha leaned over to whisper to Rachel, "Hope Luke doesn't get a crick in his neck looking up at Pete. At least he doesn't need notes for this service. He loves to do weddings."

Pete and Annabelle stood before Luke as the pastor led them in a recitation of the wedding vows. Another pang of envy surged through Rachel as she watched her friend's beaming face. Would she ever know the happiness that Annabelle felt today?

I'm sorry, Lord. You know I'm glad for Annabelle. It's just that I . . . The waiting's so hard sometimes.

"I now pronounce you man and wife."

Luke's words brought her back to reality. Daniel scrambled from the bench as they stood.

Rachel joined the small crowd clustering around the newlyweds. She gave Pete a quick kiss on the cheek and hugged Annabelle, who whispered in her ear, "Trust God, remember."

Rachel whispered back, "I'll try."

The next hour flew by as Rachel helped Martha serve coffee and slices of Mr. Gunther's wedding cake. Only after Pete and Annabelle had driven away in his buggy and the last dish had been washed and put away did Rachel manage to do what she had longed to do all day—escape. Something deep within her craved solitude.

Changing quickly into her riding clothes, she saddled Sunshine and headed to the same place she had gone every evening for the last week. She let Sunshine pick her way along the top of the ridge that pointed fingerlike to the river, bending the stream in the shape of a narrow horseshoe. From here, Rachel could look back to the town, the buildings dappling through the trees, the church steeple reminding her whom to look to for all things.

"Trust God." Annabelle's words came back to her as she gazed northward, where Michael and the posse had ridden more than a month ago. Alone with her thoughts, her prayers, she searched the horizon for a sign of their return. She remembered her words to Michael: *"Come back . . . so we can get to know each other better."*

Yes. Come back. She pictured his face, those hazel eyes with the flecks of green. Could she trust the man behind those eyes?

Come back. I'm willing to find out.

Was he?

Seven days she had made this trip, seven days since the image of Michael flashed across her mind. Was he safe? Was he alive? Something in her spirit told her he was, but she sensed something profound had happened to him, something that could affect both their lives.

She dismounted, allowing Sunshine to wander and graze, knowing the horse would never leave her, wishing she could summon that kind of trust in people. So many times in the past month she had prayed for wisdom, but she still didn't feel very wise.

"God," she finally said out loud, "Annabelle said You will give me the desires of my heart, but that's hard for me to imagine. So I guess I'm just going to have to leave it with You. You know what is really important to me, and I'm willing to wait to see what You have in mind. Only, You'll have to be real clear about what that is, because I don't want to make a mess of it."

She held her elbows and scanned, searching for a smudge that would be the dust of the posse returning. Nothing. Heart thumping like a bass drum, she prayed again.

"And, God, I would really appreciate it if You could bring Michael back safely. Even if he's not coming back to me."

She stood there a long time more while the sun sank behind the horizon. The only sounds were birdsong and the clink of Sunshine's bridle while she grazed. Rachel sighed and took a step toward the horse, ready to go home.

Suddenly the scene before her—the ridge, the river, the ranches—vanished. Now, she stood looking over a beautiful, lush valley. No houses or fences, just untouched land stretching to sun-soaked mountains in the distance. A river meandered through it, sun glinting off the blue water. Myriad shades of green colored the grass and the trees. A breeze, soft and warm, caressed her cheeks. The fragrance of wildflowers wafted lightly through the air.

And a voice rumbled inside her, deep, resonant, filling her with warmth and peace. It spoke words from the Bible, those words Pastor Luke had spoken over Annabelle and Pete: "Therefore shall a man leave his father and his mother, and shall cleave unto his wife: and they shall be one flesh. . . . What therefore God hath joined together, let not man put asunder."

Someone stood next to her. She turned. Michael took her hand, and she looked into those eyes.

The voice continued, its softness like an arm, warm and loving, around her shoulder.

"This is the man I have chosen to be your husband."

Acknowledgments

WRITING A NOVEL is never done in a vacuum. It involves so many people that the author runs the risk of missing someone when it comes to this page.

The first person I want to acknowledge is our Father. Without His giving me the desire to write, this novel would not have happened. And He sent people to cross my path, divine appointments sent at precisely the right time to help bring this dream to reality. May this novel and all my writing bring Him glory and honor.

I thank my test readers: my wife, Linda; Frances Anne Butler; and Cassie Sunshine for their diligence in reading the entire manuscript and for their honest feedback.

Thanks to my local North Texas Christian Writers critique group, the Super Scribes, and my online critique group, Fearless Fiction Writers.

The Christian Writers Guild taught me to develop a thick skin, to hone my craft, and to grow as a writer. Thank you, Jerry B. Jenkins, and all the staff and mentors who worked with me. A special thanks to my Craftsman class, especially our mentor, John Perrodin, and my friend Ann Fryer.

Thanks to Stephanie Broene and all the staff of Tyndale House who saw promise in this book and took a risk.

Thanks to my editor, Anne Christian Buchanan, for helping me and guiding me to make the novel better than I could have on my own.

A most profound thanks to my mentor and friend, DiAnn Mills, who saw some talent in the first few pages of this novel and who encouraged, challenged, and inspired me to keep writing. She wouldn't give up on me or let me give up on myself. Her commitment to what she saw in me is a huge part in why *Journey to Riverbend* is a reality today.

About the Author

HENRY MCLAUGHLIN is the 2009 winner of the Jerry B. Jenkins Christian Writers Guild Operation First Novel Contest. He has a master's degree in social work and spent many years working in the public child welfare system. It was in this role that he first honed his writing skills in preparing concise and accurate court reports and petitions. He retired from that career in 1999 to work with Kenneth Copeland Ministries.

To improve his craft, Henry belongs to several Christian writers organizations; attends writers conferences, workshops, and retreats; and participates in online and local critique groups. He completed the Christian Writers Guild Craftsman course in April 2010.

Henry and his wife, Linda, have been married for over forty years and live in Saginaw, Texas. They have five children, the oldest of whom is in heaven, and one grandchild.

Visit his Web site at www.henrymclaughlin.org.

Discussion Questions

1. When *Journey to Riverbend* begins, Michael sets out to reconcile a father and son. But at some point his mission seems to become about more than just fulfilling his promise to Ben. Do you agree or disagree? What else do you think is driving Michael?

2. Many of the townspeople in Riverbend judge Rachel because of her past, even though she's no longer a prostitute. Do you ever make snap judgments about people based on things you've heard about them? Other than gossip, what leads us to jump to conclusions about people before we get to know them? How can we stop ourselves from doing that?

3. Though Rachel has accepted Christ's forgiveness, she still has a difficult time trusting in that forgiveness and often allows her insecurities to overshadow the new person she's become. In chapter 16, she says, *That's me. Ever alert. Always* waiting *for something else bad to*

happen. That's partially why, in chapter 21, she mistakes Michael's act of kindness for something else. Have you ever experienced this yourself? Why do you think you reacted this way?

4. Michael is haunted by an event in his past that he never had the courage to face. Have you ever had a similar experience, one that was difficult to look back on?

5. In chapter 37, when Michael asks Jeremiah Turner how he became a gunslinger, Jeremiah replies that during the war, he saw such cruelty. Though it drove some men to disbelief, it had the opposite effect on Jeremiah and drew him closer to God. Why do you think people can have such opposite reactions to adversity or evil? Have you ever witnessed or experienced this yourself?

6. The townspeople of Riverbend risk a lot to save Sam's life—time, resources, even their own lives. Do you think that they were right to do so? Why or why not?

7. At the end of chapter 42, Rachel gets the sudden and inexplicable urge to pray for Michael and the rest of the posse. Have you ever experienced a call to prayer or action like that?

8. In chapter 45, Caleb tells Michael that he can't reconcile others' views of a good God with a God who would allow pain and sickness, like his wife experienced before she died. Would you have responded the same way Michael did? Why or why not?

9. Did you feel sympathy for Sam at any point in the story? Why or why not?

10. Romans 8:28 assures us that "God causes everything to work together for the good of those who love God and are called according to his purpose for them." What are some examples of this throughout the story?